PASSION'S PROMISE

"We are enemies, Maren, you and I, but our conflict will be laid aside this night." Brettan de Lorin pulled the raven-haired beauty to him, knowing he had longed to possess her from the first.

"If you choose to use force, milord, I am powerless to stop you, but let it be known I shall never yield to you. I shall fight you until my last breath." Maren's eyes narrowed with fury as she struggled anew against his hold upon her. But then Brettan's lips found the hollow of her throat where her pulse raced and, at that searing contact, Maren's cry of protest died unborn.

She gasped in sudden shock as his lips began to roam over her silken flesh. Then his mouth claimed hers, bruising, demanding, and a warm, strong hand gently caressed the soft curve of her hip, making her moan with aching ecstasy.

Maren responded with a need she had never known. She was unable to deny him as he awakened her body to the pleasures of love. Her fingers traced the broad expanse of his chest, and she met his gaze without fear. Entwining her slender arms about his neck, she held him closer, seeking to fulfill a desire she did not fully understand . . .

IRRESISTIBLE ROMANCE FROM ZEBRA!

MOONLIGHT ANGEL (1599, $3.75)
by Casey Stuart

Dashing Captain Damian Legare, seeing voluptuous Angelique, found his blood pounding in his veins. Though she had worshipped him before with a little girl's adoration, her desires now were those of a passionate woman. Submitting to his ardent caresses, she would surrender to one perfect night of unparalleled ecstasy and radiant rapture.

PASSION'S DREAM (1086, $3.50)
by Casey Stuart

Beautiful Morgan Fitzgerald, hating the Yankees for having murdered her parents and destroying everything she cherished, swore she'd kill every last one of them. Then she met Lieutenant Riordan. Though she tried to hate him, when he held her in his arms her lips longed for his fiery kisses, and her heart yearned for the Yankee's searing love!

RAPTURE'S CROWN (1570, $3.95)
by Karen Harper

As the King's favorite, blue-eyed Frances could have had anything, but she was mesmerized by the heated emerald gaze of Charles, Duke of Richmond. Previously faithful to their royal master, the two noble subjects now risked treason, submitting only to the rule of desire, the rule of RAPTURE'S CROWN.

ISLAND ECSTASY (1581, $3.75)
by Karen Harper

Lovely Jade Lotus, kidnapped from Canton by sea-roughened sailors, was left to die on a beach in the fragrant Hawaiian isles. Awakening in the arms of the handsome Don Bernardo, she found him a cruel master—whose slightest touch made her ache with desire. Their passion burning in the tropical nights, Jade craved that his moment of kindness in saving her could become a lifetime of love!

Available wherever paperbacks are sold, or order direct from the Publisher. Send cover price plus 50¢ per copy for mailing and handling to Zebra Books, Dept. 1587, 475 Park Avenue South, New York, N.Y. 10016. DO NOT SEND CASH.

DESIRE'S FLAME

BY CARLA SIMPSON

ZEBRA BOOKS
KENSINGTON PUBLISHING CORP.

ZEBRA BOOKS

are published by

Kensington Publishing Corp.
475 Park Avenue South
New York, NY 10016

First printing: May 1985

Printed in the United States of America

For David, Braedon and Brooke, who gave me the gifts of time, love and patience, to create *Desire's Flame*.

Chapter One

March 6, 1282

A late afternoon breeze whispered through the branches of the massive oak and pine trees, caressing those giant guardians of the forest with its warming breath. The snows of winter had been long, but now, in the golden glow of the spring day, the forest had come alive, as new leaves budded forth and ferns once again grew tentatively in vivid green colorations after shedding the cold, white mantle of the winter past.

The thick foliage overhead filtered the warming sunlight as golden rays split through the dense growth on their journey to the forest floor below, casting a soft glow on the two women who worked, carefully sampling the earth's bountiful treasures, so well guarded within the wooded copse. Their voices floated softly through the sheltered woodland, seeming to blend with the forest sounds.

Maren de Burghmond stopped and straightened against the growing stiffness in her back. She shaded her eyes with her hand as she gazed toward the sky. She knew of a certainty that several hours had passed since she and her maid had first entered the heavily wooded copse in search of the herbs and mosses that abounded there. The cloth pouches they had brought were now filled to overflowing with those gifts of nature that could bring healing magic.

The ancient art had passed from mother to daughter, through long hours attending her mother on journeys to the surrounding villages near Cambria Castle. Those who lay sick or injured knew they could trust the gentle ministrations of the Lady Julyana.

No longer the curious, spindly child, but a young woman of near a full score years, Maren had grown in figure as well as manner. Her striking resemblance to her mother often made them seem more like sisters. Her hair matched her mother's ebony tresses in its own raven-black color, holding the lustre of light as richly as any satin. Maren often cursed the heavy mass, which seemed to defy restraint, as she labored to confine its unruly tresses, as if it were a live creature seeking its freedom. Lady Julyana soon abandoned any hope of proper headdress for her young daughter and allowed the girl to leave her hair loose and flowing. Only occasionally, as now, did Maren pull it back from her fair face by binding it securely at the nape of her neck with a cluster of woven ribbons. Her face was tinged with the bright pink of glowing good health. Her jawline was wide and her nose small and fine-boned, slightly uplifted at the end. Creamy, soft skin gave stark contrast to the raven hair, and caused more than a few admiring glances from the young men about Cambria. Her full, generous mouth seemed forever on the verge of a radiant smile that revealed even, white teeth, and the dazzling beauty of that smile and the softness it brought to her flawless face were often used teasingly to gain a special favor. Her beauty was perhaps inferior only to that of her eyes, for they were the color of large, blue sapphires, and wide

8

with a look of unexpected innocence that somehow made her seem deceptively vulnerable.

Gazing about the clearing, Maren was aware of a sudden stillness that had settled about them, as if every living creature sat in hushed silence. She looked back at the maid, Agnes, crouched a few feet away beside a fallen timber, deftly prying the green mosses from the gnarled bark of a downed tree. The woman worked on, undisturbed, humming a tune to herself as she stuffed the green velvety patches into one of the cloth bags.

"Agnes, listen," Maren whispered, as she cocked her lovely head to listen for sounds in the forest.

The maid halted her labors and stood for a moment, straining for the sounds she should hear. "I hear nothing, milady," she shrugged, as she turned back to her work.

"That is my meaning. There is not one sound to be heard. Do you not think it odd that in the middle of the forest, abundant with wild creatures, we hear nothing?" Maren questioned, suddenly uneasy.

In sudden alarm, a covey of gray dove burst forth from a nearby thicket, the silence momentarily lost to the wild frenzy of their flight. Maren vividly recalled her father's warnings of wild boar that roamed the forest. Many tales were told before the blazing hearth at Cambria of brave hunters, well armed, who were no match for the large, tusked boars, and who fell severely injured or maimed for life after meeting those tines of death. Maren stepped cautiously back toward Agnes and watched the perimeter of the forest clearing carefully, wishing now they had not ventured so far from young Thomas, who had accompanied them to hunt.

Maren strained to see through the dense foliage. She watched a sudden movement in the brush, her breath suddenly still in her chest, but when a lone figure emerged from the bushes and low-hanging branches,

9

her sigh of relief was clearly heard, as she recognized the long, lanky strides of the gamekeeper's son.

Thomas moved easily in spite of the weight of his fare, thrown casually over his shoulder. His long swinging gait carried him easily across the clearing, where he promptly deposited both his long body and the lifeless pheasants upon the massive trunk of the fallen tree beside the two women. A lopsided grin split his face as he regarded his young mistress.

"The animals are restless today, and much too wary. I have walked this entire edge of the forest and have only these five birds to show for my efforts. I fear the cook will be tempted to wave her sharpest cleaver at my head for failing to bring anything more substantial than these meager hens." He gestured in mocking imitation of the cook at Cambria, rising to lumber about in mimicry of the cook's ponderous size and rolling gait. He waved his long arms about as if giving chase with that imagined blade and turned back to the two women, rolling his eyes and wiggling his eyebrows in feigned anger. Maren dissolved into fits of uncontrollable laughter at his wild gestures. Her fears of the moments before faded as Thomas imitated the stout woman to perfection. Thomas gave himself over to Maren's infectious humor and collapsed helplessly upon the soft grass of the clearing in the grip of laughter, tears filling his eyes.

The moment passed and was gone, and Maren reminded him of the lateness of the hour. "We still have a good ride ahead of us. It is best that we return to the horses. I have no desire to be about after dark," she added, her manner now more serious.

Thomas regarded his young mistress soberly. He had felt the unusual quiet of the forest and was at a loss to explain the sudden stillness. The air was unsettled, much as before a storm, though the sky had held only the promise of bright, clear weather since early morn. He

10

rose unceremoniously from his perch and retrieved his longbow. Next he gathered the pheasants and, shifting their weight over his shoulder, moved off through the trees in long easy strides.

"Aye, 'tis best we were on our way," he agreed as Maren and Agnes followed him, emerging at the edge of the forest a short while later.

Maren glanced upward. The sun was still high in the sky, though it was indeed later than she had guessed. Her stout maid good-naturedly poked fun at Thomas as he brought their horses over to them.

"It would seem, Thomas, that the cook has already banked the fires at Cambria in anticipation of the feast she will make from your good fortune at the hunt today. Look well, for you can see it from here. Oh, she will certainly have your hide upon the tanner's wall when she sees the meager fare you bring."

Pretending indifference to the woman's teasing, Thomas shrugged absently.

"I will merely explain that it was your tuneless crowing that drove the animals to shelter, making it impossible to find better birds. And on the morrow, I shall leave you seed-gatherers behind for more womanly tasks and return to Cambria with a score of birds, and mayhap a buck or two."

Maren ignored their bantering, but watched the smoke that filled the sky beyond the crest of the distant hill. Her uneasiness returned. She mounted her gray mare with ease, keeping a firm hand on the reins as the mare sidled nervously, seeming to sense Maren's unsettled spirit. She gave the gray free rein down the gently sloping hillside, and reveled in the rush of the wind against her face and the feel of the lean, hard-muscled animal beneath her. The mare took firm hold of the bit and stretched her slender legs out into a full, running stride that carried them swiftly over the even, grass-covered

11

fields. Thomas and Agnes soon found no small task in catching that fleeing figure, each silently wondering at the frantic pace their young mistress had set.

The slope flattened into the valley floor, and Maren slowed the mare with a steady hand, to allow the two who followed to catch up. She rode lost within her own thoughts, her gaze fixed on that distant gray haze that formed ominously over the ridge beyond. Maren felt an unknown fear she could not escape, and a deep foreboding took hold as they rode toward that distant hillside.

The sun moved across the afternoon sky, and they rode on silently, unable to ignore the thickening haze before them. The fading sun cast its golden glow along the horizon, the gray meeting the glowing light to form a deep red color along the entire crest of the hill, like candles glowing in the waning light, drawing them onward.

Maren's thoughts were haunted by earlier warnings of raids about the countryside, for those loyal to the fugitive prince, Llywelyn, brought death and destruction to those who resisted the rebellion. She knew Cambria to be well protected in its remote safety near the sea. The land was prosperous, the herds numerous. The sea held its own rich bounty for the fishermen. Indeed, war seemed very far away. But Maren recalled with a deep longing those last evenings before her father's departure for the north. Sorely feeling his duty to his king, Gilbert de Burghmond had taken half the garrison of Cambria with him to join the battle near Anglesey. Later, reports had come almost daily of the English army forced further south in an effort to gain control over the maurauding loyalists who desperately sought to rouse the sympathy of the Welsh people against the iron hand of the warrior king. Within Maren's family, loyalties were divided. Her father was English, and a knight and lord of the English

12

crown. Her mother was Welsh, with ties and ancestry deep in the history of their tiny, independent country. Maren's grandfather had fought against another English king, throwing off the oppressive yoke of English domination, but the years of constant warring had greatly taken their toll. When the English had finally established their coastal fortresses, they had brought peace and prosperity, for a time. Her grandfather had easily recognized that endless years of war must cease, whatever the cost, and he had taken part in the treaty of Conway, pledging himself to that peace. His home had been opened to the English and his allegiance to the English throne sealed by the marriage of his only daughter to Gilbert de Burghmond. In all the years since, when peace was constantly threatened, the Lady Julyana had never spoken of the conflict that raged within her heart; a conflict between the love for her people and love for the English lord who was her husband. The people of Cambria came to know Lord de Burghmond as a fair man, and the vast holdings that were Cambria flourished under his hand. To those who knew her well, it seemed Maren was the finest blend of the fire and vitality of her mother and the fierce pride and strength of purpose which were a gift from her father.

Maren rode on silently, letting her horse lead the way along the base of the ridge. They followed the river where it narrowed and slowed to a gentle stream. Thomas insisted on taking the lead, and they rode single file across a wooden footbridge to the other side of the river, where the village of Penhryn lay nestled in the shelter of the mountainside that sloped away to the sea beyond.

A foreboding silence surrounded the village. A few scattered head of sheep grazed on the hillside, but the shepherd was absent, the flock unattended. Sparing no time to find the cause of such unusual quiet, the three riders followed the bend of the river past the old fortress

13

of Cambria, which stood at the foot of the hills, set apart from the newer castle. The ruins of the fortress loomed before them as they urged their horses on through the waning afternoon light. Maren glanced briefly at the old stone edifice, pushing the mare as fast as she dared along the shadowed footpath, and silently spoke a prayer that all was well at Cambria. Her thoughts were full of her mother and young Catherine, barely thirteen. Her younger brother, Edmund, was only ten years old, but a strong lad, fiercely loyal to his Welsh ancestry. So unlike her older brother, Andrew, who rode beside her father with the English armies at Anglesey.

They could see the west barbican of the castle as the upper watchtowers came into view, and they halted at the crest of the hill. Beyond them, the massive stone fortress of Cambria Castle rose majestically into the blue sky. Swirling clouds of dense gray smoke billowed forth from the heart of the castle, and shouts could be heard from within. Panic seized Maren at the sight of the flames that leaped from within the stone walls; no cookfires laid for the evening meal, but flames that ate at the wooden structures within the bailey. A long column of riders caught Maren's attention as they entered the main gates with no show of resistance from the guards at their posts. The sight of brilliant blue banners, resplendent with the emblems of the English king, alarmed her.

"Merciful father in heaven! What has happened?" Agnes' face paled as she caught sight of the flames that engulfed the buildings.

Brettan de Lorin, Duke of Norfolk, whirled the giant warhorse about while he shouted orders to his men, dispensing them to secure the castle, and then to see to the fires that raged within and threatened to lay waste to most of its buildings. The afternoon sun glistened off the intricate design of the woven chain mail protecting him from unseen attackers. His hands, encased in heavy gauntlets, rested warily on the great sword sheathed in the leather belt that bound his waist, as he restrained the steel-gray stallion easily with a firm hold on the reins. Soldiers had been posted to guard against any who might attempt escape, but for naught. Few remained alive.

The heat and weight of the steel helm became unbearable, and the tall knight swept the mail coif from his head, perspiration beaded across his forehead and temples, rivulets of moisture running down his cheek. Golden-green eyes surveyed the death and destruction all about. Bodies lay askew where the castle guard had fallen, slain before any could reach their weapons. With little satisfaction, he noticed that the great hall, where no flame had been set, stood secure, and a frown creased his starkly handsome face as he guessed his men had indeed surprised the attackers in the midst of their ransacking of the castle, causing them to flee. At the sight of his knight Sandlin, he spurred the nervous stallion forward.

"Milord, we shall need to find some other entrance to the main hall. The doors have been barricaded from within. I find no reason for what I have seen. Valued possessions, worth a goodly amount, have been left untouched." Sandlin noted the look of disapproval that crossed Brettan's face.

Brettan de Lorin surveyed the great hall before him, keeping a firm hand on the reins.

"What of the lord of the hall, and others of his family? Surely there must be some who have survived and not yet managed to flee to the hills. The rebel army is responsible for this. It is their manner of attack. I want all survivors found and questioned. Someone might have some knowledge of the attack. Any prisoners are to be well cared for and brought to me immediately."

Sandlin nodded curtly. He had served the Duke of

Norfolk for many years and knew the unspoken words that lay behind those orders. No prisoner taken that day would be harmed, but he would yield the information they sought and he would do so eagerly, for there were ways to make a man talk.

Brettan de Lorin watched as his man departed, then turned his horse about and rode hard the length of the courtyard. Waste angered him. And all about him, this day, he had seen nothing but waste, senseless waste. There were those who would pay for this, and he would see that they did. Often he had argued openly with Edward the king, for they were fellow soldiers, as well as friends, and he had not hesitated in speaking his disapproval of war in this cold, unyielding land. Beyond the burning walls of a nearby building he could hear the distinct sounds of horses caught within their stalls as the flames crept close to consume them, and he shouted new orders for his men to rescue the crazed animals from certain death.

Watching the smoke as it poured from the castle beyond, Thomas glanced back at his mistress and saw the firm resolve that glowed within those deep blue eyes. Thomas grabbed her arm with a restraining hand.

"Mistress, we cannot know what we may find. We are only three, and I cannot risk harm to you. We must ride from here and seek help in the village."

Maren turned stormy eyes upon the lad as she pulled her arm from his grasp. She turned her troubled gaze to the besieged castle that stood before them.

"There is no time, and I will not sit calmly upon this hillside while you ride for others. Nor will I leave my family to seek shelter elsewhere." Maren brushed him aside, in her mounting concern for her family, then urged the gray mare forward and headed for the

16

gatehouse at a furious pace.

Reaching the west wall of the castle, Maren threw herself from her horse. The heavy portcullis had been lowered against any entry to the inner bailey. Maren gazed up toward the tower and became aware of the absence of the guards at their posts. Close behind her, Thomas finally caught up with her. Agnes followed, desperately trying to control her horse while the animal nervously pawed the ground, as if sensing the danger within.

"Mistress, we must take great care," Thomas cautioned. Maren nodded her agreement, her eyes scanning the battlements, shrouded in the growing clouds of smoke.

"Where are the guards, and the soldiers of the garrison?" A note of urgency sounded in her voice as she fought the panic that threatened to overwhelm her. Maren quickly remounted and, whirling the mare about, rode along the west wall, determined to gain entrance to the bailey.

"We will use the postern by the sea tower. Very few know of it. Perhaps it was left open."

Carefully, the three made their way back along the outer wall until they rounded the far side of the tower.

The small gate near the entrance stood open, and Maren dismounted at once and moved to enter. Instantly beside her, Thomas caught her arm in silent restraint and moved ahead of her.

Maren's senses were assaulted by the sights within, and she halted, stunned by the destruction that lay before them.

The entire courtyard seemed awash in the blood of battle. The bodies of Cambria's soldiers lay about them in horrifying disarray, like so many limp and torn rag dolls carelessly thrown aside. Already, the stench of their death fouled the air and mingled with the gray clouds of smoke that poured forth from the buildings within the bailey. Maren leaned heavily against the stone wall, her eyes filled with the sights of the recent struggle that had robbed so many of their lives. Beside her, Agnes clung fearfully to her arm.

"Mistress, I think it best that you and Agnes remain here, so that you may flee if necessary." The young man spoke earnestly.

Maren grabbed at his arm with a sudden, fierce strength. "No! No. I will not remain here. I cannot." Maren turned pleading eyes on the lad. "We must remain together and find what we will."

Thomas nodded hesitantly, unwilling to endanger his young mistress by allowing her to continue into uncertain danger, yet also realizing she would have her way, no matter his objections. Bending down and reaching inside his boot, Thomas brought forth a long hunting knife he always carried and handed it to Maren.

Maren accepted the blade and slipped it up the length of her sleeve, tight against her forearm.

Moving ahead carefully, Thomas flattened himself against the stone wall of the courtyard. Maren and Agnes followed close behind him, making their way around the inner wall of the tower toward the open courtyard. Smoke billowed angrily around them in thickening gusts, blinding them so that it was impossible to know in which direction they traveled. They groped their way along the side of a building, and Maren stumbled. Glancing down to see her way to more even footing, she realized she had tripped over the body of one of the Cambrian guards, the man unrecognizable, his face smashed by a great war-ax imbedded in his head. Maren gasped, and her hand flew to her mouth at the sight of the mangled soldier. Agnes turned away and pressed Maren forward past the crumpled form.

Through the smoke and confusion, Maren heard

Thomas' voice as he shouted back over the noise of the roaring fire that surrounded them. Maren fought for breath to clear her head only then realizing the building they passed was all that remained of the garrison hall. In the blinding smoke Maren's eyes smarted with tears, and she was aware of others moving past them, shouting for water to put out the fires. The wind suddenly shifted the direction of the smoke, and Maren now recognized their location, across from the stables, which stood completely engulfed in flames, flames which were spreading quickly along the rooftop to the kennels beyond. The sickening smell of burning fur and hides mixed with the agonized screams of the horses trapped within, overwhelming her sense of caution. The hunting dogs, securely held within the kennels, added their frenzied baying to the uproar, and Maren could not bear those tormented sounds. She bolted from the safety of the stone wall in an effort to reach the stables across the yard, that she might release the tortured animals within. She did not see the crumbling timbers which restrained the fear-crazed animals giving way beneath the assault of flames and the maddened beasts. A warning shout was heard behind her, and Maren suddenly knew her own death was certain beneath that toppling wall of flames. But just when she expected to feel her skin melting from that searing heat, Maren found herself seized from behind and dragged across the back of a horse, the animal's churning muscles quickly carrying her away from the rain of death as the building collapsed.

Maren fought to regain her breath. She was turned over and laid unceremoniously across the saddle before the rider, while he spurred his mount forward, away from the flames. Some of the embers that showered about them burned through the woolen tunic she wore, blistering the tender flesh underneath. Momentarily stunned, Maren remained flattened against the saddle, the motion of the large warhorse jarring her until her bones threatened to break.

Maren was acutely aware of the rider who bore her away from danger, and of the rock-hard firmness of a long, muscular thigh pressed firmly against her cheek. Her temper flared at this crude handling, and at the unseemly position she now occupied in the stranger's saddle. Maren turned her head against that muscular leg in a futile attempt to push upwards and gain her freedom. She strained against the strong hand at her back, holding her securely across the horse, and her gaze was filled with a brilliant blue color. She stared at a fearsome gold lion emblazoned across the rich velvet tabard worn over the heavy chain mail. Then she lifted her head and saw the piercing green eyes, looking straight ahead, and she was startled by the fierce strength she saw. He was the one who led the English. The richness of his tunic left no question as to his rank. Maren gathered all her strength and pushed with both hands against his grip, which held her firm. Her eyes smarted and teared from the blinding smoke, and she wiped them with a soot-smudged hand to clear her vision.

Brettan, holding his captive securely before him in the saddle, swung the stallion about and searched for a place of safety to deliver the girl. Maren struggled anew against that iron grip, and she was suddenly alarmed by her intimate contact with this stranger, and by the raw power she felt flowing through her where his hand touched her. Maren twisted about and finally managed to loosen his hold of her, causing him to release her unexpectedly, while he sought to control the horse, which had grown nervous under his hand. Maren gave a last push and felt herself tumbling to the ground close under the hooves of the mighty destrier, which pawed at the sod not a hair's breadth from where she lay, momentarily stunned by her sudden release. The giant warhorse sidled from the noise

20

and confusion about them and would surely have trampled her to death. Maren felt herself lifted from her spot in the dust and dragged back just when those hooves would have smashed her to death.

"Ho! What have we here, milord? A survivor? Why, 'tis no more than a mere slip of a girl and, to be certain, one of the few we shall find this day."

The clear, flawless English was not lost on her, for Maren understood the language as well as the Welsh her mother spoke and, at the mention of survivors, her head suddenly shot up. Her hair was pulled back and tucked within the confines of her rough, woolen mantle. Her soot-smudged cheeks gave her the appearance of a young servant girl, and she made no effort to change that impression, as she carefully pulled the mantle more closely to hide her face from prying eyes.

Brettan de Lorin turned about to see to his men and to find what might yet be saved from the fire.

"See that the hall is secure, and put the girl to work where she might be of use in bringing some order to it. I want to know the name of the master of the hall. The girl might know something of it, if you can make her understand you. Send out twenty of the guard to secure the perimeter of the castle. I want no surprise attacks, such as this." Whirling the grey about, he left to survey the damage to the castle.

The English knight stood before Maren, looking somewhat uncertain. "You, girl, I have not the time to be bothered with you. Get yourself to yonder hall and see what food there might be. My men will be sorely starved after their work here."

Maren hesitated as the knight moved closer to look upon her face.

"Do you understand anything of what I say?" At her wide-eyed expression, the man surmised she understood little, if anything. He approached closer as if he might

21

make her understand what was expected of her. He made wild gestures with his hands to indicate the hall, and then made the motions of eating.

An expression of understanding shown in those blue eyes, as Maren decided to take matters into her own hands and, lunging forward, gave the man a strong push. The English knight stumbled backwards and fought to maintain his footing. Turning on her heel, Maren fled the courtyard for the hall beyond, in search of her family. Her fears were strong in her heart for she saw nothing but death all about her.

Chapter Two

Maren pushed her way through the blinding smoke to the large double doors that led to the inner bailey. Fighting for breath against the searing heat that assailed her, she felt her lungs would burst if she did not breathe fresh air soon. Finally reaching the massive oaken doors, the main entrance to the great hall, she leaned her meager weight against the portal, and tried to raise the latch. The handle moved freely, but the doors would not open. She could only assume they had been barricaded from within. No amount of pressure would move the door even the smallest space. Maren moved along the stone wall of the castle, feeling her way through the smoke that had changed direction and now surrounded her. Carefully she moved toward the back of the courtyard and the kitchen entrance. Here the air was clearer, for the wind gusted the smoke away from her, and moving quickly to the kitchen doors, Maren easily gained access.

The inner corridor along the kitchens to the great hall was mercifully cool, and her eyes soon cleared and adjusted to the dim light within. The noise in the courtyard was muffled behind the stone walls. Indeed, the unusual quiet that surrounded her gave stark contrast to the confusion beyond, as if those stone walls had indeed held back the carnage, protecting those within.

As she moved past the servants' chambers, Maren was uneasy that she found no one about, and when she reached the hall she found that indeed, here also the violent hand of destruction had moved swiftly and surely to leave its mark.

Chaos loomed before her. A guard lay slain at the main entrance, where he had valiantly attempted to stay the intruders and met his own death. A second guard lay sprawled at the foot of the massive stairway in a pool of his own blood, his left arm nearly severed from his body. Maren turned from the sight, nausea threatening to overcome her. In a desperate effort to quell her weakness, she forced her attention away and moved about the big hall to survey the damage better.

Chairs and tables had been overturned and scattered about the large room. No piece had been left untouched. The morning meal having been interrupted, broken platters and goblets lay scattered about the stone floor where they had been thrown. The large woven tapestry of the hunt scene, her father's favorite, was half torn from its moorings and dangled precariously from one corner. As Maren moved through this great hall that had been her home and known so many joyous occasions, it seemed that nothing had escaped the intruders.

In the dim light of the hall, Maren moved forward uncertainly and stumbled over a soft form. In the half-light that cast lengthening shadows in that room of death, she knew it to be the faithful hound her father had given her three summers before. Sadly she knelt beside the animal, knowing he would not greet her this day. She gently nuzzled her cheek against the soft furring of the large, noble beast and felt a tear roll down her cheeks.

Maren lifted uncertain eyes to stare at the senseless destruction she saw all about her.

"Mistress?"

The sound came raspily from the darkness across the room, near the large hearth, so quietly that she almost thought she had not heard it at all. Maren sat momentarily frozen in fear, as a figure now moved and seemed to reach out to her.

Maren stood uncertainly and started across the hall, picking her way carefully among the debris that littered the room. When she reached the hearth the figure suddenly slumped forward and sprawled face up at her feet. Maren's breath caught in her throat at the sight of her father's faithful steward. The blood coursed freely from a gaping wound in his shoulder, and his face carried a deathly pallor. She quickly knelt beside the man and raised his head upon her lap. His ancient eyes opened slowly to stare blankly back at her. Maren carefully pulled apart the torn fabric of the man's tunic in order that she might inspect his wound.

"Quickly, child, a length of cloth to bind the wound."

Finding no fabric within reach that might suffice as a bandage, Maren lifted the skirt of her woolen gown and tore away a length of linen from the chemise she wore underneath. Gently she pulled apart the torn fabric to reveal the wound, and with a firm and sure hand pressed the folded cloth against the flesh to stop the flow of blood.

Feebly, William held the cloth in place, while Maren tore a second length of cloth from the undergarment and wrapped it about his chest to secure the crude bandage. Silently she worked, agonized questions racing through her thoughts, but held in check by a growing fear of the silence within the great hall.

The faithful steward closed his eyes against the pain. Many long years of service to his lordship had seen other injuries, and he would not yield to his pain before his young mistress. When he again opened his eyes, he found dark blue eyes staring keenly back at him, and he wondered at the true strength of this slender girl who now attended his wounds, their roles oddly reversed.

Maren's voice failed her as she forced herself to ask questions of the injured man. "What of the others, William? What of my mother and the children? Surely they are about."

Before William could answer her, they were startled by a loud pounding on the large oaken doors. Those outside sought entrance to the hall.

Alarmed that the attackers might have returned to finish what they had begun, Maren moved toward the portal as if she alone might protect her home from further attack.

The heavy wooden doors groaned from the weight of many who now tried to gain entry, and she was thrown aside as they finally swung open. The slain guard who lay sprawled across the entrance was gently pulled aside, and Maren backed away uncertainly in recognition of the English soldiers who swarmed through the entry in their search of the fortress. In the press of the soldiers, Maren saw two familiar faces. Thomas and Agnes moved cautiously through the cleared opening, and the maid halted in stunned disbelief, just inside the doorway, as her eyes met the devastation within the hall. Thomas quickly rushed to give Maren assistance as she returned to care for the old steward. Carefully the younger man lifted the injured servant with an ease borne of youthful strength, and set him in one of the few remaining chairs that stood with all four legs attached. Settling William into the chair, Thomas turned worried eyes to his mistress. "Are there any others about?"

William answered him as Maren turned uncertain eyes to the old man.

"Nay, lad, they have gone. And as quickly as they came upon us, too." William struggled to sit more erect in the straight-backed chair, which offered little comfort to his injured shoulder. His pained eyes turned to Maren.

"Mistress, there is much you must know; there is much danger still about." The faithful servant sighed heavily at the thought of the sadness she would have to bear.

"There was no warning of their attack, mistress. There was no time for any of the guard to raise their weapons to defend the castle. I cannot even remember their assault, only that they were about us all at once, before any could raise their swords." William moved with great effort, and he motioned Maren closer, for his voice was failing him. His whisper rattled in his throat barely enough for her to hear him.

"We were betrayed, mistress, by someone within the castle. It is the only way they could have taken Cambria."

Maren looked over the man's head, her shocked expression clear upon her face, and she knew by the grim set of Thomas' mouth that the lad believed the steward's words.

"It is the only way anyone could have struck with such surprise, Lady Maren. This castle is well fortified and protected against attack."

A deep frown played across Maren's face as she tried to find some understanding of what she had just learned. If treachery were involved, then it was possible that the traitor was still about, and all their lives were still in danger. Maren rose and looked to where Agnes stood in the darkness of shadows at the doorway, as if she feared venturing into the room. Maren crossed the room, the English seemingly oblivious to her presence as they continued their search of the castle. She picked her way carefully through the rubble and for the first time noticed the slender girl standing quietly beside the maid.

27

Her head was bowed, the long strands of her matted hair hanging forward about her face, completely obscuring her features. Maren glanced questioningly at Agnes, who stood protectively near the girl. Maren reached out her hand to raise the girl's chin and gave a sudden gasp as the girl cringed away from her touch, pulling back with such wild-eyed terror that, had it not been for the soft, green velvet of the tunic she wore, Maren would never have known the frightened girl to be her sister, Catherine.

"God's mercy, Agnes! Wherever did you find her?" Maren's voice broke with emotion as she reached for the young girl, who cringed into the corner and regarded her with blank, unseeing eyes. Maren could only guess what her sister had suffered at the hands of those who had been there, and she forced her mind to close against the terror that welled within her.

"Oh, Agnes, she does not know me." A deep fear took hold of Maren as she looked upon the young girl, once so lively and spirited, now sadly pathetic, and she fought with all her strength against the scream of anger that welled within her.

Agnes reached out a comforting hand to Maren to ease her distress at seeing her sister so transformed.

"Thomas found her not far from the stables when the building started to collapse, and would not have known her but for the song she was singing, as if her mind could remember nothing more. Thomas recognized it as the one I taught you when you were small; about a shiny black pony with yellow satin ribbons." Agnes looked up at her mistress and Maren knew the woman's anguish by the tears in her eyes. Agnes' voice cracked as she struggled to continue.

"She has said nothing more, and I hardly think she knew who we were. She followed so willingly, just like a lamb, and mindless to anything else about her." Agnes

28

reached up to dab at her eyes with a soiled cloth, then wrapped an arm protectively about Catherine's sagging shoulders. Maren reached out slowly for the girl's hand. When she made to resist, Maren persisted, taking Catherine's hand firmly in her own. Maren began to sing the verses she remembered of the song, and for a moment she thought she saw a glimmer of recognition pass in those pale, blue eyes, so fleeting, and yet enough that she believed the girl's mind not completely lost.

Maren sighed heavily. "Agnes, take her to the servants' chambers. Those rooms seemed untouched as I passed them. I do not want her to see more of what is in this room, for I fear her mind is too fragile for what she has already seen. Care well for her, and see if there are others about. I will need food and drink for William, and fresh cloth for bandages. I must see where my mother and the others might have gone. I only pray they are safe."

Agnes nodded bleakly. She put her arm about the young girl's waist and guided her down the long hallway, past the kitchens, away from the disorder and mayhem that ruled the hall.

Physically drained, Maren leaned against the long dining table for support, fearing she had just begun to know the full extent of their loss that day. She desperately needed her father, with his cool judgment and strength, to set right the confusion that surrounded her, yet she knew they must all now rely on her mother's firm hand, as mistress of Cambria.

Several of the English soldiers moved about the hall and chambers of the ground floor. Though none had threatened her or the others, she regarded them warily. Her thoughts were of her mother and young Edmund, and she returned to William's side. Eyes closed, the steward seemed to be dozing, and Maren hesitated to disturb his much needed rest. Uncertainly she bit at her lower lip while she gently touched the old man's hand. Slowly he opened tired eyes, seeming at first not to know her. Maren thought surely she could not bear the sight of that blank expression that stared back at her. She had seen enough of sightless eyes, with minds closed out of terror. In mute appeal, she looked helplessly at Thomas. Again she tried to draw the old man's attention back to reality.

"William, what of my mother, and Edmund? Did they escape to the forest or to Penhryn, or perhaps to some nearby farm?"

Slowly the fog seemed to clear from those watery eyes. William gazed up at her, and then his glance wavered as he indicated the stone stairway across the hall. Maren followed his gaze, at first unsure of his meaning. Slowly the realization of his unspoken words came to her. Then fear gripped her, tearing at the last shreds of her composure, and she pushed her way past Thomas, stumbling in the meagerly lit hall. Familiar shadows of the hall guided her, while she ran across the stone flooring to the stairway that led to the second floor apartments. She was oblivious to the English soldiers she passed, scrambling up the cold steps, tripping in the darkness, bruising her knees when she fell, unfeeling of any pain as she pushed her way up.

Returning with fresh linens to bind William's wounds, Agnes saw Maren's desperate flight up the stairway. Without being told, she already knew what Maren would find at the top of the stairs, and followed at her slower pace, soon panting from her efforts, to reach the girl.

Gaining the top landing, Maren tripped headlong over a discarded shield in the darkness and, regaining her footing, moved with deliberate slowness to the lord's chamber. Coming to a halt before the opening, Maren slowly pushed the heavy framed door aside.

The chamber was bathed in the soft glow of afternoon

30

sunlight that streamed in through the narrow windows, where the shutters had been opened early that morn to catch the cool spring breeze. A low table across the room had been overturned, the small jars atop it scattered across the room. The large high-backed chairs that sat before the hearth to catch the warmth of the evening fire had been scattered, one thrown against the opposite wall. Disorder ruled the chamber.

Maren pushed the heavy oaken door open wider, her senses raw at the destruction she saw before her. She tried to breathe, but felt as if an unbearable weight pressed against her chest, so deep was her foreboding.

Brettan de Lorin went down on one knee beside the bed in the large chamber. His gauntlets cast aside, he gently felt for some sign of life in the slender neck of the woman who lay on the cold, stone flooring. Her skin was cold and wore a deathly gray pallor, but somehow that could not diminish her beauty. Long raven-black hair, still untouched by the passage of time, lay tangled beneath her. In her youth, he knew well, there would have been none to rival her beauty. Sadly, he could feel no signs of life, and he brushed back a tendril of dark hair covering the ugly bruise that had spread across her temple. She had been badly abused, but that one blow had ended her life.

The room gave proof of the battle she had waged against her attackers. Brettan gravely wondered that the lord of the castle would leave one such as her unprotected. Although, judging by the death and destruction he had seen in the courtyard and outer bailey, there had been no time for defense. He turned at a sound from the doorway, and Brettan's golden gaze locked with that of a young servant girl who stood there motionless. The hood of her gown was drawn high over

31

her head, hiding all but her stunned wild-eyed gaze as she looked first at him and then at the dead woman.

Maren stared disbelievingly at her mother's crumpled form beside the bed where she had fallen, and then her brilliant blue eyes rested on the English knight who knelt beside the bed. Maren saw only a warrior in the armor of battle, a stranger in her home, kneeling beside her mother, the blood still fresh on his fingertips. Hysteria welled within her, and Maren grasped the handle of the door with such unnatural strength that her fingers went white. With a wild lunging movement, she screamed her agony and descended on the man before her, clawing wildly at him wherever her hands might touch. She fought with all her strength, unaware of anyone but the lean hunting beast she saw before her; the beast responsible for her mother's death.

Brettan sprang to his feet when the girl flew at him, like some vengeful winged creature, talons bared to tear at him. His lean strong fingers closed over her slender wrists, and he strained to protect himself against the madness he saw in those wide, blue eyes. He held her at arms' distance with a gentle strength that was unyielding, and still she fought him, until her screams broke into agonized sobbing. She lunged against him, then tried to twist free of his grasp, but in her desperate struggling he could feel her begin to weaken. Tears streamed down her face, and she swore at him in the Welsh language that was unknown to him. He could well imagine her confusion and fear upon returning to find her mistress slain. Vainly he shouted, that he might break through her wild, mindless ravings. His efforts were useless, and the girl continued to rail at him, so that he feared she might do herself harm. Grasping both her slender wrists in one hand, Brettan slapped her, the stinging sound of his hand against her cheek suddenly quelling her wild screaming.

The force of the blow threatened to separate Maren's head from her shoulders, yet in the reeling confusion that ruled her thoughts she somehow sensed for a brief moment that, had he intended it, the bold knight who held her firmly could have done her greater harm. The shock of that blow drew her reluctantly back to reality, and she stared at the man before her. Maren's heart ached as if it might burst from the tragic reality that was cruelly forced upon her, and though she longed to go to her mother, she could not, for she was held within an iron grasp that would not release her. Her home was in ruins, those that she loved mercilessly struck down or abused. She should have felt fear in the face of such brutal strength, which could easily have delivered her to the same fate. But oddly she felt no fear as she stared back into the emerald-green gaze that seemed to hold hers as if she had no will of her own. Maren struggled to overcome the silent sobs that welled within her. She would not allow the English swine to see her weaken. They stood locked in silent confrontation, and Maren valiantly fought the rapid beating of her heart, for fear that the great hunting beast before her might hear that softly muffled sound within her breast, and strike her down as he had her mother. A strange, vibrant warmth flowed through her from where his strong fingers remained closed at her wrists, imprisoning her in a grip that she could not hope to break. It was like a river of molten heat spreading down the length of her arms and reaching deep within to her very soul, so that it drove back the cold, gripping fear that had threatened to rob her of all reason. Maren longed to strike down this tall English knight, to wipe the smug sense of power from that starkly handsome face, and yet she saw no satisfaction in his lean, bronzed visage, only surprise, perhaps as great as her own. Vainly, Maren struggled not to yield to the torment of her emotions before this stranger. She fought back the flood of tears that threatened, and stubbornly shook her head back and forth, as if she might deny this flood of sadness, but then weakly yielded, all her resolve fleeing before the undeniable truth of her mother's death.

Brettan stared hard at the young girl he held soundly within his grasp. The hood of her woolen tunic had fallen back, in her wild strugglings, to expose her delicate fairness. All her anger and ravings could not diminish the exquisite beauty of her face. Her eyes, wide with surprise, oddly held no fear of him, and their brilliant blue color drew his breath away, robbing him of clear thought, so that for a moment they stood, face to face, the girl completely defenseless against the armed intruder. Her long hair was drawn back, exposing the delicate oval of her face. His senses were filled with the sight of her, the feel of her vulnerable beneath his hand, yet possessing unnatural spirit, so that he knew of a certainty, here was one that might never be conquered. She had this day witnessed the full weight of loss in the death of her mistress, perhaps even her family, yet she stood before him unafraid. Brettan saw the barely perceptible tremor of her lower lip as she stared back at him, and he longed to hold her against him, to quiet her ravings and soothe her anguish, to protect her forever from harm. Tears welled within those wide, blue pools that stared back at him fearlessly, and his heart constricted that he could have brought pain to one such as her. Desperately the girl bit at her lower lip while she fought to maintain control.

In renewed anger and frustration, Maren wrenched one wrist loose from that unyielding grasp and lashed out with her one free hand. In her pain and anguish she saw only her mother's murderer. She beat frantically at his other hand and felt his grip loosen. With a quick twist of her wrist, Maren momentarily gained her freedom. In desperation, she reached out and seized the slender blade sheathed in her captor's belt. Her hand closed over the small but deadly blade and, drawing her arm back, Maren struck out with all her strength. The blow glanced off the heavy chain mail that protected his broad expanse of chest, and Maren knew with sickening reality she would not have a chance for a second strike.

At the girl's sudden movement, Brettan realized he had trusted too much in her lesser strength. He turned toward her just at the moment she drew the blade from its sheath, and saw she would have driven the blade home to do its greatest damage in the slender opening between the chain mail that protected his chest and the woven mail sleeve that protected his arm. Loudly cursing his own foolishness, as well as her boldness, he brought his fist down across her wrist, smashing the blade from her grasp and sending it clattering loudly across the flooring.

Only momentarily stunned from the force of the blow, Maren struggled with renewed effort, that she might yet do him some harm. She gave little thought to the other soldiers that filled the hall.

Brettan fought to subdue her hands, his fingers closing around one wrist. Yet even as he held her captive once more, Maren refused to yield, but threw him a murderous glare that could have split his head in two. Brettan was taken aback at the spirit of the girl who, though completely trapped, steadfastly refused to succumb to the growing fear he saw behind those brilliant blue eyes which held him transfixed.

Glowing green eyes of the hunting beast bored into her azure gaze as they stood, alone, each firm in purpose, refusing to yield. In a sudden, swift movement, Brettan crushed her slender frame against his lean, muscular body, the flame of her anger exciting within him a deep hungering passion, long restrained by his soldier's life.

35

With a practiced hand, he grasped her head in his strong grip, his long fingers playing along the corded muscles of her neck.

Maren reacted in stunned surprise at his touch of her and pulled back against his embrace, but her resistance seemed only to further excite the hunting beast.

Brettan stared into wide, deep blue eyes that mirrored his passion, and then pulled her closer within his grasp, his head suddenly lowering, his lips crushing hers in a kiss that was meant to proclaim his authority over her.

Maren's head was forced back by the pressure of his kiss, so that she felt her neck would surely break, yet she sensed the firm support of his hand behind her head, and knew there was no escape. Her mind revolted against the very thought of his boldness with her, while his lips moved across hers, his tongue warm and surprisingly sweet as he probed between her own lips, and he seemed to draw the very breath from her. His lips burned across hers, so that she felt branded by his touch. Her thoughts were that she must struggle with all her strength against this English knight who was an enemy in her father's house, but her body would not obey her feeble commands, but seemed to have a will of its own, for she felt a raging heat burst forth and spread through her entire body, building to consume her. Through her confused emotions, Maren felt herself leaning into his well-muscled, mail-covered chest. She was crushed against him, and her mouth moved against his in sudden response, igniting a fire of its own as her lips parted willingly beneath the new and pleasurable sensations of his kiss.

Unprepared for the heated response he felt within the slender girl, Brettan fought to regain his composure, though he felt a familiar stirring deep within. Roughly he pushed her from him before he could yield to a stronger desire to bed her there, with little regard for the slain woman who lay before them.

Maren's cheeks flamed crimson, then her eyes closed in her silent agony, and she yielded to her sorrow, crumpling to the stone flooring beside her dead mother.

Gently Brettan released her wrists. Her grief washed over her, the sobbings barely heard, and she reached out to the dead woman. He longed to comfort her, to take her sorrow for his own. Oblivious to all else about them, Brettan de Lorin reached out to stroke her head gently, that he might ease her grief, but he pulled back suddenly when the old maid entered the chamber. Brettan drew to his full height and retrieved his gauntlets, then turned to the stout woman.

"Your mistress is slain. See to her as you will." Brettan quickly turned on his heel and pressed past Agnes, not waiting to learn if she understood his words.

Maren grasped her mother's slender hand in her own. She lifted it tenderly to her cheek, that she might yet feel the gentle warmth she had known in that touch. Her tears fell unchecked, and she let her sadness flow completely, when within her grasp she felt the coldness of metal. A small object fell from her mother's hand. Her fingers closed around a small medallion which glowed golden in the fading light within the chamber. The figure of a lion's head gleamed back but held no meaning for her.

Agnes stepped back and left the chamber. There were no words of solace she might offer her young mistress that could ease her pain.

Maren had no idea of how long she remained in that chamber of death. She roused herself and attempted to stand, her knees nearly giving way beneath her from having bent so long. Slowly she made her way to the hall below.

Some semblance of order had been restored to the room. Broken furniture had been removed, and the large tapestry now hung securely. Agnes' hand was evident all about the great hall. Thomas stood before the hearth, glancing up when Maren slowly crossed the room. She sank wearily into a chair before the open hearth in an attempt to drive the coldness from her body, as well as her mind.

"Thomas, what of Edmund? Has he been found?" Maren asked, but the lad remained strangely quiet. She glanced at him sharply.

"With what I have already seen this day, what more might there be that could be worse?"

Thomas glanced uneasily at Agnes, who had entered from the kitchens, and mutely appealed to her for some aid in what he must tell his mistress.

Maren rose from the chair, her temper rising at the lad's silence. Thomas dared much in the face of her shattered composure.

"You must tell me what you know. What of my brother?" Maren pressed, her voice quavering.

Agnes reached out a hand to her young mistress in an effort to calm the growing hysteria she saw in those wide, blue eyes. But it was William, rousing himself painfully from his pallet before the hearth, who tried to answer Maren's questions, the agony in his shoulder overcoming him, his face pale from his efforts.

"Those who have attacked the castle have also taken young Edmund captive," the old man whispered weakly.

Seeing the sudden distress clear on his mistress' face, Thomas quickly continued for the man.

"I do not believe they mean to harm the lad. I am certain they intend to ransom him for a costly sum from your father, or perhaps gain some advantage against the king."

William nodded his agreement weakly. "If they had intended to harm the lad, they would not have bothered taking him with them. Nor would they have left anyone

38

alive to tell of the matter."

Maren closed her eyes against the rising panic that threatened to overcome her, pressing her fingers tightly against the growing ache at her temples.

"They! Who are 'they'? Who has done this, and why? I cannot understand why anyone would attack Cambria. There is nothing here anyone might want." Maren missed the look that passed between Agnes and the wounded steward.

"William, you must tell me everything you can remember."

The steward spoke slowly through the pain that clouded his memory. "We knew nothing of the attack, mistress, until they were among us and drew their blades to strike us down."

Maren's voice softened as she noticed the man's distress. "What of the captain of the guards? Surely the alarm was given?"

William shook his head in denial. "The captain of the guards was one of the first to fall. Of the entire guard, numbering four score men, few more than thirty have survived. I ordered the hall barricaded against their attack, and you saw well how the guard fell before the enemy. They were cut down from within the hall, by ones who knew their path well. The element of surprise served their purpose, and our men ran about putting out fires, while their men cut us down where we stood. They carried no banners nor crest upon their shields. Indeed, they wore no armor. They stole quietly among us, dressed as we in simple garments, so as not to draw attention to their presence. I cannot give names to the men who were here, but they fought like skilled soldiers. And the words they spoke were Welsh, for I heard them clearly after they thought they had finished with me."

"William, the Welsh would not dare attack here. My mother's family is one of the oldest in all of Wales.

39

Llywelyn's soldiers would not attack their own people."

"Aye, mistress, I know well your thoughts. But remember too, your father is English and holds these lands by virtue of his marriage to your mother. You, your brothers, and young Catherine are of his blood, half English and half Welsh. Llywelyn and those who follow his cause consider you to be English."

"But we are Welsh, and my mother is of Welsh blood. Her father, and his father before him, were lords of this land. They too fought against the English. It cannot be that Llywelyn would strike against a family older than his in loyalty to Wales." Maren fought against the doubts that flooded her thoughts.

Thomas spoke. "Mistress, I would more readily believe that those same English, who now roam your father's hall and pretend to give us their protection, are the very ones who attacked Cambria. The one who leads them, the English duke, gives his orders to our men for the fortification of the castle, as if he had assumed command of the place. Nay, mistress, look to the English for your mother's murderers, and guard well that they not know you to be mistress of this hall, lest you should suffer the same fate as the others we have found."

Maren felt the coldness of the gold medallion in her hand and raised her eyes to stare at the young man.

The steward added his agreement. "We know not these English, nor their purpose at Cambria. We must guard well."

She shook her head in disbelief. "Do you forget so quickly, Thomas, that your lord and the master of this hall is English? I think my father would hardly tolerate such disloyalty were he to hear your words."

Alarmed at the anger he saw in those stormy blue eyes, Thomas held up his hands in supplication. "Mistress, I sought only to remind you that Llywelyn makes his war on the English. The English who now occupy this hall know not our loyalties, nor would they easily believe that our sympathies lie with the English king. They would see only treachery in any truth we might offer them."

William feebly nodded his agreement with Thomas' words. "These English are not your father's men and, though I would strongly deny that they are guilty of the crimes committed against this house, we know not their mission or their character. It would serve no purpose for you or the young mistress to suffer further for those who are now dead. Let them continue to believe you are merely a servant in this hall, and at the first opportunity we will send you from here to a place of safety until such time as your father and brother are returned from the north country."

Maren considered the old man's words and saw the wisdom of them. Indeed, they knew not the character of these men. A warm glow spread across her cheeks as she remembered that bold knight and his handling of her. She was silently grateful for the lengthening shadows that fell across the hall and partially hid her face from William and Thomas. She could not easily have explained the strange emotions that flowed over her at that vivid memory. Maren sighed heavily. She knew old William was right, and there were others to consider. She studied the emblem of the fierce lion emblazoned across the face of the medallion. Her reverie was broken when the large doors to the main hall were abruptly thrown back to allow more soldiers to enter, and her attention was drawn to the tall man who walked before them, the brilliant blue tabard he wore over his chain mail smudged with soot and dirt, from his labors with his men to quell the fires within the keep.

With sudden urgency, Thomas pulled Maren back into the shadows near the hearth. Desperately he tried to hasten her along the far wall to the servants' chambers near the kitchens, but Maren waved him back, hesitating

41

in order to gain a better look at these English who had invaded her home, and more particularly their bold, arrogant leader.

The one known as the Duke of Norfolk turned to speak with his men, and Maren could barely discern his features in the waning light that glowed within the hall. When he glanced about to survey the hall, Maren shrank back into the safety of darkness. Her breath caught in her throat to see his face in the light of the nearby candles. Those golden-green eyes were as she had remembered them, and they held her transfixed. They seemed to see into every corner of the room, and she felt certain he had seen her in the darkness, for certainly nothing escaped that piercing gaze, those orbs glowing like live coals upon the hearth. A deep consuming warmth spread over Maren as she stared at the man. His dark hair was longer than the style worn by most men, with natural waves curled to frame his lean face, bronzed golden by long hours in the sun. His aquiline nose was set between finely arched brows of that same rich, dark brown color. A long, thin scar ran the length of his left cheek just beyond the browline, the pink of the freshly healed skin giving stark contrast to the golden brown of his face, and she wondered what hand had caused such injury to so bold a knight. Maren stared openly at his handsome profile, and a soft gasp escaped her lips when he raised his gaze, his finely shaped mouth curved into a slight frown with the efforts of his concentration, while he discussed some matter with his men. Maren was horrified at the sudden thought that a smile on those lips would indeed be a pleasurable sight to see. She steeled herself against her thoughts. He would not find her the easy prey he had found her mother and brother. Her gaze lowered to the brilliant blue field of the tabard worn resplendently upon his broad chest, and the emblem she saw there was the figure of a golden hunting lion woven in the luxurious fabric. An unbearable coldness swept over her, for the full memory of that same figure on the medallion glared in her brain.

Maren steadied herself against the coolness of the stone wall at her back. At Thomas' insistent pulling at her arm, she flattened herself against the wall and quietly retreated to the temporary safety of the servant's chambers.

Brettan de Lorin gave no indication that he had seen the figure stealing silently through the shadows to escape the hall. He instantly recognized the slender form of the servant girl, and his thoughts were filled with the memory of her beguiling form and his unmistakable stirring at their earlier meeting. He turned to his knight Sandlin.

"Have the girl watched. If she attempts any treachery, have her brought to me immediately. I know not yet the truth of her presence here, but it is more than we are led to believe."

Sandlin nodded curtly and left to give other orders to his men. The Duke of Norfolk studied the crudely drawn map that lay before him, but his thoughts were not on the markings and locations to be found there. His men would guard well against any treachery should the girl be other than she appeared. But although he would have preferred to take his ease in the hall, perhaps taking the girl to share her warmth, he would make his pallet with his men upon the open ground, for he trusted no one. He was now certain the attack upon the castle had come from within. He folded the map and wrapped it within its leather bindings. They would not remain longer than was necessary for his men to restore order to the fortress, and for the steward to take command until his master returned. It would take them more than a score of days to reach the English border from this remote outpost, to rejoin the king, and he did not want to risk his men

43

further in this game of chase they played with the Welsh rebels. Already he had pushed deeper into Wales than was clearly wise in his unrelenting quest for revenge.

A worried frown furrowed his sun-bronzed visage as Brettan tried to gain some understanding of why the Welsh would attack their own people. He knew well that the lady of the castle had been high born, and her father one of the powerful marcher lords of the region, commanding vast holdings of land and wealth. He had learned nothing of the others that might have survived, only that none of the family had been found within the castle, and that in itself seemed odd. There remained only a few servants who had chosen bravely to defend the castle against great odds, and for the most part had lost their lives for their cause. He glanced across the room at the wizened old steward being lifted by a young lad and removed to the servants' chambers. Brettan knew well the old man understood the words they spoke, for he had seen a spark of response at the mention of King Edward. But Brettan's questions of the family or their whereabouts had drawn only a blank, unyielding expression that masked complete understanding.

Brettan took no great comfort in the evening meal. His men ate silently, the somber mood of the day hanging over all of them. They retired from the hall to seek their beds of straw in the courtyard beyond, preferring the cool night air to the atmosphere of sadness and death that ruled the hall.

Maren stepped from the small chapel and softly closed the door behind her, gently lowering the latch into place. She had ordered her mother taken there, and with Agnes' help prepared her for burial. Later she had sent the maid from the chapel and remained for a time staring at that face—still beautiful in gentle repose, as if her mother but slept—trying to find some meaning in her mother's death.

Now, her legs ached from standing so long. A shiver ran through her weary body, and she noticed the last embers had long since died upon the hearth in the large hall. Mercifully, she found the English had chosen to camp outside the main hall, leaving some measure of privacy to those within, with only one guard posted at the main entrance. Her head throbbed and, to her horror, she knew an unrelenting hunger that gnawed at her and would not be willed away. It only added to her misery that, in the face of such death and destruction, simple needs went on as before.

Her fatigue heavy upon her young face, Maren crossed the room. Thomas had moved William to a small chamber near the kitchens, where he might be more easily cared for. She found him there and carefully checked the bandages. The bleeding had stopped. Maren sighed her relief that the steward might yet recover from his wounds. Gently she tucked the bandages back into place and looked up when she felt his steady gaze upon her. His eyes were glassy and marked by the heat of the fever that spread through his body, but he reached out a weak hand to touch her arm.

"Mistress, there are matters we must speak of. I have already sent word to your father and brother of the attack. But it may be days, perhaps even weeks, before they can return to Cambria."

"Surely this may wait till the morrow," Maren pleaded gently.

Stubbornly, William persisted against the mounting pain in his shoulder.

"The hour is late. Already it is the morrow, and this cannot be delayed. I must follow the orders your father gave me before he left for the north country. And perhaps in this small way I may yet redeem myself." The man's voice came as little more than a whisper, and Maren was forced to lean forward so that she might

45

clearly hear his words.

"You must leave Cambria, mistress, at once, until such time as your father can return to defend this hall."

Maren shook her head sadly. She knew well the wisdom of his words. The longer she and Catherine remained at Cambria, the greater the risk they might be found out. Though she might be willing to take that chance, she did not have the right to risk further harm to her sister.

"Yes, good William. Well I know the truth of your words, but there are matters which carry more import than my safety. I must first see my mother properly buried. It must be done by loving hands. I could not bear the thought of strangers seeing the matter done, nor could I easily trust them with it." She spoke softly.

"I understand what you feel, child, but your safety falls to me, and as long as there is strength in me, the decision is mine. I pray you will forgive me for it."

Maren smiled gently, knowing her argument already lost. She placed an affectionate kiss upon his coarsely whiskered cheek.

"I understand your duty to my father, but you must also understand mine."

Seeing his mistress would not easily be dissuaded, William sighed his resignation for the moment and retreated to his fitful dozing. When she was satisfied that he rested comfortably, Maren rose and quietly left the chamber.

Maren sat on the narrow bench in the kitchen and contemplated the empty platter before her. If starving oneself was a measure of one's grief at a loss, then she had none. Arguing with Agnes that she could not possibly eat anything, she had avoided the woman's smug look of

46

satisfaction when the platter was cleaned with hardly a crumb remaining. She drained the goblet of wine for the second time, drawing a slight frown from the maid, but she chose to ignore it. The warmth that spread through her from the liquid was welcome compared to the aching cold which seemed to grow deep within her from the sadness and death she had seen that day.

The fire beneath the cook-pot danced merrily before her and suddenly seemed to set the room aglow. Her jangled thoughts would not respond when she tried to remember the day. She again emptied the goblet, concentrating on the bright embers at the hearth, which glowed back at her like cat eyes, stalking her. Her memory was filled with the vision of the golden-green eyes of that English knight, and she remembered those moments in her mother's chamber when he had held her firmly in his grasp. Her cheeks flamed brightly at the memory of his hard chest pressed firmly against her, and his bold kiss that had seemed to burn against her lips. All her senses suddenly seemed aflame, as if that lean, stalking beast had entered the room and but watched her with his glowing eyes which seemed to see into her soul. She struggled to forget his face and the brilliant blue of his tunic, with the fierce lion woven in rich, gold threads, but she found herself too weak to turn away from the eyes that glowed at her from his bronzed face. Her hand had become quite heavy and would not obey her. She reached for the goblet, completely unaware that it teetered, precariously balanced on the edge of the table.

Only Agnes' quick movement saved the goblet from tumbling to the stone flooring.

Maren rose on unsteady feet, the golden glow from the wine spreading through her body, and she leaned forward to grasp the edge of the table for support, her knees unsteady beneath her. Vaguely she saw Thomas' lanky

47

frame outlined in the doorway, but little else. The golden glow from the hearth seemed to vanish, and the room darkened.

Maren offered no resistance when Agnes hurried Thomas forward to carry his young mistress to a bed that awaited in a small chamber at the far end of the servants' hall. She saw only the lean, handsome face that crowded her memory, finally yielding to the thick fog that seemed to reach out for her, surrounding her like a thick, soft mantle as she sank further into the deep abyss of slumber.

Agnes carefully removed the woolen tunic, smeared with soot and dirt, and then the light linen shift underneath, leaving Maren naked beneath the heavy coverlet. She tenderly smoothed back the curling, raven tendrils that circled her exquisite face, now peaceful in sleep.

Maren stirred against the chill in the darkened room, and Agnes pulled the coverlet high over bare shoulders and tucked the edges in, as she had done countless times before, since Maren was a child. She placed more wood on the dying fire at the hearth to warm the chamber through the rest of the night, then left to take up her vigil beside the younger girl who slept in the chamber across the hall, haunted by dreams from which no potion could free her.

Chapter Three

Maren awakened to the sounds of horses and soldiers in the courtyard, muffled from behind the stone walls but nonetheless distinct.

Vivid memories of the day before flooded over her, and she sat up quickly. Her head felt twice its normal size, and the loud persistent buzzing in her ears would not be silenced. Slowly pushing aside the heavy coverlet, Maren could see the glow of sunlight through the cracks of the shutters. Wrapping herself against the chill in the chamber, she moved slowly across the room to the windows and unlatched one of the shutters so that she might see out.

Beyond the mass of men who assembled, ready to ride, she could see what remained of the stables and the garrison, both buildings now reduced to little more than charred rubble. In the cool of the morning air, an occasional wisp of smoke could still be seen rising from the blackened ruins. Maren shuddered to remember the sounds that had come from those buildings while the horses and dogs trapped within had died slow and agonizing deaths in the flames. Her stomach lurched uncertainly, and she pushed the shutters closed. She turned abruptly when Agnes entered the chamber, carrying a tray amply laden with fruits and fresh, warm bread to break the fast. Beside it she set a mug of steaming, dark liquid, then went about setting some order to the room.

Maren sipped the brew carefully, gently probing her aching temple.

"Agnes, what of Catherine this morn?" she questioned, her words spoken softly so as not to bring on the buzzing that had for the moment subsided. She let the steaming liquid warm her.

"Your sister is as well as might be expected for now. She slept the night through but would eat nothing of the morning meal. Her mind is not clear. She sits and stares into the shadows. I must keep careful watch over her, or she is likely to wander and there is too much danger with these English about. 'Tis not a safe place for her, or for you either. William is right in his decision to send us from here. Fine protection Sir Geoffrey provided us, after his promises to your father. Where was he when he should have been here to protect this hall?" Agnes shook her graying head in despair.

Maren cast the older woman a sideways glance, knowing the direction of their conversation, and wishing to avoid the argument that always followed any discussion of Geoffrey and his proposals of marriage to her. Agnes considered her childhood friend a highly unworthy suitor and had cackled with controlled approval when Lord de Burghmond had refused to give his consent to the betrothal. Maren remembered all too well her father's steadfast refusal to consider the marriage, but his reasons had always seemed unclear. True though it was that she had never felt any all-consuming passion for Geoffrey such as her friends confessed for certain swains, she still valued his friendship and, indeed, felt a great fondness for him. Her father, however, had not felt the same fondness.

Agnes slammed down the heavy lid of the wooden coffer as she returned with a clean tunic Maren might wear, her exasperation clear on her face.

Maren smoothed the soft wool of the plain, gray gown and with Anges' help dressed before the warmth of the fire. She ran her hands down the length of the tunic and fastened the simple woven belt about her slender waist. Bending to pull on soft, leather slippers, she paused to drag long fingers through the tangled lengths of her raven tresses. She caught sight of her disheveled appearance in the small hand mirror on the table and stopped to bind the black mass with a single length of ribbon, absently tossing the thick, curling tresses over her shoulder, out of her way, before she moved to leave the chamber.

Agnes halted her flight with a restraining hand on her young mistress' arm. She insistently settled the hood of the tunic in place over Maren's head to discourage prying glances, should the English return to the hall for their morning meal. She eyed her young mistress steadily as she spoke to the girl.

"Thomas has word that the English will leave within a few days' time. It is said they await but to see there will be no further attacks against Cambria. I do not easily believe their words and, until they have gone, you must not be seen about. You could only come to harm were they to know you are mistress of this hall."

"I fear you are right, Agnes," Maren nodded in agreement. "But there are other matters which must be attended. A priest must be brought to bless the graves. I will not leave until it is properly done." Quelling any further protests with a look that tolerated no argument, she turned and left the chamber.

Maren paused for a moment at her sister's chamber and peered inside. She found Catherine sitting in a chair

51

beside the narrow bed. She was washed and neatly dressed, with her long golden hair clean and gathered back from her face. Her eyes gazed past Maren toward some distant point only she could see. Maren knelt beside the chair and gently gathered the two smaller hands into her own. Catherine's gaze never wavered; she seemed not to notice Maren's presence in the room. Maren stared at the girl, tears welling in her eyes at the thought of what her sister had suffered. She finally stood and made to leave the room, but Catherine began humming an old lullaby. The girl mouthed the lyrics in a mournful singsong voice, singing the words Maren had not heard in a very long time. Their mother had sung the verses to them as babies, and sometimes later she would sing it for the girls, long after young Edmund was no longer a babe. Catherine clung to Maren's hands with uncommon strength and continued to sing the verses.

"Dear Catherine, everything will be all right. I promise you." Maren stroked the girl's hair, desperately hoping her sister might understand some of what she said.

Gently, she withdrew her hand from the steel-like grip that clung to her as if to life itself and, reaching for a woolen shawl upon the bed, she draped it snugly about Catherine's shoulders for extra warmth. With a final thought before leaving the chamber, Maren stopped and lit a small candle in the alcove across from the bed. The golden light from that one slender taper cast a softness about the room, as if it would protect the young girl, who sat lost within the confines of the prison terror had made of her mind.

A deep raw anger grew in her heart as Maren straightened her shoulders and turned to leave the room. Her decision was made. She must see Catherine safely away from Cambria, and then she would begin her search for her brother. She silently vowed her own revenge on those who had caused the girl's madness and taken their

52

mother's life.

Maren moved quietly down the long hallway toward the main hall beyond, stepping discreetly among the shadows that lined the passageway. Sounds of men's voices came to her, and she knew the English soldiers had indeed returned to break the morning fast. Reaching the end of the narrow hallway, she peered carefully from her secluded vantage point in search of Thomas, but drew back at the sight of the Duke of Norfolk, who stood only a few paces from where she now hid from view. His height marked him from the others, the brilliant blue tunic replaced by common leather garments, and she could not help but notice the strikingly handsome figure he cut in those simpler clothes. The leather breeches fit snugly, seeming to have been cut just for his muscular thighs, and long leather boots reached well above his knees. A linen shirt was worn over his broad chest with sleeves that flowed loosely to his wrists, the deep bronze of his skin marking sharp contrast with the lighter fabric. Over the shirt he wore a leather jerkin lined with fur against the early morning chill which, even in the warmer months of the year, sent chilling fingers stealthily through thin garments.

Maren leaned back into the safety of the shadows. Sensing the uncertain beating of her heart, she felt certain that all must certainly hear it. She closed her eyes against the rising warmth that flowed through her when she stared at the bold knight whose authority seemed to command the hall. Some small comment drew his attention in her direction, and a startled gasp escaped her lips. She seemed to be staring straight into those glowing eyes, as if he knew very well that she hid in the shadows of the corridor.

Maren moved back along the wall, unaware of a second gaze that watched her intently. Strong arms reached out through the darkness, soundly trapping

53

her, pulling her back along the passage to the kitchens, a hand firmly clasped over her mouth against any outcry.

Maren struggled in blind panic against the strong grasp. Both her arms were firmly pinned to her sides, so that it was impossible to strike out. She was hauled back into the kitchen, and wildly glanced about for the cook or one of the other servants. The room was deathly silent except for her strugglings and the soft sound of her slippered feet against the stone flooring as she sought to maintain her footing. Refusing to yield easily, Maren twisted about in an effort to loosen the man's hold of her, and she brought her slipper down sharply upon her attacker's foot. She heard a muffled curse, and the words came clearly to her in the heavy Welsh language. Her name was grunted in pain from between clenched teeth while the stranger sought to restrain her movements and prevent further harm. Her strength rapidly fleeing, Maren hung limp, pinned helplessly between the man's body and the stone wall. She fought to regain her breath, struggling with one last effort against the hold about her.

"Maren! Cease before you do us both harm." A harsh whisper pierced through the wall of her fear.

She stared to gain some recognition of the shadowy figure, but she could barely discern his face under the hood the man wore. Numbly she nodded her understanding of his words and was slowly released until she was held but a small distance from that face.

"Geoffrey!" Maren gasped at the sight of the man who stood before her, supporting her slender frame. She could have fainted from sheer joy at the sight of him.

"Geoffrey, are you not harmed? What of the English? Do they know you are here?" Maren's questions tumbled one over the other as Geoffrey gently laid a quieting finger upon her lips, warning her to silence.

"There will be time enough for this later. For now I

54

must find a place where the English will not find me. I vow, they leave no stone unturned. I was nearly found out early this morn."

"I know of a place where you might hide. The storeroom on the far side of this kitchen will be safe enough, though I warrant there is no place they have not searched." Maren whispered from the shadows.

"At least here I shall have a roof over my head and food aplenty to ease my hunger. It will suffice for now."

Maren pulled Geoffrey along with her as she moved past the huge hearth, down a short passage to a heavy wooden door that led to the large storeroom.

Geoffrey sank wearily down upon the uneven mounding of grain sacks that lined the floor, while Maren searched for a candle. He leaned back on the bed of bulging sacks, closing his eyes against his fatigue, then slowly opened them to stare, through the dim light that poured forth from the kitchen, at the girl who sat expectantly before him. A slow smile spread across his lean face as he regarded her radiant beauty clearly outlined in the dreariness of the room. The coarse wool of her simple garments could not hide the ample curve of her breasts, nor the slender waist that tapered from those full, firm orbs. He vividly recalled when he had held her in his arms, but a few moments before, and felt the softness of her woman's body, pressed full length against his own. That memory caused him no little discomfort as he sought to hide from her the stirrings her youthful beauty caused in him.

"Maren, how I prayed I would find you safe. When we first saw the fires and the smoke, I could only fear the worst." Geoffrey spoke softly. He leaned forward, his face smeared and creased with dirt and soot from having crawled among the ruins the night before. Taking one of her slender hands in his, he bent low to place a kiss upon it.

Maren pulled back uneasily and then turned, somehow relieved, when Agnes' bulk filled the doorway. The maid regarded Geoffrey contemptuously.

"And where might you have been, Sir Geoffrey, when Cambria was under attack, young Edmund abducted, and the Lady Julyana so cruelly murdered? 'Twas your Welsh guard that was given the safekeeping of the castle in my lord's absence." Agnes glared at the young man.

"Agnes, please." Maren pleaded with the woman. Behind her Agnes huffed her disapproval but spoke no more, regarding him suspiciously.

"Maren, I did not know of your mother's death, nor that Edmund had been taken captive," Geoffrey spoke carefully. "We only chanced upon an English patrol just beyond Cambria. Several of my men were killed as they gave chase." He spoke convincingly, gazing into those deep blue, velvet pools.

"Geoffrey, who are these men you speak of? Do you know anything of them, or where they might have taken Edmund?" Maren questioned anxiously.

"Your surprise to find the English here at Cambria could have been no greater than mine. They must surely have known that your father and a good number of his guard are away to the north. We received word that the English might strike in the south. We guarded against it, Maren, but their numbers were too great." Geoffrey hesitated, seeing her uncertainty at his words.

"The English have harmed no one that I can see. They offer aid and protection, and Thomas has told me they remain only to be certain that Cambria is secure, and will soon be gone." Maren said nothing of William's report of the Welsh who had attacked Cambria. Could the old man have been mistaken? The thought that the attackers had indeed been her own people gave her more fear than the English who now held the castle, for it meant there were none she might trust completely. Maren shivered uncontrollably against the fears that rose within her.

Geoffrey reached out a comforting arm and gently pulled her within his embrace, the very nearness of her, the fresh smell of her skin and hair teasing his firmly restrained passions. How long had he patiently awaited the time when she would at last be his? And now that opportunity had presented itself so much more clearly than he could ever have planned.

"Maren, could you but send the woman on an errand? I must speak with you, and I cannot be certain who may now be trusted."

"I have no secrets from Agnes. What you would say to me, you may say before her."

Geoffrey cast a menacing look over Maren's head at the older woman who stood firmly inside the opened portal, yet he knew the bond between Maren and the maid was strong, and if he were to gain Maren's favor it was necessary that he not make an enemy of the old woman.

"Maren, you must leave Cambria at once. The safest place for you, and the Lady Catherine of course, is at Meyrick Hall, where you will have the protection of my guard. These English are not to be trusted, though I know well your doubts of my words. These men are the ones responsible for your mother's death. Can you not see? They know not of your father and are pledged to one cause, striking against our people. And now they have taken Edmund. Maren, come with me to Meyrick. There we can send word of this to your father in the north, and see to Edmund's release," Geoffrey pleaded earnestly.

"Geoffrey, I know well your fears, for they are also mine. I have decided that I must take Catherine to the abbey of St. David's. I know it would be my father's decision. But we must await our chance when the English are not about, for I fear they might prevent our leaving. For now you must remain here, for it is the only place

57

they are not likely to search. I will make the necessary plans and return as soon as I can." Maren reached out a reassuring hand to his arm.

Geoffrey seized her hand and pressed an impassioned kiss upon her fingers.

"You must take great care, Maren, and do not let them know that you are mistress here. You have seen well how your mother suffered for it."

Maren pulled her hand back, uneasy at Geoffrey's eagerness for her to believe the English responsible for her mother's murder, when William had spoken his doubts of it.

"I will return when it is safe." Maren rose and followed Agnes from the storeroom, closing the door securely behind them to guard their secret.

"I do not trust him," Agnes whispered vehemently as they left the kitchen. "Why is he here now, and not before, when your mother and Edmund needed his protection? Nay, do not trust his words, mistress. Sir Geoffrey cares for nothing beyond his own gain. I have seen it in the child these long years. It is no different in the man. Your father saw it also. Can you not see it to be the reason your father refused to allow your marriage to him?"

"Agnes, please. This argument is old between us. Geoffrey means only to offer us his protection. I know not the reasons for his absence when Cambria was attacked. For now I can only accept what he has told us. The one thing I am certain of is that I must take Catherine from here. And I will need Geoffrey's help in that."

Agnes followed Maren down the passageway toward the main hall.

"If we are to leave Cambria, we will need clothes for the journey. I must try to find some more suitable garments in my brother's room." Maren looked across

58

the hall at the knights who stood before the hearth with the Duke of Norfolk.

"It is far too dangerous. The more you are seen about, the greater the risk that the English will become suspicious of you." Agnes tried to reason with Maren.

The large oaken doors of the hall were thrown open, a cold gust of early morning wind swirling in around the knights who now entered the hall. Maren seized her opportunity while the attention of the Duke of Norfolk was drawn to his men, newly returned from a patrol about the countryside. Brushing off Agnes' restraining hand, Maren flattened herself against the stone wall and quietly slipped through the shadows near the hearth, behind the soldiers and the English duke. She felt the coolness of the stones beneath her hands as she felt her way along the wall toward the stairway to the second-floor chambers.

Agnes wrung her hands fretfully, watching Maren's progress, barely discernible among the play of shadows across the far wall.

Maren quickly crossed the dimly lit landing and moved silently up the steps, the soft-leather of her slippers noiseless on the stone steps, and those below her seemed oblivious to her movement.

Andrew's chamber was at the far end of the long hallway from her own. How very odd that his room had been left untouched by the attackers. Maren crossed to the long narrow table where her brother kept the few precious books he had acquired from the priests at the abbey. Thoughtfully she ran her fingers across the heavy leather binding on the one that kept all the entries of the activities of Cambria since before her grandfather. Her father and Andrew seemed so very far away now, when she needed them so desperately. Maren sighed heavily and willed herself not to yield to her sadness. She was now responsible for Catherine's safety, and she must see it through, then see what might be learned of Edmund. She refused to believe that her younger brother might have met the same fate as her mother.

Maren moved to the heavy wooden coffer at the far side of the room. Searching through the neatly folded garments that Andrew had chosen not to take with him to the north country, she quickly found the well-worn but sturdy leather tunics and breeches she had hoped to discover; functional garments which would serve far better for a long journey than the long, flowing woolen gowns which only hampered ease of movement. Better, also, to disguise the form of a young girl as that of a lad.

Loud voices came through the door from the hall below, and Maren stopped to listen. It seemed as if the voices were drawing closer.

The door to the chamber was thrown open with a loud crash that seemed to echo against the stone walls. The heavy lid to the wooden coffer slammed shut when Maren jumped back in startled surprise, her gaze suddenly filled with the sight of the tall, imposing form that seemed to fill the portal with his menacing presence. Golden-green eyes glared at her with deadly intent.

From the hall below, Maren could hear the sounds of struggling, and then Geoffrey's belated warning as he screamed her name.

"No!" Maren screamed her indignation, as she flew across the room, in an effort to reach Geoffrey below, her fear strong for his fate at the hands of the English. But her flight was suddenly halted when she was grabbed firmly about the waist by a lean, well-muscled arm. The Duke of Norfolk barred her retreat.

Maren's first fear faded into blind, seething rage, as she struck out against his hold on her, but even as she struggled, she realized she would not easily break it, for his grasp was like a band of steel firmly about her. She lashed out with her hands, for the moment still free, and clawed with fingernails that were like deadly talons. But they found only air where they struck, and Brettan fought to restrain her hands.

"Hold! Hold, I say, lest you find yourself chained and flogged to restore order to this hall." He glared down at the girl he held firmly against him.

"I know well you understand my words." Brettan tightened his grip painfully about her slender waist, holding one of her arms pinned to her side, his other hand fighting to control hers.

Maren could hardly draw a breath, so tight was his grasp about her. She was held firmly against that hard expanse of chest. She could feel the play of his muscles beneath her breast, separated only by the smooth softness of their garments. Her senses were filled with the powerful warmth of his contact, driving from her all fears, all anger, all thoughts except that of his presence. That realization tore through her and angered her more than his discovery of Geoffrey in the storeroom. Maren's wrath flew to new heights, and she would have struck at that arrogant, bronzed face if she could have freed her hands.

"Maren!"

Her name on his lips shot through her like a molten shaft burning deep as it penetrated her anger, and she remained still within his grasp.

Brettan felt the fierce struggling ease within her. She regarded him warily, her head held proudly away from him, so that all she yielded was the perfect profile of her exquisite face, all her anger and fear set in the deep, vivid pools as brilliant as precious sapphires. He felt again, as he had one time before, a deep longing to see a smile upon the soft line of her mouth. He could almost feel the warmth of her lips against his, the velvet softness of her lithe young body, as he had held her the day before.

Maren strained away from his touch, aware of the

intimacy of his contact. She struggled anew at the unfamiliar closeness that kindled a deep glow within her, a glow that seemed to spread through her with a life of its own, a glow that brought with it a fear of what she had never before known.

Through barely clenched teeth Maren fairly spat at him, her gaze never wavering from the handsomely bronzed face where she refused to see anything but her enemy.

"Unhand me, you illgotten son of a swamp viper. I will not be treated so, not by you nor any English swine."

Brettan carefully eyed his beautiful young captive, who proudly stood her full, slender height before him, barely reaching his chest, yet defiant, as if she would have stayed the whole of King Edward's armies single-handedly, given the chance. He was silently impressed by her boldness, for no woman, English or Welsh, had shown him such uncommon spirit. Nor could he deny the sudden glow of warmth he felt beneath his hand, the same he had felt the day before, when he had first seen her in that second floor chamber with the dead woman. He was suddenly seized with a great longing to taste the fire upon her lips as he had felt it then, and the response he felt certain she was capable of. Gently he set Maren down, not trusting enough to release his hold of her wrist. One of his guards suddenly appeared in the doorway of the chamber.

"Have the prisoner bound and chained, until we may learn his purpose here," Brettan commanded, and the guard nodded, then left to carry out the orders.

Maren glared back at the man who towered above her, fully aware of his power over her. The Duke of Norfolk slammed the heavy portal closed, only now releasing his hold of her wrist, and then turned back, the feral, threatening glow in his green eyes now masked behind lids that concealed all emotion.

"You are called Maren. Who is your family, and what is your purpose in this hall?" Brettan leaned easily against the closed portal, crossing his arms casually across his chest, as he eyed the young beauty before him.

Maren's fists opened and closed at her sides as she fought for control, lest he know the fear that threatened her composure. Here was one who must be met with equanimity. If he knew her fear, he would use it against her, of that she was certain.

"You have your answers. I am but a servant in this hall. I have no family." Maren bit off her reply angrily.

"No, Maren. I have the answers you wish me to have. But I feel they are far from truth. I will have your answer, mistress, or by heaven, heads will roll. And I think yours shall perhaps be the first, for I value not a fair face that conceals disarming lies. Who is the mistress of this hall whom we found slain?" Brettan pressed her, a note of deathly calm in the rich timbre of his voice that seemed to caress her.

Maren fought to quell the trembling of her lips, determined not to cower before the towering knight. Oddly, she felt no fear for herself, only the desperate need to protect her sister. Guardedly, she raised her small chin a bit higher, gazing unafraid at the Duke of Norfolk.

"I am not one of your Welsh rebels, milord." Maren fairly choked over her words as she addressed him according to his title. "The lady who was slain was the Lady Julyana of Cambria."

Brettan regarded the girl keenly. The high spirit of the girl was surely far more than dared by any other servant, yet he could see that she would not easily tell him more. Reaching out, he gently lifted her chin, forcing her to meet his gaze.

Maren bridled at his casual treatment and tried to jerk her chin away from his touch. It burned her skin, leaving an invisible glow, and spread through her entire being.

63

Her confusion grew by the moment, that the man, whom she fully acknowledged as her enemy, should cause such stirrings within her. Maren raised her uncertain gaze to find that his green eyes held the same momentary confusion she had felt, and she knew a growing need to run from the hall and hide from this Englishman whose searching, glowing gaze seemed to touch her intimately, so that she somehow knew it would always haunt her.

Maren's breath became uneven. She tried to look away from his darkly handsome face, but found herself unable to break the contact of his golden gaze while his strong fingers firmly held her chin. That golden gaze burned into her like live embers from the hearth, and her vision was filled with his nearness. How she longed to pull away from him, to flee the uncertainty of her own feelings, but she found herself secured by bonds stronger than any chain. His lean, handsome face blurred before her, and Maren's breath caught in her throat at the feel of his warm lips so exquisitely soft against the corner of her mouth. Beyond her own will, Maren felt herself yielding to the heat of his touch, longing to feel again that kiss that had drawn her from herself. She sighed her silent torment, and her eyes closed, the long sweep of black lashes brushing against her cheek, as she turned trembling lips towards his instinctively.

Brettan drew her to him, his mouth moving across hers with deliberate slowness as he sought to taste her response fully. His long arms closed about her gently yet with a power that was unyielding. He molded her slender length against his own, the firm fullness of her breasts beneath her gown crushed against him. He felt her sudden hesitation and her feeble efforts to free herself.

Maren fought against the flood of uncertain emotions that threatened to destroy all her resistance to the bold English knight. She flattened the palms of her hands against the soft leather of his jerkin in an attempt to push

64

him away. His mouth sought hers, and then pressed fevered kisses along the delicate outline of her cheek, and down the gentle contour of her neck. She strained against his hold of her, unable to comprehend the emotions that washed over her. Again his lips pressed a kiss against the hollow of her throat, and Maren ceased her struggling. She longed for him to stop, to release her, to end his assault, and yet she slowly became aware of a subtle, almost imperceptible awakening deep within, while his lips traced the gentle curve of her neck.

Brettan reached up and buried his hands in the silken mass of her hair, freeing the raven-black tresses from the satin ribbon, breathing in the sweet fragrance of her hair.

His breath was warm against her skin, setting her aflame, as he murmured softly, drawing her resistance from her. Maren reached up, her hands closing around the neck opening of the leather jerkin, again trying to push him away. Her fingers brushed against his warm skin, that contact igniting within her a flame that destroyed all further resistance. Oblivious to anything or anyone beyond the walls of the chamber, Maren turned her face to his, and then drew him to her with a fierceness to match his own. Her lips responded to his, with a longing and a hunger she had never known.

Brettan tasted her sweet, honeyed response, her lips parting softly beneath his. As he explored the warm softness of her mouth, his hands gently pressed her to him, her slender hips molded against him. In any other he would have thought the move deliberate, yet he sensed a certain innocence within her.

From the depths of oblivion, Maren fought to regain her senses. She was horrified and angered at what she had allowed to happen. A deep anger welled within her, and she thought of what Catherine had been forced to endure. Her hands were pinned between them, flattened against his chest. Maren tried to twist away from his kiss but found herself powerless to restrain him. She felt as if she might smother if she did not break his hold of her. Desperately she pulled away.

Brettan pushed Maren from him, a flood of curses filling the air of the chamber. He stared at her in stunned surprise as he tasted the trickle of blood upon his lip where she had bitten him. Eyes the color of emeralds suddenly glowed menacingly, as he descended upon her.

Maren fled to the far side of the chamber, realizing she had dared much, and that further retreat was impossible. She might yet suffer Catherine's fate. She darted around the wooden coffer and flew for the doorway, but a moment too slowly, for his hand caught at her sleeve. He pulled her back, and Maren heard a sickening, rending tear as the fabric of her gown separated. She was drawn backwards and stumbled clumsily, nearly going down on her knees. Maren whirled about to face her attacker but halted in bafflement as she felt the coolness of air against her bare skin. Her gown had torn down the length of her back and at the shoulder and now fell away, exposing the fullness of her breasts beneath the gossamer sheerness of her chemise. Her strategy of attack now changed into a struggle to hold her gown together.

Gleaming skin caught the golden light of day and blushed faintly beneath his gaze. Brettan stared at a slender shoulder and the gentle rounded curve of one breast momentarily exposed, for the chemise had suffered the same fate as Maren's gown. Driven beyond all caution, he reached out, seizing a slender wrist, the gown now revealing more than it concealed from his hungering gaze. With ease he pulled Maren within his grasp and lifted her from the floor before she was aware of his intent. He quickly bore her to the bed at the far side of the chamber and fell with her across the mounding of the soft coverlet, pinning both hands to either side of her lovely head while she struggled to free herself.

Maren stared at her captor with an expression that bordered on complete terror. Whatever her fate might now be, she had only her own foolishness to blame for the matter. She silently cursed herself, closing her eyes in misery.

His beautiful young captive soundly trapped beneath him, Brettan gazed at the delicate outline of her face and the perfect skin, flushed a gentle pink from her efforts. His head lowered, and his lips gently caressed the heaving roundness of an exposed breast.

Maren's eyes flew open at the unexpected contact, and then her anger flared. "I demand that you release me at once."

Brettan's laugh was vibrant and warm from the depths of his throat as he nuzzled his fiery captive at her delicately curved ear. "I think, Maren, that you are in no position to make demands."

Maren struggled anew, realizing well the truth of his words, as his hands slowly wandered across every curve of her body. She groaned silently. A loud pounding sounded at the door, and her desperate gaze sought that portal. Above her, the Duke of Norfolk cursed under his breath, and then shifted away. In one easy movement he had reached the portal. "What is it?"

"Milord, riders, well-armed, have been seen north of the castle. They carry no standard, nor shield. They ride hard for the shelter of the forest beyond." The man spoke quickly.

Brettan de Lorin hesitated only a moment, then gave his orders to the soldier. "You have done well. See that my horse is ready. We shall follow these riders and see where they will lead us." Stepping into the hallway, he bellowed his orders to his knight below.

"Sandlin, see that guards are posted within the hall until my return."

The Duke of Norfolk turned back to gaze at her from

the doorway, his glowing gaze burning through her.

"We shall finish what we have begun, mistress. You have my promise of that."

He bowed mockingly before her, then turned on his heel and descended the wide staircase, followed by his soldier. Maren listened to their leaving, the noise that had filled the hall suddenly silenced with the slamming of its oaken doors. She sat in stunned stillness upon her brother's bed, trying to hold together the torn pieces of her gown, and a single tear trickled down her cheek.

Agnes moved up the wide stairway as fast as her aged legs would carry her. Fearing the worst, she entered the chamber at the end of the hallway. Maren sat on the end of the bed, her gown torn, her long hair in wild disarray.

"Dear child." A sob broke the old woman's voice, and she rushed to her young mistress.

Maren brushed back her tears, shaking her head fiercely. "I am all right, Agnes. He did not harm me, though I warrant I may not be so fortunate next time."

"Next time?" Agnes reached out a weathered hand to comfort her.

Maren's voice shook so that it was hardly more than a whisper. "Agnes, we must leave here at once. It is not safe for any of us. You must tell Thomas that we will leave before the Duke of Norfolk returns. What of Geoffrey?"

"He has been bound and chained, and is well guarded in the main hall."

"We must find a way to free him, for we cannot leave without him."

"Nay, mistress, it is impossible. There are two guards that keep constant watch, and two more guards at the door. How can we leave without their knowing of it?"

"We will not leave by the main hall. We must leave Cambria through the dungeons below to the seawall. From there we may be able to reach the forest. It is our only chance." Maren spoke, gaining confidence of her plan with each passing moment.

"But the guards—" Agnes wrung her hands frantically.

"Somehow we must find a way to draw their attention, so that we may free Geoffrey and leave the castle. If only it were night, we could slip away while they were sleeping," Maren mused thoughtfully.

A light gleamed in Agnes' eyes, and she clapped her hands together in sudden delight. Maren looked at her as if the old woman had suddenly taken leave of her senses.

"Aye, it might just work," Agnes cackled gleefully.

"What are you about?" Maren eyed the woman suspiciously.

"A potion, I think, for the midday meal, disguised within a hearty stew for our English invaders and, for just the right seasoning, a bit of a certain powder to bring on a nice, long nap." Agnes winked at Maren, knowing well where she might find such a powder.

Maren laughed excitedly, catching the maid's meaning. She rose and retrieved from the wooden coffer the garments she would need for their journey.

"I hardly think this gown will suffice, or I shall have Geoffrey to defend myself against."

Agnes' mood suddenly darkened. "Do not trust to his decisions. Trust only in what your dear father would have in this matter. Mark well my words, all is not as it seems with that young man. I am well favored to leave him to the English."

"Nay, Agnes. I cannot allow it. He is here because of me, and I will not betray him. I fear what his fate might be, if the Duke of Norfolk were to return and find we are gone, while Geoffrey remained. I fear he might end as my mother. And Geoffrey has pledged to see us to safety. We may well need his help to reach the abbey."

Agnes huffed her displeasure at Maren's decision. "I

shall go to help cook prepare the midday meal. We shall have hearty appetites, I'll warrant."

Maren smiled reassuringly at the old woman. "Make the stew one of the finest to be served at Cambria, Agnes. Much depends upon your skills now."

The knight Sandlin again checked the last of his guards and stood now staring at the leadened sky. The threat of rain had grown full force since the morning hours, only adding to his restless mood. His gaze scanned the battlements, and he carefully eyed his guards at their posts in the drum towers. He felt an uneasiness that had first set in when the Duke of Norfolk had ridden in pursuit of the unknown riders. The first droplets of rain fell and spattered on the stone steps. He entered the large hall and stood inside the massive portal for a few moments, letting his eyes adjust to the light within. A fire crackled at the hearth, sending golden flames dancing about the logs. Sandlin glanced about and found his two guards seated at the dining table. Suddenly aware of the uneasy silence that surrounded him, Sandlin crossed the hall in great, long strides. He placed a gloved hand firmly on the shoulder of one guard, and was not surprised when the man suddenly lurched forward onto the table, his face completely buried in the thick stew before him. His hand flew to his sword to guard against attack, and a loud snoring came from the opposite side of the table. Cautiously, Sandlin moved around the table, his eyes wary, searching the shadows of the great hall for unseen enemies. He stood in stunned disbelief as the soldier continued the loud snoring, and Sandlin realized the man was hardly slain, but fast asleep. A quick shake failed to rouse him. Sandlin persisted with rougher handling, but the man slept on, undisturbed. The knight stood back in shocked wonder at the sight of his fearsome soldiers reduced to sleeping babes. He yelled a blood-curdling oath for the trick played on him, for he was certain that he would find no one about; all had flown. His guards swarmed into the hall and searched each chamber, finding only the old steward, greatly weakened from loss of blood and delirious from fever.

Sandlin stared about the hall, his anger at his own foolishness clear upon his face, as he ordered his men to remove the two, who slept like babes in their mothers' arms. When the Duke of Norfolk returned, they would all face his certain anger at their failure that day. And that was not a moment he eagerly awaited.

Maren huddled within the entrance of the dark passageway, her arm firmly about Catherine's slender waist, as she guided the girl through the opening. Behind her, Agnes followed closely so as not to lose her way in the darkness. Geoffrey had remembered the old passage with amazing accuracy, moving along confidently in the meager light of one lantern.

Huddled closely together, they made their way along the twisting passageway that descended into the depths of Cambria Castle. The air became chilly about them, and Agnes wrapped a heavy woolen shawl about Catherine's shoulders when they stopped to rest. All about them were the sounds of the creatures that lived within the bowels of the castle—mice and rats that scurried about, and an occasional bat that whisked down on silent wings, the only sound of movement the stirring of air. Maren waved her arm to protect against one of the winged creatures, which had ventured too close to Catherine. The doeskin cap Maren wore offered little protection from the bats, but she was indeed glad she had chosen the leather breeches and tunic to keep her warm against the penetrating chill of the dark passage. Her feet fell silently

71

on the dampened stone steps, shod in leather boots that hugged her legs. A fur-lined vest gave her additional warmth and helped disguise her well-curved figure against prying eyes. Agnes plodded along, greatly hindered by the dragging skirts of the long gown she had steadfastly refused to relinquish. Beside the maid Catherine moved along mutely, no more than a puppet whose movements depended upon others, with no will of her own.

The old chambers they passed would have served as dungeons in another time, and Maren shivered uncontrollably as they continued their descent, feeling their way along the dampened and slime-covered walls, so scanty was the light from the lantern. The air grew fetid and seemed to disappear as they approached the sea level, before reaching the caverns. They stopped to rest one last time before moving on, and Maren found herself fighting for each breath, so rancid and foul was the air. She noticed for the first time that here the sounds of the bats and other creatures had ceased. Even those low creatures thought better than to venture here.

Maren pulled her sister more closely to her and talked to the girl in a low, sweet voice that belied their surroundings, seeking to quiet some of Catherine's unspoken fears.

They emerged at last into the cavern that led to the sea beyond. The sound of rushing water could be heard, and the pounding of the waves upon the rocks beyond the seawall was distinct from the rush of the wind, which brought the tangy welcome sea air to their nostrils. Almost as one, they inhaled deeply of the refreshing, cool air, which seemed to clear the spirit as well as the head. Moving in single file, they finally emerged beyond the seawall, onto the greensward which bordered the sandy beaches. Geoffrey hurried them into the shelter of the rocks which climbed the high cliff to Cambria Castle,

72

above them. Once they had reached the crest of the hill, they quickly made their way to the heavily wooded copse, taking shelter in the thick growth, while Geoffrey went to find his men. True to his word, he returned within two hours' time, and Maren pondered the ease with which he had obtained extra horses, another question that for the time must be left unanswered.

They wound their way through the woods away from Cambria, and Maren turned to take one long, last look at her home. She thought again of her mother, and her heart was heavy that she had not been allowed the time to lay that gentle one to final rest personally. But she felt a reassuring calm that William would see the deed properly done.

Solemnly Maren turned back in the saddle, the castle disappearing from view beyond the thick growth of trees that surrounded them. Hot tears flooded her eyes and spilled forth to roll down her cheeks, dropping softly on the leather vest. The warm saltiness mingled with the first droplets of rain that fell from the leadened sky.

The travelers were soon drenched on their way through the heavily wooded forest, the branches of the trees, sparsely leafed with new growth, offering little protection from the persistent downpour. The cloying dampness of the leather clothing only added to her misery, and Maren thought of young Edmund, whose fate she could not know. She shivered against the growing coldness of the spring rain, yet in her anguish she drew some small measure of comfort that Catherine would be safe.

The storm hampered their progress, the wind coming to drive gusts of rain like lashes at the huddled riders. They dared not risk stopping to seek shelter. Their only chance lay in continuing through the storm, putting as much distance as possible between themselves and Cambria, and hoping the Duke of Norfolk would await

73

clear weather before giving chase.

The storm raged about them and tore at their clothing, removing too all traces of their passage through the forest. But it could not remove the memory of glowing green eyes that bored into Maren's soul, or the searing heat of that impassioned kiss that had awakened within her unknown desires, placing bonds about her that no amount of time could ever remove.

Chapter Four

The riders continued their relentless flight through the long hours of the afternoon and far into the night, striving to escape the English. Only when exhaustion had set in and none could travel further did they seek shelter in the forest, among an outcropping of rocks. They made their beds upon the unyielding stones, oblivious to the storm that raged about them.

Maren rose at the first gray light of dawn. Slowly she felt a warm, tingling sensation from the blood moving through her cramped limbs. Beyond the secluded ledge where they had huddled through the night, Maren could see Thomas moving away from the camp, his long bow slung over one shoulder.

At the sound of her movement behind him, Thomas turned to smile grimly at his young mistress.

"Stay and rest. The ride shall begin soon enough, and you will need your strength. There is a stream nearby, and I but thought to fill the skins before we leave."

"I shall join you. Two more hands will make light work, and the walk will be welcomed. I hurt in places I did not know existed." Seeing the disapproving look that crossed Thomas' face, Maren gave him one of her most beguiling smiles. "I will come whether you allow it or not."

Thomas handed her two of the skins and headed through the brush at the edge of the clearing, knowing well that to refuse her would only have made her more determined in the matter.

Maren removed the leather vest as she worked and then, setting the skins aside, pushed back the sleeves of the linen shirt and plunged her hands into the icy depths of the water. The coldness brought shivers to her skin, but she splashed her face several times in an effort to wash away the fatigue that dragged at her. Shaking the last droplets of water from her arms, Maren sat suddenly still at the sound of a twig breaking underfoot. She turned abruptly, thinking Thomas had returned, but as the sounds came closer, Maren felt a sudden prickling of fear at the unmistakable noises of riders approaching on horseback, the gentle clinking of harnesses filling her with a sense of dread.

The riders moved through the heavy undergrowth, and Maren stepped back quickly into the low brush at the edge of the stream. She could only hope Thomas would remain hidden in the forest. Through the sparse leaves she could see the approaching horses and their riders. One by one the horses drank at the stream's edge. Voices came to her and, in her silent agony, Maren recognized the English words they spoke. They must have ridden most of the night. One of the soldiers dismounted and approached very near where Maren hid in the brush. Her labored breathing caught in her throat when she realized what had caught his attention. Her vest lay where she had left it on a nearby rock. She knew they would not be satisfied until they had searched the entire area. Her only hope of warning the others lay with Thomas. Her decision firm in her mind, Maren suddenly bolted from her hiding place. Her sudden movement from the brush drew the attention of the entire guard, and a full score of riders bore down on her.

"Well, what have we here? A young lad lost in the forest?" questioned the knight who had found her vest, doffing his helm and turning toward her. Taking his broadsword from its sheath, he leaned forward and scooped the vest from the rock.

With hands that trembled visibly, Maren reached for the vest and quickly slipped it on. She lifted her gaze and found the lethal tip pointed directly at her heart. She met the man's gaze evenly, refusing to yield to the fear she felt within. From the corner of her eye, she thought she saw a face poking through the brush across the clearing; or had she been mistaken? She prayed Thomas knew of her plight. A second glance, and the face was no longer there. She could only hope that he carried a warning to the others. As for herself, she could not hope for rescue. She must bravely face the consequences of her choice.

The armored soldiers moved apart to allow another rider within their circle. Maren backed away a few paces at the sight of the knight who now rode toward her. He was unmistakable among his men, the brilliant blue and gold colors of his crest glaring in her memory. His finely made hauberk was interwoven with gold links, and the surcoat worn over was of a deep blue and matched the mantle which draped his huge gray warhorse. The breastplate the knight wore was emblazoned with the figure of a golden lion. Maren fought to control her fear as the knight halted before her, his voice rumbling like distant thunder from behind the steel helm.

"I seek the Welsh rebels, not a mere scrawny lad."

"Milord, we have searched the entire forest and found nothing," one of the knights answered.

Maren could feel the heat of those glowing eyes boring into her from behind the slits in the steel helm, but she refused to raise her gaze, terrified he would recognize her.

"Where are you from, lad?" Brettan de Lorin looked down on the youth, unable to raise the slightest response.

At Maren's silence the Duke of Norfolk spurred his horse forward, as if intent on riding over her. The giant warhorse pushed against her with a massive shoulder that could easily have smashed her to the ground. Maren glanced about frantically, seeking some last escape. Her nerves grew taut when the knight drew his broadsword and brought it to rest menacingly beneath her chin, demanding her attention. Stubbornly, she refused to yield to her fears. Maren reached out and boldly brushed aside that threatening blade. The blade was returned, the tip pressing dangerously into the soft flesh of her neck.

"If you desire to live, then I will have your answer. Where are your people?"

Uncertain to trust her voice to carry out her disguise, Maren felt the cold sweat of her fear on the palms of her hands. She forced her straining muscles to relax, unaware of the menacing glow that crossed those green eyes behind the helm. In the next instant Maren was lifted clear of the ground. The Duke of Norfolk seized her by the neck of her shirt and dragged her up against the side of the tall steed, who stood firm.

Suspended by only his hold about her neck, Maren felt the breath choked from her. She lashed out with both hands, pummeling the broad expanse of steel-covered chest.

In surprise at the sudden spirit of the lad, Brettan de Lorin grabbed both her free hands in his one to prevent further attack.

Maren flew beyond control, panic blotting out any thought except survival. Like a wild animal caught in a snare, she struggled frantically against his hold. If her life was to end, then she would cause him some harm that he might remember. Wildly Maren thrashed about, her head snapping back while the Duke of Norfolk shook her viciously to force her into submission. In the course of her struggle, the doeskin cap loosened and fell to the ground, freeing her masses of long, raven-black hair to flow about her shoulders in wild disarray.

A sudden quiet fell over the other knights, who watched in stupefied disbelief at the lad of a moment before, suddenly transformed into a wild-eyed maid.

Maren immediately knew the foolishness of her actions. Blue eyes, wide and fearful, stared into the narrow slits of the steel helm. She could feel the heat of his wrath beneath the cold of the steel.

The Duke of Norfolk held her in a grip like a band of steel, so tight about her that she could not breathe. Again Maren attempted to break his hold, and she felt herself drawn even more tightly against the steel breastplate that protected him. She began to feel lightheaded in her struggle to breathe, and a strange coldness swept through her. Slowly, darkness crept over her with stealthy fingers, and Maren slipped from consciousness, her memory filled with the vision of a steel-headed monster whose eyes burned like live embers, searing her soul. Maren's struggling gradually ceased, and her slender body went limp against the steel-clad warrior.

Brettan de Lorin pulled the girl in front of him, so that her unconscious form rested against him in the saddle. The contact with her softness sent a glowing warmth coursing through his veins. This was the prize he had sought. The others would be caught in time, and he would have his answers.

A buzzing sounded in Maren's ears, and her head ached through the dense fog which shrouded her senses. She brushed aside the tangled mass of her hair and gazed with confusion at her surroundings. Then the fog cleared, and

79

a vague memory returned.

The walls of the tent were draped with silks of vivid blue and gold, and she remembered the sight of those same colors on the helm of the knight who had dragged her atop his horse. She was now prisoner of the Duke of Norfolk.

Maren gazed about her in silent wonder at the rich trappings of her cloth prison. A long wooden table, ornately carved, stood across from her, with two matching high-backed chairs, the intricate design of the hunting lion carved into the soft grains of their wood. A finely woven tapestry laid to cover the floor of the tent held the same motif: two long and lean lions seemed to spring toward each other beneath a golden crown woven into the brilliant blue background.

Maren turned back abruptly at the sound of someone approaching, and her vision was suddenly filled with the sight of the Duke of Norfolk entering the tent. Maren scrambled backwards onto the soft pallet and stared warily at the English knight from the shadows at the edge of the tent. If he was aware that he was being watched he gave no indication, but called for his squire. The gleaming broadsword was removed and carefully laid aside, then the lad returned to accept the mail coif and helm. Maren's eyes widened in wonder at the sight of the tall warrior, freed of his armor. Instead of a man, she had expected to see the body of a lion spring forth from the chain mail, and she was not surprised to find that his eyes glowed green and catlike, and seemed to pierce her through. He regarded her for the first time, with an intensity that took her breath away. Maren felt his gaze move over the length of her, and instinctively she moved away from the heat of that gaze, confused by the uncertain emotions she felt, which had nothing to do with fear. He removed the heavy gauntlets and laid them within the helm. Maren studied him closely from behind the veiling mass of her unbound hair. His tall, wide-shouldered stance and his lean, handsome features wore the look of the hunter. The long, thin scar shown pale against bronzed skin just beside his eye and was almost hidden by his mane of dark, curling hair, dampened from the confines of the helm and waving softly about his head and neck. The Duke of Norfolk abruptly turned toward her, just as the lion regards his prey before striking.

Brettan crossed the distance that separated them in long, easy strides.

Maren attempted to retreat further but found her way blocked by a wooden coffer. Cornered, she turned on him, as does any desperate creature that can do naught but face the mighty hunter.

It was that look in her eyes that gave Brettan cause to change his manner. He had seen that same look once before, and he knew her proud, defiant spirit would never allow her to yield to the fear he saw there. Brettan took in the full measure of her beauty, as he slowly reached out and lightly touched her cheek, turning her face so that he might see her better in the light filtering into the tent. Merciful father in heaven, but she was beautiful. The softness of her skin against his battle-scarred hand caused him no small amount of surprise and pleasure, for it seemed as if he had touched the finest of satin, and his only thought was that here was one that must be protected and treasured like a rare jewel. Surely, even dressed as a boy, she was far more beautiful than any richly gowned lady at the English court.

The warmth of his touch against her skin startled Maren, and her confusion grew at the gentleness she felt there, when those powerful hands could have ended her life, had he chosen to. His fingers left a glow upon her skin long after his hand had moved away. Holding herself rigid lest she betray her uncertain thoughts, Maren was

81

surprised at the sound of his voice, no longer muffled by the steel helm, but rich and vibrant, as she had remembered it.

"I see you are recovered," Brettan observed, watching her stiffen at his words. He moved to check the bonds that held her fast.

"If you give me your word you will not attempt to escape, I will remove them." He regarded her evenly, and Maren instinctively knew she could trust him.

Maren nodded, and the Duke of Norfolk removed the slender estoc sheathed at his belt. She drew back, fearful of that menacing blade, but found herself firmly held by one wrist. He severed the bonds in one easy motion. Maren jerked away from him, gently rubbing the bruises on her wrists where the leather ties had bound too tightly.

Brettan's hand closed around her wrist, drawing her close, and he raised the slender blade so that its tip rested lightly against her throat.

"I will tolerate no foolishness. This chase through the forest has cost me a goodly amount of time, and I will waste no more. I know you understand me well, for you speak the king's English as well as I."

Moving to the opening of the tent, Brettan gave his orders for food to be brought in. Within moments a vast assortment of fresh fruits, meats, and cheeses appeared. Platter after platter, heaped to overflowing, was brought and set on the long table. Silver goblets, platters, and utensils for two were also brought, and wine to quench thirst. Maren watched silently, warily, from her temporary safety in the shadows.

Brettan motioned to her from the table, and when she refused to move, he descended upon her with rapidly fleeing patience. Roughly he shoved her into one of the high-backed chairs. He poured wine into the two goblets, setting one before her. Maren sat in silence, refusing to yield to her ravening hunger, although it grew with each passing moment before the sights and smells of the amply spread table.

"Eat! I will not have you starving yourself. You shall be of no use to me dead. Now, eat!" Brettan leaned toward her menacingly from across the table. When she still refused and only stared back at him with wide-eyed obstinacy, he leaned forward and with one swift movement drove the tip of the blade he still held into the table, not more than a hair's breadth from her hand.

Maren's composure failed her, and she pulled back in sudden fear of the bold warrior who glared at her so threateningly. There was no doubt in her mind that he would not hesitate to use that blade more effectively should she continue to refuse him. Though he might not allow her to starve, he might well content himself with leaving her a few permanent markings for her stubbornness.

Maren's voice nearly failed her, her throat bruised from their previous struggle. "You are most generous, milord, but I care for nothing. I wish only to return to my people." She glanced uneasily at the lean, handsome face, fully expecting him to use that blade. But she saw nothing to fear in the emerald-green gaze that stared back at her speculatively.

"Who are your people, Maren?"

Again the questions. Maren shifted uneasily in the hard chair. "I have told you, milord. I am but servant to the master of Cambria. My family is far from here."

Again that piercing gaze which seemed to see into her soul and must certainly know the lies she spoke.

"I find it strange indeed that a mere servant should be so well versed in the English language. Such privileges are usually reserved for the nobility." Brettan challenged her, the sudden widening of her eyes telling him that he had perhaps struck close to some truth.

"Milord, the master of Cambria is a knight of the realm. There were many in his house well spoken in the English language. The steward, William, is himself of English birth." Maren watched him for some indication that the Duke of Norfolk might already have known that fact. She saw only a momentary flickering of surprise quickly masked behind his golden gaze.

"Who is your master, and where was he when the castle was attacked?" Brettan continued, watching his beautiful captive carefully.

Maren's thoughts tumbled one over the other. She weighed the consequences of telling him more, then continued cautiously.

"Lord Gilbert de Burghmond is master of Cambria. He fights with the English king in the north country. He thought Cambria too remote to be of great import in this war between England and Wales." Maren's voice broke suddenly as her thoughts were filled with memories of the last days.

"I fear he greatly misjudged its importance. There is obviously one who considers your master's home to be of great import, enough to leave your mistress slain."

The Duke of Norfolk rose suddenly and walked to the entrance of the tent, gazing across the clearing in the forest at some distant point, while he contemplated her words. Turning back to her, he narrowed his eyes at her, approaching the table.

"Who were the others who fled with you? I know of the girl and the old woman. What others were there?" At her continued silence, Brettan de Lorin leaned across the table.

"At this very moment, my men continue their search of the forest. The others will be found. Their lives could well depend upon your cooperation now." Brettan searched her blue eyes, set within the fragile width of that flawless face. He knew well there was much she had

84

not told him, and until he learned the truth, she would remain his prisoner. Brettan fought his doubts of her and gazed into those eyes, which were like early spring flowers upon the heath, so deep was their blue color. He was momentarily lost to his desire to feel his hands within the masses of ebony hair which fell enticingly to her waist. He imagined her to be not more than a child, yet he remembered well her woman's body pressed firmly against him, that time he had found her in the chamber at the castle. The memory of that thick, silken mane and the sweet fragrance of it against his face, when he had brought her to the camp, came back to him, and he grew suddenly angry at the stirrings he felt from her closeness. He crossed the enclosure and retrieved his helm and gauntlets.

"Be warned, my men will not hesitate to use their weapons, should you be foolish enough to attempt another escape. Their lives depend on following my orders. Be certain that your life depends on those same orders. My knight, Sandlin, will see to your needs in my absence, but do not be foolish enough to think you can deceive him again. He is most eager to redeem himself for your first escape." Brettan spun on his heel and was gone, leaving Maren in stunned silence. She followed him to the tent entrance. Her guards were posted along the entire perimeter of the tent. Her freedom from the English would not be easily won.

Maren sighed heavily and turned back toward the table. Her stomach growled noisily, and she felt deep pangs of hunger from not having eaten since early morn the day before. Surely no one would notice the absence of a small piece of fruit, or a crust of bread.

Maren wiped her hands carefully upon the soft linen cloth and pushed back the platter. Her fine intentions had flown before the demands of her appetite. She emptied the ornate goblet and gazed slowly about the tent which was now her prison. Somehow, she must find a way to escape. Carefully she wrapped several pieces of cheese and a thick crust of bread in the linen cloth and hid it behind the wooden coffer. She would have a need of food if she was to escape the English, for she could not know how long it might take her to reach Cambria.

Maren retreated to the soft pallet to contemplate her predicament. The long hours of the afternoon passed slowly, the sun rising high in the sky. The tent became warm, and Maren fought her growing sleepiness, straining to hear the sounds from the camp beyond. The wine had worked upon her, making her drowsy, and soon her lids seemed far too heavy. She curled up on the soft pallet, resting her head in the crook of her arm for just a moment.

When she awoke some time later, Maren realized several hours had passed. The sun was no longer directly overhead, since the heat in the tent had eased and long shadows fell across the encampment. She gazed past her guards at the entrance of the enclosure, then rose to ease some of the stiffness in her tired muscles. Sorely feeling her confinement, Maren paced the breadth and width of the tent, coming to a halt before a small table beside the wooden coffer. A basin of fresh water had been poured, and beside it lay a silvered mirror. Maren stared at her reflection. Her hair was a tangled mass, and smudges of dirt streaked her face. She held up the mirror and stared at the dark bruises that had formed on either side of her neck, where the linen shirt had cut into her flesh when she had been grabbed from above. Her hands trembled as she reached for a linen cloth and, wetting it in the basin, wiped the dirt from her face and neck. She removed the doeskin vest, pushed up the sleeves of her shirt, and washed her hands and arms. The linen shirt gaped away from her slender form while she gently washed the bruised column of her neck, oblivious to one who watched from the shadows.

"It was never my intent to cause you harm, had I but known the true form beneath the boy's clothes."

Brettan de Lorin approached from the opening in the tent, where he had been watching her.

Maren whirled about, a spark of defiant anger gleaming in the wide depths of her eyes.

"Is it your habit, sir, to go about spying on people? Am I to be allowed no measure of privacy?" Maren threw the linen cloth into the basin of water, her surprise bringing all her carefully controlled anger dangerously close to the surface. Yet within her sparked a warning that she must proceed with great care. She stood before him, desperately hoping he did not sense the fear that welled within her. She raised her chin slightly, refusing to yield before his incandescent gaze.

"You are my prisoner. You will have what I offer you, nothing more," Brettan answered softly, reaching out his hand to turn her head. A scowl darkened his handsome features, when he saw the bruises and raw marks that marred the silken perfection of her neck.

Maren jerked away from his touch, feeling the lingering warmth of his fingers against her skin, her composure deeply shaken at that contact.

"I am certain these are merely the first marks I am to receive as your prisoner. But do not think that I shall remain here to feel the sting of the lash, for I shall soon be gone."

She strained away from his touch when his hand returned to cup her chin gently, drawing her gaze back to his with a strength that was unyielding.

"The hand that draws the lash loses its anger in the presence of such beauty, Maren. Do not force me to draw the blade against you."

His face was very near hers. He bent low over her, and his breath was warm against her cheek. Maren felt her resolve weaken before the warmth of his nearness. She forced herself to think of Cambria, of her mother and Catherine, and the great danger of remaining a prisoner of the English. Her lips trembled as she turned away from that haunting gaze.

"Please, milord, I—" She faltered, and his strong fingers again turned her gaze back to his. Maren stared into those emerald depths, her uncertainty mounting with each passing moment. Her lips parted, struggling for words that might stay him, but her voice failed her. What was it she saw in those glowing depths? Was it her own fate, perhaps her own death? Maren felt the warmth of his lips against hers. She longed to draw away from him, and yet within her flamed a response that she could not deny.

Brettan's arms closed gently about her, drawing her against his wide expanse of chest, and his lips traced a molten path along the gentle curve of her neck. Almost without a will of her own, Maren arched away from him, trembling at the exquisite tenderness of his lips against her skin, her protests dying on her lips.

Desperately Maren fought to regain her composure. Vainly she pressed against that rock-hard chest that she might push him away.

"No Maren, there will be no anger between us now. I will not hurt you. Whatever your cause, I will face it on the morrow. You may resist, but the choice is mine." His voice was vibrant and low in his throat as he bent over her.

Maren moved away from him, her panic taking hold. He reached for her and, missing her arm, his hand closed over the thin fabric of the linen shirt. The garment split in one motion and fell away as Maren lunged from him. She halted at the sudden coolness of air against her naked skin. In one desperate move she turned to flee but found her escape barred. Once more she was drawn against him.

In one quick motion, Brettan lifted her in strong arms and carried her to the pallet. It mattered little that she struggled with all her strength. He carefully deposited her upon the soft coverlet, and Maren rolled on her side, quickly scrambling to her feet to escape him, but wherever she turned, he met her. She sought to trip him, and his arms went about her waist, pulling her with him backwards onto the pallet, his lean, hard body cushioning her as she fell across his chest. Maren's head shot up in surprise at the shock of that contact against her bare breasts. Vainly she struggled to break his hold of her. Grabbing both her arms, Brettan skillfully flipped Maren onto her back, so that his weight pinned her down. Frantically she clawed at his arms, causing no small amount of pain and drawing blood beneath her fingernails. Undaunted, Brettan grabbed her wrists with strong hands and pinned her arms back over her head.

Maren could hardly breathe for the weight of him across her. In an effort to regain her strength, she lay still beneath him. The rapid rise and fall of her firm, full breasts, and the quickened pulsing at her neck, that beat just beneath the surface of silken, creamy skin betrayed her. Brettan's gaze lingered on the thin gold chain about her neck and the gold medallion that lay in the hollow of her throat. His fingers traced the length of chain until they closed over the medallion. In the dim light of the tent, Brettan could plainly see the unmistakable form of the gold lion. Anger replaced his passion of a moment before. He seized the medallion, pushing Maren from him, tearing it from her neck, the chain cruelly tearing at the tender skin before giving way.

"Where came you by this medallion?" He roared at her, his anger distorting his handsome face until he seemed transformed into some wild, crazed beast.

"I will have your answer, or by God I shall have you drawn and quartered. How came you by the medallion?"

Brettan's anger knew no bounds, and his words tore at her.

Bewildered, Maren could only stare back at him, thinking him surely gone mad. She backed away, fearfully clutching at the coverlet.

Lunging for her, Brettan seized the coverlet and tore it from her. Maren glanced about frantically for some point of safety, but she hesitated a moment too long, and Brettan's hands closed about her wrist and drew her painfully toward him. Maren clawed at him frantically in an effort to save herself from death at the hands of this maddened beast. His grasp tightened, and Maren felt her arm would surely break. She struggled against his hold of her, her free hand grasping for anything that she might use as a weapon against him.

"There are ways, Maren; ways to drag the truth from you. And I shall have the truth." He bellowed at her. Moving over her with sudden calm, Brettan unsheathed the slender blade from his belt and, twisting her arm cruelly behind her back, drew her to him, the blade of the knife pressed menacingly against her throat.

"Be aware, Maren, that here, just beneath the tip of my blade, lies a most vulnerable spot. When it is cut, your blood will flow quickly and surely, and will not stop. Not a very pleasant way to die," he threatened, pressing the blade more firmly against her skin.

Maren was convinced he must surely be mad, but the blade was too dangerously close she dare not provoke him further.

"Please, I but found the medallion and, thinking it of some value, I kept it against a time when I might have a need of it. I know not its meaning. Until these days past, when I saw that same crest upon your shield, I had never before seen it." Maren closed her eyes against her growing panic that her life would end in the next moments. But at his continued silence, she knew he considered her words.

Brettan's rage of the moments before waned at the sight of her desperate tears. Her words tore at him. Did she indeed know the importance of the medallion? Lowering the blade, he held her away from him, momentarily lost in the depths of wide, frightened blue eyes that stared back at him. The dark mane of her hair cascaded wildly over her shoulders, and her lips were slightly parted as she regarded him warily. Gently he pulled her to him, unable to resist the innocence he saw in that velvet gaze.

Suspicious of his sudden gentleness, Maren struggled against his hold, all the while knowing well the futility of her efforts. In mounting frustration she hung within the confines of his embrace for a long moment, and he leaned over her, his words soft and gentle against her ear.

"We are enemies, Maren, you and I, but the conflict will be laid aside this night." Brettan stared into the brilliant depths of her defiant gaze, knowing deep within that he had longed to possess her from the first moment he had seen her.

"If you choose rape, milord, I am powerless to stop you, but be it known I shall never yield to you. I shall fight you until my last breath." Maren hissed from between teeth tightly clenched to still the chattering from her mounting fear.

"You may scream or not, the choice is yours, for it matters little if every knight of my guard would know what passes between us. None will interfere in matters that are mine."

Maren's eyes narrowed venomously, glaring her wrath. She struggled anew against his unyielding hold upon her. Moving over her, Brettan's lips found the hollow of her throat where her pulse raced and, at that searing contact, Maren's cry of protest died in her throat. She turned her head aside in silent agony, desperate to avoid his touch, knowing the words he had spoken were true. There were none who might save her now.

Maren turned back in sudden shock at the velvet touch of his lips against her breast, that intimate contact before unknown to her. Immediately Brettan shifted up, his mouth claiming hers, bruising, demanding, causing a multitude of emotions to flow through her. A warm, calloused hand closed over her breast, gently kneading, caressing, teasing that soft peak to a taut hardness while he had his way with her. Maren revolted against the firmness of his hips against hers, arching upwards to escape him, finding it only increased his desire for her. In one quick movement he loosened the belt of her breeches and, when she twisted away from him, they fell away from her legs. She gasped in stunned surprise and, his hold of her momentarily relaxed, she rolled away from him. She hardly waited to contemplate her sudden freedom, but sought safety at the far side of the tent, darting behind the wooden coffer. She waited in silence, shivering at the chill of the air against her skin. Early evening shadows filled the tent. She carefully crept around the end of the table and sought her garments on the floor. Her nerves tingled her ears straining for some sound of his movement, hearing only the noises of the camp beyond. Spying her shirt only a small distance away, Maren reached out, drawing the linen garment against her.

In that same instant, a long, muscular arm stole out from the shadows and whirled her about. Maren was drawn against the naked expanse of his hard chest, as Brettan swung her into his arms and quickly bore her to his pallet. In one easy motion, he laid her down, the full length of his naked warmth pressing her into the soft mounding of the coverlet.

"The choice is mine, Maren." His lips moved over her cheek to her jawline and down the side of her neck, gently caressing the bruised flesh. He kissed her lips, the molten heat of his touch drawing her will from her, his kiss branding her, searing her lips. He traced a path achingly along the soft mounding of her breasts, nibbling gently, teasingly, causing shivers of pleasure to tingle along her spine. Confident in his power over her, his kisses fell across her face, and his hands caressed her intimately. His mouth returned to hers, gentle now, warm, consuming, as he seemed to take her breath for his own. Deep within Maren a spark kindled, a flame growing brighter, demanding, consuming as it grew, driving away all resistance. In innocent confusion, Maren moved against him, and his long, muscular thigh moved between her legs, forcing them apart. Maren hesitated at the warmth of his body entwined with hers, feeling herself becoming one with him. His voice was oddly muffled against her ear as he whispered her name, burying his hands in the thick mass of her hair, smelling the sweet fragrance that was hers alone.

Maren responded with a need she had never known, feeling herself unable to deny him. His hands gently released hers, and her fingers fanned across the broad expanse of his chest, now lost in the thick curling dark hair that spread across his chest and tapered thinly down his stomach. Maren stared into the depths of his golden gaze without fear, only an awakening awareness of herself. She felt the molten heat of him pressing against her, and her eyes widened in surprise. A chuckle of deep pleasure escaped his throat when Brettan's larger hand closed over her own and he guided her, his long fingers closing her smaller ones over him. Maren would have pulled away at that sudden pulsing contact if Brettan had not firmly held her, so great was her shock. Carefully, skillfully, he guided her, at once amazed and impassioned by her innocence. And as he entered her, Maren would have cried out at that first tearing pain, had not his mouth covered hers at the final moment, taking her pain for his own.

Tears formed within those wide, blue pools, and Maren closed them against the pain that threatened to consume her. Brettan lay still above her, his mouth traveling along her cheek, until he tasted the salty wetness that trickled along a path to the delicate curve of her ear. The resistance had surprised him, for indeed he had not expected her to be a virgin. His memory was filled with thoughts of others who had pretended to possess that virtue, surrendering it only to him.

Blocking out all other thoughts, Brettan's mouth returned to claim her lips tenderly, and he tasted her fully, his hands caressing her, feeling the rapid beating of her heart beneath his hand at her breast. Slowly he moved within her, carefully taking away the pain and building within her the fires that had flamed briefly moments before.

Against her will, Maren moved with him, the pain less each time. Soon she met him equally, her silken arms entwined about his neck, pressing him closer as she sought to fulfill a need she did not fully understand.

Brettan's passion soared at her response, and he moved with increasing urgency. Yet he held back, his thoughts of her pleasure as well as his own.

Maren arched upward to meet each thrust, and she was pulled higher with him, their mounting passion engulfing them, sweeping them along the path to the pinnacle of their desires, blocking out all conflict, all hatred, stripping away all desires save one, their ultimate pleasure in one another. Brettan carried her with him to that final moment, and Maren stared in wide-eyed wonder at the pleasure that awaited her, a cry escaping her lips as their desires were met as one; yet it was no more than a soft whisper. Brettan drew her to him, as if she truly were a part of him that could never be separated

94

from him.

He relaxed against her, his arm laid gently across her breasts. She attempted to pull away from him but found all retreat soundly blocked, and his voice rumbled deeply in his throat, for he found some humor in her dilemma. Tenderly he kissed the curve of her ear. She turned away from him. Those strong fingers that had seared her skin drew her back to him against her will. Maren's lower lip trembled, and she refused to meet his warm gaze.

"Did I hurt you?" Brettan's voice was soft against her ear, and he gently reached up to brush aside a raven tendril that curled enticingly across her breast, his fingers like molten heat against her skin. A startled gasp escaped her lips, and Maren turned surprised eyes on him.

"It is of little import. You have taken what you wanted. Can you not leave me in peace?" Maren tried to jerk her chin away, but found his grasp tightened upon her.

"Can anyone, once having tasted of the finest wine, turn away from a filled cup? You are wrong, Maren. I never sought this end. The choice was yours. Had you not escaped to the forest, forcing my hand, all might have been much different."

"Will you now release me?" Maren turned her uncertain gaze toward those unrelenting, glowing orbs.

"Will you now give me the truth, as I have asked for it?"

Maren groaned her agony from between tightly clenched teeth. "I have given you the truth, yet you refuse to believe it. There is nothing more I may tell you."

Brettan rolled from her side and rose to his feet in one easy motion, the lean, muscular line of his body bold before her, the golden light from a nearby campfire dancing across the rippling planes of his body, leaving no part of him to her imagination. The color rose high across her cheeks, and she thought of what had passed between them.

"Until you are willing to tell me what I would know, you shall remain my prisoner," he answered, retrieving his doeskin breeches and the linen shirt. "You will find, Maren, that there is more to be found in cooperation than in stubborn resistance. The price of silence can be dear, though I vow a most tantalizing tribute to collect."

"Is death, too, the price for resistance? Perhaps the death of innocent women and children?" She sat up angrily, pulling the coverlet high over her breasts, against the warmth of that heated gaze.

"I do not make war on women and children, Maren, but that is a truth which, for now, you must accept upon my word," Brettan answered as he turned to leave the tent. "Nor do I usually take unfair advantage of prisoners, though I must say that I have no regrets of this one exception." A devilishly handsome smile pulled at the corners of his lips.

Maren found his humor unbearable in light of what the last moments had cost her. She would have given a king's ransom for a heavy object to heave at that arrogant head, taking a great deal of pleasure in seeing it cloven in two. She pounded a small fist into the soft coverlet in mounting frustration and humiliation. When she turned about, he had left the tent to join his men.

Chapter Five

Maren stirred sleepily against the unfamiliar presence wrapped about her. Coming more fully awake, her mind cleared while Brettan moved in his sleep. Carefully she slipped from his side. Standing in the darkness, she shivered in the early morning cold, trying to move about without disturbing him. Quietly she crept around the edge of the pallet, bumping into the large oaken table; another bruise, she thought ruefully, to add to the others she now felt. Groping along the table, Maren stumbled, her feet caught in a garment upon the floor of the tent. She bent to retrieve her linen shirt, quickly slipping into the thin garment.

With a quick glance to see that Brettan still slept, Maren moved quietly through the tent opening out into the early morning air, the sky just beginning to lighten on the horizon, the last stars twinkling before disappearing in the growing light of dawn. The guards that had surrounded the tent the evening before were gone, with only one remaining. The man stood before the dying embers of a nearby campfire, warming himself against the early morning chill. A horse nickered softly from

97

across the camp, and though Maren was sorely tempted to make her escape, she knew the futility of it when she caught sight of the heavy guard placed near the animals. She would have to wait for a better time, perhaps when the English prepared to break camp. For now she could think only of the stream beyond the camp, and her longing to wash the feel of the Englishman's touch from her body.

Maren waited until the lone guard moved past her, then darted into dense foliage and underbrush which easily concealed her. A momentary thought of escape was soon dismissed. She could hardly flee afoot into the dense forest, with half the English army in pursuit. No, she must wait a better time, when she would have a horse and be able to give the cursed Duke of Norfolk a good chase.

Reaching the stream's edge, she hesitated only long enough to shed the long shirt before plunging into the cold depths. With long strokes, she swam to the deepest point, where the water reached her neck, and began washing her arms and shoulders with a vengeance, realizing that, if she did not keep moving, the chilling cold of the water would drive her to the shore before she finished. Wading to a shallow pool near the shore, Maren scooped a handful of sand from the bottom of the stream and scrubbed furiously, until her skin was reddened and raw. The pain helped remove the agony of what she had suffered at the hands of the Duke of Norfolk. Bending over, she rinsed her legs, hesitating only a moment at the sight of the dried blood stains on the insides of her thighs. She removed all visible traces of his ravaging of her, just as she blocked out the memory of those moments past. Her anger raged anew with each passing moment, and she silently swore she would have her revenge on the Duke of Norfolk.

A twig snapped underfoot, a tall form approaching on stealthy feet through the early shadows, to stand near the water's edge, taking in her beauty with eyes that hungered to see her bathe.

Startled from her thoughts by the sound of something breaking the water's surface, Maren whirled about. On the bank of the stream, Brettan leaned his long, muscular frame against the gnarled bark of a massive oak, silently drinking in the vision of her youthful beauty. Indeed, she seemed like some mystical young goddess, as in stories he had heard in his youth, suddenly sprung from the depths of the water to cast some magical spell over him. His thoughts were drawn back to the hours before, when her youthful innocence had yielded a prize he had not anticipated, and his thoughts were again troubled with unanswered questions of his young prisoner. A frown pulled at the corners of his mouth. He stared across the rippling water at that slender form, and he noticed she had begun to shiver violently. An unexpected breeze brushed across the surface of the water, wrapping icy fingers about her chilled body. He noticed the stubborn set of her slender jaw, steadfastly refusing to retreat from her icy refuge. Brettan thought he heard the distinct sound of teeth chattering, and she threw him a glare that only added to the early morning chill. A soft chuckle rumbled from his throat as he compared her now to that fiery wench who had occupied his pallet only a short time earlier, and he considered that here indeed might be one worthy of more than one night's passing. He swung the heavy mantle from about his shoulders and approached the stream's edge.

"It would seem, Maren, that I must retrieve you from your bathing before your fair skin turns as blue as this mantle. I am not fond of a cold pallet, Maren. I much prefer warmth beside me to drive away the chill of the air."

Maren gritted her teeth to still their chattering, for she knew well his meaning. "Can you not leave me some measure of privacy? Is it not enough that you have taken me against my will, and hold me prisoner? I will not play the eager whore to do your bidding. I would rather die from the cold than yield to you again," she fumed, her frustration and anger giving her false courage.

"'Twould do no good, Maren. You may rant and rave as is your wont, but I will not allow you to endanger yourself by remaining in the icy waters. I have no need for an ailing maid to slow my journey. You will come of your own free will, or I shall come in and get you." Brettan gazed at her keenly.

"Be assured, I do not welcome the idea of joining your icy bath. I shall await that pleasure until such time as we may enjoy the comforts of an inn and a steaming hot tub of water, to take our leisure. As for now, do not test me further in this, for you cannot hope to win."

Maren hugged her arms about her in the icy water, feeling it swirl gently about her hips. She knew the cause to be lost. She had little doubt he would indeed come in after her. And she knew the anger he was capable of, if she chose to force his hand. Her body ached from the cold, but she hesitated, struggling with a proud spirit which cried out to defy him.

Brettan suddenly took several steps toward the water's edge, and Maren held out her hand to halt him.

"Please, if you will but turn your back I will come out," she pleaded earnestly, hardly feeling the strength to persist in her defiance of him, numbness spreading through her limbs.

"Now, Maren! Or I shall come in after you!" Brettan warned again, in a manner that would tolerate no more foolishness.

Maren gritted her teeth in vexation, fully realizing he taunted her deliberately, and yet no other choice remained. Slowly and with great effort, Maren moved through the water to the bank, attempting to shield herself with her arms, and stepped from the icy water, the early morning breeze causing her to shiver violently. Her knees buckled beneath her, and she felt strong arms surrounding her, as Brettan wrapped her within the soft folds of his mantle and swept her into his arms, the warmth of his body glowing through his garments. He drew her to him.

"You are a foolish maid," he whispered hoarsely against her ear, carrying her back to the encampment.

"And you, milord, are a pompous ass. As soon as I have the feeling in my arms and legs, be confident I shall make you regret your treatment of me," Maren hissed from between teeth that chattered violently, as she tried to hold herself away from him.

Brettan chuckled heartily at her show of spirit. He would most certainly like to see how she intended to vent such anger, clad as she was only in the heavy mantle, which hardly provided adequate cover from prying eyes. His mood sobered at the realization that he must see she had something to wear that would provide more protection from his men. He could ill afford her shapely form being exposed to the eager glances of half the English army.

In long, easy strides, Brettan crossed the camp. Trapped for the moment within the confines of his arms, Maren curled against his warmth, telling herself it was only to drive away the aching cold from her body.

Brettan halted when they entered the tent, abruptly setting her to the ground. Maren turned on him defiantly, her spirit greatly restored by the warmth of his touch.

"I would ask, milord, that you not handle me before your men. Would you have them think me no better than some whore?" Maren fumed, clutching the mantle about her.

"I would suggest if you intend to protect your 'virtue,' that you cease your early morning bathing. My men are knights true, and loyal beyond question. But they are, after all, only men, and subject to the passions a woman's presence might stir. Lest you find yourself fine sport for my entire army, I think it wise that you remain here, under my protection. They shall not venture here."

"Protection?" Maren seethed. "And who, pray tell, is to protect me from you?"

Brettan turned to her, his mood carefully guarded. "You will find garments in the coffer. Choose what you will. For now, sit and eat. I do not have a liking for skinny maids with their bones all poking through. I need a softer form to ease my nights."

Maren's eyes flashed her silent rage as she sat across the wide table, unable to touch the food that had been set before her. She stared back at Brettan warily, her one thought that she must somehow find a way to gain her freedom.

The knight Sandlin entered the tent to deliver a message, casting a surprised glance at Maren, then bending very near Brettan to whisper words she could not hear across the table. She knew immediately by the frown that appeared on his face that the duke was not pleased by the news he had received. He remained silent while he finished the meal. Maren felt his careful scrutiny, as if he considered some matter of import that concerned her. Feeling the color rise to her cheeks, Maren raised her eyes and glared at him with open defiance. Her boldness rapidly faded when she saw the cold hardness that had returned to those emerald-green eyes.

"A messenger has arrived from the king. I have orders to leave immediately for the northern border. I have no great fondness for keeping prisoners. We shall have this matter settled now. You will tell me what I wish to know of the attack on Cambria, and I shall consider releasing you."

His arrogance was insufferable.

"You shall consider it? Nay, I demand it!" Maren's temper flew out of control as she sprang out of her chair, practically leaping at him from across the table, so great was her anger. Maren failed to notice the warning flicker of light that crossed his countenance.

Brettan sat back in his chair, his voice carrying a note of deathly calm, and gazed back at her, his anger tightly controlled.

"You shall make no demands here. You are my prisoner and, until such time as I give the order for your release, you shall continue to be my prisoner. If you choose to be bound, it may easily be done. If you choose to defy me, I have other methods for obtaining the information I seek. It matters little to me what you would demand. You hold no authority here. And be warned, I have no tolerance for your show of temper. You will gain naught for it but the sting of the lash. And though it might be a shame to mar such lovely skin, be assured, I will not hesitate to hand down the punishment. You will give me the answers I seek, or you shall remain prisoner until I have them. The choice is yours."

Maren stared back at him in stunned silence, knowing the truth of his words. She sat down slowly, willing to offer him nothing, yet well aware she might yet gain her freedom if she gave him the information he sought.

"I have told you all I know of the attack. There is nothing more to tell." Maren felt her mounting

103

frustration, for indeed she knew nothing. Her own questions raced through her mind.

"The choice is yours, my lovely Maren. You may bargain for your freedom, or cast all aside and feel the lash, and then surrender the information I seek. One method shall merely take longer than the other." Brettan regarded her with a detached coolness that she found maddening, as if he might truly strip the hide from her back and care naught for the matter.

"First, you shall tell me how you came by the medallion. I seek the man who carried it to Cambria."

Maren ground her teeth in frustration. "The medallion carries your crest. You should know well who bore the medallion. I have spoken the truth, I but found the medallion. You may have me flogged, but I know nothing more of it."

"You lie! I have followed the man who stole the medallion across the whole of England and Wales. His path led me to Cambria. Unless you would have me believe you are the one I seek, then give me the truth!" He roared at her as he slammed his fist down upon the table.

Maren faced him boldly. "I have given you the only answer I have. There is no other. I could easily offer you lies, but I know nothing of the man you seek!" she cried in desperation, fleeing to the far side of the tent, her hands clenched into fists of mounting frustration.

"Very well, Maren, you have made your choice." Brettan rose from his chair and turned to leave. "We ride within the hour. Sandlin will return for you shortly. See that you are ready when he comes." Whirling about on his heel, Brettan left the tent.

Maren's anger with Brettan faded before her misery at her complete helplessness. Unless she gained her freedom, she would soon find herself traveling further and further from Cambria. Morosely, Maren gazed about the lavish tent, feeling for the first time a great fear that she might never see her family again. Gloomily she searched for her own clothes and, seeing they were nowhere to be found, she went to the wooden coffer. Reluctantly, she searched among the garments neatly folded within. A quick glance among the linen shirts and tunics proved most of the garments to be far too large. She carefully set them aside and found other garments of a lesser size in the bottom of the coffer. She held a richly cut blue tunic against her slender frame to see the fit. The tunic was cut for one of lesser size than Brettan, and the breeches could be altered to fit her slender legs. Remembering Brettan's warning that Sandlin would soon come for her, Maren quickly searched the bottom of the coffer for a belt. Her hand brushed against the coolness of metal and closed over a small, gold medallion, identical to the one she had found in her mother's hand. Maren whirled about and searched every corner of the tent. Nothing escaped her as she sought the medallion Brettan had torn from her neck in his rage. Pulling the pallet aside, she searched among the covers but found nothing. Maren stopped for a moment and gazed about the tent, her eyes finding the small medallion that reflected a shaft of early morning light. Her hand closed over the original medallion just as Sandlin entered the tent.

"The Duke of Norfolk awaits." He glanced briefly over her slender frame, still clad only in the mantle.

"I shall await your leave." Sandlin added hesitantly, then turned and left to stand just beyond the opening of the tent.

Maren tucked the second medallion back underneath the clothing and closed the lid of the coffer. She hastily donned the blue velvet breeches and tunic, holding them

105

together with a leather belt she found in the coffer. There was time for little else, so she twisted the tangled lengths of her hair into a long braid and tucked it underneath the hood of the tunic. She would see about altering the garments at a later time. She remained barefoot, for her leather boots were also missing, and decided she indeed presented a sorry sight in the ill-fitting garments. Still, she was grateful to have found something more than the mantle to wear. While it offered warmth, she would hardly have felt safe from the stares of the English soldiers. Carefully she tucked the gold medallion with the broken chain safely inside the fichet of the tunic, then left the tent and walked closely behind Sandlin, who led the way across the encampment.

Maren gained some small measure of satisfaction at the disapproving look that crossed Brettan's face at the sight of her costume. It eased her anger somewhat to know she had caused him some small moment of frustration at her ridiculous attire. But all satisfaction faded before the heat of his anger.

"You play the part of the prisoner well, Maren. Did you think perhaps to gain some measure of pity from my men by coming like some barefoot child?" Brettan derided her.

"You braying ass. Had you not taken my clothes, I might well have had something to wear of a more suitable nature. As you have taken it upon yourself to strip me of my garments, as well as my honor, I hardly see that I am responsible for my appearance." Maren choked through tightly clenched teeth.

"Maren, do not test me further with such idle nonsense."

"Nonsense!" Maren fumed. "Release me, milord, and I shall be gone, never again to bother you with such matters."

Brettan grabbed her arm roughly and guided her to a group of prisoners a small distance away. "There are other matters of importance beyond one simple-minded maid. Now, see what you may learn from these prisoners, for not one among them seems able to understand the English language. And mind you, any treachery shall mean their deaths, and perhaps your own," he cautioned.

The prisoners regarded Maren with suspicion as she approached, rubbing her bruised arm. She translated Brettan's questions as he asked them, but received only their silence for their answers. One lad, hardly older than herself, regarded her with barely concealed hostility and spat into the dirt at Maren's feet. Brettan immediately ordered the lad taken away. Moments later, the sounds of his punishment could be heard by the others. The lash fell heavily, its cracking sound mingled with his tortured screams. The other prisoners glanced among themselves uneasily, knowing well that the same might also be their fate. The lad was dragged back into the clearing and dumped upon the ground, so the others might stare at the ugly welts that raised across his back.

Maren again asked her questions and again met only a cold resolve to remain silent. A second man stubbornly refused to answer any of Brettan's questions. A third man was questioned, and she saw his uncertainty reflected in eyes that shifted nervously. He regarded her uneasily, fully understanding her words spoken in the heavy Welsh language. In the next instant, the prisoner found a menacing blade pointed at his throat, and knew the guard would not hesitate to use it. Maren cringed at the thought that Brettan could be so ruthless as to kill an unarmed man. Yet she remembered well the bodies of the unarmed guards at Cambria, lying where they had been cut down.

Fearing for his life, the prisoner broke, the words

spilling forth in a mixture of Welsh and English. Maren reached a comforting hand to him, only to find herself thrown back when he roughly pushed her away, the look upon his face telling her more than any words he might have spoken. She saw hatred that glowed brightly, and fear which forced him to betray others.

Brettan turned to his guard, and Maren seized the moment to press the man for further answers, determined to learn what he knew of the raid on Cambria. Unaware that Brettan now watched her, she was startled to be seized abruptly by the arm and dragged away from the prisoners.

"You dare much, Maren, when there is but one thing you still possess. I think you value your life very little. What treachery spoke you to the man?" Brettan raged at her, and in the glowing depths of his eyes, Maren saw her own certain death.

Maren twisted about as she sought to loosen his painful hold of her. "I but sought some word of the attack on Cambria. The man knows more than he speaks." She tried to ease the pain in her arm from strong, unrelenting fingers.

"What more does he know?" Brettan pressed her, his face very near hers, his eyes glinting yellow sparks that seemed to burn through her.

"He refuses to say more, only that he was not part of the attack." Maren flung at him. She stared up at his fearful visage and was taken aback by the tired and haggard look that crossed it, as if he were suddenly very weary. A slight frown played across his lips while he studied her, and she wondered again how much truth he knew of her. He was not a man easily deceived, and she knew of a certainty she would be foolish to believe she might delude him.

"Milord, have you learned what you wanted about the

108

Welsh rebels?" Maren questioned.

"Yea, I have learned what I wanted to know, and perhaps much more," Brettan added, his green eyes boring deep into her blue gaze, as if searching her soul. Maren looked away from that gaze, suddenly unsure of herself.

"Sandlin will see you have a horse. We ride immediately." Brettan suddenly released her, so that she nearly fell to the ground.

Maren gently rubbed her bruised arm and glared her wrath after that tall figure, so arrogant, so proud, so damnably handsome. She steeled herself against such thoughts and silently accepted the reins when Sandlin approached with the horse she was to ride. The chestnut was a fine animal, long of limb, and absently Maren wondered if he might be capable of outrunning the English horses weighted down with cumbersome armor. She felt certain of it and for a moment longer considered a quick escape through the trees. Her thoughts fled at the sight of Brettan de Lorin leading the tall, gray warhorse, which could easily best any steed.

Brettan spoke gently to the fine gray stallion, who halted and stood completely still without the slightest restraint on his reins, which hung loosely along his finely arched neck. Maren became suddenly wary as Brettan approached her, mentally preparing herself for some further barb.

"I thought perhaps you should have these." Calmly Brettan held out her soft leather boots. "They will protect against rocks and thorns which might cause you injury." He offered them almost kindly, and Maren regarded him cautiously. Gently he seized her ankle, and as Maren made to resist, he firmly but with complete gentleness kept a strong grip about her ankle, his touch sending rivulets of warmth coursing through her veins.

109

Vainly Maren tried to kick out against his touch of her, only to have the grip about her ankle tightened, not painfully, but to remind her of the foolishness in resistance. She fought a mounting desire to lash out at him with her foot, hoping to wipe that expression from his face. But where she thought to find arrogance she saw only a genuine concern, and honesty in the care he showed her. It was there for only a moment, as he slipped the boot over her foot and smoothed the leather up the length of her calf, then handed her the other boot. Then it was gone, replaced by the stern visage of the Duke of Norfolk, and he seized the reins and swung into the saddle.

Maren quickly pulled on the other boot while the long procession of knights and soldiers of Edward's army took their positions. Brettan chose to ride unprotected without the weighty chain mail, and sat easily in the saddle, with only the large broadsword for his weapon. He looked back past her, nodded curtly to Sandlin, and then moved ahead to ride before them.

Carefully the long English column of helmed riders wound its way to the edge of the forest and the greensward beyond, and emerged from the cover of the trees into the brilliant warmth of the early spring day. Rolling green hills lay before them, for the English chose to ride in open countryside, where unseen enemies might be more easily guarded against.

Maren caught sight of his auburn hair, curling thickly about that fine, proud head, and she could not deny the glowing warmth that rose within her, admiring his tall frame that so easily commanded the long line of soldiers and knights of the realm. The royal standard fluttered in the late morning breeze, and beside it the brilliant blue and gold banners of the Duke of Norfolk. Maren glanced back over her shoulder and felt a tight constriction in her chest, straining for one last glimpse of the hills that

110

guarded Cambria. She fought back the overwhelming sadness and fear that threatened to consume her.

The sun shown brightly on the silent riders through the long hours of the day, and on all the days that followed, each one taking Maren farther and farther from Cambria, and always nearer to England.

Chapter Six

The last days of winter came crisp and clear, and still the English army pressed toward England. Maren had taken a position near the heavily laden carts and maintained that place in the column on their long journey through the Welsh countryside. The rains had painted the countryside with the vivid and lush colorations that foretold the spring, and the hillsides stretching before them were like a richly woven tapestry. Maren marveled at the beauty of this part of her country, so unlike the stark coastal regions of Cambria.

Maren could have easily ridden further ahead in the long line of riders, but chose instead to maintain the greatest distance from Brettan de Lorin. She preferred the safer company of the old woman, Ada, who traveled as cook to the English army in exchange for safe passage to her family in England.

Ada remained silent through the long hours they rode together, lost to her own thoughts of the family she would soon join. Maren was grateful for the woman's silence, for she felt no inclinations to idle chatter. The silence of their hours together on the road to England gave Maren the opportunity to plan her escape, for she was determined that Brettan would not succeed in taking her to England. Since that last night when he had taken her so brutally, Brettan had maintained a welcome distance, so that she thought perhaps it might have been forgotten. Desperately she longed for that same ability, but the memory of those hours together haunted her. She slept on the hard, cold ground at night with Ada beneath the cart, and many was the night she tossed about, dreams returning to haunt her sleep. The heat of his touch and the boldness of his kisses seemed so real that she awakened, her breath coming in ragged gasps. Her hair tangled about her when she tossed and in her sleep sought to stay his fevered advances. Time, she fervently prayed, would release her from that memory. And yet within her grew a deep fear that it might live with her forever, if in the weeks to come she found herself carrying the burden of his pleasure in her, in the form of his child. That thought returned again and again, and Maren forced herself not to think of that possibility, willing it not to be, and mentally kept count of the days since her time had last come.

Though Brettan maintained a stony distance, there was no moment when she was completely alone. Even the moments of necessary privacy were carefully guarded by a soldier who maintained a discreet distance. Of late, she noticed that the knight Sandlin was her most frequent guard, and an unspoken truce was established between them. Maren knew well the limits of her freedom within the column of riders and the consequences if she trespassed beyond those limits. Yet for his part, Sandlin did not treat her like the other prisoners. She was allowed the freedom to remain with Ada, taking her meals with the woman and attending to the chores about the camp, or dressing a minor wound when a soldier grew careless with his bow, or one of Brettan's knights carelessly forgot his gauntlets, returning late to the camp with a score of

114

fresh blisters across the palms of his hands. Brettan's men soon learned to respect her knowledge of herbs and potions for treating any ailment and eagerly sought her care for whatever plagued them. Even the loyal Sandlin was given to more than one regret that she was their prisoner, for he had grown fond of the spirited young girl of uncommon beauty who graced their camp, and he sorely felt his master's dilemma as to what was to be done with her once they reached England.

A bond had formed between Maren and the stern knight who was her guardian. On the days they rode long, taking full advantage of the last bit of daylight to gain the greatest distance, Sandlin often lifted her weary form from her mount, taking it upon himself to tether the animal. And one afternoon, when they were caught in a torrential downpour and Brettan refused to halt their pace and seek shelter, Sandlin had disappeared from her side for a few moments, only to return shortly with a heavy mantle to wrap about her shoulders protectively. Her smile of gratitude was met with nothing more than a grunt of acknowledgment, yet Maren was certain that a smile twinkled in the man's eyes, which gazed at some distant point ahead. And so the days passed, and the unspoken friendship became a strong bond between them.

Brettan pressed both man and beast in his determination to reach England. The luxurious tent that had been Maren's prison required too much time to set at the end of each day, and was therefore left packed away with other furnishings of comfort in the many carts that made up the center of the column. By night, their only comfort was the glow of the campfires that blazed forth to drive away the chill of the night air. The soldiers made their pallets upon the hard earth, while others of the guard remained watchful through the night against a surprise attack. The food was always the same, pieces of dried

115

beef, a few slices of cheese, and a thick crust of bread, downed with water from the heavy skins they replenished from the streams they passed. The fare mattered little to Maren, indeed she hardly noticed it, so great was her fatigue at the end of each day. It allowed her little desire for anything more than to sleep upon the pallet spread beneath the cart, drifting off to her recurring nightmares.

By day Maren planned her escape from the English, but found no opportunity under the persistent attention of her guards. Brettan seemed not to notice her, but rode each day with his men, often disappearing for hours at a time to ride ahead with his patrol. They searched the countryside for any sign of the Welsh rebels, returning late in the day to confer with his men, redirecting their course through the valleys away from heavily wooded areas, lest they become easy prey for the wandering bands of Llywelyn's rebel army that roamed the hills. Through some rare bit of information that Ada shared with her, Maren knew they passed very near several burned-out villages and farms, the inhabitants either slain or driven off by the rebel army. And Maren wondered what her advantage might be if the English were to come under attack. She quickly dismissed that hope, realizing that her fate might be no better at the hands of the rebels, for rumors had been heard of their atrocities committed against her own people, in Llywelyn's desperation to force the Welsh people to raise arms against the English. The few farms she had seen destroyed left her shaken and horrified at the ruthlessness with which the rebels had struck down innocent people. She hardly understood the reason for it, and a deep overwhelming sadness crept over her that there was no hope for any of her people, helplessly caught between the fury of Llywelyn's resistance and the unrelenting determination of the English king to make Wales one with England. In her misery, Maren thought of her brother and father, praying for their safety. The only bright hope of her days was the certainty that her sister, Catherine, was now safe from further harm. That certainty gave her determination to survive whatever the English might choose for her fate. And indeed she could not know what that might be. Execution as a rebel? She thought not. If that had been Brettan's intent, he could easily have ended her life the first day she was captured. What other reason might there be? Maren refused to accept the idea that Brettan intended to take her to England. What his purpose might then be Maren could not guess, except perhaps for the same reason that had brought him to Cambria. Maren pushed the pain of that memory from her thoughts and forced herself to think of each day as it came. The future, whatever it might hold, would be met soon enough, and she must be prepared to take advantage of any opportunity to escape, for there might well be only one.

The days brightened while they crossed the wide expanse of the Wye Valley, the tenseness of the days before seeming to ease from the soldiers as if they had passed some unseen danger. The spirit of the camp lightened, and even the somber Sandlin attempted to draw Maren into good-natured conversation. The constant vigilance of the guards lost some of its strain of before.

Brettan no longer rode ahead, as had become his custom, but chose to ride at the head of the main column, and more than once Maren felt his thoughtful glance cast in her direction. He remained distant, and no words passed between them, but Maren somehow sensed his mood toward her had changed, though she hardly knew the reason for it.

The second day after entering the valley, word reached Maren and Ada that camp would be made early, near the Wye river. Each hand bent to a particular task. Several of

117

the guard lent skilled hands to the hunt, returning at dusk with fresh game, which provided a welcomed change from the dried meat and moldy cheese that had been their fare for the days past. Meals were prepared over the open fires, kettles set to simmer, and whole beasts set upon the spit to roast slowly above the flames, the aroma filling the cool air to remind all of their hearty appetites. Many hands were busied before the light of the campfires, polishing armor that had collected a goodly amount of dirt. Weary animals were tethered and allowed to graze on the tender shoots of the first grasses to follow the winter's frost. While the soldiers satisfied themselves from platters filled to overflowing with a wide selection of roast meats and fresh vegetables cooked in the pots over the fire, Ada busied herself at the river's edge, washing the dirt and grime from her clothes. Maren accompanied her to the river, looking longingly at the inviting water. It had been days since she had bathed properly, and she sorely felt the need for a thorough cleaning. She sighed heavily at the sight of her ever-present guard, deeply regretting that Sandlin had chosen that time to take his evening meal. She would not have hesitated to slip into those refreshing waters with him in attendance, for she knew well he could be trusted to grant her some measure of privacy for such matters. The gruff, bearlike soldier called Fairfax, who now stood his silent guard a few paces away, could not be trusted for such consideration.

Knowing her thoughts, Ada threw the man a speculative glance. She rose quietly from where she sat wringing the water from the clean garments and stepped up to speak with him. Maren watched their exchange with curiosity. A few words were exchanged, and the soldier glanced uncertainly at Maren, then at Ada. Moving back to the water's edge, Ada began untying the closures of her tunic, as if preparing to undress before the startled man. Suddenly aware that the old woman fully intended on disrobing where she stood, the soldier backed away uncertainly. "You, old woman, what are you about there?" he questioned in sudden alarm.

"I have a need to wash some of the dirt from myself. Is it your intention to stand there gaping? Surely my ancient, withered form could hold little interest for you," she teased, lifting the edge of the tunic as though completely intent on undressing.

Uncertain of his desire to view the old woman completely naked, Fairfax took another step backwards. "Hold where you are. Cease immediately," he commanded with little authority in his voice. Ada persisted in removing her boots and then reached to unbelt the tie about her ample waist, dropping it to the ground without a backward glance to see if Fairfax watched. Without further word, he whirled about and fled in the direction of the encampment. Maren dissolved into fits of laughter, for she guessed Ada's purpose. The old woman quickly retied the worn belt. "Waste no time, for I'll warrant that he shall quickly return with a handful of guards. He values his hide and would not care to feel it stripped away for lacking in his duties. Take what time you may have."

"Will you join me, then?" Maren questioned merrily, her brilliant blue eyes twinkling with pleasure at the woman's masterful handling of their guard.

"Bah! The water is too cold for bathing. I would have a need of a stouter heart and far more determination to bathe this night. I shall save my moments for a tub of hot water before a blazing hearth."

"I fear, Ada, that pleasure shall not come any time soon. It seems we are doomed to wander the countryside until we reach England. And then to what fate, who may say?"

"I shall try to delay the guard longer, but do not tarry, lest you desire to have the entire English army gaping at

119

you while you wash," Ada threw over her shoulder, gathering her clean garments and starting up the embankment in the direction of the camp.

Quickly slipping out of the tunic and breeches and pulling off the leather boots, Maren stepped gingerly upon the green grass at the bank of the river. It was like soft velvet beneath her feet, and she hesitated only a moment to catch her breath before entering the cold water.

From behind her at the water's edge, Ada called to her. "Here. It is not much, but you are welcome to what remains of it." The old woman tossed Maren a small sliver of soap before returning to the camp.

The small soap was rough and smelled hardly better than the dirt she attempted to wash from her body, but Maren indeed welcomed the lather that washed the dirt from her skin. As the soap quickly disappeared, she lathered the last bit into her hair. It would have to do, and most assuredly it felt wonderful. She silently vowed to find a way to repay Ada for her kindness. Maren squeezed the lather from the thick masses of her hair, then rinsed the heavy lengths in the swirling water. Squeezing the last bit of water from the sodden mass, she threw it back over her shoulder, then turned and waded through the shallows, gaining the grassy bank in one easy step. She quickly donned her clothes, pulling the velvet tunic and breeches over her dampened limbs, for she had no linen to dry herself. It mattered not, for nothing could have raised her spirits more than the comfort offered by that gurgling river, lapping against the shore. She pulled on first one boot and then the other just as she heard a sound behind her. Instead of the burly Fairfax, Sandlin had hastily left his meal, fully expecting to find the girl gone, escaped into the shadows of the night that fast approached. With an audible sigh of relief, he noted the dampness of her clothes and the thick mass of her wet

120

hair. A slight smile played across his stern face while he followed Maren back to camp.

Having downed a meal that could have satisfied the hunger of the strongest knight, Maren sat before the roaring logs on the fire and fanned her hair before the drying heat. She carefully worked the tangles and snarls from the glistening black tendrils which curled in wild abandon as they dried. Lost in deep thought while she stared into the flames, Maren was oblivious to the glowing eyes watching her from across the camp, more heated than any flame upon the fire.

Brettan watched her as he often had the long days past, with a mixture of bewilderment and uncertainty. The ceaseless pace he had set across the whole of Wales allowed for little other than riding and then a few brief hours of sleep, only to ride again at a furious pace that tried both man and animal. And yet there had been moments, as now, when he had stopped for a brief time to gaze speculatively at her and wonder at the truth she concealed from him. She was more than a servant. It was obvious to him. Her full knowledge of the English language belied any pretenses. No servant was granted such privileges, nor was there a need for it. But both her manner and her spirit decried much more. He had used her boldly, yet she had refused to yield in spirit, when most other maids would have cowered fearfully. But she had defied him even at the moment he had discovered her to be a virgin. The intensity he saw behind those deep velvet pools gave him fair warning that she would never cease trying to escape him. He had guarded well against the possibility that she might succeed and return to the Welsh rebels, for he believed she knew much of the attack on the fortress of Cambria. And he had been unable to learn how she had come by the medallion. His chest tightened at the thought that the answers lay so close at hand, yet eluded him. When they

121

reached England, the time would come for all truths, but for now she might still give him pleasure. He remembered well every curve, each slender limb, and the satin softness of her skin. He remembered too the wild look of her when she had fought with all the strength she possessed against the inevitable end. And when that moment had come, she had shown him something he could not name. Certainly not fear, for in that final moment he had seen none, only blinding hatred in the sapphire pools glinting venomously for his treatment of her. Since that night he had berated himself for giving in to his desire for the girl. Always before he had found any number of maids to come willing to his bed, and he would take his ease with them and think nothing more of the matter. Such was part of a soldier's life. But she had fought him at every turn, refusing him until the last moment, when she was powerless to refuse. Brettan turned the slender estoc over in his fingers and resheathed it in his belt, remembering vividly the fire in her eyes when once before she had seized the blade and attempted to drive it into his heart. Spirit beyond reason, pride beyond all suffering. Such qualities were rare in a man, rarer still in a woman, and one so young. Brettan returned to his conversation with his men. Their course was set, they would journey to Monmouth near the border, there to rejoin the king. Though he willed himself to think of other matters, his gaze returned often to that slender form across the camp, sitting before her fire. The spell was broken only when Maren stood at last, gathering the heavy mantle and the soft pallet to make her bed beneath the cart beside the old woman, her slender back turned to catch the fleeing warmth of the dying fire.

Maren's dreams returned, as always, stealthily upon silent feet, creeping through the stillness of the night to lurk near. And when at last Maren gave herself up to

122

exhausted slumber, they stole over her like a thick mist reaching to enclose her with cold, frightening hands. Vividly those last days at Cambria returned. She saw again the spiraling smoke which darkened the sky, and the expressionless faces turned with eyes that did not see. The dead of Cambria lay before her. She saw Catherine's vacant stare, but only her eyes, for the girl's face faded in the mist closing again before her. Real, so real that Maren sobbed softly in her sleep. She saw again her mother's slender form, just as she had appeared that last morning. When next she saw her, the cruel mask of death had claimed her mother's beauty, the coldness of eternal rest hushing her tender words forever. In her silent agony, Maren pushed through the blinding mist until she stood before the menacing figure of a man, darkly shrouded so that she could not see him clearly. But from the dark color of his mantle Maren knew him, and the sob that escaped her lips would have torn the stoutest heart. The face faded and was replaced by another she could not see, but the glow of golden eyes drew her nearer, and though she fought against the unseen arms closing about her, she could not fight the silent strength of the dark knight who watched her through the mist of her dream. Maren tossed in her sleep, unknowingly throwing off the mantle as if it were a live thing that dragged at her. Barely awake from the horror of her nightmares, she was aware of strong arms, warm and protective, that lifted her from her hard bed upon the ground.

Brettan's voice came low in his throat as he bore her to his pallet, apart from the snoring of the soldiers. "Whether you will have it or no, Maren, it will be."

She mumbled sleepily against the velvet of Brettan's tunic.

Brettan chuckled softly at her feeble objections, which quickly faded as she drifted back to sleep. Gently he laid

123

her upon the pallet, suddenly aware of how small and vulnerable she seemed. He could not name his mood or find reason for the sudden sadness that consumed him at the sound of her sobbing. He knew only an overwhelming desire to comfort her, to shield her from whatever fears tormented her dreams. At first he cursed his foolishness in allowing the girl to rule his thoughts, but his resolve to hold himself from her had faded before his desire to hold her close and protect her. Silently he had cursed under his breath, his features almost feral in the last glow of the firelight, while he had watched her from afar, long after she had fallen asleep. Then, as she had turned, restlessly fighting off some unseen danger that haunted her, his intentions had faded, and he had crossed that small space of ground to gather her in his arms, bearing her away in long easy strides. No more would the demons of her dreams be allowed to torment her. He would drive them away with the last of his strength if she would have it. He knew nothing of her, except that she was extraordinarily beautiful and innocent, though desirable beyond all imaginings. The lies she gave him would be found out soon enough, and then he would see of the possibility of keeping her with him. There were always arrangements to be made. Many a maid bettered her lot in life when she became the mistress of some titled lord.

Suddenly chilled without the heavy velvet mantle to protect against the growing cold of the night, Maren curled into a tight ball on the pallet where Brettan had laid her. And then she was aware of a warmth at her back and protective arms that closed about her, drawing her into the curve of his body beside her.

Brettan watched for a time the even rise and fall of her breast, while she drifted into slumber. Long, dark lashes rested against the pale glow of her skin, the faint hue of pink spread across her cheeks. Her lips parted slightly with her breathing, and he realized that he would have liked very much to roll her onto her back and kiss that gently curving mouth, just to see if the taste of her was as he remembered it. He sighed heavily at his rising passions for the slender form nestled beside him. For the time being he would be content to share his warmth with her, but the time would come again, and very soon he vowed, when there would be much more between them, and the thought of that eased his torment some small measure, though he highly suspected she might voice some objection in the matter. Brettan pulled the heavy weight of his fur-lined mantle about them, closing them within as in a cocoon. Maren snuggled closer within his embrace, her vulnerability reaching into his heart. Her one hand extended to the edge of the pallet, and he reached out, carefully closing his lean, brown fingers over hers, sheltering her hand with his own. His own fatigue washed over his senses, and he slept at last, cradling the slender girl at his side.

When Maren awakened the next morning, she sat up in surprise not to see the wooden cart above her. Realization dawned on her, and she turned to find the pallet empty except for the heavy blue mantle, richly trimmed in its costly gold braid, which lay over her. Brettan was nowhere to be seen. Her anger flared at his boldness, but even more that she had failed to notice the change of sleeping arrangments. Most of the soldiers were already about and had rolled their pallets in preparation for the day's ride. Ada had packed the cart and waited for one of the soldiers to bring the horse. Maren stretched her legs before her to ease the stiffness of the night on the hard ground, and raked her fingers through the lengths of her ebony tresses, trying to set some order to her disheveled appearance. Sandlin approached leading the chestnut stallion, saddled and ready for her to mount. "We are to ride immediately, and the Duke of Norfolk has asked that you ride with him near the front of the guard."

"You may inform the Duke of Norfolk that I choose to ride where I have ridden these days past." She shot back at him testily, her temper high at Brettan's casual assumption that she should feel honored to occupy such a position at his side. Sandlin hesitated uncertainly in his saddle, unprepared for the girl's open defiance to a direct order from the Duke of Norfolk.

As if to add emphasis to her decision, Maren reached out, grabbing the reins from the man's hands, and then, gripping the edge of the saddle, hauled herself atop the tall horse. With a firm hold on the reins, she whirled the animal about and, giving him an impatient kick, she sent him to her chosen destination, the wooden cart, atop which Ada hefted her ample form.

Sandlin sighed heavily, not caring to give her words to the Duke of Norfolk. Resignedly he turned his own mount about and rode in the direction of the front of the column.

Maren gloated over her small victory. There was little else she was allowed, as prisoner of the English, but her choice where to ride, she decided vehemently, was one of them. Her satisfaction at having defied Sandlin's authority was shortlived, for she saw Brettan's tall, menacing form approach from a distance and knew that he had returned to decide the matter for himself. As he neared, the lack of anger on his handsome face startled her, for she saw only grim determination in the set of his jaw. Without a word, Brettan reached out and snatched Maren from her saddle, leaving her too surprised to respond. He settled her easily in the saddle before him, her slender form filling the small gap between his body and the pommel. She was now firmly positioned in his lap. A warning glared in her brain, her vulnerability to his greater power having been clear to her. She whirled about to give full vent to her wrath and frustration, but

Brettan spurred the large gray warhorse forward, and that sudden, jarring movement required all of Maren's strength and concentration for her to avoid being unseated from her precarious position. Though Brettan's arms closed around her as he urged the destrier forward, she highly doubted he would offer any assistance to prevent her from falling should she become unseated, and she clung to the saddle with both hands, desperately trying to remain upright. He hardly seemed aware of her plight, but rejoined his guard, oblivious to the questioning looks his men cast in his direction. If they found it unusual to find a beautiful, if angry, young girl seated before the Duke of Norfolk in his saddle, none offered any indication of it. At a curt nod from Brettan the column moved ahead and began the day's journey, which would bring them closer to England, and Maren's fate.

Chapter Seven

The days became warmer as winter faded into a new season, and the English army pressed closer to the English border, eager to be rejoined with their king and the army he led from the North.

Brettan remained distant during the day, preferring to ride with his men at the front of the long column, or venturing ahead with one of the patrols to search the countryside for any signs of possible attack from unseen rebels. By night, once the evening meal had been taken, he made his pallet among his guard.

Late one afternoon word spread along the column that they approached the town of Brecon, and the spirit of the men seemed to ease at their nearness to England. The main body of the army remained behind to make camp in the large meadow beyond the town, while Brettan and a smaller number of his guard rode into the town. Maren remained with the camp, and it suited her well, for she had grown weary of their forced march, and every bone cried out for rest from the endless hours they spent in the saddle each day.

Maren helped Ada unload the cart, making her pallet in her usual spot beneath the cart, only to have Sandlin appear to inform her that she was to await the Duke of

Norfolk in his tent. Her face flooded with sudden color. She seethed silently at Brettan's presumption that she but awaited his bidding and would fall at his feet in humble compliance. She sniffed her indignation, realizing her refusal would gain her naught, for Sandlin would merely be forced to take her there bound. She trudged off in the direction of the tent, Sandlin following behind to post guards outside against any attempt on her part to escape. She passed the next hour pacing about the tent, and then flounced into a nearby chair. Her eyes wandered to the pallet she had shared with Brettan, and her cheeks flamed brightly at the memory of his arms about her, the warmth of his body pressed intimately against her own. She forced those thoughts from her mind, glancing about the enclosure and desperately wishing there were a nearby stream in which she might wash, for she had seen none as they made their camp.

Maren stood suddenly at the sound of riders and peered out through the opening of the tent, to see Brettan and his guard returning to the camp. Behind them followed an oddly assorted group of people afoot, and several carts, heavily laden and neatly covered with cloths against the dust that flew up from the horses' hooves, as they churned the sod. Maren stared in amazement while the townspeople swarmed into the encampment and quickly set about emptying the carts.

Large baskets were unloaded and set aside, and others brought forth, all containing a vast amount of fresh fruits, cheese, and loaves of bread, whose aroma, still fresh from the baking ovens, filled the air. Several casks of wine were unloaded and broken open. Freshly killed game birds already stripped of their feathers and prepared for roasting were skewered and set above the open flames of the fires blazing about the campsite. A large boar, already well roasted, was carried forth on a huge platter and set on a nearby table. All about her the camp came alive, a vast array of foods and drink appearing to cover the sturdy tables. Fine linens covered the tables, and platters and goblets were set for the evening meal as elaborately as any fine table she had seen at Cambria. The procession seemed endless. Each cart entered the camp, was quickly unloaded, and then was just as quickly taken to the edge of the camp. Efficient hands set order to the vast amount of foods required to meet the appetites of an army the size of the English guard. Maren stared in open wonder when the last, large cart rumbled heavily through the encampment, the driver stopping momentarily to ask his way, then urging the horse on until he pulled the animal to a halt before the Duke of Norfolk. Sliding with ease from the back of the gray stallion and tossing the reins to his young squire, Brettan motioned to the driver and then, moving past Maren, entered the tent.

Throwing back the cover of the cart, the driver motioned to two stout lads, who removed a large, wooden tub from the back of the cart. Orders were given, and steaming buckets, filled to the brim with hot water from kettles on the open fires, were carried in behind the tub, the two lads struggling to set it in the middle of the tent. Maren was far too enthralled with the activity that had descended upon the camp to pay much attention, instead watching in amazement while the camp slowly took on the atmosphere of a country fair.

More people arrived, and benches were set at the tables for the evening feast. The smell of roasting meats permeated the air, and the soldiers and knights' good humor came to the fore as several young girls, and several not so young with the promise of experience, bustled about the camp to prepare the feast, eager to please the rich English duke who offered so much gold coin.

A group of musicians set to practice with their

instruments, and the sweet, clear sounds of the lute and zither filled the night air, while a brightly clad girl with gold bracelets swayed and moved to the music. Caught up by all the noise and excitement, Maren failed to notice Sandlin's imposing presence at her elbow, awaiting to escort her back to her prison. A deep frown etched Maren's lovely brow when he insistently reminded her to return. Her lips formed a straight line, and she wearily resigned herself and followed him back to the tent, halting just inside the opening. In the center of the tent stood the wooden tub, brimming with steaming water. All thoughts of anger fled, and Maren knew a longing to feel the soothing warmth about her. She sighed heavily, approaching the tub and trailing her fingers through the hot water. Behind her Brettan's voice was warm and vibrant. "I should think you might hasten, before the heat is gone from the water."

Maren whirled about, her eyes meeting that golden gaze, as a faint smile pulled at the corners of Brettan's maddeningly handsome mouth. When she understood his meaning Maren could have hugged him, so great was her pleasure at his surprise for her, but she carefully restrained her enthusiasm, lest he take her gratitude for something more.

"You are most generous, milord."

Brettan's gaze softened when he spoke, his eyes twinkling with humor. He seemed to understand well her thoughts. "Try to leave some measure of warmth to the water, Maren. I have need of a bath myself. If I do not find you bathed when I return, then I shall find it necessary but to join you." Bowing low before her, mockingly, he turned to leave, but not before he cast a final glance to see that she wasted little time in removing the belt that bound the tunic at her waist. Green eyes glowed warmly his pleasure at the sight of her once again in his tent, and a devilish smile crossed his fine lips, for he thought of the hours to come, and how well her enjoyment of the bath might serve him before the night was over.

Maren slipped out of the leather tunic and breeches, shivering slightly before stepping into the tub, easing herself down through the steamy comfort, until she sat fully submerged, with only her slender neck and head above the water's surface. She luxuriated in the warmth. The water seemed to caress her skin, driving away the stiffness of many hours, days, in the saddle, and far too many nights spent upon the cold, hard ground. She did not hear Ada's soft steps entering the tent. "He treats you well. Far better than any other prisoner."

Blue eyes, soft and glowing, regarded the woman levelly. Ada set out a linen cloth and handed Maren a bar of sweet-smelling soap one of the girls from the town had given her, explaining that the Duke of Norfolk had purchased it for the young lady in his tent.

"Ada, I would have paid a king's ransom for such as this, had I but known how it would feel. I swear I must have carried in my clothes every bit of dust and dirt from across the whole of Wales." Maren lathered the bar of soap, inhaling deeply the fragrant, sweet smell of roses, surprised at this unexpected gift from Brettan. She washed thoroughly, then struggled to wash her long raven hair, the heady smell of roses washing away the dirt of the long days past, leaving the thick mass glowing and vibrant. Finally she rinsed the last of the soap from her hair.

Brettan returned a short while later to find Maren combing through the dark mass, sitting before the long oaken table, wrapped in the velvet mantle. Ada quietly left the tent, taking the soiled doeskin garments with her. Brettan stood quietly contemplating the girl before him with renewed interest. It fascinated him that she now seemed so soft and beguiling, when he knew well the

133

anger and fury she was capable of, as if she embodied all the demons of hell, so fiery was her temper. She was most certainly no soft and coddled courtly maid, but a strong-willed girl who intrigued and bedeviled him. His thoughts returned to the gold medallion she wore, and his pleasure at her beauty was clouded by the frustration of having learned little of how she came by it. He had no reason to trust her, yet there was a need in him to believe her words. The thought that he might be falling in love with his Welsh prisoner came as a sudden blow to his composure and was quickly dismissed. He removed the sword at his side. Women were to be used for a moment's pleasure, then set aside. Yet even as he thought this, he knew the falseness of it. She had not come to him as others had, willingly, so eager for his title and his gold. No, she was different. She had held herself from him until he was forced to take her, and even then she had not bemoaned her loss to gain the price of a promise from him, but asked only for her freedom. And well he knew how she longed for that freedom, for he could see it in those blue eyes that haunted his thoughts. He could see too her sadness, which clouded those beautiful eyes. He seemed to see them everywhere about him, even when she was not close at hand. He had but to close his eyes, and he could see their brilliance staring back at him unfalteringly, defiantly. Yes, he thought, he wanted to know much more of the thoughts so well guarded behind the shield of that gaze. Watching her now, he felt it most natural for her to be there in his tent, scantily clad from her bath, her skin glowing warmly from the heat of the water in the tub. Clearing his throat loudly, he entered the tent, and Maren quickly pulled the mantle more closely about her as if to hide herself from his gaze, her startled blue eyes glowing warily back at him.

Brettan moved across the enclosure of the tent, tossing a carefully wrapped bundle onto the table before her. He ran his fingers through the water testing for any warmth that remained. "So cool are you, mistress, that you rob the heat from the water," he teased, before calling for his squire to bring more hot water. Seeing that he fully intended disrobing where he stood, Maren jumped from the chair to depart the tent before she was forced to stand audience before him. A devilish smile spread across his handsome face, for he had ordered the old woman to remove Maren's soiled garments to be cleaned. She stood before him in nothing more than the mantle, her predicament clear upon her exquisite face.

"Sir, I will not stand here and be subjected to your boorish behavior, yet I can hardly leave when I have no clothes."

Brettan chuckled at her fit of temper, noting that her eyes glowed a deeper blue when she was angry.

"I would not have you running about clothed as you are. I will not take on my own men in defense of a mere prisoner who, in truth, seems to prefer the garments of a boy. See to the package, for I would have you dress in the gown you will find there. I have need to see if there is perhaps a woman to be found beneath your boy's rags."

Maren's temper flared at his mockery of her, but she picked up the bundle. Her breath caught at the sight of the blue and gold velvet gown within. Surely it was the finest she had ever seen, and her anger quickly faded before her silent longing to slip into the gown.

"You will find the other appropriate garments within. The woman I paid for it assured me she sent everything you would need."

Maren turned to inspect the other items in the bundle, while Brettan discarded his tunic and breeches and stepped into the tub.

A gossamer chemise of the sheerest fabric, delicately decorated about the neck and armholes with fine golden threads, was cut long to reach past her knees. The

135

coolness of the diaphanous cloth was no more than a whisper of softness against her skin. She sought privacy behind the wooden coffer and slipped into the chemise, letting it fall loosely over her slender body. But the richly cut blue velvet gown, pleased her more than she dared say. The gown was well-fitted, clinging to the gentle curves of her body, the bodice fitting almost perfectly the full roundness of her breasts, then clinging to the small, narrow span of her waist, which sloped to gently curving hips. The fabric of the skirt fell gently to a greater width, barely touching the ground, and then swept back behind her to trail a small distance. The neck was cut low across the ample swell of her breasts, with only a glimpse of the delicate chemise exposed to shield discreetly that tempting sight, and then elaborately decorated, as were the long, sweeping sleeves, with braided gold cording woven in the design of clustered flowers. The sleeves fell away from her wrists, exposing the softness of her long, slender arms. Uncertain of her appearance, Maren turned about to find his emerald gaze glowing at her from across the tent. Brettan's motions of bathing suddenly ceased at the sight of her. The blue velvet indeed had been the perfect choice for her coloring, for the rich blue fabric captured the brilliant color of her eyes and made them seem somehow larger and more innocent. The delicate oval of her face seemed almost luminous in the fading light within the tent, and Brettan felt a deep longing grow within him, until the ache spread through his loins at the very sight of her. Her delicate beauty was both innocent and alluring, promising yet unyielding, as if there were some secret inner part of her that would always remain beyond his reach, until she herself chose to yield it.

Maren grew uneasy under that calm perusal. He glowed almost feverishly in his regard of her. Hastily she bent to pull on the matching blue slippers with soles of the finest leather, and was again greatly surprised at the perfect fit. It rankled her composure no small measure to find that Brettan knew her body quite well, and her color rose high on her cheeks at the thought of how he had come to do so. As if he knew her thoughts, Brettan tilted his handsome head in mock salute as their eyes met, and Maren quickly glanced away, unable to face his gaze. The last item within the bundle was a finely woven gold circlet. Brettan's voice was gruff, as if he spoke with some effort. "I would see your hair loose and flowing as it is now. I will not have you cover your hair and hide it from my view."

Maren flung the circlet down on the oaken table, her temper suddenly flaring at his gentle but obvious command. "Milord, I do not dress to please you, and I will not play the whore for you, for the price of the gown. Since you have seen fit to remove my own clothes so that I have no choice in the matter, then I am left no freedom in respect to my garments, but I will do as I please as regards my hair." Scooping the velvet mantle from where it lay across the coffer, Maren wrapped its voluminous folds about her, shielding herself from his view, then pointedly pulled the hood over her head so that her hair was also hidden from view. She stood her full height, the very essence of defiance, all caution thrown aside, for she dared to challenge him in the matter. Brettan's eyes narrowed, returning her gaze, and then he suddenly lurched out of the tub, rising to his full height, and in one quick, fluid motion he lunged at her from across the tent, his lean, strong fingers closing painfully around one slender wrist, his other arm encircling her waist, the tightly sinewed muscles closing about her like a band of steel and drawing her to him with impetus that drove the air from her lungs. The length of her slender body was molded to his, still wet from his bathing, and every muscle, every fiber of his body strained, as if he sought to

137

pull her within him. Her head snapped back with the force of his grasp. She could feel the dampness of her bodice where her breasts were crushed painfully against the rock-hard firmness of his chest. Maren raised her one free hand, pushing vainly against his chest in an attempt to gain some small distance that she might breathe, her slender fingers raking through the thick mat of damp, curling hair on his chest, but seemed only to excite him further. Brettan's eyes gleamed deep emerald in the waning light, locking with hers in a silent battle of wills. His breath caught in his throat at the wild, angered look he saw in those brilliant blue eyes that seemed to spark, her temper flaring at his handling of her.

"Let me go. I will not be treated in this manner." Her words were barely heard from between tightly clenched teeth. Maren fought desperately to control her wildly racing emotions. Brettan's eyes glinted brightly, almost feverishly, as he held her defiant young body firmly against his own. In one catlike motion, he released her wrist, reaching to bury his hand in the thickness of the rich, luxurious mass of raven tresses that swirled about them while Maren struggled against his hold. Twining his fingers through the silken softness, he gently grasped her hair at the nape of her neck, drawing her head back slowly, and bent his head to trace the outline of her slender throat gently with his lips, warm and feather-soft against her skin, breathing in the fresh scent of roses from her hair, the satin texture of her skin, the heat of her wildly racing pulse only driving his passions to new heights. He tasted of her sweet softness, his lips caressing, etching a molten path along her collarbone and across the heaving mounds of her breasts above the cut of the gown, bending her back across his arm.

Maren could feel the gentle brush of his lips against her skin, and Brettan breathed her name again and again, unable to deny his desire for her. Her own breath caught in her throat as she vainly attempted to stay him. "No. You must not. Please!" Further protest died on her lips, for she felt deep within her the desperate longing to be held forever within that unyielding grasp, to feel his warmth blending with her own, to feel his fingers like whispers against her skin. Brettan raised his head to stare into the dark, stormy depths of her eyes, wide, uncertain, searching, all defiance gone before the realization of her own awakening passions.

From beyond the tent came the unmistakable sounds of laughter. Someone approached. With a muffled curse Brettan set Maren gently from him, the abrupt release sending her backwards against the wooden coffer. There in the shadows of the tent, Maren sought to regain her badly shaken composure, as the dancing girl she had seen earlier unceremoniously entered the tent to find the Duke of Norfolk leisurely drying the thick waving curls of his hair with a linen cloth, a second cloth casually draped about his lean, muscular waist. Unmoved by the sight of a near-naked man, the girl curtsied deeply and then boldly moved to stand before Brettan and offer him a silver goblet of wine from the tray she bore. Her eyes missed nothing, raking Brettan's broad-shouldered length shamelessly, her open wantonness clear on her face. Maren's breath caught in her throat in utter dismay when the girl flaunted the sweeping low neckline of her shirt, bending before Brettan to retrieve the woven circlet Maren had flung to the table. Brettan reached to take the headpiece from her, and her fingers boldly caressed his hand, then traveled up the length of his bronzed arm in open invitation. The linen of the girl's shirt fell away from the rounded fullness of her breasts, the strings in the bodice loosened to provide Brettan an unrestricted view of her ample charms, and she swayed her hips provocatively before him. Brettan seemed to enjoy her performance, an amused smile

139

playing across his lips. His eyes traveled the length of the girl, then glanced past her into the shadows where Maren stood concealed, as if hurling a silent challenge to her. Desperately hoping to gain Brettan's favor for the evening, the girl reached up to caress the expanse of his chest, her fingers moving slowly across the play of muscles beneath his skin. At her vantage point in the shadows of the tent, Maren's cheeks flamed brightly at the girl's wanton display. Or was it more that forced Maren to look away? She raised her uncertain gaze to find Brettan's emerald green eyes boring into hers, and her breath caught in her throat when Brettan ignored the servant girl, slowly crossing to where she stood. Reaching out, Brettan's hand closed over her arm, drawing her out of the shadows. Behind them the servant girl scowled deeply at his choice, having wondered for whom the richly made garments were intended. The girl turned abruptly and fled the tent. She had seen the look of uncertainty and then defiance on the other girl's face. And she knew from words she had heard about the camp that the raven-haired girl was held as a prisoner in the English camp. She would press her cause later, when enough wine had flowed in abundance, and see then if the English duke did not prefer a more willing form to one of defiance.

Refusing to release her, Brettan bent to press a kiss into the palm of Maren's hand, forcing her slender fingers to open the tightly clenched fist she had made. She felt his warmth surging through her veins, that one contact building within her a soft glow which all her defiant Welsh pride could not stay. Gazing into the depths of her blue eyes until she felt that her very soul lay bared before him, Brettan gently laid the woven gold circlet across the palm of her hand, closing her fingers about it with his own, his silent command for her to wear it clearly written in the glowing heat of the gaze that held hers fast. She reluctantly accepted the circlet, and he released her arm, allowing her the freedom to leave.

As she brushed past him, the soft velvet of her gown caressing his leg, Maren felt as if she had accepted something more than the gold band, as if his hands had branded her skin where he touched, so that she would always carry his mark on her. So great was her confusion when she fled the tent that Maren nearly collided with Sir Bothwell. She stumbled and would have certainly fallen had the knight not caught her arm, steadying her with his strong grasp. She saw the questioning look in the eyes of the knight, who gazed at her quizzically. "What is it that troubles you, milady?"

Maren's head shot up at the use of the title she had not heard since Cambria. What did he know of her? And if he knew the truth, then Brettan must also know. She smiled her bravest smile into the kind eyes that searched hers. "'Tis nothing, milord, merely the creatures of the night that stalk the camp!" she retorted uneasily. Staring back at her uncertainly, Bothwell could not resist the sad beauty of the small upturned face that smiled bravely at him. "Then I shall have to hold my sword fast to protect you."

"Which is it to be then, milord, to protect me or to hold me prisoner?" she questioned plaintively.

"You ask questions, milady, that have no easy answers, for there are too many truths left unspoken. Come, let us enjoy the feast that has begun. I vow that with so much noise, and so many stout hearts about, all evil creatures will cower in the shadows and dare not venture forth to cause you harm." His gentle smile comforted her, and he led her to the tables near the blazing campfires, where Brettan's knights already seemed to have enjoyed a goodly amount of wine. A tremulous smile which could have melted the fiercest heart formed at her lips, and Maren laid her hand across

141

Bothwell's arm, allowing herself to be led across the wide circle of the encampment to the tables that awaited beyond. He quickly delivered her to the table that had been set for the Duke of Norfolk. Maren hesitated, then chose another place at the far end of the table. It was a small act of defiance, but it gave her confidence to see that none of the English knights pressed the matter of her choice.

Her attention was soon drawn to the vast array of platters that had been set on the tables, heavily laden with roast meats and fowl, the aroma filling the cool night air, reminding her of her raging appetite. Roast birds of every size and kind abounded, some stuffed with nuts and berries, others split apart to reveal a breaded stuffing with pieces of apple cooked within the cavity of the bird. The boar she had seen earlier had been placed on a large carving tray before Sandlin, and the knight drew his great sword and, in mock preparation for battle, made as if to slay the fearsome beast. His efforts were met with loud shouts of encouragement in the face of such an adversary. He brought the heavy blade down across the neck, separating the head from the body. A loud shout of approval rose from his men, seated about the tables, as he heartily applied his sword in quick slicing motions, cutting away great portions of the succulent meat, which were then passed on platters to other tables. Baskets of fresh apples and other fruits abounded, and hot steaming loaves of bread were brought forth from warming pans laid in the coals of the fires. Goblets overflowed with the wines brought from the inn of the town, and several toasts were offered up among the men. The servant girl, who was called Neala, was hard pressed to keep each filled. She moved about the tables, her shoulder pressing seductively against one knight, a hand lazily caressing a cheek, or hips swaying to the sounds of the music that floated about the camp. Maren's cheeks burned, whether from the heat of the large fire that burned nearby or from embarrassment at the girl's wanton display, she could not know.

A platter was filled with some of each of the assorted foods and set before her. Maren felt an unexpected heat and raised her eyes to find Brettan's gaze resting casually on her. He was like some lazy feline creature quietly contemplating his prey. Maren forced herself to look away, fearful that he would press the issue of the seating arrangement, but he made no move toward her. Maren's fears eased, and she concentrated on satisfying her hunger. She astonished even herself by cleaning the platter, and blushed in embarrassment sometime later, when she looked up to see Sandlin's wide grin of approval beaming down on her. "You find our fare not too distasteful, I trust?" he teased her, refilling her empty wine goblet.

"In truth, sir knight, I find the fare no different than that set upon the tables at Cambria." Maren caught herself, for a moment, afraid that she might have betrayed herself with her casual conversation. "I meant only that it is a welcome change from the crusts of bread and moldy cheese of the last days."

"Ah, and it is good to see you smile. I see too much sadness within your eyes. For one so young and beautiful, it grieves me deeply to see so much sadness. Would that I could take away your sadness, fair maid." The words were honestly spoken without the slightest hint of the sarcasm she had come to expect from the Duke of Norfolk.

"My greatest sadness is that I must be so far from my family. And I can see no way to change it, though I know not why I am held prisoner."

Sandlin grew suddenly quite sober. "I am oft reminded that the sworn duty of a knight of the realm is not always a pleasant one, milady. Would that I could see you returned to your family. But my allegiance must fall to the Duke of Norfolk, Edward the King, and England. Though I swear yours is the first pretty face that has easily tempted me. These past days and weeks you have earned my respect. Be of good faith, milady, the Duke of Norfolk is a man of honor. Give him the truth he seeks, and you shall have your freedom."

Maren stared at the rich color of the wine. The lights of the candles flickered in the evening air, casting a thousand lights to dance across the red liquid, which had sent a golden glow through her veins, making her speech bold. "I have given him the truth, and he has chosen to believe otherwise. Tell me, then, what shall my fate be for a man blind to the truth when he has it within his grasp?" Maren's eyes suddenly shone bright with tears welling at the corners of her wide blue eyes, and she searched the face of the knight who sat beside her. He had no words to offer her, for he knew well his master's fierce stubborn nature in matters past. In his heart he saw only the girl's innocence, and he silently grieved that he could offer her no solace. Gently he covered her slender hand with his larger, calloused one, a comforting gesture that somehow eased Maren's torment.

The evening gave itself to merriment, and Maren's mood softened, for she found it impossible to ignore the good humor and high spirits of the men about her. Sipping from the goblet, she failed to notice the number of times it was refilled by eager hands from one side of her or the other. As spirits livened and the knights grew bold, they took turns in coming before their leader in contests of song or sport. Brettan enjoyed their good humor, but kept a watchful eye toward the other end of the table. As the evening progressed and the wine flowed in abundance, the words of carefully prepared verses seemed to jumble on wine-thickened tongues, until the last knight stopped in the midst of his song and, having forgotten the words, added a few of his own, relating a story of loyalty to his horse, rather than to the fair maid of the story. Maren dissolved into fits of laughter, and the good-hearted knight stood before her in complete bewilderment. Ending his ballad, he returned to his cups to contemplate wherein lay the humor of his song. Stifling her laughter behind her hand, Maren's eyes caught the burning gaze of the Duke of Norfolk, all thoughts of anger or fear of him gone. She felt herself drawn within those green eyes, glowing warmly at her, a slight frown playing across his lips. He rose and slowly walked toward her. Carefully he reached out and took her hand in his. The wine had made her brave, and Maren stood before him, her wide-eyed gaze meeting his equally without fear. "Do not frown at me so, milord, for I swear the power of it would lay low the bravest knight, and I am naught but prisoner in your camp, and have no weapon to hold against you."

The innocence Brettan saw behind her eyes seemed to beckon to him, and he felt a longing deep within to crush her to him, to hold her, to kiss her, to taste of her honeyed sweetness, to feel the resistance of her proud spirit melt away before the heat of her own passions, and finally to feel the response that he knew her capable of. Still holding her hand in his, Brettan raised her fingers to his lips and gently kissed them. "Do not play games, Maren, unless you are prepared to pay the price, should I be the victor. And have no doubts as to the outcome, my sweet."

Maren's eyes sparkled like brilliant blue sapphires, catching the flickering light of the campfire. "I shall take my chances," she challenged. Brettan crushed her small hand within his iron grasp, fiercely fighting his desire to bear her away from the feasting to his pallet, to see then how bravely she taunted him.

The pleasure of his touch shot through her and,

though Maren struggled to remember he was her enemy, she found her defiance giving way beneath the assault of his warmth. Their attention was suddenly drawn back by the loud shouts of his knights. They had enthusiastically responded to a new source of entertainment. The girl, Neala, had replaced the wine skin in her hand with a long silken scarf and, lowering the shoulders of her shirt, stepped to the center of the circle. Neala clapped her hands in an even rhythm, tapping her slippered foot in time to the tune the musicians provided. Keeping pace with the music, she moved boldly between the long tables, the look in her dark eyes promising. She moved in front of Brettan, where he had taken a seat beside Maren. Slowly the pace of her dance quickened. She whirled and swayed before the soldiers, the heat from the campfires and her fevered dancing causing her skin to glow with a fine sheen of sweat as her movements increased. Swirling about in a wide circle, she bent low before Brettan, her shirt gaping open to leave nothing to the imagination as to the charms she offered. Maren turned her gaze from the girl's lively dance, for she realized Neala's open invitation to Brettan. Neala moved closer to the table, her message clear upon her face and in every movement of her lithe body, swaying wantonly before him, her lips parted enticingly. The music built to a fevered pitch, and Neala whirled about the entire camp, taking the long silken scarf from about her neck as if it were a banner flowing out behind her. Several knights tried to grasp that silken piece in their hands. She drifted past them, only one destination in mind. She stopped before the head table and, leaning across the width of it, delivered her challenge, wrapping the shimmering length of silk about Brettan's neck, throwing a taunting glare at the raven-haired girl at his side. The dance ended, and Neala collapsed upon the ground before the table, her skirt fanned out about her, her head thrown back and tossing

146

the wild mane of her hair, her eyes closed as if in a trance, her bosom nearly fully exposed to the entire guard and heaving with the strain of her performance, her skin gleaming in the glow of the firelight.

Maren sat motionless, her own breathing labored, as if she too had swayed as one with the music before Brettan, sending him that message of longing and desire. Aghast at her own emotions, Maren turned away, unable to comprehend her mood, and silently wondered at the effects of the wine.

A faint smile crossed Brettan's face. He stood and with slow, deliberate movement reached up to remove the silken fabric from about his neck. Maren watched, her breath held in her throat. Was she fearful that he might yet choose the girl, Neala? She hardly knew her own thoughts as she watched him, awaiting his choice. Slowly he drew the silken length away and studied the hopeful girl who lay before him, as if he were considering her offer. Brettan then gathered the scarf and, turning to Sandlin, placed it about his knight's shoulders, his rejection of the girl plain to all. Then, turning back to Maren, he seized her hand and, bending from the waist as if to bow before her, he placed a kiss upon her hand. The full meaning of his choice was lost to none, and he lingered over her hand, his eyes full with his meaning.

Maren could feel the heat of his gaze, and she tried to look away. Whether from the fire or his touch she could not know, but she was aware only that of a sudden she could not breathe, as if some weight pressed down upon her. Standing abruptly, she turned away from the table, upsetting the goblet close under her hand, and struggled to free herself from his grasp. "Please, milord, I—" Her voice broke. She fought against a sudden light-headedness and reached to the table to steady herself. Her thoughts confused, Maren felt herself swept up in well-muscled arms and carried into the coolness away

147

from the glowing fires. Oddly, she felt safe and secure within that unyielding grasp.

Maren was oblivious to the wild hoots and shouts of encouragement that followed them as Brettan bore her to his tent. Maren relaxed against the firmness of that wide expanse of chest until he laid her upon the soft pallet. In the soft glow of light from the distant fires she was pale, but her eyes glowed with a sudden warmth. Carefully he released the lacings of her gown, allowing Maren to take a full, deep breath, the color already returning to her cheeks. The gown was drawn over her head, the chemise followed, and Maren shivered in the cool night air. He drew the heavy coverlet high over her gleaming white shoulders, removing his belted sword and then the velvet tunic and breeches. He tossed aside the linen shirt, then slipped beneath the coverlet, drawing it about them against the cold, the warmth of his long body curled around her, driving the chill from her skin. Maren responded to the feel of his warmth about her. Strong arms encircled her waist, and pulled her closer to mold her to him. In the darkness that surrounded them, she stared with wide, blue eyes, searching for the golden gaze she felt upon her, unable to understand why she did not fight against his nearness. Brettan's lips sought hers, brushing across her forehead, then lightly touching her eyes, the tip of her nose, and finally as soft as a feather upon her own lips. Maren sighed shakily, feeling from deep within a response so long denied and, with no hope of containing it, she yielded to the touch of his mouth against her own. Her slender arms reached up, encircling his neck, drawing him to her in a grasp he would not have broken for all the wealth in the kingdom. Her mouth, eager, demanding, opened against his, seeking, her small tongue touching the softness of his mouth. Brettan's lips crushed down on hers, and he savored the sweetness of the wine and the honeyed taste of her. His desire raged

148

within him, a desire to take her now, while he felt the sweet response within her slender body, to feel himself within her warmth, to satisfy his own need of her. But in the far reaches of his mind he lingered, desiring more, for he sought to build within her the full pleasure of their union. He kissed the corner of her mouth, her finely chiseled jawline, and a delicately curved ear, sending shivers of excited pleasure down her spine. Her long, raven-black hair surrounded them, wrapping them as if in a shroud. Maren abandoned herself to the pleasure of his touch, her senses, her skin suddenly aflame from the heat of his caress. It mattered not that he was English, or her enemy. It mattered not that war alone had brought them together, and she was his prisoner. Maren slid her hands along his shoulders, reveling in the play of muscles along his back and down his arms. Lightly she traced the line of his collarbone until her fingers were lost in the thick furring of hair upon his chest, as if she stroked a lean panther. She raked long fingers through that curling thickness, feeling the rapid pounding of his heart beneath her fingertips. His lips lowered to her throat, tracing a molten path along the vein that pulsed in her slender neck. His mouth then sought a taut peak, and his lips closed over her, her hands buried in the soft dark curls about his head, holding him to her, as if she could not bear for that contact to be broken. Brettan teased her, tormented her, nibbling gently at her breast, his hands expertly stroking, kneading, caressing, exploring, moving over her. Maren felt as if he had taken her to the far reaches of her being. Her senses came alive at his touch, and she felt her youthful body responding. He took her higher, his hands moving lower over her body, where no man had touched before, awakening sensations within her that she had not known existed. Gently, slowly his large strong hand moved over the flatness of her stomach, and Maren arched against that touch, only just beginning to realize her need of him. Her breath stilled in her throat when she understood his intention, and she parted her legs slightly to accept his contact. Gently Brettan continued caressing, stroking, building the fires of her own passion, and Maren responded by exploring his lean, hard body with hands that hungrily explored each muscle flexed with the tension of his passion, the long hard length of his back, the cording of the tendons in his neck. Maren sought to fulfill her passion, and her hands moved over him, tentatively, questioning, light as silk against the flaming heat of his skin. Remembering his reaction at her touch once before, Maren slid her arm down the length of his flat, hard stomach, her fingers trailing the thick furring of dark hair as it narrowed at his waist, and slowly her hand closed over him, and she lifted her eyes to see his gaze glowing golden in the darkness above her. His breath was labored. One arm encircled her waist, and the other hand rode gently on her hip, holding her to him. He moved over her slowly, his knee moving between her legs, gently forcing them apart, for he saw the desire in the wide, blue velvet pools that stared at him. Everything but his touch was lost to her. She saw nothing, felt nothing, except his warmth, his strength, his desire for her. Carefully Maren guided him to her, arching her hips to take him fully. As he entered her, Brettan sank slowly so as not to cause her pain this time, moving gently, and Maren moved with him, closing about him, feeling his heat deep within her. He seemed to fill her more completely with each thrust, her body responding to his subtle demands, the flames of their passion building to consume them. In the wild abandoned pleasure of his body moving with hers, Maren's hands were like silken wisps along his back, caressing him, pulling him deeply within her. His impassioned thrusts increased, for he felt her passion, and she met him equally. He felt within her a growing urgency, a deep

150

longing, her body arching against him, giving as well as taking from him. Maren's eyes opened wide, and her breath stopped in her throat. The flames that had merely warmed them now consumed her, and she felt the waves of pleasure moving over her, and she took him with her, feeling that exquisite fulfillment that was almost painful, the sweetest agony. Brettan responded to the heat of final passion that passed through Maren by thrusting deep within her, his muscles lean and hard against her, a long shudder passing through his rigid body as he found his release within her, the recurring waves of her ultimate pleasure easing the passage of his seed. He bound her to him in an embrace born of desperation. Then his breathing eased, his lips brushing across her temple, his glowing eyes closed. He inhaled deeply of her scent, her forehead dampened with a film of moisture. Reluctant to break his contact deep within her, longing to prolong their shared pleasure of one another, free from all hostility and deceit, Brettan closed her slender body firmly with his grasp and pulled her gently with him as he rolled onto his side, their legs entwined, that intimate contact preserved. He molded her to him, as if he might draw her within and hold her forever, a part of himself. Maren's deep blue gaze searched through the darkness for his glowing green eyes, now softened with the passion of his pleasure in her. Her unspoken words were stilled on her gently curving lips, for Brettan pressed a kiss tenderly, silencing any questions, any protest she might have spoken. Feeling the safe protection of his arms about her, Maren surrendered to his greater will, pushing back for a time all doubts, all fears, beyond the veil of darkness that surrounded them. She closed her eyes to her silent torment, seeking to steel herself against the stirrings of her own emotions of the moments past, and the rush of tenderness she felt for the man who held her so tightly. Her cheek pressed against his shoulder,

151

her soft breath warm against his skin, her slender hands resting gently against his chest. Her fingers caressed his skin, the pale white of her fingers disappearing into the dark, curling hair. Slowly she stroked the rounded muscles that lay beneath his skin. She tilted her head back so that she might see him. Like live coals that hold the promise of the flame at rest, his eyes glowed above her. The darkness hid his expression from her. Had she seen the look upon his face at that moment, all her fears and doubts would have crumbled before his desperate longing. Her fingers traced his collarbone. She stared unafraid into his golden green eyes, and then in one fluid motion her hand slipped behind his neck, and she buried her fingers in the thick, soft, dark waves of hair that curled about his neck, pulling him to her. Carefully she rolled on top of him, their union unbroken. Gently she held his lean, handsome face between her two hands and, closing her eyes, lowered her mouth to his. Brettan's eyes closed in complete abandon to the impassioned caresses that fell across his body. Deep within him he felt the rise of his passion at the bold yet innocent explorations of the young girl who lay over him. A deep longing surged within him, an awakening to the unexpected pleasure that her audacious touch roused within him. He opened his eyes to stare into liquid blue pools that held his gaze. She again pressed her lips against his, her longing, her passion fanning the flames of his desire, her tongue thrusting tentatively between his lips as he had instructed her, questing, seeking, tasting of him until her senses reeled with the scent of him, the taste of his skin against her lips. Maren raised herself above him, the wild mane of her raven hair cascading about them. She watched the play of emotions that crossed his handsome face in the flickering light from the campfires outside the tent, and she marveled at the lean hard strength of his arms, while his hands moved across her hips and he

152

sought to move within her. He seemed like some mythical warrior of ancient legends, only he was very real beneath her hands, the heat of his body setting her aflame, his bold hands exciting within her a response. Slowly, savoring each moment, Maren lowered herself over him, taking him fully within her. Their first passion spent, they now moved slowly together, each luxuriating in their full pleasure of the other. Maren leaned over him, her full, ripe breasts crushed in the soft furring of his chest, her lips drawn to his by a strong hand at the back of her head. She could feel the silent strength of his muscles, his mouth crushed against hers. She could feel the deep longing in the heat of his kiss, his breathing soft and warm against her cheek. His lips traveled down the length of her neck, only to return to her lips, as if his thirst for her could not be quenched. Brettan's head reeled at the assault of her innocent abandon, for the slender girl poised over him responded freely, without reservation. She was like a child, seeking, exploring, only just beginning to know the depths of her own passion, and yet she was a woman. He saw in those blue eyes that she was without deceit or guile, and in his heart he felt a sudden tightening that these moments they now shared were the only truth, and that nothing else mattered, not even the blind quest for revenge that had set him against her. And there was no despair in that realization, only passion, and he sought to build again within her the passion of the moments past. In one quick, effortless movement Brettan turned and pulled Maren beneath him, moving deep within her soft flesh. A soft moan escaped her lips, and she rose against him, her slender arms wrapped tightly about his neck, drawing his lips to hers. They moved as one, reaching higher toward that unseen moment that awaited them. And as the heat of their passion consumed Maren, she choked back a sudden cry of his name, her young body trembling with

153

the waves of her final pleasure of him. Brettan lifted her against him, his release coming as one with hers. For long moments Maren could feel his pleasure deep within her, and she closed her eyes in complete rapture at the heat of his body against hers, and bound him to her as if she might never let him go. Gently Brettan lowered her to the soft pallet, then stretched out beside her, content to hold her against him. Later, her breathing came deep and even with her slumber, and he curled protectively about her, pulling the heavy coverlet high over her bare shoulders against the cold of the night. Beyond the tent the sounds of the night's festivities were now low. His knights made their pallets upon the ground, seeking their own comfort with the willing maids of the town. His golden, green eyes shone brightly through the night, and he knew with sudden clarity that he could never allow her to be taken from him, for it would be to surrender his very soul.

Chapter Eight

"You cannot mean what you say! This is madness. It's quite impossible," Maren stammered, staring in wide-eyed disbelief at Brettan across the table where they sat to break the morning fast. Then her surprise turned to anger at his bold decision, those deep blue pools glinting with her barely suppressed rage. "I cannot, I will not, go to England, and there is no power that can force me to do so."

Brettan turned his glowing green-eyed gaze upon her, his eyes traveling the full length of her body, the gently heaving bosom, the stubborn set of her jaw, the flush of bright color that spread across her cheeks as her temper mounted, and he seemed to strip the very clothes from her with his deliberate perusal. He sighed heavily, reluctant to enter the conflict yet knowing there was no way around it for the decision he had made. "There is no question in the matter, Maren. Unless, of course, you would rather I hand you over to the king and let him do with you as he will. I do not think that a fate you would care to tempt. Edward has proven no great fondness for rebel traitors. Many a fair maid has found herself much the worse for stubborn pride and high spirit."

"Yea, I know well how Edward leaves his mark upon my people." Maren slammed down the empty goblet, her wrath pushing her perilously beyond all caution. "I know well, for I have seen it myself, how they lay waste to our land, killing innocent women and children, plundering till there is naught to feed the most meager beggar through the winter months. And always the English return, again and again. I fail to understand how your king in all his wisdom hopes to have anything left to conquer once his armies have ravaged our land and our people. Tell me, milord, what is the reason that would leave an innocent woman, loved and respected by all, slain at the hands of her English murderers, her youngest daughter left to madness and her son, no more than a mere child, taken for hostage? You speak of the wisdom and compassion of your king, yet I see only death and destruction across this land that is my home. Explain it to me, if you can, so that I may understand what I cannot see with my eyes." Maren stood beside the table, her tiny hands clenched into fists of rage and pain. All the passion of the night before, all the tenderness was now replaced by anger, and a fear that Brettan had only glimpsed before. And yet she remained the beautiful proud temptress who had enticed him so beguilingly the evening before, for even when angered as now, her long, raven hair waving about her shoulders and tumbling down the length of her shapely back, his only thoughts were to crush her to him, to silence her tormented ravings, to soothe the pain he saw in the wide, velvet pools of blue, which suddenly flooded with unexpected tears. And Brettan suddenly realized that, through all he had forced her to endure these last weeks, he had never seen her cry. Angrily Maren dashed the tears from her eyes with the back of her hand, her frustration at such weakness goading her beyond all reason. "Tell me, milord, how could you possibly trust me not to run you through should you turn your back for a moment? Or perhaps when we are abed, for it seems that is your true purpose, to flaunt me before your king and all of England as your mistress?" Maren gritted her teeth, her fists clenched tightly at her sides to still the trembling fear that belied her boldly spoken words. They were both oblivious that Sir Bothwell had entered the enclosure and now stood uncertainly, witnessing the heated exchange. Brettan rounded the end of the table that separated them, golden, green eyes narrowed keenly. Reaching out with lightening-quick swiftness, his hand closed over her slender wrist, drawing her to him cruelly, his other arm encircling her waist. "I think that you know well the futility of such threats. But if you should be successful in delivering me to that fate, be it known there is no place in either heaven or hell that could keep you safe." His face was like a mask of death, his threats spoken with calmness. His lids lowered over that piercing gaze and, unable to meet his gaze lest he know of her fears, Maren glanced away, her obstinacy made only more obvious by her silence. Slowly the pressure of his grip eased, and he released her. Her bones ached, but Maren remained motionless in his grasp, her mind tumbling in her desperation to outwit him, to best him and leave him bleeding before the assault of her hatred. Gently, with almost imperceptible tenderness, Brettan reached up to cup her small face, turning her reluctant gaze to face him. "You cannot deny the advantages of my protection nor, I think, can you deny the pleasure you have found in sharing my bed." Before she could give argument to his words, his head lowered, his lips closing over hers in a kiss that seared and burned with his passion. Her senses reeled beneath his bold assault, and she vainly sought to push him away with her hands, shoving against the firmness of his chest. But instead of his usual brutal forcefulness against her, Brettan hesitated for a moment, his lips leaving hers, so that she sighed with obvious relief that he would release her and torment her no further. But that was not his intent. He sought to make plain his authority over her, and gently his lips returned to reclaim hers, only now with infinite tenderness, almost as if he caressed her. Maren's eyes flew open in surprise at the sudden change in his manner, uncertain of his intentions. But his kiss carefully traced the corner of her mouth, the gentle curve of her jawline, and Maren realized his game. And indeed he knew his game well, for he sought to humiliate her before his knight—they had both seen him by now—by plying her with gentleness, hoping to tear down the wall of defiance she had so carefully placed between them. Deep blue eyes sparked a forewarning of vengeance. Had Brettan not concentrated so completely on his enticement of her, he would have proceeded with greater caution. Maren parted her lips invitingly beneath the soft warmth of his kiss, and just when he thought she would yield that velvet softness, she bit him, her sharp teeth sinking in deeply, seeking retaliation in the only way left vulnerable to her. With a loud oath, Brettan pulled away from her, his surprise complete, the mounting fury obvious in the dark cloud of anger that spread across his bronzed features. A small trickle of blood appeared at the corner of his mouth. He stared at her in stunned surprise, and behind that golden visage she detected the fury of his tightly restrained wrath. For a full, long moment, she expected him to strike her, the scar below his eye turning white with his barely suppressed rage. Trapped as she was within the circle of his grasp, Maren was left nothing save her pride, to which she clung desperately. She had thrown down the challenge and now stood defiantly rigid, willing to accept her fate. But a faint warning checked his actions, for he realized she knew not what she risked, that only stubborn pride had pushed her beyond reason, and that perhaps he had pushed her too far before his man. Brettan raised his hand. Maren flinched from an imagined blow that never fell. Brettan buried his hand in the thick, swirling masses of her hair, his long fingers twining through the satin softness, then twisting sharply, forcing her head back. A gasp escaped her parted lips while his mouth tasted the sweetness of her neck, the heat of his touch forcing her to strain away from him. His kisses traveled lower along the arch of her neck, across the wildly racing pulse that hammered under gleaming white skin. With sudden clarity she realized the path he traveled, for the low cut of the gown stretched taut, exposing the heaving mound of a vulnerable breast. His hold about her waist tightened, restricting her breathing so that she felt smothered by his unrelenting assault. Any protest she might have uttered would not come, and she felt the fog of unconsciousness slipping over her, his hold persisting with greater pressure. He was the devil incarnate, and any defiance she offered only heightened his cruelty. Maren felt herself slipping from reality, until she became aware that he had released her. She fell backwards against the table, her lungs filling with cool, refreshing air that brought with it a soft buzzing somewhere in the back of her head. She opened her eyes and stared in dazed confusion to see Brettan retreat the width of the tent, then snatch up his sword and gauntlets, turning back to her with a final warning before leaving with Sir Bothwell. "We ride within the hour. Make yourself ready, and be certain, milady, that any decision I make shall be final."

With great determination, Maren willed her hands not to tremble as she clumsily unfastened the velvet gown and, stepping to the wooden coffer, flung the gown inside, preferring her own leather tunic and breeches, relenting only where the chemise was concerned, for she had not the time to discard it. Hastily she pulled on the

159

soft doeskin garments and then the soft leather boots, her thoughts flying at a perilous pace. Her life was worth nothing. She knew now that whatever might have passed between them meant nothing to Brettan, and she was suddenly horrified that, while her every thought had been determined on her escape from the English, her heart had defied it, only to bring her to this moment. She knew that each passing day brought them closer to England, and she knew of a certainty that Brettan would carry out his intentions to take her to London. Maren closed her eyes against the torment she would feel, the daughter of an English lord, being flaunted before all of England as the mistress of the Duke of Norfolk. She also realized that, had she chosen to tell him the truth, he would never have believed her. Maren fought back angry tears of frustration. Her only hope lay in her escape. Whirling about, she stormed from the tent out into the bright light of the early morning sun. The camp was alive with the activity of preparation made for the day's ride. Behind her the stakes of the massive tent were pulled, the last furnishings loaded into the carts. Ada sat atop her cart, clucking softly to the horse, guiding him behind the trail of wagons already following Brettan's guard. At the edge of the clearing she saw the young girl, Neala, preparing to mount a shaggy brown mare, the girl tossing Maren a withering glare while she reached up to the saddle and pulled herself aloft, settling herself atop the ancient nag with an unmistakable pout firm on her young face. So lost was Maren within the misery of her own thoughts that she collided headlong with Sandlin, who was crossing the small clearing leading the large chestnut. Only his quick restraining hand prevented her from tumbling headlong to the ground when she attempted to recover her footing. "The Duke of Norfolk has asked that you ride with his guard. We must make haste to catch them before they gain too much distance."

Maren's eyes sparked fire, staring back at Sandlin, and he felt momentarily defenseless before the wild-eyed beauty of the young girl before him, like some wild creature cornered, now turning to face the foe openly in one last confrontation with only one possible ending. Maren knew this man was not her enemy, for he had shown her only kindness. Reluctantly she yielded the moment, accepted the reins, and with his assistance pulled herself atop the tall horse. "Be it known, Sandlin, that I will have my freedom before this journey is ended," she promised him passionately, grasping the reins firmly in one hand, as Sandlin also mounted and rode to keep up with her.

"Beware, milady, that I will do all in my power to prevent it, though I can plainly see your cause in the matter."

"If you see my cause, then allow me to slip away. None would be the wiser until I gained some good distance. And what would be the loss? For I vow I am of no import but to my family."

"You are wrong, milady, for you are of considerable importance to the Duke of Norfolk and, be he right or wrong, I will do as he bids me in the matter."

"Then you, sir, are a coward!" Maren flung from between tightly clenched lips.

"Nay, milady, I am knight of the realm, and true to my sworn duties to his lordship and my liege. I have sworn to lay down my life for their cause, and if that is the price I must pay, then I will gladly pay it."

Maren's anger fled before the man's honesty. He had spoken bravely and without hesitation, and she knew of a certainty that he would carry through with his duty no matter what the cost to himself, for she had seen that same intense loyalty in her father and brother. She smiled sadly across at the knight who rode beside her. "And you would see me imprisoned and bound in chains, to see your duty well met? I could not deliver you to that same fate by my escape. You have been a friend to me, even against your judgement, and I value that beyond all else." Maren reached out to touch a slender hand upon his strong arm.

Sandlin cleared his throat uncomfortably, suddenly ill at ease before her beguiling beauty.

"The Duke of Norfolk is an honorable man, milady, and a good man, even if he is English. Trust in him, and he shall protect you against all who would do you harm."

Startled, Maren stared wide-eyed at the gruff knight, who turned abruptly, as if embarrassed at what he had said. "We have a long day's ride ahead of us." He motioned her to ride ahead and join the guard. Maren had plenty of time to consider the man's words over the long hours of the day, while they rode through the early spring morning, each hour bearing her closer to England.

A nagging uncertainty plagued Brettan, and he strengthened his guard by night. By day his men rode hard, searching the hills for some sign of the Welsh rebels, always returning unable to find a trace of the elusive enemy, whose presence he felt but could not see. His patience wore thin, and he often responded with only a quick temper or sudden disapproval, retreating to brooding silence. His doubts of Maren troubled him constantly, and often she would feel the heat of his gaze upon her, to find him staring at her as if he sought some unspoken truth. They rode long, hard hours by day, and Maren soon discovered that the guard around her had also been strengthened. Resolutely she waited and watched for her opportunity at freedom. By night her dreams were haunted by Catherine's eyes so void of any emotion, her mother's lifeless body so cold, and young Edmund's smiling round face, and she often awoke crying her anguish at the small boy's fate. Whatever distance remained between them by day, always at night there was Brettan's silent strength about her, and warm hands to brush away her tears gently, his resistance crumbling beneath the assault of her silent, tormented dreams.

Nerves grew taut, each knight, each soldier remaining alert to any signs of possible attack. Maren's request to ride beside Ada's cart was coolly denied, and Sandlin remained her constant companion when duty required Brettan's attention away from the main guard.

A torrential spring storm left them soaking beneath their heavy mantles, but the sixth day from Brecon dawned mercifully clear and warm. Though Maren's spirits soared with the change in the weather, she soon found that Brettan's uneven temper of the days past persisted. He remained lost in his own thoughts and rode silently at the front of the guard, leaving Maren to contemplate his ill humor, staring at the broad expanse of his back, the brilliant blue and gold of his tunic hidden beneath the heavy mantle, the mail coif pushed back from his head. But the morning sun rose high in the sky, bringing an uncommon warmth to the day.

Brettan sat stiffly upright in the saddle, the gray warhorse dancing nervously in the column of riders. They continued across a small valley to the gently sloping hillsides at the base of the Black Mountains. He glanced back toward the center of his guard, searching among the riders until he found the slender, boyish figure he sought. Raven-black hair, bound into one thick braid, trailed across Maren's shoulder. Her small face made her seem no more than a child, yet as their eyes met briefly his breath caught at the brilliant blue of sapphire eyes. They held his gaze for but a moment and then glanced away, her discomfort at that contact obvious in the slight frown that marred her perfect beauty. In the days since their last confrontation over his decision to take her to London, there had been few words exchanged, indeed

163

only the barest nod or acknowledgement that she was even aware of his presence, so cold and unyielding was her manner toward him. Yet beneath that mask of indifference, when her dreams returned to haunt her sleep, Maren reached out to his warmth and welcomed his closeness, so that he knew the falseness of her hatred for him. The sight of her now, well protected by his guard, somehow calmed his unspoken fears some small measure.

Maren welcomed their midday stop to rest the horses and take a light meal of cheese and bread. Carefully she guided the chestnut to a nearby stream and let him drink of the cooling waters. The leather tunic and breeches she had stubbornly insisted on wearing had grown unbearably hot and stifling, and she now loosened the ties at the front of the tunic. Trailing a length of linen in the water, she wrung it out to wipe the dust and dirt from her face and hands. The mass of her hair, plaited in one long braid, was pulled casually over her shoulder, and she wiped the back of her neck with the cooling cloth. Lost to her own thoughts, her gaze wandered across the stream to the gonfalons, resplendent with the colors of the Duke of Norfolk, the blue in the banners waving brilliantly in a clear azure sky. She sighed heavily. Her efforts of the last days to find a means of escape had been for naught. With the guard about her, escape was now impossible. She glanced ruefully at the small band of camp followers gathered about, taking advantage of the cooling stream to fill their skins with water. She was much the same as they, her existence dependent upon the English army that bore her further and further away from her home with each passing day. The only difference was that they were free to leave when they chose, and she was not. Knowing his anger of the past days, Maren had pressed Brettan no further on the matter of her release. He remained steadfastly determined in his decision to take her to England and Maren now realized her only chance to remain in Wales lay in a direct appeal to King Edward. What fate that might bring, she could not know. Her father had often spoken of his friendship with the king, but she could not be certain the friendship would extend to her even if the King were to believe her words. Her deepest fear remained that Brettan was responsible for her mother's death. She felt certain her own safety lay in keeping her secret for the few days that remained before reaching England.

The rest was brief, all too brief. Maren wearily pulled herself into the saddle and resumed her position beside Sandlin, the loyal knight casting her an encouraging smile. "These mountains are called the Black Mountains. They are called that because when viewed from afar they seem black, even in the brightest light of day. We will travel through a pass that will take us beyond the mountains, to England. Monmouth lies only two days ride beyond the last ridge. This time of year all of England comes alive with wild flowers, the grass is rich and the soil fertile, and the sun shines warmly. It gives strength to the weary soul."

"There is great longing in your voice, Sandlin. I would not have thought you to care for such things. How long has it been since last you saw your beloved England?"

"It has been near a full year since last we rode from England. When we have won this war, we shall return to stay for a long while." Sandlin glanced hesitantly at the young girl beside him, remembering that they were enemies in this conflict. Victory for England meant defeat for her people.

Maren smiled gently at the big knight.

"I meant no harm, milady."

"Yea, I know, Sandlin. You are a knight of King Edward and a soldier of many campaigns. Surely you are accustomed to being away from family and home."

"'Tis true that I have fought beside the king in the crusades, with the Duke of Norfolk. There are many among us who have seen many a battle upon foreign soil, but always for a cause we could name. This war with Wales weighs heavily upon me, for it seems to me as if we make war needlessly. In truth, milady, I would gladly see us gone from this place, for I cannot abide this cursed cold that robs a man of health and stamina, but I am sworn in my duties to the Duke of Norfolk and therefore sworn to his cause."

"And what is the cause of the Duke of Norfolk? Is it not one and the same as that of the King?" Maren glanced at Sandlin speculatively.

"The Duke of Norfolk has always been a man to follow his own path. When he has found that which he seeks, he will then return to England." He answered her cautiously, abruptly ending their conversation, and spurred his horse forward to speak briefly with Sir Bothwell at the head of the guard. Maren's delicate brow furrowed slightly in contemplation of the knight's last words; if not to carry out Edward's war against Wales, what then was Brettan's reason for venturing the length and breadth of the countryside, risking his men in the face of battle? Was it the vengeance he had once spoken of so briefly?

Maren was startled from her thoughts by a warning cry that sounded along the column of the guard. She reined in the large chestnut, her eyes searching for the cause of the alarm. Ahead of her Sandlin spurred his mount forward to the lead of the column. All about her swords had been drawn from their sheaths. The knights prepared for battle, whirling about to face the rear of the column. Maren glanced about her in sudden panic, realizing that the attack Brettan had feared was upon them. Behind her she could see carts scattered hastily, their drivers seeking some point of safety in a small stand of trees nearby. Her horse pawed nervously, and she saw a

166

distant swarm of riders descending upon the English guard. Seeing Ada struggling to control her panic-stricken horse, Maren urged the chestnut forward. Behind her she could hear the shouts and cries of the English as the battle was joined, the sound of steel striking against steel sending shivers of fear down the length of her spine. Confusion descended all about her. Reaching the old woman, Maren leaned over to grab the lead rope of the frightened horse, while Ada fought to control the animal, which backed up awkwardly, almost turning the cart. Maren was nearly pulled from her saddle, but attempted to keep her hold of the rope. Instantly beside her, Sandlin retrieved it just as the animal jerked away with fear, pulling the rope from her grasp.

With his sword outstretched, Sandlin pointed to the safety of an outcropping of rock beyond the stand of trees. Maren whirled her horse about and directed him toward that safety, frantically urging Ada's horse ahead. From behind her came the agonized cries of battle, the clash of steel cutting through chain mail. The sounds of her nightmares became stark reality. Through the haze of dust that rose from the battlefield, Maren saw the huge gray stallion and the knight who rode him hard, the blue and gold of his tabard now covered with blood, whose blood she could not tell, as he swung the mighty broadsword against those who would cut him down. From side to side Brettan wielded that mighty blade of death, but behind him Maren saw one plainly clothed attacker rise feebly from where he had fallen, a lethal blade clutched desperately in both hands as he moved with great effort toward the English knight astride the warhorse. All about him the battle raged, while Brettan and his knights fought the rebel attack, the blood of English and Welsh mixed on the field of their struggle. In that one man's desperate efforts, Maren saw Brettan's certain death. From deep within her came the cry of his name lost in the tumultuous uproar of the battle that surrounded them. With an urgency Maren hardly understood, she whirled the chestnut about, driving him headlong into the crush of the battle, her only thought that she must warn Brettan. Again she cried his name in warning. This time he turned about, her cry carried to him on the wind. For the briefest moment his emerald-green gaze locked with hers, and he saw her fear for him mirrored in the depths of her brilliant blue eyes.

Brettan whirled the gray warhorse about just when the deadly blade would have sliced into his back. His anger seethed at the coward who would have struck at his back, and in one swift movement he ended the rebel's life. Both hands wielding the heavy broadsword, he guided the massive steed with the slightest pressure of his knee, whirling the gray in a wide circle to sweep his gaze over the bloodied field. Only a short distance away, Maren lay pinned beneath the fallen chestnut, struggling to free herself. An arrow protruded from the neck of her mount, and the beast lay still where it had fallen when she had cried her warning.

Maren pushed against the saddle of her horse and felt the soft sod beneath her leg yield, allowing her to free herself. She felt the ground beneath her tremble. A horseman advanced on her before she could gain her footing. She whirled to face her attacker.

Shifting the heavy broadsword to his left hand, Brettan reached down, his right arm encircling Maren's slender waist. Easily he lifted her and set her before him in the saddle. He turned the gray warhorse about, while Sandlin rode hard toward them from across the greensward. All about them the dust of battle settled, and Brettan's guard gave chase to the last of the rebels, who fled to the safety of the hills, leaving behind their dying and wounded.

Maren cringed back against Brettan from the horror of death that surrounded them, and they rode back across the stilled battlefield. All about them lay the bodies of the Welsh rebels who had struck with such surprise but paid heavily. Among them lay the fallen few of Brettan's guard. The wounded were carried to a place apart where even now Ada moved among them, offering water and bandages to those in need.

Brettan guided the gray toward the scattered line of carts and gave his orders for the camp to be made. His lips brushed hastily across Maren's temple, and she felt the warmth of his arm about her in a momentary embrace before he gently set her to the ground. Maren watched him ride down the long line of carts, his concern for his men worn heavily upon his broad shoulders. She turned to help Ada unload the cart. Their work that day would carry long into the night.

Chapter Nine

For an entire day they remained camped beside the stream in northeast Wales, attending the dead and wounded English soldiers. The wounded of the rebels were given equal care, but well guarded, for Brettan felt certain that the rebels who had escaped into the nearby hills would attack again. His thoughts as to their reasons for so bold a strike so near England were kept silently to himself. Guards were posted along the entire perimeter of the encampment, and a heavily armed patrol continued to ride the hills surrounding the wide valley.

Maren worked tirelessly, dressing a multitude of wounds or bringing food and water to the injured. Long after Ada had slumped wearily before the blazing camp fire, Maren was sought by yet another soldier of the realm with an injury he had before pleaded was minor, but now suffered from greatly. Requests were met with a gentle smile, while she moved among the pallets of the wounded, replacing a cool cloth on a fevered brow, or stripping away a dried poultice and replacing it with another. She constantly sent Sandlin or Sir Bothwell foraging to the nearby streams for mosses and lichens that could be found on the embankments, growing in lush abundance. Though some cast a wary eye at the strange potions she mixed from an assortment of unknown herbs and crushed powder, none could deny the relief her gentle touch brought to those in pain.

Very near dawn that first day after the battle, Maren straightened when she had finished binding a last wound. Every bone in her body cried out for rest, and her leg pained her greatly from the bruise of the fall she had taken. She glanced up at the tall shadow approaching from across the camp, realizing for the first time that there had been no moment for words between her and Brettan.

Brettan noticed the weary droop in Maren's slender shoulders, her face drawn and pale with her fatigue, and he realized with a sudden heaviness that it was near first light and she had not stopped to rest or eat since late the afternoon before. He expected that much from his own men, but hardly from one such as her, much less one considered prisoner in his camp.

"I must have your knowledge to bind one more wound. Sir Aiken took an arrow and, though the tip and the shaft have been removed, the wound bleeds badly. I fear for his life, for even now he is greatly weakened by the loss of blood."

Maren gathered clean linens from the cart, and a foul-smelling bowl of liquid that simmered over the hot coals of the fire. "Then let us bind this last English wound. I will not allow Sir Aiken to die for want of my care."

Brettan led the way to where several pallets had been lain for the night. Sir Aiken stirred and rose on one elbow when his lord and master approached. His face paled to an ashen color with his efforts, and he slumped back upon the pallet, his breathing shallow and warm with the fever from the infection that had already set in.

Maren touched his brow, her hand burned by the fire she felt there. Sir Aiken opened his eyes weakly and

172

managed a faint smile.

"It was not my intent to take you from others in greater need, mistress," he sighed heavily.

"My work is not done until the last wound is bound. It would not do to have you die from lack of care. I fear the Duke of Norfolk would hold me responsible for your loss." She teased gently, pulling open the tunic and drawing back the blood-soaked linen of the shirt beneath. Already the wound had festered badly and continued to bleed, not profusely but enough that Sir Aiken could easily lose his life. Maren quickly asked that the shirt be stripped away and ordered hot water from a nearby campfire. Soaking a clean linen in the water, she gently cleansed the wound, drawing away dried blood and dirt that had caked over it during the long hours of the night. She knew well the heat of the water caused him pain, but he bore it as a true knight of England, a clenched fist the only outward sign of his agony.

"It is not my intent to cause you pain, Sir Aiken, but the wound must be closed, or I fear for your life." Maren glanced from Sir Aiken to Brettan. He knew well the truth of her words, and silently nodded for her to continue, then called for Sandlin and Sir Bothwell to restrain the wounded knight.

Maren layed a broad, flat-bladed knife across the glowing coals of the fire, then bent to prepare the poultice to bind the wound. When the blade glowed as golden as the coals, Maren seized it carefully, wrapping a heavy cloth about the handle. She glanced uncertainly at Sir Aiken, knowing the pain she must cause him. Bravely the knight bade her continue. Maren inhaled deeply to calm her nerves, and with a sure and steady hand drew that glowing blade across the torn, gaping wound. The stench of burning flesh filled the night air. Maren laid the blade back on the stones and closed her eyes for a moment to steady her reeling senses. Brettan's strong hand closed over hers, his warmth flooding through her in an unspoken message of his faith in her. When she opened her eyes, she found his warm gaze staring back at her, and she was startled by the gentleness she saw there.

Sir Aiken drew in a ragged, uneven breath, fighting against the pain the searing blade had caused. Maren quickly applied the oozing poultice of warm liquid, packing it with a thick pad of linen cloth and then tying it firmly in place with a long strip of linen. Carefully Sandlin eased the injured knight back onto the pallet. Maren drew a warm coverlet high over the wounded shoulder.

"The fever will continue for the next few hours. I will remain with him. The poultice must be changed frequently to draw the infection from the wound." Wearily Maren replaced the bowl of liquid over the live coals, then sat down before the campfire to take up her vigil. Her head nodded once, then twice, and Brettan lifted her sleeping form gently, giving his orders for the wound to be dressed. In long easy strides he bore her to his tent, thinking that she had well earned the reward of freedom that day, yet knowing he must deny her for reasons that went beyond the secrets she kept from him.

Maren snuggled closer to Brettan's warmth, her breath a soft whisper against his neck, and unknowingly reached a hand to caress the soft furring beneath her cheek, while he held her against him in sleep.

Brettan stirred, feeling the warmth of the sun penetrating the fabric walls of the tent, then he slipped from the covers, careful not to disturb Maren. She slept, oblivious to his departure. For a long moment he stood and stared at her fragile beauty, the thick cascade of her raven-black hair sweeping across the indentation in the soft pallet he had occupied a moment before. After pulling on leather breeches and boots, Brettan slipped

174

the leather tunic over his shoulders. Stepping to the small basin of water, he doused his face with cold water, running his hands over the barbed stubble on his face, and silently vowed to find his squire and relieve himself of the uncomfortable bristles. Shaking the droplets of water from his hair, he swung about at the sound of Sandlin's hesitant entrance.

"Good morning, my friend." Brettan spoke heartily, his lightened mood obvious in his voice.

Sandlin cast an inquiring glance at Maren's sleeping form, undisturbed by their exchange. "How fares our Welsh captive this day?"

Brettan regarded his man evenly. "I think your concern for her rivals mine. She has slept soundly these last hours, and I warrant that upon waking she shall be fit to take on the entire English army."

"She has shown great kindness to the wounded, and there are many among your guard who have a great fondness for her, milord."

"Yea, Sandlin, it would seem our prisoner now holds us captive." An uncertain look crossed Brettan's lean, handsome face, and he stared at the beautiful young girl who slept soundly on his pallet.

"You are troubled, milord?"

"There are many unanswered questions, Sandlin; secrets that she holds within. To what purpose I cannot name, surely not fear, for I believe she is without fear. She risked her life to save mine, without question, and for that I owe a great debt. No, my friend, I am not troubled over her, only of what she may know of the medallion I found."

Sandlin gazed somberly at Brettan. "You are certain it is your brother's medallion?"

Brettan stiffened. "It is the same. How she came by it, I do not know." He turned gruffly away from Sandlin's gaze.

"So, then, you are caught at cross purposes, caring for

175

one who has saved your life, yet may have been responsible for your brother's death. But it is not reasonable that she could so easily cause one man's death and then risk her own life to save another, one she is forced to call her enemy."

Brettan glared at his knight for the man's boldness, the truth in Sandlin's words sorely testing him when he had no patience for such matters. His good humor fled before the truth he could not deny. His temper darkened, and he reached for the heavy broadsword, hastily belting the blade at his side. "We will speak no more of it. Time will see the matter well out."

"Perhaps, but very soon we reach England, and I think she will not easily accept your decision to take her to London." Sandlin spoke bravely, daring much before the rising temper that sparked in emerald-green eyes.

"She will do as I say, and for now I say we shall speak no more of it."

Sandlin bowed his head in obedience and departed the tent before the unyielding wrath of his master.

Brettan stared through the opening of the tent across the encampment beyond. He could not deny the man's words. He knew well Maren would refuse to leave her homeland. And the thought came to him that he might yet learn the truth from her in exchange for her freedom. But could he easily keep his part of the bargain if she agreed? He leaned over her quietly sleeping form, his gaze suddenly warm and devouring as he studied the delicate contours of her face. Her lips parted for some unspoken words. Brettan was at a loss to understand the peacefulness he felt deep within just having her near. Gently he reached out and traced with the back of his fingers the silken softness of her cheek, tinged with a faint glow of color. One strong finger caressed the outline of her lips, and a gentle smile curved his handsome mouth at the memory of the past hours, when she had

176

unknowingly reached out to him in her sleep. Deep within him a soft glow stirred like a small flame, flickering, then glowing brightly. At a loss to understand the strange emotions that welled within him, Brettan rose hastily and departed the tent. Seeking out the gray stallion, Brettan swung easily into the saddle, his fatigue of the last days falling away. He urged the gray into long, even strides and joined his men to patrol the hillsides. His spirits soared, and he attributed it to their proximity to England. The last months had been long and grueling, resulting only in more unanswered questions in his search for his brother's murderer. Once they were returned to England, he would decide their next course. The cool wind pressed him back into the saddle, and the sun high in the spring sky warmed his back, while his muscles worked with the surging animal beneath him. His weariness faded with the rhythmic, even strides that carried him swiftly across the valley floor, and for a time he was content to feel the strength of the animal he rode, and the companionship of the trusted knights who had fought so many battles by his side. He pushed aside the lingering memory of deep blue eyes, so brilliant that they made him ache with a longing to look at her, and raven-black hair that swirled about him, caressing him with her sweet, honeyed scent, and soft, silken skin glowing warmly under his touch. But only for a moment, for the memory again intruded, and he drove the magnificent steed harder, so that the rushing wind might force that memory from his thought.

Maren awoke to the sounds of activity about the camp, the day already well advanced, a brilliant warm sun shining into the tent. She rubbed her eyes, not yet quite awake, and felt the empty space on the mat beside her. Her senses cleared, and she grew angry with herself that

177

she should be concerned with Brettan's whereabouts. Her anger was shortlived when she realized that what had awakened her were the sounds of horses and armor. They were preparing to leave. She had little more than a moment to contemplate that thought before Brettan entered the tent from his morning ride, followed closely by his squire. He quickly gave orders for the furnishings to be packed in the waiting carts. He turned as if suddenly aware of her presence, and Maren was aware of the cold tone of his voice.

"If you are sufficiently rested, we shall be leaving shortly. There have been several attacks about the countryside. Your rebel friends are intent on causing as much death and misery as possible. It has become too dangerous for us to remain here any longer. The wounded seem sufficiently rested. We ride within the hour."

At a loss to understand his coldness or the harshness of his words, Maren glared at his assumption that she was somehow responsible for the attacks by the rebel army.

"We have a shortage of mounts. You may ride in the cart with the old woman."

Maren's head shot up at his last words, suddenly fearful that her last chance for escape might be fast disappearing. If she was forced to ride in the cart, there would be no escape. She had to have her own horse.

"Milord, I would prefer to ride; perhaps one of the wounded would be more comfortable in the cart," Maren suggested casually.

Brettan eyed her keenly. "Very well. You may ride with me." Then, turning on his heel, Brettan left to give further orders for the preparation of their journey.

Through the long hours of the afternoon, Maren had cause to regret her insistance that she be allowed to ride. Brettan had settled her in the saddle before him,

178

cushioning her with the heavy thickness of his mantle folded across the saddle, and there she remained, well guarded beneath his strong hand. She soon gave up any hope of escape until she might be given her own horse, and settled against the firm support of his chest, allowing his hands and arms to hold her securely in the saddle, finding his strength and closeness somehow made her feel safe.

The course they followed wound through the narrow valley surrounded by the Black Mountains. With nightfall, they made their camp, and Maren curled contentedly against Brettan pushing aside the haunting uncertainty of her fate. She had the long hours of the next days to contemplate her future. She realized now that the English king might well be her only hope for freedom.

The Wye River flowed through the valley, and Maren marveled at the vivid green of the gently rolling landscape, sprinkled with the vastly arrayed colors of white, yellow and dark blue flowers that marked the new season. The sun glowed warmly down upon the column of the English Army as they stopped for a noonday meal. The guard dismounted, allowing their horses to graze on the fresh, green grasses, and Brettan gave the gray stallion free rein, allowing the horse to wander into the cool, swirling waters at the river's edge, while he gazed at the peaks of the distant mountains they had left behind.

Maren knew of his impatience to reach England, though he had set a slow pace over the past days in deference to his injured men, the day's ride often ending long before the setting of the sun.

"How many more days before we reach England?" Maren ventured casually, twisting the silver-streaked mane through her fingers.

Her offhanded question broke through his deep concentration, and Brettan turned to stare into her wide, deep blue eyes, which caught the blue of the sky so much

179

that he thought he might lose himself in her gaze forever. His green gaze held hers warmly for a moment, and he studied the alluring innocence of her beauty. Her profile was perfect, as if cut from the finest stone, each contour flawless, the gentle curve of her small nose slightly uplifted at the end, before dropping a small distance to the perfect lips he so enjoyed tasting. He sighed heavily that the back of a horse did not afford the opportunity for him to examine more closely the beautiful young girl seated before him.

"My dear Maren, look about and behold England." A smug smile pulled at the corners of his gently curved mouth, for he enjoyed her startled reaction. She turned her wide-eyed gaze back at him.

"You mean that we are already in England?" Maren stared at him in astonishment.

"Aye, these two days past, we have been in England."

"But how can that be? It looks the same as before, the hills, the valley, all are the same," Maren exclaimed, an obvious frown creasing her forehead.

"Aye, the same, and perhaps the reason Edward desires to make Wales one with England. Indeed it is the same. At least here, so close to the border between our two countries. But do not look so distressed, Maren. Or had you perhaps hoped yet to make good your escape?"

Her sharp intake of breath confirmed more to him than any words she might have spoken, but she stared across the expanse of the river at some distant point, refusing to meet his gaze.

"Did you think I was not aware of your plans, my love?"

"Surely such an attempt would be foolish, milord. I am too well guarded," she retorted.

"I much prefer the sound of my name from your lips, Maren, even if it be in anger."

Maren scooted as far forward in the saddle as possible to avoid his touch of her, her anger rising. "You are insufferable. All these days past you deliberately kept me under your hand, pretending there was no other horse I might ride, when your only purpose was to keep me well-guarded. And I thought—" Maren stopped abruptly, biting off what she would have said in anger.

"What is it that you thought? That perhaps I desired your closeness? Indeed, little one, such was part of my plan, for I do take great pleasure in your company." His wry smile twisted the blade of his insults deep within her. In one quick motion, Maren drew back her hand to strike at his handsome face, suddenly throwing herself off balance in her precarious perch on the back of the stallion. The animal, startled by her movement and sharp words, nervously side-stepped, and Maren slipped from her position in the saddle, while Brettan sought to control the wild-eyed horse threatening to cast them both into the cold waters of the river. Unable to stop her fall, his hand closed around empty air where he would have grabbed at the cloth of her tunic, but he heard only her muffled gasp and a loud splash, as she fell backwards into the river.

It took all of Brettan's strength to control the frightened steed, fearful that those sharp hooves might crush Maren or cause irreparable damage. In the splashing and thrashing that followed, her muffled curses were lost. She took in a good measure of water and came up choking and sputtering, the sodden mass of her hair weighing her down, while she struggled to stand upright in the waist-deep water. Brettan whirled the gray stallion about to offer her assistance, pulling the nervously pawing animal to a halt a few feet away. He dissolved into fits of uncontrollable mirth at the sight of her bedraggled form standing in the water, hardly a beautiful young maid at her bath, but more like some creature sprung from the depths, several long water reeds caught in her thick, wet tresses, obscuring her face from view.

Maren's humiliation was complete. She parted the mass of her hair so that she might see. She tried to pull her feet from the sandy bottom in an effort to reach the bank, but fell forward, the sand holding her foot firm, reluctant to release her. Maren's temper flew to new heights, and she gave full vent to her wrath, loudly uttering every Welsh curse that came to mind. Then, when the river bottom had yielded its hold, Maren stood with stiff-backed dignity and strode from the icy waters, staring straight ahead, past the group of English soldiers and knights who had paused in their meal to line the shore in stunned disbelief at the sight of the Duke of Norfolk practically unseated by that gray brute of a stallion, but even more surprised at Maren's sudden entry into the river. Sandlin watched, his high humor of the scene before them carefully suppressed behind the mask of his stern expression. The soldiers turned away to hide their obvious delight at the moment, while still others of the English guard coughed loudly to stifle a sudden burst of laughter. Maren strode to Ada's cart nearby and with quiet deliberation set about removing the squishing leather boots. Wringing as much water from her garments and hair as she might manage, she stoically refused to acknowledge Brettan's presence. He urged the stallion from the water and approached the cart, halting the big animal a few paces away.

"I appreciate your determination to escape, milady, but I should think, given the coolness of the water, that perhaps another time might be more appropriate." A satisfied smirk creased the corners of his mouth, and Maren thought that if he said one more word, she would throw herself at him and claw that taunting smile from his face.

"You seem quite certain that was my intention."

The expression on Brettan's face sobered for a moment, as he spoke low. "Of course it was your intent, as it has been since the day I made you my prisoner. Indeed, it was to be expected, since we neared England. You have never hesitated to voice your hatred of England and all Englishmen."

Taken aback that she had not fooled him for an instant, Maren sniffed indignantly that he should know every thought before it was spoken. "I do not hate 'all' Englishmen," she spat, her nerves on edge, irked that she seemed to have no thoughts of her own.

"Can it then be, sweet Maren, that I have found a place in your heart?" His voice was teasing, but his manner deadly serious. He stared back at her, his catlike eyes glowing at her with a warmth that surpassed the glare of the sun beating down on them.

"You arrogant, insufferable—" Maren fumed, struggling for some words that might injure his pride, the heat of her anger making her oblivious to the cold, cloying dampness of her garments.

Brettan held up his hand as if to halt the barrage of insults. "I am fully aware of your opinion of me, at least what you would say in the light of day. But perhaps I should speak loudly and clearly of your response to me in the dark of night." His tone was menacingly serious, and Maren stared back at him in stunned disbelief that he would dare be so crude. Yet a silent warning held her anger firmly restrained, for she knew full well he would not hesitate to tell of all their nights together before the entire guard, if indeed he had not done so already during the long hours before the evening fires, when he and his men took great delight in exchanging tales of their past glories. She silently yielded the moment, and a soft smile appeared in Brettan's eyes. All the qualities of a true lady, gently born, yet still clinging to the guise of a servant. Very soon, he thought, all her secrets would be known. He smiled gently at her, taking in her sodden appearance.

"It would seem you have determined the location of

our camp this day. I will not have you taken ill for want of dry clothes, even though it is your own foolishness that gained you such. Perhaps next time you shall not struggle so much under my hand." And giving her a mocking bow, he whirled the stallion about to give word to his men that they would ride no more that day.

Later, as evening approached, Maren stripped away the limp tunic and breeches in the privacy of the rocks at the river's edge. She slipped into the cool depths of the river, leaning her head back to let the gently swirling water fan her hair out behind her. In her hand she clutched the small bar of fragrant soap Brettan had purchased for her, reluctant to use the gift, yet unwilling to allow the opportunity for a thorough cleansing to escape. She lathered her raven tresses and then spread the sweet-smelling lather across her skin, ignoring the coolness of the water, aware only of the clean feeling of her skin. She rinsed the soap from her slender body and leaned back to cleanse her thick hair, squeezing the water from the lengths that fell about her hips before she turned back toward the bank.

Maren halted short of the water's edge, gazing through the fading light. Almost indistinguishable in the deep shadows, she saw another form approaching at the shore between her and her clothes. Thinking that Brettan played some game, Maren's anger began to rise at his unwanted intrusion of her privacy.

"Can I not have a moment alone? Is it not enough that half your guard is constantly by my side? Now you take it upon yourself to invade my bath?" Maren stopped suddenly, for her words seemed to have little effect on him. It was not like Brettan to let one of her barbs go by without some retort. There was something haunting about the way he stood there watching her. A sudden prickling of fear tingled along the length of her spine, as some inner sense warned Maren that the man who

184

watched her was not Brettan. Before she could retreat into the depths of the water, the man sprang at her through the shadows. Defenseless against any attack, she cried out, and her terror-filled scream cut through the air.

In one motion all hands flew to their weapons. Easing from the back of the gray warhorse, Brettan instantly recognized the scream. He quickly unsheathed the broadsword and ran toward the river, where he knew Maren had gone to bathe.

Maren struggled in blinding fear at the hands that closed about her, her attacker attempting to drag her across the river to the far side. She stumbled over the uneven river bottom, fighting with all her strength against this new terror. The man's panting breath was close at her ear, and with sickening reality she felt his strong arm closing about her bare waist, through the mass of her hair that hung like a damp mantle about her. Maren thrashed wildly against that hold, realizing when she was again hauled to her feet that her attacker was intent on taking her with him. A second hand clamped down over her mouth, and Maren bit wildly at that touch, causing the man to grunt loudly in pain, drawing back for a moment. As air rushed into her lungs, Maren screamed again, knowing she could not hope to win against her assailant's greater strength.

Maren's second scream came just as Brettan reached the river. In the fleeting light of day, he recognized her struggling form. With a bloodcurdling cry he lunged into the water, not waiting for the rest of his guard. The man whirled about at this unseen danger, his grip about Maren firm, holding her before him like a protective shield, his other hand pressing a deadly blade to the hollow of her throat, in mute warning for Brettan to come no further.

Brettan halted when he saw that menacing blade

pressed against the silken white skin. Maren's eyes, closed in fear, now opened in wide-eyed terror of the man who held her.

"Harm her, and I vow your life is forfeit." Brettan's words came low, across the small distance that separated them, the warning like a molten current in his voice. The man stood uncertainly before the menace of Brettan's threat. He felt the raw, animal strength of the English knight, like that of some feral beast defending something of great value. He hesitated a moment longer, until the sounds of the approaching guard reached them.

Her attacker seemed to weigh the possibilities of escape from the silently raging beast who stood before him. Maren's wide blue eyes gazed through the darkness at Brettan, yet she saw no sign that he watched her, his gleaming golden eyes locked on the man who held her. Maren's breath caught in her throat when the man took a lunging step backwards, dragging her with him, the blade pressing deeper against her throat, so that she felt her blood would flow if he pressed it any further. Brettan advanced carefully, his eyes never leaving that blade, which could end her life at any moment.

The attacker made his decision. Maren felt his grip loosen, and then she was roughly pushed forward. He had released her. Brettan rushed forward to catch her, while the man thrashed across the shallows of the river and scrambled up the opposite bank into the darkness. In a rush, the English guard swarmed past them from a multitude of places where they had stood poised, awaiting only Brettan's command.

Brettan pulled Maren against him, his warm protective embrace shielding her from the view of his guard. He quickly scooped the mantle from the rocks and enclosed her shaking form in its voluminous folds, then bent to lift her into his arms. Whirling about, he stepped quickly from the shore and carried her to a spot before

186

the blazing campfire, which cast leaping shadows across the circle of carts at the edge of the camp.

Maren lay against him, her fears giving way to a flood of tears that threatened to drown them both. Her sobs were softly muffled against the soft leather of his tunic, and she clung to him as if she might never release him. Brettan felt a surge of warmth as she reached out to him. Soothingly, he stroked the damp mass of her long, dark hair, murmuring soft comforting words to calm her.

Sandlin approached from across the camp, and Brettan spoke to the man over the top of Maren's head, her shoulders shaking visibly.

"Fetch the old woman."

Maren sniffled loudly against Brettan's shoulder. "Please do not leave me."

"You will be safe now," Brettan replied gruffly.

Maren clutched at him with her hands, her fingertips grazing the bare skin at his neck, and he felt a deep longing to bear her to his pallet, where he might draw her closer and lie with her to share the growing passion he felt deep within. "He cannot harm you now. Sandlin will bring Ada to stay with you."

Brettan gently set Maren beside the warmth of the fire, wrapping the mantle securely about her, Ada quickly following Sandlin over.

"I will have my personal guard posted nearby. No harm will come to you, and Ada will see that you have dry clothes." Unable to resist her any longer, Brettan bent over her, pressing a hasty if passionate kiss upon her slightly parted lips. The feel of her softness blocked all else from his thoughts, and his senses were filled with the rose scent of her still damp skin.

"I shall return to force the chill from every part of you. That I promise you." The full meaning of his words was not lost on her, and Maren blushed warmly, pulling away from his embrace.

187

Much later Brettan returned, having failed to capture the man who had attacked Maren. He found her curled upon the thick mat beside the fire where he had left her, the heavy fur-lined mantle wrapped about her like a protective cocoon. Gazing down at her sleeping form, he was taken aback at how young she was, and how very beautiful. Tenderly he lifted a raven curl from the pallet, feeling its silken softness between his fingers, and he sighed heavily before pressing it to his lips. Soon their journey would be ended at Monmouth, and he knew in his heart he could not bear to send her away, for she was not like others found in a soldiers' camp. She was a rare prize, to be kept and well guarded with one's life if necessary. That realization did not disturb him greatly. Brettan set aside the broadsword so that it lay within easy reach, and settled himself beneath the mantle, drawing Maren's slender body within the curve of his own, and his last thoughts were filled with the vision of eyes the color of sapphires, and raven-black hair that cushioned his head beside hers.

Chapter Ten

Monmouth lay beyond the Black Mountains, on a gently sloping hillside overlooking a wide valley below. The green grassland was bordered with stands of tall trees budding forth with tender new leaves, the warm spring days having enticed the new buds.

Maren spent those last hours lost in thoughts of how her life would be after this day.

The huge towers of the castle loomed behind the small buildings that crowded the town, like a protective mother guarding her flock.

The bustling streets of the town were lined with shops of such a vast array of merchants that Maren found it difficult to see it all while they passed along the cobbled streets. The largest town she had seen in Wales had been Fishguard, a small seaside village a mere three days ride from Cambria, and the size of Monmouth with its winding streets overwhelmed her. Added to the normal population was the press of soldiers of the English army newly returned from the north of Wales and, in their company, Edward, King of England.

Maren had chosen to wear the blue velvet gown Brettan had purchased for her, for her other garments, the tunics and breeches, were far too worn and ragged. She had angrily ignored Brettan's smile of smug satisfaction at her choice of the gown, pointing out to him that the only other garment she might wear was the blue velvet mantle, and she hardly thought it appropriate for her to be presented to the king dressed thus. Brettan had smothered a conceited smile when he left the tent, mumbling something about the king perhaps preferring such meager attire. Maren had chosen to ignore any other comments he had seen fit to give her. Over the blue gown she decided to wear the blue mantle against the chill in the air, with the fur-lined hood pulled high over her head, concealing the long cascade of raven-black hair from view. Though Brettan had insisted she wear her hair loose and flowing about her shoulders, she had chosen to dampen his pleasure in it by keeping her head well hidden, gaining some small satisfaction from the frown she had seen cross his face when he had first turned to look at her among his guard.

The long column threaded its way through the cobbled streets of Monmouth, and Maren was silently grateful for the protective ring of his guard that rode closely by her side. Brettan's tall, commanding frame was impressive in the brilliant blue velvet tunic, edged with gold threads finely woven in a complicated design at the sleeves and neck of the garment. The entire guard wore matching tunics emblazoned with those striking colors, and Maren could not help but notice the appraising looks drawn by the guard while they passed along the main street of Monmouth. Closely guarded, with Sandlin's large black steed pressing against her smaller bay mare, she felt an unexplainable sense of pride well within her to be a part of this magnificently displayed column which paraded through the town. Brettan swung about in the saddle to glance back over his shoulder, and for a long, appraising moment his glance lingered over her fair form, his emerald gaze boring into hers in silent communication. He took in the vision of her fair beauty among the masculine strength of his guard, the brilliant blue of her eyes the same as his colors, which she wore, as if giving evidence to his claim upon her. Maren felt the warm glow of color spreading to her cheeks under his keen appraisal and lowered her eyes, suddenly uncertain of her feelings, now that they were at their journey's end. When she looked again he bowed his head to her, that devilish, mocking grin spreading across his face, and she felt a sudden racing of her heart at the sight of his handsome, broad-shouldered frame, astride the fiery gray stallion that walked with barely restrained nervous energy through the press of people who stood to stare at the Duke of Norfolk. Word of their arrival in the city passed quickly.

Brettan had chosen to send the greater number of his men around the town, to the gently rolling fields between the town and the fortress of the castle beyond. There they would make their camp, while the Duke of Norfolk and his guard were received as guests of the lord of the manor, and of the king.

Lord Charles Kennerley, Maren learned from Sandlin, was master of the magnificent stone fortress which graced the sweeping hillside overlooking the town. Established as one of the border fortresses, it was well fortified, with a heavily armed garrison of soldiers. It gave stark evidence to the war between their two countries. As they passed the last row of stone cottages and shops and continued along the road that led to the castle, Maren stared in wonder at its massive outer wall, which formed a complete circle of well-manned towers to guard against attack. The large wooden gates stood open to welcome them. The guard within the castle stood impassively at their posts, watching silently while banners ornately decorated with the king's emblem fluttered gently in the evening breeze. A swarm of stable-boys, identically dressed in the royal colors, gathered about them, and they stopped before the large steps which led to the main hall. The fortress was well guarded against any attack, and Maren sadly realized that, had Cambria been this well fortified, no enemy could have gained access. The high stone walls that reached into the darkening sky before the last golden light of the day reminded her of another fortress of another day, and Maren's memory was filled with thoughts of her home and the last days she had spent there, with so much death and sadness. Although only a few weeks past, it now seemed that someone else had lived that tragedy, certainly not she, for it all seemed so far away now. Maren closed her mind to the pain of those memories when she felt Sandlin's strong hands lifting her from the back of the mare. She stared into his kind gray eyes, and in the reassuring smile that greeted her she felt the fears and uncertainties falling away.

A royal page announced their arrival to those within the hall, while the guard, with Maren at its center, mounted the stone steps behind Brettan. He glanced only briefly at her before entering the large hall, his look unreadable to her.

The main hall of the castle was easily four times the size of that at Cambria, opening wide on both sides of the main door to accommodate the large dining tables that had been set end-to-end in anticipation of the additional guests for the evening meal. Clusters of large candles that burned brightly had been secured in sconces along the entire perimeter of the hall, the light driving back the shadows of evening, while more candles flickered brightly in ornate holders at each table. The royal colors were brilliantly displayed from moorings on the walls, draping the stonework in festive decoration. Vivid tapestries of battle and hunt scenes were hung on the farthest wall, which supported the stone stairway leading to the upper floor chambers. A fire crackled invitingly at the huge hearth across the room, easily dominating the large group of men clustered about, who now turned to take notice of the latest arrivals. Maren's senses were assaulted by the scents that came to her from the kitchens beyond the hall, whence servant after servant carried out heavily laden platters with abundant fare for the evening meal.

Introductions were begun and greetings called from across the great hall, those who knew the guard welcoming them. Maren watched a tall man separate himself from his companions and approach Brettan. She felt Sandlin's reassuring touch on her arm and suddenly realized that the tall man who now approached in warm greeting was Edward, King of England.

The two men greeted each other like long lost friends, quickly grabbing each other by the arms, their wide smiles spreading across their faces. And then, as if suddenly aware of the gaping crowd about them, Brettan dropped to one knee in formal greeting of his monarch. Edward quickly bid him rise. Maren watched the two men in fascination, realizing that here was a special friendship, which went beyond a king and his subject. They were of equal height, and the king's bearing was that of a warrior, confident in his strength. His wide-shouldered stance rivaled Brettan's, and Maren realized that in an even contest the king would have been a formidable match for Brettan's well-muscled strength. The man who was King of England, enemy to her people, exchanged several words with Brettan, and when the duke made some reply, a wide smile spread across the king's face. And Maren became aware that this noble king, this fearsome warrior who had vowed to make Wales one with England, was also a man. A strong, unyielding man, a fierce contender, and yet still a man.

He wore no crown before his men, but the ornate cut of his tunic, with the boldly woven design of his crest, set him apart as their king, yet made him seem as one with them, the mark of a true leader. The Welsh prince, Llywelyn, led by fear and threat of reprisal. She sensed that here was a man who had been destined from birth to be a true leader of men, holding his power by undying loyalty, given freely, willingly, by men who found in him something of themselves. And with a sudden wrenching thought Maren realized, without knowing more, that Llywelyn's cause was already lost.

Others joined the warrior king in his greetings of the Duke of Norfolk, and Sandlin stepped back behind her a small space while the rest of the guard parted, standing aside when Edward approached. Brettan followed, and panic seized Maren, for she realized there was no escape from the introductions that were to follow and, she silently wondered how Brettan had explained her presence to his king. She struggled with her growing turmoil, since he would not, could not present her as his mistress, although she was certain that was the conclusion most would make. She glanced uncertainly at Brettan, trying to convey a last silent plea in her wide-eyed gaze, but she thought she read a faint twinge of humor in his glowing green eyes, and her panic turned to barely concealed anger, for she realized the game he played with her. She could not know the exact words that had passed between Brettan and the king, but by the self-satisfied smirk that played around the corners of Brettan's mouth, she could guess the content of their discussion. Her cheeks flamed, and her large, blue eyes sparkled like brilliant sapphires, accenting the blue velvet of her gown. Her bosom heaved with barely concealed rage, yet for the sake of her own cause she dared not speak out in the presence of the king. Brettan obviously held great favor with Edward, and she could

194

not risk herself when she needed the aid of the king in returning to her family. With great determination, Maren smothered her raging temper to gaze fully at Edward and bravely return his keen perusal, refusing to cower before his towering presence, although she would have preferred nothing better than to hide in some dark corner.

Edward approached and took her slender hand in his own. Maren bent in a low, wide curtsy, bowing her head slightly but never once breaking her unyielding gaze with the king. He gently pulled her to her feet, his eyes missing nothing, taking in the proud tilt of her head, the shining mass of her raven-black hair, unbound, like a live thing swirling about her in a wave of softness. But it was her eyes that held his attention, for he had never seen eyes of such blue color. One moment they seemed as true blue as the velvet she wore, and then next the color of darkest night, as some deep thought crossed her face, held in check while she contemplated the man before her. He smiled at her graciously, enthralled by her open curiosity and childlike innocence, yet aware of the woman that stood with quiet grace in the slender form before him. Edward turned to Brettan. "She is possessed of great spirit as well as beauty. My friend, you must take care not to lose yourself completely." The warning was given lightly and with good humor, and Maren decided that in fairness to this man who was king, she might find in him a worthy protector, for she saw nothing but sincere approval in his keen gaze. He smiled at her, and Maren found herself warming to his gentle manner. Carefully he turned and spoke to those about him. Maren caught Brettan's gaze fastened upon her, and she felt a momentary confusion at the proud look she saw in those glowing eyes.

Maren turned back as Lord Kennerley came forward to make other introductions. "May I present Roger de

195

Monfort, Earl of Rothesey, and Lord Gilbert de Burghmond." Lord Kennerley halted briefly, turning back to her. Maren stood in shocked silence and then responded as if in a trance, but the words would not come. Her heart seemed to stop beating, and an unbearable coldness drained her of all feeling. She responded vaguely to Lord Kennerley's questioning stare, but saw nothing except that face, and those eyes that stared back at her in utter incredulity. Unable to draw a breath, Maren felt the room begin to move about her, and she suddenly felt so weak that she feared her legs would not hold her weight. Feebly she reached a hand that trembled visibly to her head, as if she might push away the nightmare that had closed in on her. Her mouth was dry, and in that last moment she felt as if the stone flooring had suddenly reached up to seize her, and then she felt nothing. The veil of dark oblivion closed about her, releasing her from all thought, all feeling, and she plummeted into a sightless, soundless void. She saw neither her father's look of stunned disbelief, nor the momentary look of shock that appeared on Brettan's face when he at last learned the truth she had held from him. Sandlin caught Maren as she collapsed.

Brettan's look of shock quickly turned to anger, and then to embarrassment before the questioning gaze turned upon him by Gilbert de Burghmond at the sight of his daughter in the company of the Duke of Norfolk.

Edward sought to stay the anger he saw building within both men, and he gave orders for calm in the hall. Lady Kennerley saw only the disheveled form of her young guest, while Sandlin turned uncertainly with Maren in his arms. Quickly taking command of the uneasy situation, Lady Kennerley called for her maid and led the knight up the long sweeping stairway to the second floor chambers. Maren was carefully laid upon a soft bed, Lady Kennerley seeking to rouse the stricken girl.

Maren felt a soothing coolness across her forehead. She opened her eyes and stared uncertainly through the meager light of the chamber. Her thoughts were confused, seeking to bring back some memory of the moments past. She heard the sounds of a newly laid fire at the hearth, the golden light from the tentative flames dancing about the room. Her vision cleared, and she turned her head at the touch of a calm soothing hand upon her own. Lady Kennerley carefully watched the young girl's face, the color starting to return to her pale cheeks. "You must lie quietly until you are stronger."

Maren gratefully accepted the goblet Lady Kennerley pressed into her hand and cast the woman a surprised look at the rich taste of the wine.

"It will help to calm you. Now you must rest. I shall attend my other guests, and then I shall return. My maid, Mary, will bring a tray for you."

Maren nodded her gratitude, not trusting her voice to uncertain words. She felt oddly calmed by the woman's gentle manner, so much like her mother's. Maren smiled faintly when Lady Kennerley gently patted her hand, then left the chamber, leaving her to her confused thoughts.

"I demand an answer, and I will have it now!" Gilbert de Burghmond threatened, turning back to face Brettan. "I will have the reason for my daughter's presence here, and under circumstances that are completely unacceptable." The older man glared his anger at the younger one who towered over him, undaunted by Brettan's presence or his reputation as a soldier upon the field of battle. With great effort Maren's father sought to maintain some measure of control before their king.

Edward laid a restraining hand on the older man's arm, hardly wishing to see his knights come to blows. "We will

197

have a full explanation, but after we have set to the evening meal. Our hosts await." Edward turned purposefully toward Brettan, his manner grave. "We must have the matter settled, and without letting blood. I still have a great need of all my knights, if I am to succeed in bringing this war to a successful victory. But I will have a worthy explanation." He gazed from one man to the other to see that they understood well his meaning, then turned back to Lord Kennerley. The smile returned and his manner was once more relaxed while he led the procession of guests into the large dining hall. Only the most observant would have noticed the hardened demeanor that rested just below the surface of his effortless smile even as he spoke amiably to one guest and then another.

Brettan and Maren's father each took their places at the king's table, which was reserved for those of title and the knights of Edward's guard. Across the table, a silent confrontation was met when Brettan's golden gaze locked with the light blue one of Lord de Burghmond, who watched him unwaveringly through the long hours of the evening meal. Though the meal was indeed fit for a king, two appetites faded in the presence of barely suppressed anger, and the air held a foreboding, like a sky charged with the mounting fury of a storm which gathers waiting only for that final moment to unleash its fury.

Several toasts had been drunk, and the spirit of the evening livened for those about the table, but Brettan found little humor in the events of the last hours. Bitterly he twirled the wine about the rim of the silver goblet, considering his own stupidity at not guessing the truth Maren had held from him. Why had he not seen the resemblance between the girl and the slain woman his men had found at Cambria? He remembered well that the woman had been a great beauty, but beyond that he had paid little attention beyond the fact that the lady of the manor had been slain. He had dismissed the memory of the woman as he had dismissed the faces of so many other dead, a forced habit, acquired from fighting many battles in nameless fields and plains throughout his life. He quietly contemplated the older man who now sat across from him and wondered what were his thoughts. He could well understand Lord de Burghmond's anger and shock to find his daughter in England when he had thought her elsewhere. Unable to calm his churning thoughts, Brettan rose abruptly from the table and, without asking leave of the king, turned on his heel and fled the hall, not caring if all the royal guard descended upon him. At that moment he would perhaps have welcomed a good fight to release some of the anger he felt. His long easy strides quickly gained him the row of stables, and he whistled to the gray stallion, who tossed his head and snorted a greeting. Brushing aside the young stable boy, Brettan quickly saddled the gray. The tall animal chomped expectantly at the bit, attempting to pull the reins from Brettan's firm grasp. Whirling the steed about, Brettan sent him flying out the large oaken gates of the keep and, ignoring the protests of the guards, sent the animal charging into the cool night air, the large hooves churning up clods of dirt. The spirited animal had gained his freedom and Brettan enjoyed the rush of the cold wind, which pressed him back in the saddle and cleared his thoughts. He was aware only of the heat of the surging animal beneath him. They became one and rode through the night, his senses keenly heightened to any unseen dangers that awaited. Silently Brettan dared any to challenge him. He would gladly have welcomed that challenge and the opportunity to vent some of the dangerously seething anger that boiled within him. He urged the gray to the crest of a hill, where he brought the animal to a sudden halt. He listened to the night sounds that surrounded them, and watched the torch lights that glowed warmly from the fortress below. Brettan reached down to soothe the gray, then started at the sound of a screech owl in a distant tree. Darkness surrounded them, with only those faintly flickering lights in the distance to guide them. But even in the darkness Brettan was haunted by the vision of eyes the color of brilliant sapphires, and he cursed under his breath that the girl should cause him such trouble. Finding the gray still worked at the bit, eager to be off, he urged the large horse down the sloping hillside toward those distant torches, giving the gray free rein, as if the rushing wind might drive from his thoughts all traces of her gently beguiling beauty.

Maren paced the length of the chamber and then back again, while the long evening passed. She had barely touched the food, her appetite lacking before the uneasy churning of her stomach. It was impossible to guess the hour. She strained for the sounds that drifted up from the dining hall below, but was unable to understand anything that she heard. She wrung her hands anxiously, thinking what her father's thoughts must be at finding her in the company of the Duke of Norfolk. Maren jumped when the door to the chamber opened and the servant girl, Mary, entered, casting a disapproving look at the tray of food, untouched, the food cold and uninviting. Two young boys followed her into the room, laboriously dragging a heavy wooden tub across the flooring. The tub was filled with bucket after bucket of steaming water brought into the room. Mary carefully laid out several fragrant cakes of soap and fresh linens, then eyed Maren thoughtfully. "Lady Kennerley has asked that I bring you whatever you may need for your bath. If there is anything else you care for—"

"No. Please, there is nothing I care for," Maren replied, her voice edged sharply, turning toward the warmly glowing fire. Then she turned back to the young girl to soften her harsh words. "Your mistress is most kind. But there is one thing I desire." Maren stopped to gaze at the young girl. "I must speak with my father, Lord Gilbert de Burghmond."

Mary gazed at her uneasily, having heard of the earlier confrontation from the servants in the main hall. "Milady, I am not certain that I can help you."

"Please, you must take a message to my father. You must tell him that I wish to speak with him, It is most important." Maren pleaded with the girl.

"Milady, I cannot. The man you speak of, even at this moment, meets with the king and Lord Kennerley. I would not dare go to the private hall with the king there. I will tell milady that you wish to speak with your father. She will find a way, I am certain."

Mary turned back to her chores, oblivious that Maren held little interest in the bath the girl had prepared. Maren could well imagine her father's anger, and she closed her eyes in silent torment of the words Brettan would tell him. She knew well he would have little regard for her feelings in the matter and undoubtedly spare little detail of their weeks together, once confronted by her father. If only she had known her father would be there, she might have had time to ease the shock of that first meeting. But how she might have accomplished that she could not begin to guess. If only she had managed to make good her escape before the English reached Monmouth, then no trace of her presence in the English camp would have remained, except the stories Brettan would have told, and she knew well her father would never have been the wiser, believing her safe with Catherine at the abbey. But now there was no point in thinking of what might have been. The reality of the matter was this, and somehow she must find the time to speak with her father before he could be hurt by the half-truths he would hear from Brettan. Maren stared into the

201

flames that licked at the logs upon the hearth. She pressed her fingers to her temples to ease the persistent ache that had started there. In sudden decision, she whirled about. Mary had left the chamber, no doubt to seek out Lady Kennerley with Maren's request. She could well guess Lady Kennerley's firm if gentle refusal to allow that until her father had met with Brettan and the king. Maren could not allow Brettan's lies to hurt her father, not when he still must face so much sadness when he returned to Cambria.

Quietly, Maren slipped out the door of her chamber. She glanced quickly in either direction, against the possibility that Lady Kennerley might return and, satisfying herself that she was alone in the hallway, she quickly reached the landing at the top of the stairway. She listened carefully for the sounds that reached her from the dining hall below. The hour was late. The candles in the silver sconces at the bottom of the steps had melted low, though lively voices still came from the hall. Maren moved in the shadows of the stairs, descending slowly, taking great care that she not be seen. Reaching the last step, she glanced carefully about the hall. Boisterous voices raised in a cheer, as some story was told before the large hearth. Her vision was filled with the blue and gold of the tunics of Brettan's guard. That could only mean that he had not yet left the hall or, worse yet, that he would remain the night in the hall. Unable to find any sight of her father or the king, Maren could only assume that they had left the large hall for some other place to meet, as Mary had told her. Across the hall was another hallway and, keeping to the shadows, Maren made that her destination. A young servant girl approached very near where Maren stood, to refill an empty goblet, and Maren quickly motioned the girl aside. The chamber she sought was indeed down that hallway. Maren breathed deeply to calm her fears, then

202

she started toward that point. A voice behind her halted her steps when she reached the arched hallway.

"Maren, what are you about?"

She whirled about at the sound of that familiar voice, her eyes suddenly filled with the comforting sight of her brother.

"Andrew, I must speak with father." She gazed pleadingly into her brother's face.

"Maren, it is impossible. At this moment he meets with the king."

"Oh Andrew, that is why I must speak with him, so that he may know the truth. Please, you must help me."

"What is the truth, Maren? Can you possibly understand his shock at finding you here at Monmouth, and in the company of the Duke of Norfolk?"

"Andrew, I must speak with him. There is a simple answer to all of this, but I must be certain that he hears the truth and not lies."

"What lies might the Duke of Norfolk tell him, Maren?" Andrew glanced at her uncertainly.

"Andrew, can you not see how this must seem? So much has happened these last weeks. That I must make father understand. Please, Andrew!"

Maren gazed pleadingly at her brother. This was not how she had thought their reunion might be. It had become a nightmare, and she must somehow soften the blow her father had received. She could see the doubt in Andrew's eyes, and her frustration grew that he might prevent her from entering the chamber.

"Maren, you must wait until father has spoken with the Duke of Norfolk. You must not interfere in this now." Andrew gazed at her keenly, seeing something different about the girl who stood before him, so passionately determined to set the matter aright. Was it just the months that had passed that marked the change in her, or was it what she had endured in the time they had been apart? He felt the sadness she must have known, and the fear, after the attack on Cambria, and he could see the mark of that tragedy in the deep blue of her eyes. Or did he see something else that somehow made her seem so different from the girl he remembered from that day so long ago?

Maren could see her hopes for his help wavering in the uncertain look that crossed his face. Did Andrew also assume the worst from her presence among Brettan's guard? Merciful father in heaven, how could she possibly hope that they would believe her? Realizing that each moment was precious if she was to speak with her father, Maren twisted within Andrew's grasp and, gaining her freedom, did not hesitate to seek permission to enter the chamber, but rushed inside, the heavy chamber door crashing back loudly, drawing the full attention of the three men who stood before the blazing hearth.

Maren stood uncertainly before the lingering scrutiny of the king. Andrew charged into the room behind her in hopes of drawing her away, but halted when he realized he had arrived too late.

"Lady Maren, you honor us with your presence, but I think perhaps it is best that you await our discussion. There are matters of import to be determined." King Edward greeted her evenly, and she could not determine if he was angry or merely sought to be the intermediary in the discussion she had interrupted.

"Maren, you will leave. Now is not the proper time for our discussion." Her father's voice held the sound of quiet authority. She had never heard him speak to anyone in their family in that manner, and her heart constricted at the pain she saw in his face. She refused to meet Brettan's steady gaze, but calmly approached the king.

"Your Majesty, I beg your forgiveness for my intrusion." Maren's voice quivered, and she summoned all her courage before the stern countenance of the king. "I beg your indulgence, that I be allowed to meet privately with my father, so that I may explain what has passed this evening. My family has suffered great sadness, and I would not be the cause of more."

King Edward approached her slowly and gently reached for her hand, drawing her to a large chair before the warmth of the hearth. "Pray tell, Lady Maren, give us your words, so that we may know the reason for your presence among the English army."

Maren glanced uneasily at her father and then at the king. She had not expected that he would ask her to tell of the weeks past. And she realized with growing discomfort that he deliberately sought to find the truth, against what Brettan had already told them. Maren folded her hands in her lap to still their shaking, then told of the attack on Cambria and her meeting with the Duke of Norfolk. She spoke of her escape with Catherine through the dungeons below Cambria, and her capture by Brettan's guard in the forest beyond. She halted for a moment, seeking Brettan's gaze for the first time since entering the room. She tried desperately to discern in that stony visage some indication of what he had told them. She saw nothing behind the mask that guarded well his thoughts of that moment. She continued her story, telling only that she feared the English and let them believe she was merely a servant at Cambria. Hoping to make her escape before they reached England, she had remained a prisoner in their camp. Maren was amazed how simply the story of the last weeks was told, with so few words. She carefully left out any mention of what had passed between her and Brettan. When she had finished her story, she sat quietly in the chair, the silence in the large room unbearable, feeling the unbearable scrutiny of all three men who considered her words.

Brettan leaned back into the shadows across the room

and stood quietly contemplating her story. With great skill she had refused to tell anything more than a most innocent story, so that none would be the wiser for the time they had spent together, or know that she had been anything more than prisoner in his camp. He knew well that she sought to withhold that truth from her father, but he also knew that his earlier words to the king that evening, of the lovely girl among his guard, belied her simple story.

Edward carefully considered her words and turned back to her, his gaze momentarily locking with her father's. "Lady Maren, you have presented me with a most difficult task. For if a wrong has been committed, then I must see that it is set aright."

Seeing that he did not readily accept her story, Maren rose from her chair. "Your Majesty, what wrong has been committed? In truth I can see none, save a simple mistake."

"Lady Maren, it would seem that your story is true, as much as you have chosen to impart, but I fear you have chosen not to tell all of the weeks past."

Maren felt her knees weaken, for she realized that indeed the king knew much more of what had passed between her and Brettan.

"Your Majesty—" Maren fought back her rising panic, realizing that he would force her to tell all before her father. She had dared hope to spare her father his certain pain at the truth, and now to her horror she knew that he would be the one to deliver that blow. Whether she chose to tell the truth or steadfastly deny it, her father would know as he had always known, even when she was a child. She was soundly trapped, and she could see no way out of it. Her large blue eyes were filled with grief as she stood bravely before her father's questioning gaze.

"No more! There will be no more questioning in this."

206

Brettan emerged from the shadows, his lean, muscular frame filling her vision. In his silent strength, she felt his quietly restrained anger, hidden behind that glowing gaze.

"I have already spoken the truth of these past weeks, when I thought the Lady Maren to be nothing more than a servant from the fortress. I will not now given denial to my words with lies. As a knight of the realm, I accept full responsibility for what has passed between the Lady Maren and myself. But I offer no apologies." Brettan's words tore through Maren, and she realized with frightening clarity that with his words her father knew all.

"Maren?" Her father approached from across the room and stood before her, silently awaiting her answer.

Her eyes filled with hot tears, her gaze remaining downcast, unable to meet her father's, knowing he would see his answer there.

Gently Gilbert de Burghmond reached out to lift her face so that he might look into her eyes. "Maren, what has passed is done."

"Father, I—" The words she longed to speak would not come. Her vision blurred, and she felt a rising anger within her that she was unable to say what she had hoped to tell him; of her love for him, of how she had tried so desperately to return to Cambria. But where she had expected to see sadness, perhaps even anger in his face, she saw only grim determination, as if he had decided a matter of grave importance.

Tenderly, Gilbert de Burghmond reached up lovingly to caress his daughter's cheek. So fair, so beautiful, so like her mother. His grief so new within his heart eased some small measure at seeing Maren before him now, no longer the child or the willful young girl, but a woman. Looking into her deep blue eyes, so very brilliant, he knew that now beyond anything else he must keep her

207

safe from the death she had escaped at Cambria. "Go now, with Andrew. I must speak with the King and the Duke of Norfolk." He smiled reassuringly at his daughter. She was so very innocent, for all that she had endured in the past weeks. There was so much that was beyond her capacity to understand, that he felt only a father's duty to protect her, no matter what the cost. How could he possibly make her understand the events of all those years, now past? How could he keep her from the harm that even now reached out to her with desperate hands? He clasped her gently about the shoulders, then kissed her forehead. "Go now with Andrew, and leave us to speak of matters of import. All will be set aright. I promise you that."

Seeing that any further efforts to speak with her father would be futile, Maren humbly complied. Andrew escorted her from the chamber. Though she felt the heat of Brettan's unyielding gaze, she refused to meet those eyes, more than aware of the silent accusations she would see in that golden visage. His words haunted her, that naught but harm could come from her lies. Unable to find any other path, she had chosen deception, but now paid dearly for that choice.

Maren remembered little of the moments that followed, only that Andrew delivered her to Lady Kennerley's care, that kind and gentle woman mercifully choosing not to press Maren as to what had passed in the chamber.

When she was finally alone in her chamber, Maren released herself to her anguish, collapsing on the large bed and giving full vent to the strain of the evening, her sobs flowing from her in waves. All the anger and frustrations, and fears of the past weeks were at last brought forth from her tightly held control. So great was her misery, while her tears flooded the coverlet, that Maren did not hear Mary enter the chamber. The young girl stood in confusion before the large bed, hardly knowing the cause for such sadness or the remedy for it, but could only gaze at the grief-stricken girl who lay across the bed. Behind her, Lady Kennerley shook her head sadly and approached the far side of the bed, gently reaching out a comforting hand. "You must not be so sad. There is naught in the world that is worth such sadness from one so fair. Come, Mary has brought more water from the hearth. A hot bath will help ease some of your misery."

She numbly complied when Mary helped draw off the blue gown and then the thin chemise Maren wore underneath. Shivering at the feel of the cool night air against her bare skin, Maren quickly stepped into the tub of steaming water. She sank back into the soothing depths of the water, her thoughts confused, refusing to come together. She stared into the flames that licked at the logs upon the hearth. In their soft glow she thought she saw again her father's silent torment, that care-worn face, as the truth was given, and she closed her eyes that she might block out that memory, only to find it replaced by the vision of golden, green eyes boring into hers, so that she felt certain she might never escape that haunting visage. Maren reached for the nearest cake of soap and lathered the linen cloth for her bathing. She washed absently, trailing the cloth over her arms and shoulders and across the ample swell of her breasts. She tilted her head back on the edge of the tub, thinking of those moments now past when she had stood before the king of England, forced to accept Brettan's admission of what had passed between them. She felt the warm tears again welling in her eyes, and she closed them tightly as if she might halt their flow. And always her memory was tormented by the heated gaze that sought hers. She drew the lathered cloth across the fullness of her breasts, slowly, lost in her thoughts, and her body betrayed her.

She remembered gentle, feather-soft caresses, for Brettan had touched her where her own hands now lingered. The rose-hued peaks of her breasts tautened at that memory, poking impudently above the surface of the water. Her skin tingled and, though she would have denied it, her body reacted to the heat of that memory. Maren willed her thoughts to other matters and finished her bath, for the temperature of the water cooled. She rose abruptly, reaching for the linen to dry herself, since both Mary and Lady Kennerley had left the chamber to give her some privacy. She stepped carefully from the tub before the roaring fire, to catch the warmth while she dried herself, and she noticed with great relief that her many bruises from the fall were all but gone. That much less would she need to explain to her father. Her garments had been removed from the chamber and, with no others to replace them, Maren wrapped the linen about her slender body, closing the fabric in front by knotting the two ends above her breasts. The bottom of the cloth barely reached beyond the slender curve of her bottom, but there was nothing more to be done until Mary returned. She sat before the wooden table and began the task of removing the tangles from the ebony tresses which fell about her shoulders in wild disarray. So intent was she upon her task that she failed to notice the quiet opening of the chamber door above the sounds of the crackling fire, which popped whenever searing heat found the pitch in the pine logs.

Brettan stood quietly just inside the closed portal, taking in the vision before him of the young maid barely clothed against the raking heat of his gaze. He watched her attend to that gentle task, and felt a stirring deep within, in spite of the anger he had brought to her door.

Staring at some distant point among the glowing flames upon the hearth, Maren gently worked the comb through the long masses of her hair, the flickering lights of the fire dancing in the lustrous shine of her hair, which waved enticingly down the length of her back and about her hips. She stopped, her hand stilled in the midst of a stroke, when she caught sight of his long well-muscled frame reflected in the silver mirror before her.

Maren whirled about on the small bench, her deep blue eyes wide in stunned surprise at his boldness. "You!" she breathed.

Brettan stepped from the shadows of the doorway, his long body completely at ease while he approached her. "My compliments, Maren. Or should I say, Lady de Burghmond. Indeed, you seem to fare quite well in all situations." He bowed low before her, that inane, mocking smile spreading across his handsome face, causing a faint dimple to crease his cheek. And yet there was something silently menacing in his manner.

"You must leave now. Have you not caused me enough trouble?" Maren fairly hissed at him, crossing her arms before her, suddenly aware of the thin, damp linen that was her only garment.

Brettan stared warmly at the heaving roundness of her breasts, his desire plainly reflected in those glowing emerald eyes. Frantically Maren glanced about the room for some means of protecting herself, but found nothing that she could reach without causing a confrontation. "Leave immediately, or I will call out." She had long ago learned the foolishness of appealing to Brettan's sense of honor; indeed, where she was concerned he had shown no such inclinations, her agonized pleadings always meeting with his stony refusal to see her part in the matter. She could hardly hope for such from him now.

"You will not call out. For that would require the explanation of my presence in your chamber, and while I most certainly have no fear of the truth, it is my belief that you would not choose to answer any more embarrassing questions." Brettan taunted her, the deep

211

timbre of his voice warming her, vibrating through her. Was he aware of the effect he had on her, even now, when he was the source of so much pain and misery for her? Did he know how the very sound of his voice, rich and achingly gentle, tore through her composure?

"I once warned you against the danger to be found in telling lies. Now you find yourself soundly caught for the lies you spoke to me. Had you spoken the truth as I asked for it when first we met, you would now be spared." He spoke somberly, coming closer to stand before her. Uncertain of his intentions, Maren rose from the bench and tried to move away from him, unwilling to trust him even for a moment. But even as she did so, Brettan reached out with great swiftness, one well-muscled arm encircling her slender waist, drawing her against him in a crushing embrace. Unable to breathe or to cry out against his hold of her, Maren stared wide-eyed into his menacing green eyes, her panic rising like a consuming flame within her. She tried to gather her senses. Surely he must be mad to come to her like this, when Mary might return at any moment and find them. He must surely be mad. It was the only explanation for him to do this, to risk being caught in her chamber. Refusing to yield to her rising fears, Maren stared back at him, while Brettan glared into the depths of her blue eyes, fighting to maintain control of his anger. His grip tightened about her, as if he intended to crush the life from her.

Maren's cheeks flamed brightly, and her first fears now turned to rage in the face of his assault. With a will born of stubborn pride, she refused to cower before him, trapped though she was with no defenses against his strong grasp. Slowly her first panic ebbed to be replaced by an unwavering gaze of persistent defiance.

"So, brave knight, would you take me now as you have in the past, before my father, before Lord and Lady Kennerley, before your king? And to what end, milord?"

212

Maren questioned heatedly, her anger pushing her dangerously beyond reason.

The glow of the fire played evenly across the planes of his face, one moment lighting the yellow-green eyes which glowed at her threateningly, the next shielding his visage from her. With a sudden violent cruelty her head was jerked back. Brettan buried his hand in the mass of her loose hair, pulling her back painfully so that her back arched, forcing her against him, the full length of her slender body pressed to his, her firm, full breasts crushed against the woven gold of his tunic. Cruelly his mouth twisted across hers, searing, demanding, his tongue penetrating her lips to taste the tender softness of her mouth. A muffled cry died in her throat when she felt the faint stirrings of her response deep within. Desperately she willed it not to be, and pressed the flattened palms of her hands against the soft, blue velvet that covered his broad chest, but slowly closed her fingers over the soft folds of his tunic, drawing him to her. Her lips parted slightly, and he probed between them, and she felt herself yielding to him that softness he sought with such urgency.

In one desperate movement, Brettan pulled away from her, pushing her back as he tore away from her grasp. He stared into the depths of her blue eyes, searching for some reason to hate her, but finding none in the heated passion of her youthful gaze. With great effort of will, Brettan calmed his churning emotions, and his composure returned. He made a low, mocking bow before her. "My compliments to you, milady. You possess great skill. Even in the hour of your greatest sadness, you gain much. But soon we shall see who is the more skillful. There are still matters unsettled between us, Maren. I vow to you, they shall be resolved." The grim set of his finely curved lips faded and was replaced by that mocking grin. He quickly turned on his heel and was gone, the heavy portal closing softly behind him.

Maren's emotions were in such chaos, and yet all about her was calm. The fire danced lazily upon the hearth, the only sounds in the room the occasional popping or hissing of the wood as the flames consumed it. Indeed, all about her seemed strangely calm, so that he might never have been there at all, except for where her skin glowed warmly from his touch. She sat down upon the small bench beside the table, gently rubbing the marks on her arms where he had held her, and she could still feel his mouth bruising hers. She sat there, lost in the torment of her thoughts, oblivious to the growing chill in the room against her thinly clad body, nor did she hear Mary's voice uncertainly urging her to slip into the chemise. Absently she allowed the girl to dress her for bed, the gossamer fabric of the chemise falling like a silken cloud against her skin.

The hour had grown late, and beyond the heavy oaken panel of her chamber the feasting of the English ended with a last round of toasts.

Fatigue claimed her, and she curled upon the large bed, until even her greatest fears and sadness were unable to hold back the heavy veil of sleep that finally closed about her.

Chapter Eleven

"Never! Never! Never!" Maren whirled about, the soft velvet of her gown brushing against the stone flooring, and stomped a slender, slippered foot emphatically. Her hands were clenched into tight fists, and she glared across the room at her brother, Andrew, who stood quietly before the onslaught of her mounting anger. At first she had thought he taunted her with some cruel jest, but when he had continued, his face completely serious, she had realized the grim truth of what he had come to tell her.

"I will never consent to this marriage. Andrew, I must speak with Father. Surely he will not force me into this marriage."

Andrew's face was grave with the news he had brought her, and vainly he sought to calm her. She had changed so much over the months past. She now seemed so much a woman, not the young girl he remembered last at Cambria, but then so much had happened since that day so many months before, and she had been forced to endure so much sadness and danger, and now this. He sought some gentle words that might ease the shock of what he had brought her. He shook his head as if he too were unable to understand, but he knew well that more than her honor was at stake.

"The decision was not Father's."

Maren turned back from the window to stare at her older brother uncertainly. "If not his decision, then who is responsible for this outrage, without even considering my will in the matter?" A light of heavy suspicion began slowly, and Maren raised questioning eyes. "Surely not the Duke of Norfolk?" She laughed at the absurdity of the idea, but her laughter died on her lips when her brother remained silent. She stared aghast at Andrew, unable to accept that Brettan would have offered this, when his intentions had been for her to return to London as his mistress. No, she could hardly believe his offer of marriage for the sake of her honor.

Andrew's voice clearly showed his strain, and he gazed at her uneasily. "The king has ordered the marriage."

Maren looked at him incredulously. "Surely you jest. I cannot believe what you say. Of what importance is any of this to the king?" Her vexation grew with each passing moment, that the King of England would dare command who she might marry.

Andrew could see the suppressed anger in the nervous twisting of her small hands and the stubborn set of her slender jaw. He knew well the defiance that welled within her.

"The King's decisions are of little consequence to me. He is not my king, and I shall not marry the Duke of Norfolk. I wish only to return to Cambria and, I swear by all that is holy, so I shall." Her voice was soft but filled with determination.

Andrew crossed the room to stand beside her at the large window that opened out onto the courtyard below, then reached out a hand to touch the sleeve of her gown. "Maren, you cannot defy the king. He has ordered the marriage by royal decree. Even now the plans are made

216

for the ceremony to take place this very afternoon."

Maren turned to face her brother, all her proud Welsh obstinacy reflected in those deep blue eyes, and Andrew groaned silently when he realized she was prepared to refuse the king with her last breath, for he knew her temper well in matters past and was certain she would not yield in this.

"Edward is not my king. I am Welsh. There is no need for him to concern himself with matters of my lost honor. I will not marry the Duke of Norfolk, nor any other Englishman the king may choose. Andrew, I wish only to see Father."

Andrew's hands dropped to his side, for he realized well that the battle of wills had only just begun. "I will speak to Father, but I can give you his answer now, as he bade me give it to you. He accepts the king's decision."

Maren turned away from him, refusing to listen to him any further, but only gazed out the window. She hardly heard the gentle closing of the chamber door when Andrew departed, so great was her confusion.

When she was left alone in the chamber, Maren's misery was complete. She could not accept that her father had so willingly given his consent to the marriage, yet what other purpose would there be for Andrew to bring her word of the decision? It was not true, it could not be true. Edward was not her king, he could not order her marriage to someone she loathed with all her being. And yet beneath the mask of her anger and confusion, Maren knew well that if the order had been given, her father as a knight of the realm would have no choice but to comply. She knew her father well, and she knew that he would never defy his king. Her heart wrenched achingly at the thought of her father's betrayal of her. All at once the stone walls of the chamber seemed to close in on her, and Maren felt as if she could not draw an even breath of air. She whirled about, suddenly desperate to be

217

away from there, anywhere that was away from the cruel reality of Edward's decision.

Maren quickly stole down the shadowed stairway until she reached the main doors of the great hall. Across the main room, she heard the faint sounds of voices raised in serious conversation, but she hardly waited to hear what was spoken or who the men were. At that moment nothing mattered but her ability to leave the confines of the fortress. She lifted the metal latch that secured the portal and, stretching up on her toes, set the latch back in place, moving the massive door open a small space that she might slip out.

"You must allow me to accompany you, milady." Those mocking words halted Maren's flight. She stopped, abruptly frozen where she stood. After a long moment, she inhaled uneasily before turning back to stare into the emerald gaze she had felt boring into her back. With all the confidence of the hunter stalking his prey to its lair, Brettan stood before her, his tall, well-muscled frame almost relaxed with the quiet ease of one who constantly guards against the unexpected. The light that flooded through the tall windows across the hall was barely enough to discern the dark scowl she saw on his handsome face. Maren ground her teeth in vexation, realizing that his appearance alone set her nerves on edge. He was most certainly the most arrogant man she had ever known, always so certain of himself.

"I have no need of your company or your protection, now or ever." Maren seethed, for she realized any plan for escape was now lost.

"So eager to be away from me, my sweet? And after all we have shared." His tone cut through her like a well-honed blade, shaking her confidence with every moment that passed.

"I have never chosen your company. You will remember well, milord, that your presence has been forced upon me at every turn, with little regard for my desires in the matter." Maren wished the conversation ended and turned back toward the stairs, to seek what little privacy she might find in her chamber.

"I know well your desires, Maren." Brettan's voice had lost none of its mocking tone, but was spoken in quiet, as if he cared for only her to hear the words he spoke. She whirled about, her cheeks flooded with bright color at the unmistakable meaning of his words. And yet she could find no reply to give denial to them. Any protest she might have given would only have amused him.

"I will not discuss this with you," Maren retorted, turning to flee up the wide stairs.

"If not with the man who will be your husband, then with whom, pray tell, will you discuss them?"

Maren stared at him in stunned disbelief. "There will be no marriage. It is a lie, a deception, and I will not be a part of it," she responded brittly, her lips pressed together with her fury.

"But you shall be part of it, Maren, perhaps the most important part. Edward has decreed that the wedding will take place this very day, against what you or I may say in the matter." Brettan quickly reached out, his arm closing about her slender waist in a grasp that was as unyielding as a band of steel.

"Unhand me. I demand that you release me immediately, you lowlife Englishman, you. . . ."

With sudden fierceness Brettan pulled her tightly against him. "I am completely aware of your opinion of me, Maren, and be certain it matches my own of you. But that is of little import in the matter we now face. The king has ordered the marriage, and it will be done. You see, I vowed to have the truth from you, and I shall have it. As my wife, there is no place that will keep you safe from me."

Maren struggled within his grasp, that she might loosen his hold of her, but found all her efforts in vain before the assault of his unrestrained fury.

"You are a fool, milord. You have the truth. You have always had it. I know nothing of the man you seek." Maren glared back with blind determination, her senses were suddenly filled by his physical contact. And though she willed it not to be, she felt his glowing heat searing through her veins at his closeness. She closed her eyes in frustration and anger, as much with herself for her response to his touch, as with him for touching her.

"Do you still deny any knowledge of the medallion? Your possession of it condemns you, Maren. You know of the one I seek, and you shall lead me to him. And then your part in this shall be known."

Maren twisted within his grasp, at the same time lunging away from him, her anger reaching new heights before his mindless accusations. "Murderer! Liar!" Viciously Maren struggled to free herself. She lunged at Brettan using the only weapon available, clenching her hands into tight fists and beating at him furiously. "You have blood on your hands, yet seek some nameless revenge upon me through this marriage. I shall never yield to you." Maren hissed her angry threats, seeking to wound him wherever her fists or her toe might find a vulnerable spot. Brettan clasped his arms firmly about her, pinning her flailing arms to her sides, and swung her off the floor.

"Cease your mindless ravings, Maren!" His voice echoed loudly in the large hall. Still she struggled against him like a wild, frightened creature.

"You will stop this. I will not have you harm yourself for this foolishness." Vainly Brettan tried to hold her while she struggled against him, her back pressed into his chest. He knew by the uneven edge in her voice, that she bordered on hysteria. Roughly he jerked her back

220

against him, so that the air left her lungs, forcing her into submission. "I know well you think me responsible for the attack against Cambria and your mother's death, but you are mistaken." Maren gasped and attempted to renew her struggling, but Brettan clamped down even harder on her ribs, so that she feared they might crack.

"Maren. Your mother was already slain when my men and I entered Cambria. I am responsible for many things in my life, for which I offer no apologies. Murdering innocent women and children is not one of those, and as for this marriage, milady, there is naught you or I may say against it. Edward has given his order." Brettan leaned over her, his lips brushing very near her ear. He gritted his teeth in frustration when his senses reeled at the sweet, fragrant scent of her silken hair, which brushed against his cheek. His voice was very low against her ear. He sought to calm her. "I seek a truth above all others, Maren, for I too seek that murderer and, whether you will have it or no, you shall lead me to him, whoever he may be."

Maren wrenched free of his grasp, at the same time turning around to face him boldly. What madness was it that he should know her very thoughts? Was there no safe haven from those glowing eyes that seemed to see into her very soul? "Do you believe me to be in league with that murderer?" She rubbed the bruises that already formed on her arms, where he had held her with such brutal force.

"Only you may answer that question, Maren. But given your talent for lies, what is there that you could say that I might believe?" Wearily Brettan held up a hand to halt her reply. "No. The only truth that either one of us might be certain of is that before this day has ended you shall be my wife, and there is naught that can save us." Brettan stared down into wide sapphire eyes, feeling himself drawn against all reason into the depths of those

221

orbs. She glared silently up at him, proud defiance giving her strength against a greater desire to run as far and fast as she might.

With the very nearness of her, Brettan felt a quickening within. He longed to take her now, to crush her against him, to bear her away from all the half-truths and deceptions that had set them against one another from the beginning. He longed to still her ravings with kisses, then taste her honeyed response as she fought vainly against her stubborn pride, at last yielding to her own passions, as he knew she could. And he would draw her with him into that abyss of their passions united as one. He ached to feel the silken soft smoothness of her skin beneath his hand, to stroke gently the full, ripe firmness of her breasts. His head reeled with the very nearness of her, and he remembered their nights together, the silken thickness of her hair draped about them in the wild abandon of their lovemaking. For only then did he feel certain that all her defenses were laid aside, freeing her to respond honestly to his caresses, matching his desire with her own in a truth more ageless than any that might be spoken with words. What madness was it that, when angered with her, as now, he could think only of taking her into his arms and quieting her ravings, so that he could feel her gently molded against him? What was it that he fought against with all his strength, and yet felt such desperation to keep near him? He saw no answers in the wide blue eyes that stared back defiantly at him.

"The truth may be your cause, but you are blind, Brettan de Lorin, for you do not know it when you have it within your grasp. You take and use whatever you can, as long as it will aid your cause. You speak well of the truth, but tell me, what lies have you spoken to turn my father against me, so that he accepts this marriage?"

"I have spoken no lies, Maren. You have heard all that

I have said before the king. He knew well your position within my camp, long before we arrived at Monmouth."

"Yea, milord, and who delivered me to that fate, but you who claim all innocence now?" Maren looked away, suddenly pale at the realization that there was little she could say to alter the decision the king had made. She closed her eyes in silent agony at the pain she had caused her father. "You go beyond yourself, milord. What has passed is better left forgotten."

Brettan sighed heavily. "It would have been impossible to forget such a comely maid, or the charms she carried beneath the disguise of a boy." He smiled teasingly, recalling her costume and the well-curved form she had sought to hide beneath the doeskin garments. "You see, Maren, my reasons for keeping you by my side are threefold; it was indeed my intention to keep you with me upon my return to London and, even if this differs somewhat from my original plan, the result shall be the same. But I warrant this alliance, as you call it, will not be entirely unpleasant for either one of us."

"You, sir, are insufferable. You care only for your own purposes in this and look not to mine. I do not understand how you could consent to this marriage, when you have spoken against such bonds."

Brettan looked down at her soberly, his own eyes glowing brightly. They bored into her blue gaze with such intensity that she was forced to look away. "Do not misunderstand my reasons in this matter, Maren. I have but one true cause, and that is the matter of the medallion, for it shall lead me to the one I seek, and I shall keep you near me until I learn the truth of it, perhaps taking some ease in your company as well. That is the added pleasure. But the third reason for such an alliance, little one, is to guard against the unforeseen possibility that my seed might have found fertile ground within your slender frame, for in truth I have no desire to bear bastard sons. Had you been a mere servant, as you would have had me believe, then the matter would have had an easy solution. Many a maid who finds herself with child from such a dalliance is well cared for, and her child as well. The fact that you are titled, and the daughter of a knight of the realm, makes the matter somewhat more difficult for the king. He can ill afford disgrace and humiliation for one of the oldest and strongest families in all of Wales, when he desperately seeks to align our two countries as one."

"So it seems that this arrangement is much to everyone's advantage, except perhaps mine. What of my feelings in the matter? Be assured, milord, it matters little to me that in the weeks and months hence I might find myself with child. There are remedies for such, and I am certain a cure might be found for that malady. Be assured there will be no sons and daughters, bastard or otherwise." So great was Maren's anger that she failed to notice the cold light that glistened in those sparkling green eyes at her threats. Brettan reached out with such quickness that she was aware only of intense pain. His lean fingers closed around her slender wrist, cutting off all movement or protest, beyond her struggling to endure the sudden excruciating agony.

"Heed my words, Maren, as if your life depended upon them, for in truth it does. The marriage will take place this very afternoon, and with the marriage I shall impart that which I am bound to according to my vows as a knight of the realm. As my wife you will submit all to me, and that shall include, in time, all you know of the medallion. Be certain that you shall also impart all your wifely duties, which shall include but not be limited to bearing my children, should that come to pass. I have little tolerance for those who would attempt to still a new life to spare some discomfort to their own. Believe me as you never have before, Maren, I will not tolerate such treachery against an innocent life, and if the only way to insure that you bring no harm to yourself or the child is for you to be chained and bound, then so be it. It would not be the first time that was required. Many a young maid has held such grand ideas of vengeance but failed in her cause. Do you understand what I say?"

Maren knew now there could be no escape. Brettan had made no pretense of what he sought from the marriage, his intent brutally cold and clearly purposeful. The act of marriage meant little to him, save for the purpose of legitimitizing any bastard child she might now carry. And for her, what was there that she could hope for in such a marriage? Her tears threatened anew, and Maren fought back the uncertain wave of emotions that waited to consume her. She tilted her slender chin slightly, an odd light glinting in those sapphire blue pools. There were no words she could have said that would have held any meaning for him, so she struggled to maintain her composure.

"The matter is not that easily done, milord." While she and Brettan stood in silent confrontation they were unaware of the two men who watched them from the doorway of the conference chamber.

A look of grim determination set on the younger man's face, his regal bearing unmistakable in his broad-shouldered stance. The older man seemed unbearably weary, as if he carried the weight of great responsibilities. Sadly he turned to stand before the blazing fire at the hearth, knowing there were no words he could have offered his daughter that might have explained his decision to see her safely removed from the harm which seemed so near at hand. Hesitantly the young king approached his knight and sought to ease the man's anguish at the decision he had made.

Maren at last gained her freedom, twisting her arm from Brettan's grasp. He watched her turn on her heel and leave the hall, her slender figure still unyielding, leaving Brettan with the bittersweet taste of uncertain victory.

Lady Kennerley and Mary spent the early hours of the afternoon attending to the infinite number of last details for the wedding. A ceremony of such import was usually planned months in advance, but the King had given one order, that the marriage take place immediately, and the whole of Monmouth Castle was plunged into a whirl of activity to see those plans met.

The marriage was to take place in the small chapel at Monmouth Castle. The priest had been summoned from the town and arrived a short time earlier. Mary had excitedly announced his arrival, and was completely bewildered at Maren's lack of response when she stood staring absently out the leaded, paned window of the chamber. The maid looked questioningly to Lady Kennerley, who only pressed her lips together in silent concern for such sadness in one so young and beautiful.

The last arrangements for the ceremony were complete. Maren had made no further efforts to speak with her father. His silence was answer enough for the hurt she had caused him with her disgrace. But it was Andrew's failure to come to her that was so difficult for her to understand, that he could be so unyielding as not even to wish to see her. Andrew, who had always forgiven her every childhood mischief and trick. Andrew, who had been her protector and had now become a stranger to her. She felt indeed that she understood well the thoughts of the condemned after they have been sentenced to die and await execution. For Maren all emotion save that ceased to exist. She felt as though she moved through a horrible dream which she but watched from afar, and would soon awaken and find that everything was as it had been before her mother's death. And yet she realized with silent desperation that she was the center of all that now happened, with no possible escape. Desperately she wished that she might change all that had happened in the weeks past, but she quickly pushed the thought from her mind. Within her grew the seed of willful pride and stubborn defiance. A ragged sob escaped her throat, the only outward sign of her torment.

"Dear child, you must not despair. This should be a most happy day for you. I was no older than you when my father arranged my marriage to Lord Kennerley. I knew only his name, and it brought to mind a wizened old man. Indeed, before the ceremony I had never seen Lord Kennerley. Imagine my surprise when at last we met. After the marriage I came to love my husband, and that love has continued to this day. Very few of us are given to a marriage of choice. But who could say that the choice we might make would be any better than the one made for us. I see in you the same thing I too felt at the idea of such an arrangement. But I knew my father loved me and made that decision out of his love, and that gave me great courage."

Maren raised dark blue eyes to gaze at Lady Kennerley, all her anguish welling forth in those azure pools. "If I could believe that I still had my father's love, it would indeed make his decision easier to bear. But in truth, I believe I have lost his love."

"Dear Maren, you must not think that. Indeed, your father loves you very much, and the decision he has made has been made out of that love. I am not wrong in this, and you must trust that what I say is true."

Maren turned away to stare at the flames in the hearth, which drove the damp chill from the stone walls of the chamber. Mary eagerly bent to her task of seeing Maren properly dressed in a richly embroidered gown, which had been cut and sewn in the last few hours since the

227

announcement of the marriage. Precisely measured from the cut of the blue velvet gown Brettan had purchased for her, and with well-placed stitches from Mary's efficient needle, the new gown clung to Maren's slender figure with perfection. Made of a rich, gray velvet, the gown flowed gently from her hips to a wide skirt that brushed the flooring, sweeping into a long trail behind her. The long sleeves were cut wide into a bell shape, instead of the usual tight-fitting style, and were lined with a lustrous satin of rich blue that extended over the sleeve edge and turned back, then was stitched into place along the edge, creating a wide band of that bright color at her wrists. The same blue satin lined the sweeping neckline, exposing the slender column of her neck, and coming low to expose daringly the ample swell of her breasts above the bodice. The brilliant blue color gave vibrant and rich contrast to the soft gray of the velvet and caught the deep blue of Maren's eyes. Gray slippers with soft leather soles were placed on her feet, and Mary stood back with a critical eye, gazing at the fit of the gown, searching for any flaws. Lady Kennerley insisted on perfection, and the maid would offer no less, when her work would be seen by the King of England. With the glow of the fire behind her, the light played through the soft waving tendrils of her raven-black hair, which poured about her shoulders and spilled down the length of her back. Lady Kennerley decided against a concealing headpiece in favor of the simple woven circlet Mary had made to hold back the heavy weight of Maren's ebony tresses.

Maren was only vaguely aware that the young servant girl worked the long waving mass of raven-black hair, brushing it until it shown with lustrous lights and floated gently about Maren's shoulders. Mary smoothed the waves into place and then stood back to admire her work, thinking she had never before been so pleased with her fine talents, nor had she ever had the pleasure of attending one so lovely as the sad-eyed young girl sitting obediently before her. The circlet was woven of gray and blue satin ribbons to match the fabric of her gown, and the blue so close about her face drew out the blue of her eyes, making them seem wider and somehow more sad in the soft oval of her face. Noting the obvious use of blue satin that was the same as Brettan's colors, Maren carefully restrained a biting comment. She would have spoken aloud her objections to the color, but that only served to remind her of her inescapable fate at the hands of Brettan de Lorin. It was as if that color marked her as his before the words of the ceremony were spoken. Impatiently she waved aside the small hand mirror Mary held before her, thinking it of little importance how she looked. Mary sighed her resignation to the girl's mood and set the final touches to her work, bringing the mass of long hair back over each shoulder, so that it cascaded enticingly over each breast. She was just finishing brushing the lustrous waves when a faint knocking was heard at the chamber door, a signal that the ceremony was to begin.

Maren stood uncertainly and gripped the table for support against the sudden weakness in her knees. Mary darted about her, smoothing the soft velvet at her waist, straightening the gown out behind her, and Maren at last composed herself and took a hesitant step.

"Certainly no one lovelier has ever graced this hall. You do me great honor that I may be part of such an occasion." Lady Kennerley fixed Maren with a radiant smile.

Maren smiled weakly at the older woman. If only she might have enjoyed such enthusiasm, but in her heart was only an aching dread of what her life would be like from that day forward, as the wife of Brettan de Lorin. From deep within her grew that spark of defiance and pride that was hers alone, and with a great determination she willed herself not to cower at her fate. She pushed back the tears that threatened to come. She would not yield to her fears. The chamber door was opened by another young servant girl, and Maren inhaled deeply, with an outward bearing of quiet calm that belied her inner turmoil. She left the chamber and descended the wide stone stairway.

She stopped at the last step, where her brother stood waiting to escort her from the hall. There was no time for words, indeed Maren did not want to hear any more words. She saw only the reassuring comfort in his youthful smile, which for a moment drove away the lines of sadness about his face. Her own smile returned bravely, and Maren accepted his arm, her fingers trembling visibly when she laid her hand upon his sleeve, and he escorted her from the hall.

Stepping into the courtyard, Maren was aware of the soothing warmth of the afternoon sun, feeling it ease the coldness that seemed to grip her heart. Across the entire width of the courtyard stood the long line of the English guard, resplendently garbed in the brilliant royal colors of the king, and the guard of the Duke of Norfolk. Together they stood in dazzling array, creating a guarded path through their vast numbers to the small chapel. On her left stood the royal guards, their tunics marked by the royal crest, each knight standing rigidly straight, the banners flowing in the afternoon breeze, snapping as the wind played against the bright colors of Edward I. And on her right stood the entire guard of the Duke of Norfolk, their brilliant blue and gold tunics like a sea of blue sparkled with the gold of the sun, a sea that carried her to an uncertain destiny. At the front of the guard stood the loyal Sandlin, who momentarily broke the stern line of the guard to step forward and bow low before Maren, in a silent pledge of his fidelity. Deeply moved by his gesture, more than any words he might have spoken, Maren gently touched the knight on his shoulder, accepting his unspoken friendship and loyalty. Sandlin returned to the head of the guard, and Andrew gently drew her across the wide courtyard until they stood before the archway to the chapel.

They entered the double doors to the chapel, and Maren hesitated momentarily, her eyes adjusting to the dimly lit chamber. It was no larger than her chamber in the main hall, meant only as a place of worship for the immediate family of the lord of the manor.

Her eyes adjusted to the soft glow of the slender candles that burned brightly at the altar. Before the altar stood the priest summoned from the town of Monmouth, a round little man whose girth matched his height. She stepped down the two small steps into the chapel, and Andrew gently released her arm. She was suddenly aware of her father's stalwart frame beside her. It was their first meeting since the past evening. In a silent gesture that conveyed more than any words, Gilbert de Burghmond gently but firmly placed her slender hand over his sleeve, hesitating for a moment before he squeezed her cold trembling fingers reassuringly. Maren stared into the gray eyes that bored into hers, and for the briefest moment she knew his full emotion at the moment they shared. She saw his silent pain and torment, all the sorrows he had born over the last weeks, the suffering he had endured at the death of her mother and the uncertain fate of his children. And she saw too the love he carried for her within his heart, which gave her the courage she needed to believe Lady Kennerley's words.

Maren saw the imposing height of Edward, who stood apart from the priest. She was slowly escorted to the altar, and her eyes remained fastened on one figure that

231

seemed to fill her entire gaze, indeed the entire chapel. Brettan de Lorin, Duke of Norfolk, stood impassively before the altar, his attention concentrated on some distant point in the stone beyond, steadfastly refusing to meet her gaze. Against her will, Maren's breath caught in her throat at the sight of this man who was to be her husband. The soft flickering light of the candles glistened off the woven gold threads that ornately decorated his richly trimmed tunic. He wore no regal courtly garb, but the simpler garments of his knighthood. The tunic was bound at his waist with a belt of intricately woven gold chain, which secured his sword, sheathed in a finely worked leather scabbard, delicately jeweled with precious stones, from whose midst twinkled a row of finely cut blue sapphires in the hilt of that blade of death. The breeches showing beneath the long tunic were of the same blue velvet. Only a small width showed above the tight-fitting doeskin boots he had chosen to wear.

Maren was delivered to Brettan's side, her arm gently released from her father's grasp, and she strained all her senses, willing herself not to weaken before the reality of these few moments that were changing her life forever. She listened to every word, each sound that echoed within the small chapel, amazed at the simplicity of the ceremony which by its words bound her to this man for all eternity. The request was made, and Brettan knelt before the priest. Maren faltered for a moment and felt his lean, strong fingers close gently about her wrist, drawing her down beside him. The words were spoken, and Brettan answered, and finally Maren answered the priest's questions of her vows. Silence fell within the chapel and seemed to linger for an eternity. Brettan at last took her hand in his and gently placed an ornately carved ring upon the first finger of her left hand, its size being too great for her smaller fingers. She knew the ring, staring at the soft gold which glowed in the candlelight, for she had seen it upon his own hand, and now she felt the flood of his warmth so recently touched by that gold, driving the icy coldness from her hand. She stared at the crest in the soft gold, the figure of a hunting lion that stalked its prey, and for a moment her heart seemed to stop within her breast. Was she now lost to this hunting beast who seemed to stalk her at every turn? With this marriage that was the worst possible lie, had he cleverly bound her to him, so that he might destroy her? Maren raised uncertain eyes and for a moment stared into that glowing green gaze, which held hers with an expression she found unreadable. Did she see hatred in those amber lights that glinted like sparks from a flame, or was it something else that made that glow come alive, like coals upon the hearth? Maren glanced away from the heat of his gaze, realizing that the ceremony had ended, and that Edward now stood beside her and took her hand in a warm greeting.

The festivities in celebration of the marriage were a stark contrast to the solemn ceremony of the afternoon. Indeed, the spirit of the guard and the royal knights seemed joyous. The bountiful meal that was placed before them by the servants was to be rivaled by none, for no cost had been spared in seeing that the finest was laid before the king and his men, even though the short space of time had hardly allowed for great planning. Many a toast was offered to the king, wishing him long life and good health. And then toast after toast was given for the Duke of Norfolk and his bride.

Maren sat uncertainly when the king bade the bride and groom give the traditional wedding toast to each other. Was it not enough that she had been forced into this marriage? Must she now carry the pretense further with yet another lie? A deafening silence fell across the hall, as Maren hesitated. Beside her Brettan stood slowly and, seizing his filled goblet, turned to her expectantly, that mocking light shining brightly in his eyes, silently daring her to defy the king. Maren glanced uneasily about the room, realizing that all eyes were fastened upon her. A crimson blush spread across her cheeks, and her anger flared that she should be brought to such a moment. Her eyes locked with Brettan's, and she read his challenge behind that golden gaze. Maren picked up the gauntlet. She seized the goblet before her hand and rose to stand beside him, all her pride and defiance in the darkened blue of her unwavering gaze. Boldly she raised her goblet, hurling the challenge back at him. Each held their point of confrontation, and he inclined his head in mock salute. He looped his arm through hers, and together, their gazes never yielding, they drank the toast of their marriage.

Maren accepted the toasts of Brettan's knights with uncertain emotions, smiling faintly as each came forward, pledging his honor and his sword to the new Duchess of Norfolk. Brettan remained at her side, withdrawn and seemingly indifferent to her presence, as if she might not have existed, and yet always within protective distance, lest his exuberant guard become too lively with their merrymaking. Several good-humored comments were made, though with respect and a hint of envy, that he had captured a rare and priceless beauty for a bride.

Much too quickly a last toast was offered to the Duke of Norfolk and his bride, and with growing uneasiness Maren realized that very soon she would be expected to join her husband in one of the chambers above where they now dined. Frantically Maren closed her mind to all further thoughts, lest she lose the composure that she had fought to maintain. Through the long hours of the

234

evening that had passed much too quickly, she had desperately sought some private moment with her father, that they might speak, but such was not to be, for the unending celebrations of the wedding feast demanded her presence at the side of her husband. Bravely she had endured the short ceremony that united them in marriage a short while earlier. Where was her courage now? Maren drank amply of the wine poured for the toast, but gazed about the room for some sight of her father, as though she might gain some last-minute reprieve, if only she were allowed to speak with him. But always he remained beyond any contact, as if he deliberately sought to avoid her. Maren felt the flow of the wine burning through her veins. Brettan stood beside her and gently seized her hand. She refused to meet his gaze while he drew her from her chair and led her across the hall before their well-wishers to the wide sweep of the stone stairway that awaited them. Maren defiantly pulled away from his grasp, refusing to be led like some prized possession. She tilted her head proudly, gazing at the towering knight who stood in momentary surprise at her sudden display of temper, a faint warning light sparking in those emerald green eyes, pondering her game. Maren bore her slender height with dignity, and for a full moment a hushed silence fell over the hall, all eyes staring at the two locked in silent confrontation. Each man swore in silence that never had he witnessed such proud beauty. In an instant that warning light in Brettan's eyes faded into a mocking twinkle, which lit his green gaze with annoying humor. As if he had suddenly acquiesced to her greater will, Brettan bowed low before her, his humor of the moment evident in the smirk that played across his lips. In vexation Maren whirled away from him and mounted the steps, her manner stiff and unyielding. Behind her Brettan chuckled loudly, and soon the celebrating was again taken up. His men joined him and their king, and together they began yet another round of toasts, first to the groom and then to the spirited bride. All silently envied him, yet heartily cautioned him against her on their night together.

Brettan's eyes glowed warmly and wandered to the top of the darkened stairway where, a moment before, Maren had lingered before disappearing into the darkness. His blood warmed in his veins, and he felt that stirring within at the thought of again sharing with her those intimate moments that he had come to enjoy so completely. This act of marriage might yield more pleasures that he had first thought, when shared with a fiery beauty whose defiance matched her passion.

Maren reached the landing at the top of the stairway. She quickly disappeared into the chamber and leaned heavily against the closed portal, as if she might close out everything beyond. Mary rose quickly from her chair before the blazing fire at the hearth, where she had placed a new log. She rushed forward to attend Maren, who undressed, removing first the gray velvet gown, and then the thin chemise underneath. Maren's eyes fastened on the large bed she had slept in the night before. The linens had been replaced with fresh ones, and the heavy coverlet was pulled back in open invitation. A small table beside the bed had been set with a tray amply filled with fresh fruits, and a decanter of wine with two goblets obviously intended for the newly wedded couple. All about the room was the scent of fresh rose petals, and a hot bath drawn for her sat steaming in the wooden tub where Mary had kept the water at a perfect temperature for her arrival.

Maren stepped back uncertainly, as if only just becoming aware of the events of the day. Mary gazed at her questioningly when she retreated to the comfort of the heat thrown off by the logs on the fire and gathered a heavy coverlet about her. She sighed her relief at the sound of Mary leaving the chamber, only to have the girl return with Lady Kennerley following close behind.

Gently Lady Kennerley sat down before Maren. "My dear Maren, I can easily understand your uneasiness. But this is part of the wedding night. Certainly your mother must have spoken to you of such matters?"

Maren continued staring past Lady Kennerley, and the kind woman gently placed her arm about Maren's shoulders. If Lady Kennerley knew what had passed between Brettan and herself those long weeks past, she chose to ignore it now.

"You must allow Mary to prepare you for bed. Your husband will be here soon, and you would not want him to be displeased. Dear child, there is nothing to fear at being with your husband. It is all very natural, and the discomfort will pass quickly. The Duke of Norfolk is a worldly man, and he will be most gentle, I am certain." Lady Kennerley's concern for the young girl was marked in the deep lines of her brow, while she sought to reason with Maren.

Maren almost laughed aloud at the complete absurdity that she should have any fears of what the wedding night might hold for her. Indeed, she knew well what it would hold, and it was not a fear of pain that made her refuse the maid's help in disrobing. It was the fear of betrayal by her own body beneath the heat of Brettan's touch. She had lost herself before to her own passions, but always there had been the hope that she would soon be free. Now there was no freedom for her to hope for. Stubbornly she refused to step into the bath, until Lady Kennerley was forced to retreat from the chamber before the greater will of the young girl, leaving Mary outside the chamber should

237

Maren have a need of her. Lady Kennerley decided that it was a matter best left between the Duke of Norfolk and his young bride, for these things had a way of resolving themselves.

It seemed an eternity before Brettan drained his goblet for the last time, firmly refusing the maid at his elbow who waited expectantly to refill the empty vessel. He smiled warmly at the buxom young maid, his eyes lingering for a moment over her amply filled bodice, but his thoughts were of another slender maid who awaited him at the top of those stairs. He made his intentions clear to his men, who teasingly lifted him aloft their shoulders as if to torment him by bearing him away from that spot at the stairs that he sought. Their revelry was joined by that of the royal guard, who took up first one ribald tune and then another, telling of other first nights for a knight and his bride. Brettan relented to their merrymaking, for he saw little chance of gaining the landing under his own power, with so many hands restraining him for just one more toast.

The first gray light of the new day crossed the sky before Brettan finally gained the first stair and then quickly stole up the stairway to the chamber beyond. He hesitated a moment before the heavy portal, watching the young maid scurry down the opposite end of the hallway and disappear from her perch in the shadows.

Hesitantly Brettan tried the latch to the oaken door, uncertain of what he would find beyond the portal. Quietly he swung the door open a small space and, stepping into the dimly lit chamber, closed it firmly behind him. He gazed slowly about the large room, his eyes first noting the empty bed that had been turned back. He saw Maren's slender form wrapped in the thick

238

coverlet, gently slumped in the high-backed chair before the hearth, curled into a tight ball against the cold that had invaded the chamber through the long hours of the night. Heavy velvet drapes had been drawn over the glass windows to keep out the cold and the early morning light, should they wish to remain abed beyond first light. Brettan smiled softly at the sight of her hunched form, desperately seeking to maintain her position through the heavy fog of sleep. Stepping to the hearth, he carefully placed small twigs upon the live coals and, blowing gently, watched the flames once more come to life and leap among the twigs. In her sleep, Maren curled toward the glow of the warmth, her eyes opening slowly when Brettan placed a much larger log upon the fire. Maren gazed lazily at the glow and the lean, handsome man who squatted before the open fire, coaxing it back to life. Once the fog of sleep lifted from her thoughts, she sprang out of the chair, leaping away from Brettan, who came upright at her sudden movement.

Brettan was immediately aware of the defiant gleam that sprang into those wide blue eyes. He was hardly in the mood for battle, and yet it seemed that she was bent on the idea.

"I am grateful for your loyalty, Maren, but it was not necessary for you to await my arrival. Under the circumstances it would seem more appropriate to find you warming my bed, rather than sharing your meager warmth with the hearth." He might have chosen his words more carefully, but his lack of sleep and the abundant celebrating of the night before hardly left him in the mood to humor her. He stepped forward and would have approached her, but Maren backed away warily.

"Do not come near me. You shall not find me the willing maid you held as your prisoner. I am no prisoner now, and I shall not yield to you." She stood in a threatening stance, her feet set wide apart, as if she thought to spring out of his way should he approach her. But instead of moving toward her, Brettan's only response was a low chuckle that escaped his throat while he stared back at her. The growing light at the hearth glowed warmly behind him, catching the deep auburn lights of his hair, which curled in soft waves about his handsome face. The light from the hearth played across his face and caught the glowing light of those eyes that had haunted her dreams since she had first seen him. And Maren knew a moment of uncertainty when she found her gaze drawn to his finely curved lips, which smiled at her gently. She groaned in silent frustration that she should find him so maddeningly handsome, when she had sworn that she would not be affected by him. And yet when she opened her eyes again, she found that he had taken advantage of that one single moment to cross the room to her, and she knew herself lost. She was drawn helplessly into the depths of his emerald gaze. Vainly she resisted, but Brettan's arms closed about her, drawing her against him in one easy movement. His hands gently reached beneath the coverlet.

"No! I will not submit to you. Is it not enough that you have turned my father against me so that he would consent to this marriage? Is it not enough that I am now forced to remain with you as your wife, while you pursue your cause of vengeance? What more would you have of me?" Complete frustration and anger drove Maren beyond the limits of her control, and she struggled against Brettan's hold of her.

"I would have from you, Maren, all that the title 'wife' imparts, and that includes your presence in my bed. Do not be fool enough to believe that I would bind you to me with words and not take advantage of the pleasure I have known with you. You are my wife, Maren." Brettan

240

gently but firmly lifted her chin with his one hand so that he gazed fully into wide blue eyes, that she might have no doubts of his meaning.

"Be assured you shall be my wife in all ways. It is merely your choice whether it shall be by force, or if you will come willingly. Be certain, the result shall be the same."

She stared at him in stunned silence. His face lowered, and his lips closed over hers in a kiss that seemed to draw all the coldness of the long hours from her, replacing it with his own warmth.

Brettan felt the pressure of her hands flattened against his chest, and he hesitated for a moment, staring purposefully into her eyes. "I have promised you that you shall be wife to me. Can you not see that, having once tasted of your sweetness, I could never be satisfied just to look upon you, for I find having had you that a deeper hunger grows within me, and will not be satisfied with just a casual glance or touch."

Maren struggled with renewed efforts, realizing his intent. "You have bound me to you with lies and deceptions. Can you not satisfy your needs with someone more willing than I? Perhaps some mistress you keep, or a fairer form that you favor?"

"You should remember, Maren, that it was my intent to honor you with the title of mistress. And I stress the word 'honor,' for in truth many men value more highly their mistress than the woman who shares their name." Brettan's voice softened, and he bent low, so that his lips gently brushed against her ear, causing her skin to tingle at the warmth of his breath against the gentle curve of her neck. In mounting exasperation Maren shut her eyes, silently wishing she might be anywhere at that moment but locked within his unyielding embrace.

Not waiting for further response, Brettan stepped

away from her momentarily and, to Maren's horror, drew the coverlet away, exposing silken skin that glowed in the flickering firelight. The coverlet fallen to her feet, Brettan swept her into his arms in one quick movement and bore her to the bed that awaited.

Vainly Maren struggled against his greater strength, knowing well her efforts were for naught.

Brettan fell with her across the soft mounding of the bed, the force of his heavier weight pinning Maren against the soft linens. She struggled upwards but found her efforts hopeless, for the softness of the bed thwarted her, and she soon lay back exhausted. He gazed down at her, that odd look of amusement spreading across his handsome features, outlined in the glow of light from the fire at the hearth. Maren groaned in silent defeat, realizing that he would indeed have his way with her, and there was naught she could say in the matter.

Her struggles ceased, and she fought to regain her composure. Brettan studied her delicate beauty in the dimly lit room. Her thick, raven-black hair was spread across the bed in disarray from their struggling, and the fire sent blue lights dancing through the luxurious tresses that seemed to beckon his touch. With great tenderness, Brettan traced the back of his fingers along the silken softness of her cheek, feeling a slight tremor pass through her skin beneath his touch. There was within him a sudden overwhelming desire to protect this treasure he possessed from the secret torments that haunted her, to take from that blue gaze the sadness he had seen, and the thought haunted him that he had seen only sorrow and anger in those sapphire eyes. He had undeniably been the cause of part of that sadness, but there remained so much more she kept from him. Maren remained rigid and unyielding beneath him, as though she might will him away and, at the lingering warmth of his fingers, she jerked her face away as if it burned where he touched her. All her efforts to retreat from him were futile, for his heavier weight pressed her into the soft bed.

Undaunted by her reluctance, Brettan persisted, driven by a deep longing to comfort her. Slowly he turned the delicate oval of her face toward him, the strength in his lean fingers flowing like a rich wine, warm, melting away her coldness. She refused to meet his gaze, her confusion mounting at his gentleness, when she knew what he was capable of. Firmly held within the circle of his embrace, she had no escape from this lingering torture. In an effort to quiet her confused thoughts she inhaled deeply, a sob of despair escaping her softly curved lips, which trembled visibly. Maren raised liquid blue eyes in silent question when Brettan proceeded no further but seemed content to trace the outline of her face with his fingers. Gone was the feral gleam from his eyes. Now she saw only a soft golden glow that bathed her in warmth. Her name was a soft whisper upon his lips as he bent to take hers again, with such tenderness that it seemed a feather had brushed against her lips. Again his lips returned and again, tasting of her sweet softness, mingled with the saltiness of the trail of tears that trickled down her cheek. His fingers lightly traced the hollow of her neck, lingering over the pulsing of her life's blood, then traveled to the gentle curve of her shoulder, drawing her closer to him once his hand had closed over that soft rounded contour. With each caress, each touch, he plumbed the depths of her slumbering passions, which but rested, awaiting the touch that would awaken all her desires. Her awareness of him heightened as Maren felt that first soft caress and, in answer, her own faint stirrings of response deep within. It came alive within her from a multitude of secret hiding places, building with each kiss that he placed upon her lips, her cheek, the gentle curve of her throat. They burned a searing path to mark where he touched her. Her senses reeled beneath the assault of the deliberate slowness he used to arouse the passions he knew her capable of. She was hardly aware that he moved away from her for an instant to discard his clothes and then quickly return to her side, the heat of his bare skin against hers igniting a thousand fires with that first full contact. And the warmth from his touch spread through her like the warmth from wine, which when first sipped entices one for yet another sip, until one becomes lost in the golden glow spreading from the heady liquid. Brettan teased her one moment and gently caressed her the next, his touch promising yet holding back, feeling the response on her lips, tentative, questioning, for what she had only so recently begun to understand were her own desires. Her lips trembled beneath his, her vulnerability slicing through him like a well-honed blade, cutting away at the last vestiges of all desire for revenge against her.

Maren responded uncertainly, her fear of these newly found emotions keen, as she gazed at the man who bent over her, and yet she could not deny the deep longing for him that seemed to have a will of its own. She moaned softly under the assault of his heated caresses, and closed her mind to all doubts, all caution against this English knight who had taken everything from her, even her will to resist. There was only the moment that existed between them, all hatreds, all wars ceased. Maren abandoned herself to the growing need she felt deep within, a need she had known only for him, a need she knew in her heart only he could fill, and she reached up, her slender arms entwining about his muscular, bronzed neck, drawing him to her, that she might feel herself melt into him. Her eyes closed tightly, and she savored the mounting passion that built within her like a flame threatening to consume her. His lips took hers again, more firmly, demanding and giving at the same time, tasting her response. Maren's breath stilled in her throat so that she feared she might never breathe again, and yet she felt her breath become one with his, and the strength he drew from her, he gave back, and her need of him stayed all doubts, all fears, all anger.

Chapter Twelve

Maren stirred slowly from sleep. Then the commands spoken in Welsh came clearly to her, and she came awake, realizing they could only be from the Welsh captain of the guard who commanded her father's men. Pulling the heavy coverlet about her against the chill of the morning air, she ran to the heavily paned windows and pushed back the glass closures. In the courtyard below, her father's entire guard stood mounted and prepared to ride, their heavy armor glinting with the first shafts of sunlight that spilled over the far wall of the stone fortress, outlining their shadowy figures in the mist that rose in the early gray light. The festivities of the night before weighed heavily upon many a man who forced himself to remain awake in the saddle, lest he meet with his master's disapproval. Maren's glance searched among the guard for that figure she would most easily recognize. The orders were given in hastily spoken Welsh, for Gilbert de Burghmond seemed impatient to ride before first light. Down the long line of the column, she saw the leaner figure of her brother, who rode with some last minute instruction for the captain of the guard. Maren's gaze returned to her father's stalwart figure at the head of the guard, as if she might will him to turn back toward her chamber in the main hall. His gaze rose, and in the early morning light he saw her youthful figure standing before the window. For a long moment their eyes locked, and Maren's heart wrenched at the sadness she saw in the grim line of his face. He had deliberately chosen not to bid her farewell, and Maren knew any efforts to speak with him would be futile. It was a choice he had made and would abide by. The captain of his guard waited patiently for the order to ride. Gilbert de Burghmond hesitated a moment longer, and then in one last, silent gesture gave the awaited order.

Maren was unaware that Brettan had risen from the bed and stood behind her at the window, watching the long column of her father's guard depart Monmouth Castle. So heavy was her heart that she held no thoughts of the man who shared her bed, and who was now her husband. Silent tears welled in her eyes when the last man rode through the gate, their leaving marked only by a small cloud of dust that rose on the road once the horses had moved out into the open countryside, beginning a journey she longed to make with them.

Brettan watched the guard disappear from view, having known of Lord de Burghmond's intention to leave at first light. Casting a long look at Maren's profile and the stream of tears falling unchecked down the length of her cheek and then upon the heavy coverlet she clutched tightly about her, he knew her sadness and pain at that parting without a word of farewell. He had disapproved openly of the decision, but his words had fallen on deaf ears, since Maren's father had clearly refused to speak with her. Brettan sighed heavily, staring at her in that first light of day. It created a golden glow behind her, and he thought he had never before seen such beauty. He was at a loss to comfort her. There were no words that could easily be spoken to explain her father's decision in favor

248

of the marriage, that could take away the pain and confusion he saw in her eyes, when she had sought only a father's love and understanding. He sought to steel himself against her beauty, against her innocence, but found the wall of his resolve torn down piece by piece under the assault of her tears. Silently he muttered an oath that her tears should affect him so, when always before he had found it an easy matter to ignore such artful ploys by a fair maid to gain his favor. But in this proud, spirited maid who stood before him, who was his wife in name, yet wanted nothing of him but her freedom, he saw only vulnerability, unshielded by harsh words or proud denials. She was helpless with all her defenses stripped away, and Brettan knew only an all-consuming desire to take away her sadness, to shield her forever from those who might bring her unhappiness. How could he possibly make her understand all the reasons that had determined the king's decision for the marriage, reasons that went beyond protecting her against the possibility of a bastard child, or saving her honor? Reaching out, Brettan pulled her within the circle of his embrace, drawing her against the naked expanse of his chest, casting aside his own anger and desire for vengeance. The time for truth between them would come, perhaps once again setting them as enemies against one another. He ignored her feeble protests at his touch until she resisted no more, but laid her cheek against him and let the tears of her misery flow freely, dampening his skin where they fell. Gently Brettan stroked the silken thick mass of her dark hair, which fell across her shoulders and spilled to below her hips. He attempted to comfort her slender form, which shook with her softly muffled sobbing. Tenderly he kissed her hair, the rose-scented sweetness filling his senses. He pulled her back to the warmth of the bed and, beyond all passion, beyond all his raging desire to feel himself once again deep within her, he held her for

249

a long time until her sobbing quieted, and at long last her breathing was deep and even, while she lay within the curl of his body. For a time he held her, not moving lest she awaken. Quietly he watched the rise and fall of her breasts beneath the warm coverlet, thinking that he had never before known such peace. Maren's lips parted slightly, a dream invading her slumber. Brettan wondered if he were the cause of her silent torment, and knew the answer without further questioning. Later, when Maren drifted into more peaceful rest, where her dreams could not reach her, Brettan eased from her side and, dressing quickly in the late morning light flooding into the chamber, he left to seek Sandlin and Sir Bothwell, to give orders for their own departure for London the following day. Through the hours that remained of the morning he attended to the endless details of those preparations, then joined Edward at the hunt in the forest beyond Monmouth Castle. He welcomed the respite from all thoughts of war, but there was no release from the vision of sapphire eyes, or raven black hair spread across his bed, or the contrast of fair skin against his own, when Maren lay with her limbs entwined with his. Eventually Brettan abandoned all efforts to remove that memory, finding comfort in those thoughts until he might look upon her beauty again.

Maren stirred from sleep, her hand searching for Brettan's warmth beside her. Her senses cleared, and she gazed about the chamber, becoming aware that she was alone in the large bed. The memory of the event of the day before returned to her, and she fled the bed and flew to the window. The courtyard below was empty except for the royal guard and several of Brettan's personal guard. There was no sign of her father's men. She had not been dreaming.

She was startled from her thoughts by a light knocking on the heavy door behind her. She gathered the coverlet

250

about her naked body before Mary entered, bearing a tray with food to break the morning fast, although the day was already well advanced. Seeing that Maren was awake, the maid beckoned two other young servants into the room, who struggled with cumbersome buckets of hot water for her morning bath.

Later, sitting soaking in the hot water before the blazing fire at the hearth, Maren was given little time for her own thoughts. Mary laboriously lathered Maren's long hair, then brushed it tirelessly before the warmth of the fire while it dried. The girl fluffed the raven black tendrils which curled invitingly about Maren's face and waved down the length of her back. Lady Kennerley flew into the chamber chatting gaily about the grand day, coming to a halt before the warmth of the fire to gaze down at her young guest with a warmth and friendliness that would have brightened the bleakest day.

"Ah, so you are finished with your bathing. Sir Bothwell awaits in the courtyard below to escort us to the town. I have a need to purchase some items from the market, and we might perhaps find a length or two of cloth that could be stitched into some new gowns for you. You will have a need of others in London. And the Duke of Norfolk has asked that I give whatever assistance I might, to see that you are properly clothed. It shall please me greatly. Three sons who wear the king's armor hardly allow for a mother's touch."

Lady Kennerley's manner was lighthearted and meant with the best of intentions, but Maren's temper bristled at the thought that Brettan should so openly draw attention to her lack of dress, when it was he that had brought that upon her. "The gray velvet shall suffice. I have no need of anything the Duke of Norfolk might offer. Indeed, I do not intend to remain in England."

"But, dear child, you are a lady of title, and a duchess by your marriage. You shall be traveling to London in the

251

company of the king, where you shall be presented to the court. Most certainly the gray velvet is an exquisite gown, but a very special one that should be kept to wear for a very grand occasion. After we are finished at market, the king has requested that we join the men for a picnic in the meadow. It is a grand spring day. And the picnic shall be a welcome change from the matters of war."

Maren turned back to stare out the window at the brilliant blue sky, like a vast ocean beyond the walls of the mighty stone fortress. Her thoughts were of her father and brother and the journey to Cambria. Her mood hardly lent itself to shopping for trinkets or picnics. Her thoughts were flooded with the memory of the picnics she had promised her sister, Catherine, they would once again make upon the Welsh countryside. A single tear fell upon her cheek and trickled down the length to her chin. She swiped angrily at her cheek with the back of her hand, refusing to yield to her unspoken fears and the sadness that had returned to wear at her composure. Duchess indeed! She hardly felt like one, nor had she any idea of what was to be expected of her, beyond bearing children that could not be called bastard! The realization that she might already carry Brettan's child froze in her mind. She must not think of it now, yet the thought persisted and, try as she might, she could not recall when her time had last come, or even if it had come since she had been held within the English camp. Her hand moved uneasily across the flatness of her stomach, and her misery only increased at the thought that she might carry the seed of Brettan's cruel taking of her. She shook her head to throw off the thought, then turned back to face Lady Kennerley, who stood waiting for her response to the day's plans.

"You are most kind, Lady Kennerley. Indeed, I could have asked for no one kinder, when I am hardly more than a stranger to you. If you have a need to visit the marketplace then I shall be most pleased to join you, and perhaps it will help lighten the day. But for myself, I desire nothing. It matters little to me whether the Duke of Norfolk is pleased with my appearance or no, for I am hardly here of my own will."

Lady Kennerley sighed sadly at Maren's words. She knew from her husband that the girl had been greatly upset at the announcement of the wedding, and indeed her manner the evening before had born out her reluctance at the marriage. But Lady Kennerley held great hopes for the night that had passed, thinking perhaps Maren's apprehensions were nothing more than those of any bride. For assuredly, the Duke of Norfolk was an extremely handsome man, and seemed most gentle and considerate of his young bride. If the stories were to be believed, he was also highly sought by all the young maids of title in London, and even several not of title. There were also the well-known intentions of his mistress, a highborn lady within the royal circle at court, who had sought to gain those vows that would bind his title and vast wealth in marriage, but always to no avail. Lady Kennerley felt uneasy when she beckoned her maid to assist with dressing the girl. Indeed, there was much the young Duchess of Norfolk would have to face upon her arrival in London. But if Lady Kennerley's instincts were correct, she felt confident that the beautiful young Welsh girl would have the protection and devotion of her handsome husband, for indeed the Duke of Norfolk did not seem displeased with the marriage. In truth, he had seemed in fine spirit earlier in the morning, when he had departed with Lord Kennerley and the king for a day at the hunt. She would not easily forget his flashing smile, which dimpled his lean bronze features, and she greatly envied the young girl her beauty, her youth, and the brave, handsome knight who had wed her the day before. Mary put the final touches to the gown and brushed a stray waving tendril into place. Lady Kennerley quickly hurried Maren from the chamber, down the stairway to the courtyard below, where Brettan's guard awaited. Time had a way of taking care of such matters of the heart, and Lady Kennerley was not mistaken about the look she had seen, however brief it might have been, when the Duke of Norfolk had looked upon his young bride while speaking the marriage vows. The Duke of Norfolk was in love with the sad beauty, and Lady Kennerley felt it was only a matter of time before Maren would be unable to deny her own love for the tall knight.

They made a grand sight as the English knights, resplendent in all their finery, escorted Lady Kennerley and the beautiful young girl through the busy market-place of Monmouth. Sir Bothwell and Sandlin, together with four of Brettan's guards, accompanied the ladies, adding their good humor to the easy mood of the spring day, which warmed quickly beneath a clear blue sky that gave a hint of the summer fast approaching. Behind them Lady Kennerley's maid followed dutifully to take note of Lady Kennerley's purchase, making certain they reached the castle. Carefully Sandlin guided their small group through the winding, cobbled streets, crowded with merchants bartering with the people of the town, eager to part with their coin on such a grand day.

Maren was oblivious of the stares directed at her, or the whispers of speculation that followed her slender form, but gave herself to Sandlin's lighthearted mood, accepting his arm while he led the way through the crowded market. They walked in the direction of the town square, where many fine shops lined the streets. Merchants called to them, anxious that some of their goods might be exchanged for the rich coin they knew the knights carried. Beside her Lady Kennerley carried on

254

idle conversation, while they walked from one shop to another. Maren was surprised at the vast array of wares displayed by the merchants, for certainly none of the villages near Cambria offered so much. The best to be found there might be the fresh fish, brought in that day from the boats which left early each morn, or perhaps a length of soft wool to make a warm gown to protect against the cold of winter on the Welsh coast. Occasionally a merchant would venture from Cardiff or perhaps London, bringing the highly prized velvets to make a special gown. But never such a vast selection of velvets and satins as she saw displayed by the eager merchants whose fine wares she now admired. Maren ran her hand appraisingly across a soft mauve velvet, the color making her eyes seem like the color of heather upon the moors. She keenly eyed a light blue piece but hastily set it aside, politely refusing any purchase. She stepped from the shop, inhaling deeply of the fresh air, while a gentle breeze stirred the wisps of soft raven tendrils playfully about her face. Certainly she was the most pleasing sight to be found in Monmouth that day.

Lady Kennerley joined her a moment later, after purchasing some small trinket. They were rejoined by Sir Bothwell, and continued across the open square, where several long tables displayed fresh fruits that might be purchased.

They walked past the row of vendors' tables, Maren unaware of a beggarly old man who hobbled along behind that same row of tables a few paces away, or of the manner in which he stared at her when she laughed at some jest spoken by the English knight who hovered protectively near her. Nor did she see that he approached an old woman and quickly bartered to purchase the baskets of bright fresh flowers she displayed. Had Maren witnessed the exchange, she might have thought it odd that one so poorly dressed could offer such rich coin without haggling over the purchase. The old woman quickly stuffed the numerous coins into her sagging bodice, silently cursing herself that she could have demanded more for the flowers, so eager was the stranger, that he hardly bothered to count out the sum she had named. If the old woman thought his manner odd, she gave it no further thought, but she shuffled off through the crowded market, pleased that she had made in one sale the amount of coin it might have otherwise taken her a week of days to earn, in selling to the fine ladies such as the young beauty the entire town whispered about. She smiled a toothless grin, greatly pleased with her good fortune that day, and paid little heed to the stranger, who took up her place to sell the freshly cut blooms.

Maren stopped to sample a fresh pastry a young woman offered, giggling in good humor when the fruit filling dribbled down her chin. Lady Kennerley purchased several fine pastries, but Maren moved on slowly to admire a display of finely carved wooden figures, painstakingly perfect in their detailing of the animals they had been fashioned after. But what caught her eye was the figure of a proud stallion, rubbed so that the fine wood glistened almost black. The carving was extraordinarily beautiful, for the craftsman had managed to capture perfectly the animal's proud spirit in the arch of its well-muscled neck and the flare of its nostrils. For a moment Maren was given to the desire to purchase the carving, thinking how Brettan might appreciate the beauty of it. But she quickly pushed aside the thought. Such gifts were meant to be shared as a part of love, and most certainly that did not exist between herself and Brettan de Lorin. Silently she moved on, approaching a bent old man carefully tending the colorful flowers clustered in several baskets at the end of the long row of tables. Innocently Maren reached out to a cluster of violets, and found her wrist suddenly seized in a powerful grip that belied the old man's age. Uncertain of the man's intent, she sought to break his hold by twisting her hand away, but found her arm firmly grasped in his tightening grip. Sandlin and the others were completely unaware of her plight, and panic welled inside her at the man's bold actions. She felt her wrist bruised from his hold of her and, thinking the man perhaps misunderstood and suspected her of trying to take the flowers, she sought to reason with him. "Please, I would purchase the flowers. The others follow directly and will see you are paid for them. You are hurting me." She was very near panic, feeling the man's grip tighten about her wrist, drawing her across the narrow width of the table that separated them. Wildly, she glanced behind her for Sandlin's protective presence, but found that they were too far away for her to call out, and unaware of her struggle.

"Maren! You need have no fear of me. I will not harm you. Listen to me! I will not abandon you as your father and brother have!"

Maren's head shot up in stunned surprise, and her struggling ceased momentarily at the sound of the man's voice, no more than a harsh whisper against her ear.

"Geoffrey?" Her voice was a whisper. She sought some recognition through the heavy disguise the man wore.

"I must speak with you, but not here. You are too closely watched." There was no mistaking those eyes that bored into hers with such keen intensity from beneath the heavy hood that concealed his features from others. Suddenly he released her wrist, freeing her, and bent to straighten an overturned basket.

"Milady?" Sandlin's voice carried his concern when he approached. "Was there some purchase you desired?" Warily the knight eyed the odd-looking merchant, taking

257

notice of Maren's pale color.

The hunched old man glared a warning at her across the table. Maren rubbed her bruised wrist. "No, there is nothing I wish." She sought to divert Sandlin's attention from the old man. "Could we perhaps join the others?" And then, seeing that Sandlin regarded the man suspiciously, she quickly seized the knight's arm. "Sandlin, I thought perhaps to purchase that fair carved statue of the stallion. Would it not make a fine gift for the Duke of Norfolk?" Sandlin nodded briefly, gently taking her hand upon his arm, and they returned to the merchant who had offered the carvings. He made her desired purchase, then escorted her to join the others for the short ride to the meadow beyond the town. The knight cast a backwards glance in the direction of the flower vendor and was not surprised to find the old man had disappeared. While they mounted their horses and slowly made their way toward the edge of the town, Sandlin ordered one of the guard to remain behind and inquire about the vendor. It was a matter he intended to know more about, for there were still many dangers they must guard against, even in England.

Maren's mood remained thoughtful on the short ride to the meadow, remembering Geoffrey's words that he must speak with her. But when, and where? How was it possible when she was guarded by Brettan's knights? Thoughtfully she rubbed the soft wood of the finely carved stallion, which the merchant had wrapped in a piece of velvet cloth, and contemplated Geoffrey's words.

The small meadow beyond the town of Monmouth basked peacefully in the warmth of the spring day. It had been transformed by those who had taken part in the hunt, gathered at the end of the day to congratulate each other on their good fortune, or good-naturedly to tease those less fortunate. The weapons of war had been laid aside for a day and replaced by crossbows and lances, which better served the hunting of the wild stag and boar that roamed the wooded copse. Their small group returned from the market to join in the feasting, and Maren gazed in silent wonder at the encampment. Along the entire perimeter of the camp, forming a wide arc, several tables had been set by the servants from the castle, and stood heavily laden with baskets filled with a vast array of foods and shaded by the spreading branches of the trees overhead. Maren was silently grateful for the gentle breeze that stirred the warmth of the late afternoon, easing the sun's heat, for the heavy velvet gown had become unbearably warm on the short ride from town. Several stag and boar had been brought down that day and were strung up at the far side of the camp. Maren turned from the sight, which inexplicably left her stomach uneasy. Lady Kennerley was most eager to hear of the hunt and what good fortune the king might have had that day. Still shaken from Geoffrey's sudden appearance at the market, Maren pleaded to follow in a few moments, but found the good woman would accept no excuses. Reluctantly she followed Lady Kennerley to join the royal hunting party. The circle of knights parted for Lady Kennerley, her husband greeting her good-naturedly. Brettan stood beside Edward, leaning back lazily against the trunk of a tree, the friendship and camaraderie he enjoyed with his king obvious in the lack of ceremony between the two men. Dressed in doeskin breeches and tunics, they might have been any men who enjoyed a good day at the hunt. But Maren was keenly aware of the marked difference in these two men from the other knights who had joined them, a certain bearing that set them apart from the others. Maren stood uncertainly at the edge of their circle, and it was Edward who separated from the group of men and approached her. Wary of his casual regard for her, relaxed from the formalities of the evening before, Maren felt a momentary uneasiness, and a bright spot of color spread across her fair cheeks. The King of England bowed before her, gently seizing her hand to draw her within the circle of his knights.

"Milady, certainly no lovelier sight has ever graced my camp, save of course Queen Eleanore. You will permit me that one exception?" His blue eyes laughed merrily at her, and Maren realized how much he must have enjoyed the day's respite from his weighty responsibilities as King of England.

"Take heed, my friend, that you guard this treasure well, or you shall find yourself sorely tested to keep her by your side." Edward warned Brettan good-humoredly.

Brettan came to stand beside his monarch. "I fear such is already the case, for several of my knights have taken upon themselves the title of protector. I shall heed your advice and see that their 'protection' extends no further." His emerald eyes locked with hers for a moment, their first contact since the early hours of the morning, when he had retired to their bed. Maren glanced away, the heated rise of color in her cheeks sorely reminding her that she wished to be anywhere else that moment. With a warm hand, Brettan seized Maren's and the wrapped gift she had carried from the town.

"What is this? Some small treasure, that you hold it so dearly?"

"'Tis nothing, milord, merely a small trinket I purchased at the market." Maren hastily sought to withdraw the statue of the wooden horse, suddenly aware that Brettan might misunderstand the gift. The velvet cloth was drawn away when she stepped back, leaving him with the richly carved figure in his hands. Her startled blue gaze caught his when he looked up from the exquisite gift to stare questioningly into her eyes. The dark gray-black of the rare wood gleamed with a lustrous sheen, the small figure's resemblance to his gray warhorse unmistakable. Brettan reached out, his hand closing possessively over Maren's, drawing her away from the openly admiring glances of his knights. To any who watched them depart, they might have seemed like any lovers, strolling slowly across the meadow to a spot apart from the others.

"It is a fine gift, Maren, far finer than any I have ever received, and made much more so that it is from you. I shall treasure it like the finest jewel." And then, when he noticed the growing look of vexation that crossed her lovely brow, he sought to tease her. "Sandlin has told me of your encounter with the merchant in the marketplace. It seems you collect ardent admirers wherever you go. But I should warn you against such flirtations, for they will hardly be acceptable at the court in London."

Maren turned on him in frustration, her temper mounting with each passing moment. She might have known he would misunderstand her purchase of the horse. "You are insufferable and boorish. There was nothing to my conversation with the old man. Whatever Sandlin might have told you, he was mistaken. It was merely a misunderstanding." She watched him gaze down at her.

"Maren, there is much you do not understand. There are many dangers, perhaps more now that I have made you my wife. I cannot accept your foolish endangering of yourself by speaking with each person you meet. You must accept this, for there can be no other way in the matter."

Had he paid closer attention to the play of emotions across her lovely face, Brettan might have been prepared for the anger that glinted in those deep blue eyes, and the set of her slender jaw at his last words. As it was, he was not aware of the anger his words provoked in her, nor was he aware that her proud spirit set her beyond all caution when she bridled at his softly spoken orders.

"Milord, Duke of Norfolk, your wishes are of little concern to me, and I shall not defend my actions to you or anyone."

Maren's breath caught in her throat when he raised his emerald gaze, the gleam glowing in those depths more menacing than any threat he might have spoken. "Milady, you are my wife and subject to my word. Whether you would have it or no, I shall have the final say in this matter!"

All her fears and uncertainties of the weeks past, and the pain of her father's rejection, goaded Maren beyond caution. She rose to her feet, her slender body rigid with suppressed fury, her eyes deepening to almost black. She refused to submit to his will. "Wife perhaps, but by your word and that of your king, not by mine freely given. Nor could I ever yield to that title and all that it imparts."

"I seem to remember, milady, you yielded all this morn, when you shared my bed. Or do you call that also a lie?" Brettan's voice had grown louder, so that several of his knights now turned in their direction. Maren's voice was but a low whisper. She responded coldly, aware that he sought to humiliate her before his men. "You have taken me against my will, with little care for what I might say. Indeed, you have flaunted me before your men as nothing more than your mistress. Be it known, I shall not submit willingly. As you have chosen to take me from my home by force and make me your wife, for what purpose I can hardly understand, I shall not yield more to you. Perhaps you shall find a more willing maid when we are returned to London, since you are intent that I should go there; perhaps a mistress that shall willingly warm your bed for, milord, I vow I shall not."

Brettan fought to maintain his control before his men and his king, and he found himself sorely pressed to refrain from striking Maren. He descended upon her slender form, seizing a delicate wrist in a brutal grasp that caused her to wince at the sudden pain that shot through her arm. "You are quite right, Maren, for my mistress eagerly awaits. Therefore heed my words, milady, for though I am honor bound to remain loyal to my king, there is no such requirement in the marriage vows. And I swear that the one who awaits my return does not turn on me at every chance, or rail at me for some wrong she thinks I have committed, nor does she seek to turn my mind with lies to support some ill-gotten cause. Nay, Maren, in her I shall indeed find someone far more willing, and I shall take my ease in her gentle company, not with one who seeks to wound me at every turn." Golden green eyes sparked their silent warning of the rage that churned within him, and he flung her away from him, releasing his brutal hold which left the mark of his bruising fingers on her fair skin. Then he whirled about on his heel and strode in the direction of the horses tethered at the far side of the camp.

The purplish marks left by his grip upon her arm were nothing to the inexplicable pain Maren felt at his words to her. Mistresses were not uncommon among the royalty and men of title, but she had not considered the possibility that Brettan might have one awaiting his return to London. She was at a loss to understand the flood of uncertain emotions that churned within her at that knowledge, which cut through her like a knife thrust deep, to leave a wound that would not easily heal. Silently she raged against her treacherous emotions, seeking to control her embarrassment before the English guard and the king.

"Milady, do not think harshly of the Duke of Norfolk. I have always believed words spoken in anger are not words of the heart, but the emotions of the moment," Edward consoled her, approaching.

"I think, milord, that there is no difference, that they are one and the same. And you will forgive me if I fail to

263

understand the purpose of this marriage you have ordered." Maren's voice trembled, and she fought to regain her shattered composure. Edward smiled warmly, and she was struck by the kindness she saw behind his stern visage.

"I will not apologize for my decision in the matter of the marriage, milady, for I believe it to be the only way to have kept you safe in England. But perhaps it is necessary that I apologize for the Duke of Norfolk. He is a soldier and a knight of the realm, and he has spent the greater part of his life upon the field of battle, for the cause of England. The life of a soldier is a lonely and solitary existence and, when war is one's constant companion, one often forgets that there are matters which cannot be settled with force and the sword. It is a fault I am oft reminded of, milady."

"Milord?" Maren gazed incredulously at the king, suddenly struck by this common quality of his manner.

"Yea, milady, the queen is my guide in matters of the heart for, if left to it myself, I would soon find myself quite alone. In her I find the gentle reminders that I am also husband and father, and not always the warrior. Indeed, there are times when I am given to wonder who the true leader might be, so great is her wisdom and strength."

"But, milord, I do not seek gentleness or kind words, nor do I seek love, where none exists. I seek only my release from these bonds you have placed upon me. There is no purpose in this marriage. I cannot accept your concern that I might bear a bastard son to the Duke of Norfolk. Nor can I see his concern in the matter, for he takes his pleasures where he will, with little regard for any other but himself. What, then, is the reason for this great falsehood?"

"In truth, milady, I seek to right a wrong committed against one who is fair and who possesses innocence. Is

264

that so difficult to accept?" Edward questioned her, a certain light of amusement hiding any hint of greater meaning behind his royal gaze.

"I am greatly surprised to find the King of England so greatly preoccupied with the virtues of young maidens, particularly one who is not English."

"Ah but you see, you are English, are you not, by virtue of your father's name?" Edward asked, gazing intently into the depths of her blue gaze.

"But also Welsh, by virtue of my mother's blood," she answered quietly, thinking of the woman now slain. Edward took her hand gently in his and laid it across his arm, drawing her toward the tables that had been set for the feast. "Then tell me, Lady Maren, what is the one quality that would make a man a worthy king over other men?"

Maren stared back at him, wondering at the game he played, for she hardly thought he sought to draw her out in casual conversation. She carefully considered her answer before she gave it. "I believe it to be compassion, milord, for without it all else is lost."

"Do you believe me to possess that quality?"

Maren gazed unafraid into the light blue gaze of the man beside her, undaunted by the quiet strength she saw in his manner, unaware that many men had retreated from the powerful demeanor of the warrior king who stood beside her. Her own darker blue eyes were like deep velvet pools, the brilliant color of priceless sapphires, returning his unwavering gaze. The afternoon breeze gently caressed the thick waves of raven-black hair that framed her face, and Edward silently cursed his knight's foolishness in using this gentle maid with such callous cruelty. Behind the blue veil of her wide eyes, he saw that spark of pride and indomitable will, and knew that here indeed was one worthy of any man's love.

With an honesty she found difficult to understand,

Maren gave the king his answer. "Yea, milord. Though it might seem hidden behind your authority, it is there."

"Are you surprised at that, milady?"

"In truth, yes. You are king of England. By your title alone you are placed apart from your people. To see you as I have seen you today makes you seem no different from any other man. You possess compassion, and I think wisdom, that Llywelyn cannot hope to equal. By that alone, you will obtain what you seek."

"We must speak more of the matter, Lady Maren, for I find I greatly enjoy your honesty. Complete honesty, without fear of reprisal or hope of gain, is indeed rare. Will you honor me with the pleasure of your company at the feast?"

Maren's uneasy emotions at her confrontation with Brettan faded before the easy humor of the king, and a radiant smile, the first in many days, danced across her face when she gently bowed her head and dropped into a curtsy before Edward I of England. "I am greatly honored, milord. But I shall consent only if you promise to tell me more of the queen. I should like to know more of the woman who rules all of England."

"Then come, Lady Maren. That shall take the better part of the afternoon, for I find I do not tire of talking about my family. I have a son, age three years, whose strength already rivals that of my fiercest knights."

The remainder of the afternoon passed swiftly, for Maren gave herself completely to her enjoyment of the king's attentions. He was king first, and a warrior, but he was also a man devoted to his family, and Maren found herself anticipating her meeting with the young queen and the prince regent.

Brettan remained conspicuously absent from the feast. When the first stars of twilight rose in the evening sky, Maren searched for his tall frame among the knights, who gathered to tell a final story around the blazing fire before returning to Monmouth Castle.

Maren saw Brettan's unmistakable height among his knights. Sandlin helped her mount the black mare and, though he seemed to prefer their company, Maren found herself once again surrounded by her loyal guards, Sandlin and Sir Bothwell having taken up their positions on either side of the mare.

Maren sighed heavily during the short ride to the stone fortress looming before them on the hillside above the town of Monmouth. She suddenly felt very weary and longed for the privacy of her chamber, where she might sort out her confused thoughts of the day's events. Yet she was reluctant to face those moments alone with Brettan, when all her words of denial would fall away before the heat of his passion and she would again yield to her own desires. Stubbornly she resolved to hold herself from him. And perhaps he would do as he had promised that afternoon, and seek his rest in some other bed. He could easily await his return to London and there take his pleasures with his mistress. Indeed, she felt no honor-bound duty to comply with the responsibilities that the title "wife" required of her. She would not crawl to do his bidding.

With grim determination she entered her chamber, but came to a sudden halt just inside the open portal. Startled by her hasty arrival, Mary sprang to her feet and curtsied deeply before Maren, a crimson blush creeping upwards to spread across the young girl's cheeks. Maren stood in stunned silence, gazing about the room. Every possible surface, the bed, the table, the two chairs before the hearth, was vividly draped with a vast array of garments, whose number was too great to accurately measure. Gowns of soft, rich velvets and satins had been draped across the bed, and she instantly recognized the soft mauve velvet transformed into a gown with long sweeping sleeves, bordered with rich gold cording intricately woven in a chain about the sleeve edges and the neck, and sweeping low over the bodice. Beside the mauve gown was one cut from a light blue, and beside it another and yet another, so that she lost count while she stared in wonder. Surely there must have been some mistake, certainly the gowns were meant for Lady Kennerley. Having crossed the room and stopped to caress softly a heavy velvet mantle of a brilliant blue, richly lined with silver fox which was exposed along the entire opening of the mantle, she raised questioning eyes to the young maid, who seemed suddenly uneasy, thinking that Maren perhaps was displeased with the garments.

"Milady, they came to the castle early in the afternoon. They spent the entire afternoon in the chamber, cutting and sewing, and they said they were given strict instructions that all was to be finished before your return. Indeed, I have never seen any work as quickly as they. It seemed the very devil stood over them."

Maren gazed about the room, unable to understand any of what she saw before her. "Of whom do you speak?"

"Oh, milady, the merchant from town and his apprentices. Indeed, I have never seen such garments as these. You must be greatly pleased."

Maren shook her head firmly. "I cannot accept these. I must explain to Lady Kennerley that I cannot accept the garments."

"Milady, it was not my mistress who purchased the gowns, but his lordship."

"His lordship?"

"Aye, milady, your husband, the Duke of Norfolk.

And he also asked that these be given to you, that you might wear them with the blue gown for the feast this night, in the great hall.'' Obedient to Brettan's orders, the young girl stood before Maren and carefully unwrapped a tightly rolled piece of dark blue velvet cloth, bound with gold cording. In the center of the cloth lay a medallion, and Maren's breath caught at the sight of it. As large as the palm of her hand, the rich gold shone brilliantly in the soft candle light of the chamber, and from the center gleamed the figure of a hunting lion. It was the same as the medallion she had found at Cambria, the same as the medallion Brettan wore, only much larger. And the evenly matched blue sapphires that encircled the medallion held her transfixed, for they were quite perfect, and the same color as the blue on Brettan's shield. The figure of the bold lion sparkled with one large blue sapphire, much larger than the others, placed to make the animal's eye. The perfect stone caught the flickering candlelight and seemed to glow at her with a life of its own. Maren was oblivious to the opening of the door behind her, or that Brettan stood in the doorway watching her reaction to his gift. Mary curtsied deeply and hastily departed the chamber. Maren turned to question her further, her voice stilled at the sight of Brettan watching her with catlike curiosity. Her silent question was reflected in her brilliant blue eyes, like the dazzling perfection of the sapphires she held in her hand.

"I had planned for you to have the medallion before your gift to me this afternoon. I would see you wear the medallion, Maren. It belonged to my mother and to each Duchess of Norfolk before her. I know well your loathing for this marriage, and I vow I shall not press you to fulfill your responsibilities as my wife. But whether you would have it or no, you are now the Duchess of Norfolk, and by that title the medallion is yours. It would also please me

269

greatly if you would accept the gowns I have purchased for you. I hardly think you would care to arrive at court in the doeskin breeches I first found you in. Though I warrant, milady, that those garments hold valued memories for me. As for yonder bed, I shall not trouble you again in such matters. I shall make my bed with my men and leave you to your solitary warmth, praying you find all you desire there." Bowing slightly before her, Brettan turned on his heel to leave the chamber, his finely curved lips set in a grim line that made his handsome face seem as if it had been carved from stone. The heavy oaken door slammed loudly with the force of his leaving. The latch caught, and she stood alone in the large chamber. The clear meaning of his words came to her. She should have felt greatly relieved, even jubilant, that he would not press her further. But she felt only an odd emptiness inside of her, as if some great part of her had been removed, leaving a deep, gaping wound that gave her pain in her uncertain victory over him.

Maren chose the mauve gown for the evening feast that would be their last at Monmouth Castle, but deliberately refused the gold medallion with the blue sapphires. Shortly before she descended the stone stairway, Mary appeared and carefully wove the hair at each side of her head into a long lustrous braid, entwined with a fine gold cording that was the only decoration she wore. The braids were then drawn to the back of her head and bound together with another length of cording. Their ends fell loosely, joining the thick waving mass of her raven-black hair as it cascaded below her hips.

Maren descended the stone stairway to the hall below. She was uncomfortably aware of the eyes that turned in her direction, but the ones she sought across the width of the hall were turned away from her, and she could not deny the disappointment she felt when Brettan chose to ignore her arrival. Standing closest to the landing, Sir Bothwell separated from the group of knights and extended his hand to her. Heartened by the genuine warmth she saw in his smile, Maren accepted his arm and joined the procession, as each knight and then their hosts followed the king to the waiting tables. Each guest then imitated the king's gesture and took his chair for the evening meal. Bowing low before her, Sir Bothwell delivered Maren to her appointed chair across from Lady Kennerley. At some unseen signal from their hostess, an unending procession of servants emerged from the kitchens, each bearing some part of the sumptuous fare to be laid before them. Through the long hours of the meal, Brettan remained silent beside her but, while the evening progressed, some small conversation between them was unavoidable. Maren nervously tipped her wine goblet, and his strong hand steadied the teetering vessel, his lean, warm fingers closing over her hand, that one brief contact sending a river of molten heat charging through her. As if she had touched a flame, she drew her hand back, her uncertain gaze meeting his for a brief moment, causing her to wonder if he might have felt the heat of that contact, or if it was merely her imagination or perhaps the effects of the wine. With great restraint Maren forced herself to ignore his presence, fervently wishing the evening were at an end. Remaining at the long table only until the many fine pies and puddings had been brought forth, Maren rose abruptly and, begging the king's indulgence, retired to her chamber, unaware of the questioning glances exchanged by Brettan and the king.

Lady Kennerley rose to give assistance to the girl but found herself gently restrained by her husband, who glanced knowingly toward the Duke of Norfolk. Yielding to his wishes in the matter, Lady Kennerley called for the servants to replenish the empty goblets

271

about the table.

Once inside her chamber, Maren collapsed in the chair before the hearth. Not waiting for Mary or any of the other servants, she unbound the heavy braids of hair, shaking the dark mane loose about her shoulders, then unfastened the closures of the gown. Setting the gown aside, and clothed only in the thin chemise, Maren doused the one single taper on the table beside the large bed and slipped beneath the coverlet, that she might find some comfort in sleep.

Unable to find any comfort or sleep upon his soldier's pallet many hours later, Brettan retreated to the upstairs chamber for those few remaining hours before dawn. He sat quietly before the hearthstone, warmed by the dying fire. In the darkness of the chamber, broken only by a single shaft of moonlight that penetrated the windows set ajar to catch a breath of cool air, Brettan stared through the darkness, keeping his silent vigil over the slender girl who unwittingly occupied his thoughts. The silken skin that covered the gently curving column of her throat glowed softly in that shaft of light, and he watched the slow pulsing just beneath the skin. She stirred in sleep, turning over so that the exquisite line of her face was turned gently toward him, and Brettan's breathing became labored. He fought to maintain control and refrain from reaching out to gently caress the velvet softness of her arm, outstretched across the expanse of the bed that he should have shared with her. Brettan sipped of the wine, watching her in sleep, remembering when first he had seen her at Cambria, in the midst of the death and destruction after the attack. She had appeared to be nothing more than a servant returning to find her master's hall in ruins, but beneath the rough woolen mantle he had seen her beauty, so innocent, so fearful, and yet so brave in the midst of death. But more than her

272

beauty, Brettan had been held captive by the unusual color of her eyes, a brilliant blue that seemed the color of priceless sapphires.

Maren stirred again, her peaceful slumber broken by the anguish of the nightmares returned to haunt her, again reliving those last days at Cambria. Her lips moved in silent pleading for the torment to end, and her head tossed back and forth, seeking to rid herself of memories that were too painful. She sank into the deep chasm of her tortured sadness and flung out an arm, as if to push back some unseen danger.

Brettan came silently to his feet, quickly reaching the side of the bed. Remembering her steadfast vow to hold herself from him at all cost, Brettan hesitated for a moment, not wishing to repeat their confrontation of earlier in the day, and yet when he watched her tormented sleep, a deep anguish grew within him, so that above all else he could not bear to see such sadness. Setting the goblet aside, he carefully sat down on the bed beside her and gently took her into his arms, brushing aside the tangled mass of her hair and laying her head against his well-muscled shoulder. In the dark torment of her dreams, she feebly pushed away that restraint that closed about her but, once his warmth flooded through her, soothing, calming with his touch, she relaxed, snuggling more closely into his embrace. Carefully Brettan lay beside her, not daring to remove his tunic and breeches lest he awaken her and risk this tenuous peace between them. Tenderly he caressed the black hair that spread across the bed beneath his other arm, drawing her slender form more closely against his side, that his strength alone might drive away the demons that haunted her.

Maren drifted, aware only of the warmth that surrounded her, and she curled toward that warmth,

273

attempting to feel it all about her, keeping her safe at last. And in those last moments before she drifted into peaceful slumber once again, she rubbed her cheek against the soft mat of hair on Brettan's chest, where the neck of the tunic was unlaced, all her anger and defiance no match for her desperate desire of him. Golden green eyes of the lion glowed brightly through the darkness of the chamber. Brettan remained watchful, and then at last he too slept for a time, before rising so that he might be gone before she awakened to find he had broken his own promise to her, even if that promise had been spoken in anger.

In the first light of the new morning Brettan slipped from her side, content for the time just to have shared that closeness with her. Silently he left the chamber to attend to the details of their departure. He pushed aside his uncertainty of the days that lay ahead, yet could not rid himself of a growing uneasiness that some unseen danger awaited, which might yet take her from him. He belted the heavy broadsword to his side and he descended the stairway, contemplating the slender girl who slept on undisturbed, and the vows that had been spoken between them. What was the full meaning of such vows, that a man should be forever vulnerable to his own emotions, that a slender, young girl might deliver him to his fate as several armies had never done? Brettan shook the mane of auburn hair about his head, as if to shake off his growing doubts. His thoughts warmed when he recalled the sight of her, the feel, the scent of her softness against him. No, he thought, such beauty, such pride and spirit were to be protected and valued like the finest weapons a man might carry, and always keep by his side. Silently he vowed that someday she would come willingly to his side. None too gently he awakened his guard, roughly nudging Sandlin awake with the toe of his boot, amazed at the fatigue of his knights after several hours' rest, when he himself felt clear-headed. He continued down the long line of the garrison, roughly waking his men, dispensing his orders for the day, unaware of the curious stares that followed his lean shadow. The first light of day broke over the top of the walled fortress, dazzlingly bright and warm with the glow of the new season.

Chapter Thirteen

London was more than Maren could have ever imagined. She was filled with excitement at the thought of seeing the large town that was home to King Edward, and relief that their journey was at last ended.

The five-day journey had lengthened to eight before they crossed St. James bridge and entered the city. The last spring storm delayed their journey, rain having turned the road into an impassable river of mud, forcing them to take refuge in one of several roadside inns which marked their passage. When the skies had at last cleared, the sun had emerged to dry the road, and the unbearable heat of early summer had set upon them with a vengeance to add to Maren's discomfort on the tiring journey. She greatly welcomed their arrival that afternoon late in May, her only wish for a bath, that she might wash the dirt and grime of the road from her body, and then a soft bed on which to lie, for she felt as if she might sleep for days.

The last golden light of day mingled with the gray of smoke from a multitude of hearth fires, creating a haze across the skyline, much like a blanket over the town. At last their long procession reached the castle. The whole of London beyond, the cathedrals and Westminster Abbey, would wait till the morrow for her to view them.

King Edward returned to a joyous welcome after many months of absence, and it seemed all of London had turned out to welcome its king. The vast storefronts and shops had closed their doors for the remainder of the day. The townspeople, hoping to view the royal procession, flooded into every street and lane that marked the passage to the castle.

On each side of her, Brettan's guard was sorely pressed to hold back the throngs of well-wishers massed along each side of the streets, straining for a glimpse of the king and his knights returned from the north of Wales. Ahead of her, just behind his king, Maren saw the broad-shouldered form of Brettan de Lorin, and keenly wished he had chosen to ride beside her on this final length of their journey. Beside her Sandlin flashed her an encouraging smile, as if he knew of the doubts that flooded her thoughts. Uncertain of what lay ahead, Maren could only manage the weakest of smiles in return.

When their procession had reached a widening in the street, leading to a vast park that stretched as far as the eye might see, then circling back to surround the great castle, a sudden surge in the crowd pressed the guard back, and Maren found herself sorely pressed to control her nervous mare. All about them a multitude of torches flamed brightly, adding to the animal's uneasy spirit. She twisted the reins firmly in her hand but checked the mare a moment too late, for she felt the bit firmly seized in the mare's teeth, the black sidestepping, her eyes rolling wildly, the noise of the crowd unbearable. Maren glanced about for some aid from Sandlin but found that a portion of the crowd now separated her from the knight. When the mare began to stumble and then scrambled to regain her footing on the cobblestones, Maren found herself suddenly unseated.

She felt herself quickly seized about the waist and hauled upwards, the hood of her mantle falling back when her head was jerked back by the sudden movement. Startled blue eyes met emerald green, and Brettan held her firmly against his side, her slender body dangling against the mighty gray stallion, which Brettan easily controlled with the reins loosely held in one hand. "Welcome to London town, milady."

It was the most he had chosen to say to her in days since leaving Monmouth, and Maren was suddenly grateful that he had not forgotten her presence completely, for she sorely doubted that she could have controlled the mare in the press of the crowded streets.

She was unaware of her striking beauty in the light of the thousand torches that glowed brightly about them, the flickering flames from those glowing beacons dancing wildly in the depths of her sapphire gaze. Brettan's pulse raced at that contact with her, the first in many days that he had allowed himself.

"Do you approve of the welcome I have arranged for your arrival to my fair town?" The tone of his voice was slightly mocking, and Maren refused to be baited into another argument with him.

"Whether I approve or not is of little consequence. The people have hardly turned out in greeting of me, but of their king. And I am certain you have had little to do with the matter. Now if you please, milord, kindly return me to my horse, that we may continue."

"It does not please me, Maren. I had almost forgotten how the very touch of you warms my blood. No, the air has been cold these last days, and nights. For now I choose to keep you with me. And you, milady, have no say in the matter. I shall release you in good time but, for now, I do not think you would wish to cause a scene before the king and his loyal subjects." A confident smile spread across his handsome face, causing the dimples in the line of his cheeks to appear, making her ache to reach out, that she might gently touch his face. Maren ground her teeth in vexation at his high humor. She was tired and hungry, and scared of what awaited her, in no mood for his lighthearted jesting.

Seeing the weary droop of her slender shoulder, Brettan drew her across the front of his saddle, settling her in front of him while he shouted an order over his shoulder for Sandlin to secure the black mare.

"Will we stay at the castle?"

"Ay, though judging by the progress we have made, it shall be the better part of an hour before we arrive. It seems the people of London are pleased to see our return. Had you thought that I might cast you into some dark dungeon upon our arrival, milady?" Brettan questioned, a slight smile playing across his lips.

"In truth, milord, I am not certain what my fate shall be," Maren sighed wearily against his shoulder.

"If you are too weary, I know of a nearby inn, where we might rest before joining the king," Brettan suggested conspiratorially.

"I fear, milord, there might be more danger in a simple wayside inn than at court. I shall prefer the castle," Maren retorted caustically.

"Ah, but my lovely Maren, you know not what danger might await you there."

"In truth, milord, what more dangers might there be that I have not already endured? I can think of none." Maren replied saucily, turning her head away from his lingering gaze, lest he know of the uncertainty that indeed filled her thoughts at their arrival in London. Gently he drew her back against his armored chest, the soft velvet of his tabard cushioning her cheek from the cold chain mail. Brettan's strong arm closed around her, holding her firmly against him, the gentle motion of the

280

stallion lulling her into fitful slumber. It might have been only for a moment that she had closed her eyes, when she felt the warmth of Brettan's hand gently stirring her from sleep. Mumbling her protests, Maren resisted for a moment, then came fully awake, feeling the touch of his warm lips against her temple gently rousing her.

They had arrived at the castle.

The massive gates had been thrown wide in anticipation of their arrival. Edward dismounted and handed his steel helm and sword to a page. A young woman separated from the group gathered at the top of the steps and eagerly descended to greet the warrior king. Queen Eleanore was hardly older than Maren, and her youthful eagerness shone brightly upon her fair face when she greeted her husband. Their welcoming of each other was a brief moment. They touched hands, the young queen bowing slightly before the king, he in turn quickly pulling her to stand beside him, his arm closing about her slender waist, their unspoken words communicated in a single gesture. Yet Maren was aware that any further greeting was discreetly delayed for those moments when they would, for a time, close out the rest of the world and be like any other man and woman, separated so long and now reunited. Maren glanced shyly away from the scene, having witnessed a very private moment, meant to be shared only by Edward and his queen. She felt the calming strength of Brettan's arm about her waist, silently grateful for the anxious crowd that had forced a temporary truce to their silent war.

In the next moment, Edward was very much the king, greeting the archbishop and his ministers and advisors. Brettan's personal guard remained mounted, awaiting his orders. When he dismounted and then drew Maren from the saddle in front of him, they also dismounted. A multitude of pages and servants swarmed about them, leading the horses to the stables for grain and rest after

281

the long journey.

From the top of the steps, Edward extended his hand to Maren, speaking to the queen. "May I present the Lady Maren, late of Cambria, South Wales, now Duchess of Norfolk." It was a personal gesture, and the meaning of kindness and honest welcome was not lost on Maren, who returned the queen's steady gaze. The momentary lifting of a regal brow was unmistakable, for the young queen made no effort to conceal her pleasant surprise at the title Maren bore, as the wife of the Duke of Norfolk.

"It would seem there is much news I have to hear of the months past, which have kept my husband long from London. But come, there shall be time enough to hear all of it, once you are made comfortable after so long a journey." Her tone was openly gracious, and Maren somehow felt a kindred spirit to the young queen who had greeted her with such warmth.

The large chamber Maren occupied was richly decorated with ornate tapestries and several large chairs, which formed a small half circle before the massive stone hearth, which blazed warmly with the fire laid for their arrival. At one end of the chamber was a massive bed, luxuriously draped with hangings of heavy velvet, richly bordered with woven gold braid that fell loosely in braided loops along the entire border of the hangings, drawn back to admit the warmth of the fire. A thick coverlet of the same velvet covered the bed. Maren sank back wearily in a tub of steaming water and let the warmth ease from her muscles the ache of many days on the back of a horse. A young maid entered the chamber and laid out a gown for her first evening at the English court. The young girl, whose name was Sada, informed her that Brettan had already dressed for the occasion in another chamber and awaited her presence.

Maren felt a twinge of disappointment that Brettan had taken a chamber separate from hers, but clearly remembered he had declared his intentions that he would not require her wifely obligations. Sadly she realized that she might have lost more than she gained in her hollow victory. Somehow she had thought his mood to her might have softened, for he had obviously been concerned for her safety during the confusion in the streets beyond the castle. Did he now regret the momentary truce between them, since he was about to be reunited with his mistress? Unable to understand the range of her emotions, Maren angrily tossed a soap-filled cloth at the water in the tub, her mood sullen, tears threatening at the corners of her eyes. She avoided the questioning stare of the young maid and bent her head back to rinse the lather from the long heavy mass of her hair. Pulling the thick tresses over her shoulder, she squeezed the last bit of water from them and then stood to accept the linen the girl draped about her. The hour passed, the time for the evening meal grew closer, and Maren's mood darkened. Sada worked laboriously over the thick, raven-black hair, combing it tirelessly before the heat of the fire. It waved wantonly about Maren's shoulders as it dried, a rich dark mane of vibrant glowing lights that floated about her like a cloud. The girl repeatedly praised the glowing mass, but her words were lost on Maren, who sat before the hearth troubled by the demons of her own doubts and fears.

"Milady, I have never seen such hair. The color is like none I have seen. You certainly will be greatly admired at court."

Startled from her thoughts, Maren smiled wanly at the girl, who could hardly have been any older than herself.

"If you are greatly fatigued from the journey, you may have a tray brought to your chamber for the evening meal. The queen sent word that you would not be required at court."

Maren glanced uneasily at the young girl, trying to

read something in her words. Was Brettan so eager for his mistress that he chose to keep her closed within the chamber? Did he dread a confrontation between the two women, or was she now to be considered a royal prisoner, with these fine rich walls to keep her in London? A spark of defiance glinted in wide blue eyes, and she sprang to her feet in sudden decision. If Brettan sought to keep her prisoner, he might possibly find her unwilling to play such games.

"Sada, I shall join the Duke of Norfolk and their majesties for the evening meal. I think perhaps the gray velvet with the blue satin trim would do nicely. And in the bottom of that coffer you will find a piece of blue velvet rolled tightly. Please bring it to me."

A page announced the call to the evening meal, and Maren emerged from her chamber, resplendently dressed in the gray velvet that had been her wedding gown. The rich blue satin that decorated the sleeve edges and the neckline matched to perfection the brilliant blue sapphires of the large pendant she wore about her neck, their brilliance lessened only by the blue of her large eyes set within the perfect oval of her face, her skin glowing with a faint blush of anticipation that set her nerves tingling along the length of her back. If she was to be presented to the English court and Brettan's mistress, then she would do so proudly, defiantly, and with a courage born of her Welsh ancestors. She deliberately left the mass of her raven hair loose about her shoulders and waist, fully aware of the striking contrast she would cause at the English court to the pale ladies who were rumored to wear their hair tightly bound and covered. Maren clenched her hands tightly together, gathering her strength for the moments to come. She felt the heavy bulk of Brettan's ring upon her finger and oddly felt no fear of the lion ornately raised in the gold, nor the bold lion who had given it to her. Nodding to the young maid, Maren swept through the wide doors and followed the page to the dining hall beyond.

Her confidence knew a moment's hesitation when another page announced her arrival, and Maren silently panicked at her lack of knowledge of protocol in these matters. Mentally she forced herself into control, realizing she could hardly turn and retreat. It seemed as if a thousand eyes had turned in her direction, but across the multitude of curious and openly envious stares she saw only one gaze, and those golden glowing eyes renewed her confidence in her decision, for she saw the warmth of Brettan's regard. But it was Edward who separated from his knights and approached her. "It would seem, milady, that my judgment has been most accurate. You have this night defeated every stout English heart. The victory is yours, though I warrant you shall be the subject of all conversations at my court. Do you feel up to it?"

"Most certainly, Your Majesty. I think there is nothing to fear in the court of an English king that I have not already faced in the camp of an errant knight."

"You must forgive my good knight, milady. I fear he might not have been of clear thought in the matter. For in truth, if you appeared to him as you now appear before my court, I am certain he was quite beyond all good reason."

Maren smiled up at the tall man who led her to his own table, unable to resist his good humor. "Then, milord, you must hear of our first meeting, and it might indeed give you a moment's thought as to the preferences of your knight."

"Milady, I have no doubts as to the preferences of my knights. And now I think it best that I should surrender you to your husband, lest he think our conversation on other topics. For though it might be my right as his king to exercise such privilege, I should think better of it before such a worthy opponent."

"Do you then fear your knight, milord?" Maren questioned, a gentle smile teasing at the edge of her lips.

"In truth, milady, I fear no man. But the knights of the realm are the finest and strongest in all Christendom. I should not care to question one of them in affairs of the heart, particularly after they have been afar from England these many months past."

"If you will forgive me, milord, it would seem to have little consequence that they are far from England. Indeed, the knights of Edward of England seem quite adept at turning adversity into advantage."

"Milady, do you fear the English? In truth, I thought you to be without fear."

Maren gazed questioningly at the king, trying to understand the meaning behind his words. "I am Welsh, among a multitude of English, milord. Do you think that there is no one I should fear?"

"What words might I give you, milady, to make you see that you need have no fear of me or those of my court? You have great courage and pride. There are few who could have accepted the events of the last weeks with honor and dignity. You grace my court, Maren, and I value your presence. I pray you will accept our friendship." His words were gently spoken, so that no others would hear, and in them Maren found strength. Ceremoniously, Edward delivered her to Brettan's side, gently placing her hand over her husband's arm. "Guard well the treasures you possess, my friend, for there are those who would seek to take them from you."

Brettan bowed his head before his king, an odd expression on his face, then turned back to stare at Maren, who stood silently wondering at their exchange.

She glowed warmly under his lingering perusal, feeling his approval at the sight of the medallion about her neck.

She glanced away, suddenly at a loss to understand the emotions that flowed through her.

Through the long hours of the evening, Brettan remained by her side, never venturing further than a few feet away, as if he sought to protect her. Had she been aware of the cold, menacing stare directed at her from across the room, Maren might have felt less confidence her first night at court.

That feral gaze was not lost to Brettan, who bowed his head in stiff acknowledgment at the flaxen-haired woman who remained aloof, coolly waiting for the time when she might approach him. The final course of the meal was cleared by the royal servants, and the king and his queen rose to lead the way to the gardens that adjoined the dining hall, there to partake of the evening air and the entertainment provided for the lords and ladies of the court.

The fair-haired lady watched the Duke of Norfolk with a covetous glance from across the dining hall, and wasted no time in sweeping across the room, coming to a grand halt before Brettan, her hazel brown eyes staring unwaveringly into his golden green gaze. Intimately, she reached out a pale, slender hand to his arm, at the same time leaning close into his shoulder, the soft rounding curve of her bosom brushing against the velvet of his tunic.

"Brettan, my darling, you have chosen to ignore me this entire evening, when you are just returned after so much time. Do you seek to punish me for some quarrel I cannot, in good faith, remember?" With deliberate skill, she positioned herself between Brettan and Maren, her intentions bold and completely shameless, before the entire court. With obvious familiarity she traced the line of Brettan's hand with her fingers, leaving little doubt of her relationship with Brettan in the minds of those who watched, somewhat embarrassed.

Maren watched the exchange, stunned at the woman's

bold display before the king and, gazing into those light brown eyes, she immediately recognized the open challenge being thrown at her. Caught unprepared by the woman's wantonness, Maren hastily averted her gaze, unable to continue watching the performance that she was certain was for her benefit alone. Without formal introduction, Maren could have little doubt that she had just confronted Brettan's mistress. Her startled blue gaze traveled to his lean face, and she noted the slight coloration beneath the bronze of his cheek. The thin white of the scar suddenly seemed more obvious, and she was surprised to find that he seemed embarrassed by the woman's attentions. With great force of will, Maren fought back the constricting tightness she felt in her chest, as if a band of steel had suddenly been drawn unbearably tight about her, making it impossible for her to draw a full breath. Yet she summoned her courage and was the first to break the unbearable silence that had descended upon them, keenly aware that they had become the center of attention at Edward's court. "You have not made the introductions, milord." Maren's voice was surprisingly calm, and she returned the pale-haired woman's gaze unfalteringly. From behind her she heard Sir Bothwell's nervous coughing.

Brettan's voice came firm and with a clarity she had not expected, while he calmly withdrew his arm from the young woman's clinging grasp.

"Milady, may I present Lady Caroline of Blanding, second cousin to the Earl of Warwick and Gloucester." Brettan inhaled deeply, as if bracing himself for the impending storm, then reached out and calmly took Maren's slender hand in his own. "Lady Caroline, may I present the Lady Maren, late of Cambria, now Duchess of Norfolk, and my wife." The last words had a stinging effect, and the look of complete shock that spread across Lady Caroline's pale complexion was unmistakable. At last she realized the truth of his words, and a flush crept into those pale cheeks, her anger rising like a crimson wave, pushing aside all caution. She whirled upon the dark-haired beauty Brettan held possessively at his side. "It would seem that the rumors that preceded your arrival are well founded. How very amusing, Brettan, that you should take the girl to wife, though she hardly seems more than a child. Though I am certain, my beloved, that you had little choice in the matter, for it is well known that the decision was made for you by our king. I do not object to your seeking some pleasure when you are forced to journey afar, but is not marriage pressing the matter too far, my darling? That is, of course, unless the girl has forced you to the marriage by getting herself caught with child. But I shall forgive you in this, since it was not of your choice, and I assure you I would most gladly accept any child she might breed." Boldly she turned to Maren, her gaze raking Maren's slender frame, as if she sought some reassurance that such was not the situation. "You must beware, Brettan, that although Edward might extend his hospitality to her, there are others perhaps not so tolerant. She is Welsh, and there are those who have lost dearly in this war Edward wages against the Welsh prince Llywelyn, and might not look favorably upon her presence. But there are always solutions to these inconveniences, are there not, my love? If Edward seeks merely to hold her in England, I know of a secluded country estate where she might be accepted and safely guarded."

Maren stirred uncomfortably beneath the woman's assault. She had not thought that Brettan's mistress would so openly attack her, for that was all this could be considered. Nor could she hope that Brettan would take up her defense in the matter. Indeed, he had plainly said that he would continue as before with his mistress when he returned to London. Fool that she was, she had dared to hope, if but for a moment, that he might honor their sacred vows spoken before the priest at Monmouth. Coldly she reminded herself that his purpose in the marriage was plain. He had obeyed his king, in attempting to right a wrong against her and her family. Lady Caroline could hardly know how close she had come to the complete truth. Maren inhaled deeply, raising her clear blue eyes to stare at Brettan for a moment, the brilliance of those dazzling orbs penetrating, challenging, yet almost forbidding. "Milord, I would beg your indulgence. The journey has been long, and in truth I find the evening, and the company, quite tiresome. Please make my apologies to His Majesty." Not waiting for any acknowledgement, she whirled about, her steps firm and strong as she swept from the hall before the astonished stares of the entire court. She strode from the large hall, her one thought being that she would have given anything to flee the castle, to find her horse, and to leave London, nay, leave England, where none might take up the sword of vengeance against her at every turn. But she knew well, any effort to leave would have been halted by guards who remained constantly vigilant.

Once alone in her chamber, Maren slumped wearily before the blazing hearth. So great was her fatigue that she was only vaguely aware of the young maid who entered to assist her in dressing for bed. Like a child, Maren meekly submitted, all her stubborn will and defiance flown before her weary spirit. The velvet gown was unfastened and fell to her feet. Obediently she stepped from the gown, wearing only the thin chemise, and slipped beneath the coverlet. The last candle was snuffed, and the room bathed in the soft glow of the fire that burned at the hearth, while the maid closed the chamber door softly behind her.

Maren lay on the soft bed, sobbing uncontrollably into the pillow, so great was her misery. What indeed was her ate to be, now that she was in London? She had seen the venomous hatred barely concealed behind those amber eyes, and knew beyond all doubt that Lady Caroline would never be satisfied until she had driven Maren out of Brettan's life. Little could Lady Caroline know that she had come so very near the truth. And the complete irony was that Maren wished for nothing more than to be released from the marriage. Brettan de Lorin embodied all that she feared and hated. She gave herself completely to her misery, though, knowing the falseness of those thoughts. How she wished for the stark beauty of Cambria, for her family, that she might once again feel safe and protected. She was weary of constant battles of will. Why could he not have released her? It seemed obvious where his true feelings lay. Had he not told her that, once returned to London, he would continue his life as before? It mattered little to him that she was his wife, nor could she have expected anything more of him. Maren's misery was complete and, when her tears were spent and her fatigue at last moved over her, she drifted into uneasy slumber.

Brettan made no attempt to halt Maren's flight from the dining hall. Knowing well her pride and spirit, he could have expected no less than the confrontation he had just witnessed, and he wondered again at the wisdom of the decision to bring her to London. Silently he cursed his foolishness in subjecting her to Caroline's vindictive wrath. Knowing his mistress as he did, he could well guess the extent of her anger. He had sent word of the marriage days in advance to ease the shock of their arrival, yet Caroline's confrontation with Maren had been deliberate and well-planned and, at that moment, he fought a deep longing to strike the arrogant smirk from her face. Though Caroline was considered a beauty by the

291

standards of the English court, he had noticed earlier in the evening, perhaps for the first time, that her beauty was artful and practiced, as were her mannerisms, as if she played a part rather than herself. That realization plagued him the entire evening, and the fact that he should suddenly be aware of it, when he had failed to notice it before. It could well have been that too many of their moments together had been in darkened chambers, for indeed he had taken his pleasure with her often. But of late he had chosen to spend more of his hours in the company of his men, yielding to the duties of his station almost eagerly.

Lady Caroline perhaps received the greatest surprise from the little game she had played. Her irritation mounting, she stared at Brettan's back, while he gazed after the fleeing figure of his wife. The rumors had brought word of the arranged marriage. Indeed, Brettan's own message had made no pretense of Edward's hand in the matter. There had been some mention that the girl was titled, and that the marriage would bring a strong alliance between England and Wales. But Caroline was not deceived. This was more than the alliance of two prominent families to ease the unification of England and Wales, and Caroline silently wondered how close she might have strayed to the truth, contemplating the possibility of a child. With her Brettan had always remained elusive to marriage bonds, choosing to maintain their relationship as it was with no ties to bind, insisting that his bond of loyalty was only to the crown. Her anger abated some small measure, for she found some humor that the young girl with ebony black hair worn in a most heathen way, loose about her shoulders, could have so well attained what she had failed at. In the back of her thoughts, though, remained the firm belief that Brettan would soon tire of the marriage, and again find his way to her good graces, as well as her bed. Her greatest loss, though, was the title Duchess of Norfolk and the wealth that it carried. There were, however, always means by which to obtain that lofty title still. Her first husband's death had left her with vast estates and sizeable wealth, but her lavish tastes and excesses had soon greatly diminished her coin, so that she fervently sought that marriage which would grant her great power, wealth, and the most eligible if arrogant knight in Edward's realm. Caroline's eyes narrowed watching that departing figure, and she could not deny the pangs of jealousy that tore at her composure, for the girl was of uncommon beauty, and Caroline knew of a certainty that, whether Brettan would have acknowledged it or not, the look on his face while he stared after her told more than any words his feeling for the girl. Caroline would have given a great deal to have received that look, which had never been offered her.

With her most brilliant smile upon her lips, Caroline turned to Brettan, entwining a graceful arm through his, attempting to draw his attention back to the evening, completely aware of the attention she had drawn at Edward's court.

"Brettan, my darling, the evening is new, let us share some wine, and you may tell me of this absurd marriage. My heart aches for the time you have been gone, and now to learn of this foolishness! Indeed, it is beyond me, but I am of good faith that the matter may soon be set aright."

Brettan turned on Caroline with strained patience and set her from him, gently but firmly removing her hand from his arm. "Though I have long decried the marriage vows, Caroline, I find that, so like other vows I have made, they cannot easily be set aside. I shall abide by those simple words spoken before the priest. I intend to honor the marriage."

Caroline stared at him incredulously. "You cannot mean this. She is Welsh, she is our enemy. Or is there perhaps some other reason for your loyalty?"

"There is naught that you do not already know, Caroline, or shall soon learn, for I have every faith in your abilities to know all that takes place at Edward's court. But know this now, the marriage is made, Caroline, and I am honor-bound to remain true to the vows I have spoken."

"Brettan, do not be hasty. With all that we have shared, you cannot so easily cast our love aside."

"Caroline, what we have shared is no more than a common need. In truth, I do not know what love might be. Perhaps it is nothing more than the loyalty a man offers his king. As to what a man might feel for a woman, I have not yet seen anything I could, in all honesty, call love. I have no desire to cause you pain, Caroline, but I will honor my pledge." Gently he unfastened her fingers from the velvet of his tunic, by which she sought to restrain him. Brettan strode from the hall, halting before Edward and the queen to exchange a few words, and then continued through the large doors.

Caroline fought back the anger that threatened to overcome her. There would be other opportunities to press her cause with him, and she knew far better than the young Welsh girl what pleasures he enjoyed. Amber eyes glowed dangerously, staring at the spot where Brettan had disappeared through the doors, and she silently vowed vengeance on that one who now called herself Duchess of Norfolk, for the girl would have no peace for the treachery she had dared.

Within his own chamber, Brettan paced the length of the ornately furnished room, considering the evening. He had fully expected much worse from Caroline, for he knew her capable of great anger, far more than she had shown. But it was the look in Maren's eyes that had torn at him. She was completely vulnerable, defenseless, in a strange land where she had no desire to be, caught in a marriage she had not chosen or consented to, and with a man, he knew well, whom she considered to be her enemy. There was within him a need to go to her, to comfort the pain and fear he had seen on her face. He stared at the door that separated them and, crossing the chamber, reached for the latch, for a moment daring to hope that something other than anger might greet him beyond that portal. But knowing the resistance of the past, his hand dropped wearily to his side. May the devil take her treacherous soul, and he would be well rid of the bothersome wench. Yet even when he would have hardened his heart to her, he could not force the vision of her exquisite beauty from his thoughts. Retiring to his solitary bed, Brettan attempted sleep, but remained fully awake and restless, the thought of her silken skin and raven-black hair tormenting him. What if he had chosen to awaken her? What might her reaction have been? He could well guess, by her performance in the past. These many days since Monmouth, he had remained true to his vow not to press the cause of the marriage, and sorely cursed his own foolishness for such a promise. His only recourse had been to assume that she found the arrangement quite acceptable, leaving him to await their arrival in London, where he might seek his pleasure with his mistress, and yet strangely, all thoughts of Caroline only increased his aggravation, when he recalled her attempts to lure him to her bed. It seemed strange to him that he had not noticed before how easily she affected the mannerisms of lover, as if she had had a great deal of practice in such matters. And, if rumors were to be believed, there had been an endless number of lovers through the years, both during and after her marriage to the Earl of Blanding. He was greatly surprised that the knowledge of her infidelities now mattered little to him. Now his thoughts were crowded with visions of the gentle maid who slept in the adjoining chamber, all recollection of Caroline fading before the memory of eyes the color of brilliant sapphires that sparkled and glowed in the soft oval of her face, as fair and perfect as fine polished stone. He sighed heavily, closing his eyes and settling back against the thick softness of his lonely bed, aware of the emptiness without her slender weight beside his, molding into the side of his body.

Waking from restless slumber, Maren sat up in the middle of the large bed and shivered in the dark coldness that surrounded her. Her senses cleared, and she remembered her arrival in London and the past evening. A damp chill gripped the room, even in the first weeks of summer, for the fire at the hearth had died to little more than a few last embers. Moving to the edge of the large bed, Maren gathered the thin coverlet about her shivering body, searching in the darkness for a candle. She moved uncertainly across the width of the chamber, her bare feet meeting the coldness of the flooring, at last feeling the heavy stones of the hearth. Reaching out to locate the twigs and small branches of wood laid aside to rekindle the fire, Maren tripped over the edge of the coverlet, falling heavily against the hearth, bruising her knee and at the same time knocking over the heavy iron poker set at the corner of the hearth. In the silence of the chamber, the poker made a loud clattering noise, falling first against the flat stones of the hearth and then rolling onto the flooring at her feet. Tears of frustration and pain filled her eyes while she bent to rub the bruised member. In the next moment, the heavy door to the adjoining chamber was thrown open. Maren's head shot up at the sound, her gaze filled with the vision of Brettan's naked body, filling the doorway. The sight of his well-muscled body, outlined in the doorway by the soft glow of the fire in his chamber, startled her. The heavy broadsword was clutched tightly in his hand, the soft furring of his chest which tapered below his waist making a soft glow about him. "Maren, are you alright?"

"Yes." Maren's teeth chattered loudly, and she fought back the tears that threatened. Vainly she tried to reach a high-backed chair beside the hearth, the bruised knee giving way when she tried to put her weight upon it. Brettan was beside her in an instant. One arm went around her slender waist, while his other hand took hers, and he led her to the chair.

"What were you thinking, to be wandering about in the middle of the night?" he scolded her gently.

"The fire had died, and the room had grown cold. I but sought to rekindle the fire."

In the glow of light from the doorway, Brettan located the lost candle and set it beside the hearth. Reaching for some of the smaller twigs and branches, he rebuilt the fire and, blowing gently upon the glowing embers, slowly brought it back to life, the first tentative flames spreading upward through the newly laid wood. While the fire spread its uncertain warmth into the room, the golden glow of the flames drove back the shadows and cast a soft light across Brettan's well-muscled shoulders and back, bent before the hearth. Maren averted her gaze, suddenly aware that she stared at a completely naked man, even though he was quite magnificent. The color spread across her cheeks at seeing him so boldly displayed without the slightest embarrassment, and that helped warm her chilled body.

Turning back from the fire that danced brightly, Brettan lifted the edge of the coverlet and without any hesitation felt to examine her knee, his warm fingers carefully feeling for any broken bones. "You are as cold as ice. Having been born in a land known for its colder climes, I should think you would know better than to wander about dressed as you are."

"I should think, milord, that might better be said of you," Maren replied saucily, her brilliant blue eyes raking the length of his naked body, and for a moment all else about them ceased to exist. She felt a heat that came not from the fire, but from those glowing, green eyes, while his gaze held hers. His lean, strong fingers gently probed the bones of her leg and the curve of her knee. Maren pulled back abruptly when his fingers pressed against the bruise, her leg not yet healed from her earlier fall. Tears welled in her eyes when he found the spot where a dark, purplish mark swelled painfully against the bone.

"Can you not leave me alone? Have you not already caused me enough pain?"

Still holding her leg firmly within his strong grasp, Brettan raised his gaze to stare into her eyes. "I do not seek to cause you pain, Maren. Indeed, I have never sought that end." His voice was barely more than a soft whisper, as he leaned over her.

All her fears and doubts of the last days, and the pain of her meeting with Lady Caroline, had left her angry and vulnerable. "Can you tell me what you have not done to hurt me?" Her temper flaring, Maren tried to jerk her leg from his grasp, but found his quiet strength tightened painfully about her leg. With no small discomfort to her bruised knee, Maren succeeded in pulling herself free. Lunging to her feet, she tried to move away from the heat of his naked presence.

"What is it that you want of me, that you make me your prisoner and then drag me across the whole of Wales? What monstrous deed is it you think me guilty of, that you now subject me to this marriage, which is the worst of all possible lies? You have held me captive under threat of death. You have taken me against my will, taking from me the one virtue that I might call my own, and now you bind me to you with false vows and lies as your wife. Release me from this marriage! Allow me to return to my family," Maren cried, whirling on him.

"Above all, Maren, you seem to suffer the least. Truth you speak when you say I took you my prisoner, but only after you spoke your lies and attempted to wound me with my own blade. And yea, I have bound you to me with the marriage vows, in part, as I have said, to keep you near me. I took your virtue, but who would condemn a man who but yielded to the passions stirred by one so beautiful, whose memory haunted me, whose every move, every glance seemed to beckon to that end?"

"Beckoned?" Maren stared at him incredulously. Her anger flared past all reason, and she drew back her hand and would have delivered a stinging blow had Brettan not caught her wrist securely in his hand, his fingers like bands of steel, restraining her with ease. Maren struggled against him, the coverlet falling to the flooring. "Release me. Go seek your mistress. I am certain you will find her far more willing than I."

"Maren, stop this before you cause yourself further injury." With effortless strength Brettan drew her against him, to stop her struggling.

The contact of his naked chest through the thin chemise seemed to brand her where they touched, her breasts were crushed against that hard, muscled expanse. She was startled by the warmth of his body molded against her own, and her struggling ceased. She stared wide-eyed into that bronzed visage that towered over her.

"Release me." She pleaded softly, feeling her strength no match for his.

"I cannot, though that might be what you truly desire. I cannot."

"Milord—"

"I have a name, Maren, and I would hear it from your lips." His lean, muscular arm encircled her gently but firmly, bearing her slender weight against him, so that it

299

was impossible for her to escape the heat of that embrace. In silent torment, Maren closed her eyes against the prying heat of that glowing gaze, which seemed capable of looking into her very soul. Could he possibly know how many times his name had filled her thoughts?

"Say it!" he commanded her, his voice gentle but raw with emotion. He held her securely against him, only the thin chemise separating their bodies from that most intimate contact.

When his name fell from her lips, she sobbed her silent agony at the turmoil of emotions that seemed to pull at her from a thousand directions. But her sob was silenced by his lips, which lowered to hers, as if to calm her sadness, her anger, her fears and doubts. Again he kissed her, his lips leaving hers for but a moment and then returning to reclaim them, with mounting passion, for he felt the tension ease from her body against his, and then the first faint stirrings of her own response. The golden light from the fire played across the soft contours of her face when he opened his eyes to stare down at her exquisite beauty.

"Please, no," Maren pleaded unconvincingly.

"You are my wife, Maren, by your own vows. Though it might please you well, I shall not pass this night with another, though I might find that one far more willing, I know well the pleasure to be found with you, milady. And though there remain secrets we keep from each other, I shall in time know all."

"No, it cannot be." Maren shook her head in faint denial.

"Yea, Maren, it shall be, even though the truth should find my sword drawn against you. It shall be."

Maren stared up at him in silent wondering at his words, and yet she was powerless to resist the searing heat of the touch of his skin against hers. Less gently than at first, Brettan's mouth lowered to hers, his lips warm and demanding, and though her thoughts cried out against her response, she felt that faint stirring and a mounting passion to match his. So long she had resisted him and defied him, holding herself from him, while she ached for the touch of his fingers upon her skin, the gentle touch of his lips against her own, in complete honesty of their need for one another. Beyond all reason, Maren's arms reached up around his neck, drawing him closer to her, feeling the heat of his naked chest against the soft fullness of her breasts, those rounded peaks responding, tightening and protruding through the thin fabric. Her long fingers raked through the soft waving lengths of the dark hair which curled about his face and neck. Her hands stroked him and caressed him, and she abandoned herself to the exquisite agony of her need for him.

Gently Brettan bent, lifted her slender body in his arms, and bore her to the bed, now bathed in the dancing, golden light of the newly laid fire. Laying her gently upon that thick softness, their kiss unbroken, he pulled back from her momentarily to stare into the wide, azure depths of her eyes, seeking her truth.

"In anger, I vowed never again to come to you. Release me now, Maren, for it can be only by your word."

The gauntlet had been thrown down. And yet there was no challenge in his whisper, so close against her throat that she could feel his warmth, only a silent plea. She could stay him with but one word, and she knew of a certainty he would honor it. But at what price?

Everything within her cried out that she deny him, and yet she could not, and she shut her eyes tightly, warm tears sliding silently down her cheeks. Tenderly, Brettan reached to take the tears from her cheek with the back of his fingers, his touch sending a vibrant heat through her. His hand was soothing, calming, gently caressing her jawline, and she was awed by the quiet strength of this

English warrior who could slay the most formidable enemy, but now reached out to her with such infinite tenderness. What indeed was the character of this man? Gently Brettan nuzzled his cheek against the soft silken mass of her dark hair, breathing in the sweet, fragrant smell of roses. He held her tightly against him, and in that one instant he knew he would have taken the sword against any who would cause her harm, man or woman. It mattered not what differences lay between the two of them.

Slowly Maren's fears eased, and she leaned into Brettan's embrace, feeling the flood of his warmth driving away her doubts and fears. And for the first time in many days, she felt peaceful, as if everything beyond the circle of his arms had ceased to exist. What was it in this fierce knight that gave her calm, when all about her denied it? What was it in him that gave her strength, when she was certain none remained? Pushing all further thoughts from her mind, Maren pulled closer to that comforting warmth, her head tucked beneath his chin, the sound of his heart strong and vibrant beneath her cheek while she rested her head against his firm shoulder. Hesitantly she reached up to trace the outline of his chin with her finger, tilting her head back so that she might look into his face, and perhaps find some truth in all her confusion. She saw only the soft glow of green eyes that stared back into hers, the even planes of his handsome face barely visible in the light flickering from the hearth. When his lips lowered to hers, she responded, at first uncertainly and then with a growing intensity that answered his plea, giving back the vow he had made to her.

Brettan rolled her gently onto her back, his lips never breaking that searing contact with hers. One arm lay beneath her shoulders, his hand closed possessively over one gleaming shoulder. His other hand traveled the length of her slender body, caressing, stroking, kneading, slowly exploring all the soft beguiling contours of her body. Maren moaned beneath the assault of his heated caresses, feeling deep within her the first tentative heat, that glowed with a fire of its own, and seemed to draw its energy from his touch. Her hand slipped around his neck, and she responded fully to his demands, and his name was a whisper upon her lips, over and over again, as if she might say it for all the times she had denied it. His lips left hers, tracing down along the gentle curve of her neck, and across the line of her collarbone to the soft rounded hollow just inside her shoulder, above the roundness of her breasts. Maren's hands explored the lean, hard lines of his muscular body, which lay across her, her fingers spreading in wide circles across his ribs, well protected by lean, hard muscles from many hours of wielding the heavy broadsword. All her doubts and fears disappeared before the onslaught of his passion, and she responded with an abandon that surprised Brettan as well as herself, as if some deep hunger surged within her, a hunger only he could satisfy. His lips brushed across the full mounding of her breast, and Maren arched against him when he finally took the taut peak gently between his teeth, a deep shudder passing through her at the intensity of that contact, his other hand gently caressing the other peak until it was firm and hard. Brettan moved over her, momentarily breaking the contact, and she stared up at him in wide-eyed wonder, her deep blue eyes lost within the glowing passion of his emerald gaze. The soft waves of his dark hair framed his face, and she marveled at how handsome he truly was. She reached out her hand to the man who bent over her, raking her fingers through the soft matting of dark hair on his chest, and caressing lower, across his lean ribs, moving slowly over the hard

303

lines of his hip, and lower yet until her hand closed over him. The searing heat of that first contact tore through them and, fearing that she might release him, Brettan closed his hand over hers, giving her silent encouragement to guide him to her velvet softness. Gently Brettan moved between her thighs, his knee separating hers. His lips reclaimed hers in a silent message, and he felt the mounting impatience within her as she clung to him. Slowly he teased her, tormented her, leaned over her, gently tasting the sweetness of her lips, and at last he entered her, clamping a firm restraint upon his own desires to feel himself fully within her warmth, to take at last his ease within her, yet wishing that the intense pleasure of their moments together might last forever. Maren arched up against Brettan, all restraint abandoned to her own needs, for she felt that first fiery heat within her. She sought desperately to ease the deep aching she felt inside, and moved to take him fully, yet met with his gentle resistance. Slowly he made love to her, giving to her and then taking, only to give again with such tenderness that Maren feared she could not endure it. His heated kisses fell across her cheek and down the hollow of her throat, lingering over the wild pulsing beat along her neck. There was a longing, an urgency, and his name was spoken pleadingly for him to take her completely. Abandoning himself to his passions, Brettan rose above her and thrust deeply within her, feeling that unbearable yet exquisite heat of her close fully over him. Again he thrust deep within her and again, until he felt her slender body move in response. Maren arched against him, meeting each movement with an equal strength born of her newly awakened desires. They were molded to one another, joining in that most exquisite of bonds, becoming one, so that it was impossible for either of them to know where one separated from the other. Brettan could feel the growing urgency within her slender frame.

Maren responded with an abandon that matched his, her breath uneven and then silenced for a moment, while he felt within her the final pleasure of him. Once more he thrust deep within her, his own release joining the waves of passion which swept over her, binding her to him, the splendor of that moment a silent vow they would never be able to deny.

Chapter Fourteen

Maren snuggled deeper into the covers, curling against the warmth of Brettan's body, entwined with her own, attempting to ignore the sounds of voices that grew louder as they approached the large chamber, pulling her reluctantly from her drowsy sleep. Had she been more fully awake, she might have given some notice to the women's voices that drifted toward their chamber, the one firm and commanding with the authority of her station, the other obedient yet fretful, its owner running along behind the determined figure of the flaxen-haired lady.

"Were you given instructions for the meal to break the fast?"

"No, milady, but her majesty the Queen, bade me await the young lady's leisure, so that the Duchess of Norfolk might be well rested."

"I will hear no more of your objections. I would have a few words in private with our young 'guest' from Wales. What of the Duke of Norfolk? Has he joined the king for the morning ride?" Not waiting for the young maid's reply, Caroline grasped the latch at the door and breezed into the room, the rich velvet of her gown brushing softly about her. She stopped abruptly in the center of the room, her grand entrance halted before the large bed, her shocked gaze locking with Brettan's golden eyes. He hastily drew the covers over the lower half of his well-muscled body, suddenly exposed, and Maren dove under the coverlet, pulling most of the bedlinens with her. An angry scowl distorted his handsome face as he glared at his mistress, momentarily too stunned at seeing him in Maren's bed to speak.

"Do you always make a habit of entering other people's bedchambers so early in the morning, and unannounced?" Brettan glared at Caroline.

Realizing that more might be gained in remaining calm than in railing against his choice of beds for the night, Caroline smiled coolly, gazing longingly at the broad expanse of his chest, covered with the thick mat of curling hair that seemed to invite a caress. Ignoring the curve of the small, feminine form beside Brettan's length, she boldly strode to the edge of the bed, thoughtfully fingering the edge of the coverlet, richly decorated with fine gold threads. "My darling, had I but known you had taken this chamber so near my own, I would have come to you last night, and saved us both such early rising."

"You forget yourself, Caroline. You would do well to remember that a closed door serves a purpose. Unless you are prepared for what you might find behind that door, I suggest you use greater discretion in the future."

"Brettan, I hardly believe there is anything I might find behind a closed door that would surprise me. It is only that I am surprised to find you so obedient to our king's orders."

"Caroline, where I choose to sleep is of no concern to you." There was a warning edge to his voice that Maren recognized well from beneath the covers, where she sought some small refuge from Caroline's assault. She had heard that same tone only once before, at the stream where she had been attacked, and knew the deadly menace behind the controlled words.

"Brettan, my love, whatever you do is of concern to me. Can you so quickly have forgotten the promises we once made to each other? Ah, but I see you feel your sense of obligation to honor and duty. But remember my love, that I know well your desires in such matters, and but await for you to see the duty met, before we may again take our pleasures."

Each endearment was deliberately spoken, as if to reaffirm Caroline's past and future with Brettan. In her seclusion beneath the heavy covers, those words had a grating effect on Maren's nerves, so that she swore under her breath that if the woman uttered one more phrase, she would forget all promises to ignore her attempts at intimidation, and leave the bed for but one purpose, to bodily toss the arrogant woman from the chamber.

The young servant tugged nervously at Caroline's sleeve as Caroline started to move around the end of the large bed to the other side. "What is it you want, that you must persist in perching at my elbow?"

"Milady, the queen has requested your presence." The young maid indicated the royal page standing just beyond the open portal.

Caroline dissolved into laughter at some bit of humor. "So it would seem, my darling, that even the Queen is determined to see your obligations to this wench well met."

Had Maren not been fairly smothered in the heavy covers beneath Brettan's restraining hand, she would have cringed at the sight of the barely suppressed fury covering his lean face, the slender white scar vividly lined across the length of his cheek, giving him the look of some evil and sinister warrior, ready to do battle.

"Then may I suggest Caroline, that you do not keep

the queen waiting, lest you should meet with her disfavor also," he raged from between clenched teeth.

"Brettan, so often have I met with your disfavor, yet always we have settled such petty squabbles, and found our pleasure again in one another. I have faith that you shall again find your way to my chamber and the pleasures that await you there, once you have tired of playing the role of dutiful husband." Caroline's voice was as smooth as satin, lowered seductively to almost a whisper as she leaned boldly forward across Brettan, an amused smile spreading across her well-turned lips, and dared his barely controlled anger with a lingering kiss upon his lips.

The young maid turned her head shyly, having heard much of Lady Caroline's indiscreet activities.

Maren struggled beneath the covers, having had enough of Caroline's vicious little games, and fought upwards to gain a breath of fresh air from within her warm haven. Feeling Brettan's arm firmly pinning her beneath the covers only increased her ire, for she could only assume that he hoped to avoid a confrontation between his mistress and his young bride, which might prove highly embarrassing. The thought goaded her anger even more than the woman's wheedling comments about her relationship with Brettan. Caroline could well have him, and have Maren's blessing in the matter, as well.

When finally she managed to free herself from her soft prison, Maren gasped the fresh air into her lungs, then whirled about to cover her naked body when she felt a cold rush of air. For the heavy covers had been pulled away, when Brettan lunged from the bed and loudly slammed the heavy oaken portal behind Caroline's departing figure, as if to give emphasis to his irritation. He whirled around, his vexation obvious in the stiff hard line of his body, just as Maren leaned to retrieve the covers, the full length of her body exposed before his hungering gaze, the nakedness of her breasts fueling the fires of his appetite, so that his glowing green gaze seemed to devour her. Feeling the heat of that gaze that she had grown to know so well, Maren glanced up to see him standing silently across the room. His senses were filled with the sight of her so very near, and all thoughts of Caroline or their confrontation of the moments before were lost before his consuming desire for the young girl so innocently displayed before him.

Maren fumbled uncertainly with the heavy coverlet and gathered it about her once more. She could feel the heat of color spreading across her cheeks at his unyielding gaze, which seemed capable of stripping the coverlet away and seeing her nakedness completely unadorned.

"My apologies for the intrusion." Brettan's voice was strained, while he took in the sight of her radiant, youthful beauty, which he would not have believed could be surpassed, until he saw her now, with just a trace of sleep still in those deep, blue eyes. Her raven-black hair hung in a complete disarray of wild, waving tendrils to below the gentle curve of her hips, giving stark contrast to the pale, pink glow of her flawless skin.

"Apology? Milord, what is there to apologize for? Is it not customary for the mistress to visit the lord and his lady when they are abed? I can hardly believe your concern is for some inconvenience you think I might have been caused, but rather the embarrassment you suffered to have your mistress find you in my bed. Please hasten to reassure Lady Caroline that the matter will be set aright immediately, and most certainly with my good wishes," Maren bit off sarcastically.

A dark brow arched mockingly, and Maren was instantly wary of Brettan's suddenly even nature. "Then your actions most certainly belie your words, my love.

311

For most assuredly you find your own pleasure with me, and any denial you might speak would only be a lie. Always remember, Maren, only truth can be found in that final moment when a man and woman come together in their ultimate pleasure of one another. All pretenses are stripped away."

"Tell me, milord, does your experience with the Lady Caroline make you an astute philosopher in such matters of the heart?"

"Lady Caroline, most certainly. And others. Women are all much the same. Only occasionally may one find a woman who is willing and capable of finding her pleasure with a man."

"And Lady Caroline is assuredly one of those women?" Maren retreated to the far corner of the large bed, while Brettan slowly approached, the full length of his magnificent body exposed, so that no part of him was left to her imagination in the glowing light of early morn.

"What Caroline lacks in capabilities, she makes up for in her willingness. But I tire of speaking of matters that have no importance here." In one fluid catlike movement Brettan crossed the expanse of the bed, seizing one wrist in his grip before she could flee to the opposite side of the chamber. Slowly, with gentle strength, he drew her against him, carefully pulling the coverlet from her grasp so that the soft enticing warmth of her flesh was molded against his, his arm closing about her.

Maren drew in a sharp breath when she realized his intent. "Though a knight of the realm, you most certainly are not honorable." Too late, Maren moved to escape his hold. His arms closed about her like bands of steel, the touch of his skin against her like a flame searing, torturing, yet consuming her with sweet painless agony. Even once he held her captive within the bonds of his unrelenting embrace, Maren boldly defied him, arching her head away, regarding him with a wide azure

312

gaze which silently dared him. She beguiled him with her proud unyielding spirit, which gave no quarter, even when she was soundly trapped. Maren steeled herself against his bold assault but felt her body's silent betrayal, for a warming glow stirred faintly within her at his gentle touch.

"You are capable of such pleasures, Maren, though you would heartily deny them to your last breath." His voice was a mere whisper of warmth against her ear. He drew her near, and she was helpless to resist.

"I would deny it because it is a lie. You take what you want, and you may think of it what you will. I have little to say in the matter, nor do I care. But heed what I say, milord, for there will come a day when I shall gain my freedom and be done with this marriage, which is a lie for both of us. When I give my heart, it shall be freely given, for it is all I have that is mine alone. It cannot be taken by force, nor given away by another, even if he be King of England."

"The passionate words of a young maid who has not yet learned the cruelties of life. Love is one of those cruelties, Maren. Though I do not call what has passed between us love, in truth I cannot deny that you please me far more than any other maid."

Maren's anger seethed at his handling of her, but more at the cruelty of his words, this stranger, this warrior knight who had taken everything from her. "How can you say I do not know of life's cruelties?" Maren spat at him, her vivid blue eyes glinting venomously while she struggled against his grasp. "How can you say that, when there is little that I have not seen?" Tears welled within her eyes. She felt herself losing her hard-fought control, and she lunged dangerously close to telling him everything that she had concealed within her heart. "My family is all but lost, because of this senseless war Edward wages against my country. My home is destroyed and left

313

in ruins, but perhaps the cruelest loss is that of my father's love, for the dishonor I have brought him."

"Family? Home? You selfishly believe the only losses are your own. The losses are very dear to you, Maren, but in truth they touch us all. I too wonder whether the price we pay far exceeds what might be gained." His anger seemed to drain from him at the thoughts only he could know, and almost gently he set Maren from him, his hold loose, as if a greater weight pulled at him.

Maren guardedly watched him move away from her. Rising from the bed, he crossed the room to the door of his own chamber. She wondered at his sudden sadness, knowing the demons of his own memories of a dear one lost haunted him.

Throwing the heavy door open, Brettan disappeared into the adjoining chamber, not bothering to close the portal.

At the sounds at a heavy coffer being opened and closed, Maren could only assume he dressed, and when she heard the splashing of water at the basin, she hastened to take advantage of the small amount of privacy he allowed her, bending to retrieve the heavy velvet robe from the bench where she had laid it the night before. She drew the heavy garment about her as Brettan appeared in the doorway, his tall frame richly clad in a tunic of black velvet, worn over finely cut breeches that hugged his lean thighs. Soft leather boots had been pulled on and clung to the length of his legs, disappearing underneath the tunic. An ornately decorated leather belt was fitted snugly to his waist, richly set with gold medallions, the forms of a dozen lions elegantly embossed by a clever craftsman. Maren stared transfixed at those tawny images, unable to glance away, as if they cast some spell over her. The rich vibrant timbre of Brettan's voice pulled her from her thoughts, and she glanced up, that smooth voice seeming to caress her gently.

"Has the child moved yet?"

The unexpected question tore through Maren, making it difficult for her to breathe, as if the room had suddenly become quite stifling. All her unspoken fears were suddenly given reality by his words.

"You need not look so shocked, Maren. I have known for some time that you are with child. It was to be expected in one of your innocence. Your time has not come as it should have, unless of course you are barren, and somehow I doubt that possibility. A maid of your spirit and passion often finds herself soundly caught for her pleasures." His gentle smile had turned into a self-satisfied smirk that Maren found maddening.

"But do not despair, Maren. I told you once before that I would have no bastard sons. I expected this, and I am pleased."

Maren stared at him aghast. "But how could you know? I have said nothing of it to anyone." So great was her surprise that Maren did not even attempt to back away when Brettan approached from the doorway and gently reached to take her hand in his, drawing her fingers to his lips. Turning her hand in his, he gently placed a kiss in the palm of her hand, like a precious gift for her alone. Her thoughts were in complete turmoil, and she stared up at him, then snatched her hand from his grasp in sudden agitation that he knew what she had tried to deny these many weeks past.

Brettan reached out and lifted a soft silken curl that lay across her breast, his fingers leisurely caressing the well-rounded mound, giving distinct meaning to his words. "In truth, Maren, there are certain changes I have noticed in you. There is no shame in the child we have created, Maren."

Indeed, Maren could not deny the tenderness and added fullness in her breasts in the last few weeks. It

315

irritated her no small measure that he so easily accepted the fact, as if he were proud of the feat. She sought to tear away at his implacable composure as he stood before her so certain of himself. "Have you so easily forgotten that I am considered your enemy? How can you be so certain that you are the sire?"

Brettan's laugh filled the room. He threw back his head seeming to find extreme humor in her taunting. "My dear Maren, how easily you forget the weeks past. Indeed you wound me with the ease that you forget when first I took you to my bed. Shall I recall that night for you? Though I do not make a habit of taking young virgins to my bed, for they are a bothersome lot, I will confess that my mistake in taking you to share those cold nights in the Welsh countryside proved an enjoyable mistake. At first I doubted your innocence, but alas, sweet Maren, the stains upon the coverlet the morning after were proof enough and, though I vowed to make you my mistress, I knew well you would never consent to return with me to London. Now I shall have the pleasure of that for a very long time to come. Indeed we shall make the most of our time, and learn to take our pleasure of one another at our leisure, with none to say nay to it. Though your well-rounded form in the months to come shall hinder us for a time, I have all faith that I can bear the burden of time until you are able to again partake of that pleasure. Indeed, I waited a very long time to find you, and that small space of time shall prove no burden."

"That is all that holds any meaning for you, is it not? That you may find your pleasure in me. Then most certainly you will loathe the child I carry for the inconvenience it will cause you."

"Indeed no, Maren. There is a great deal you have to learn of me. And one thing that you will soon learn is that I value highly human life, and one created of my flesh and blood above all. A child born of our lovemaking shall

316

truly be a child of great pride and strength, not to mention high temper."

"I think there can be no pride in a child born of violence," Maren responded thoughtfully.

Brettan eyed her keenly, as if sensing the great sadness that weighed heavily upon her young heart, and a sudden fear great within him at the stories of other young maids, beset by knights of the realm, who when finding themselves with child had chosen death as their final victory over the conquering invaders. "Maren, I will not have you bring harm to yourself or the child for this anger between us. Heed my words, for I have no tolerance of such things. I have seen too much of death, I could not bear the loss of one I hold dear."

Maren seemed not to hear his words. "Would you then bind me to your side, each moment of every day, to guard against it?"

"You have been well guarded in the past, Maren. I could easily see the guards returned, to keep you safe."

Maren stared into the glowing depths of green eyes that seemed to look into her very soul, and was surprised at the solemn passion in his voice, as if he were promising her that she would indeed bear his child safely. Was there some measure of caring for her in his words, beyond his casual taking of her whenever his desires dictated? Why did it suddenly seem important that he might care some small measure for her? In that long moment of silence between them, all anger seemed stripped away, leaving them, for a moment, vulnerable to the flood of emotions that washed over them. Maren raised her hand and gently traced her fingers down the white line of that faint scar at the edge of his eye, wondering what blade had made the wound. It was a simple gesture, but given with such unexpected tenderness that Brettan felt all his anger slipping away.

His words had given reality to the child she knew she

317

carried, the final seal to her fate. Whatever that fate might hold for her. "I too have seen too much of death. I value life. I could never take the life of an innocent, and most assuredly the child we have created is innocent no matter what the deeds of its parents. I will carry your child, milord, and I will bring it forth. I only pray that you will not, in a moment's anger, cast it aside." Maren felt the tension ease from him, his fingers relaxing their hold on her hand.

"Your honor me, milady, with the gift you carry. I shall not cast aside the child, nor the one who is his mother."

Brettan stepped away from her when the young maid returned to assist Maren with her morning bath. Maren blushed slightly at his departing glance, but the maid bustled about the chamber, seemingly oblivious of the two, who now seemed at a loss for words. Nodding stiffly, Brettan turned and made to leave the chamber, pausing abruptly in the doorway. He turned back to gaze warmly at Maren, thinking he perhaps knew less of her than he had thought.

"Milord?" Maren questioned, lifting a lovely brow.

"Take heed to guard against Caroline's tongue. I know it well, and I swear it to be a weapon more lethal than any blade. I should not like to see you wounded by her anger against me."

"I accept your warning, milord, but in truth my people have fought the English for generations, and we have yet to be conquered. I hardly think a pale-faced, viper-tongued shrew capable of a feat that all Edward's armies and his loyal knights have failed to attain."

Brettan grinned at her devilishly. "I think perhaps such a contest would be most interesting, for I have often heard it said that the shrew is no match for the lioness."

Maren smiled wickedly back. "You might do well to remember that also, milord."

318

"I am oft reminded of that of late. Good day, milady."

The mild summer days of June faded, and the sweltering heat of July set upon London with a vengeance, forcing those fortunate enough to have country estates to flee the stagnant, oppressive weather for the cooler climes outside London.

Maren's days were well occupied. She rose early each morn to accompany the young queen on her walks about the vast gardens of the castle, telling the young woman stories of her childhood at Cambria. Often the young Prince Alphonse accompanied them. At age three, he was a chattering, toddling child, the image of his father. He often babbled nonsensically in response to any question he was asked. He was completely delighted at the attention he received from the beautiful young girl with dark hair that swung loose about her shoulders, providing him such delight in wrapping his chubby fingers in the thick masses, and more than once bringing tears to Maren's eyes when he tugged too playfully at the silken tresses.

Maren rarely saw Brettan during the day. His responsibilities to Edward frequently kept him afar from the earliest light to well into the night. Often she would hear him returning to his chamber adjoining hers, undressing there so as not to disturb her sleep, and then quietly slipping into the massive bed beside her. Even into the latest hour, it was as if she lay awake and listened for his return, unable to drift off to sleep unless she knew he was near, and then relaxing finally into the warmth of his long body curled protectively around hers. Only occasionally did his duties keep him from returning at night, when he accompanied Edward, and Maren would often stir restlessly into the early hours of the morning, finally drifting into uneasy slumber, somehow feeling

319

lost and vulnerable in the large bed without his nearness in the dark, so strangely comforting to her.

By day Caroline's vengeance continued unchallenged, and she only retreated to a more subtle attack when the queen was near, not wishing to bring a royal reprimand for her thoughtless words against Maren. And more than once, on those nights that Brettan failed to return, Maren was painfully aware that Caroline also was strangely absent, causing a flood of uncertainty to tear away at her composure at the thought that Brettan might have chosen to resume his relationship with his mistress, though always aware that it was his right and privilege, and that she should not care if he chose Caroline over her. Yet it did matter, and though she would have denied it with her last breath, there was the haunting thought that she indeed longed for the sight of his broad-shouldered frame across the room, or his lingering gaze that seemed to warm her, or the heat of his touch against her skin, and the agonizing ecstasy when he made love to her. Silently she was angry with herself that he could affect her so, drawing her will from her with a look or a touch. Would he still desire her when she grew round with his child? As the days passed, Maren was pleased that her shape had not altered greatly. The only sign of the child she carried was the slightly rounded firmness of her stomach.

July was upon them and passed with unbearable slowness. The royal family remained in London, making it impossible for many at court even to hope for escape from the summer heat. After her morning walks with the queen, Maren often retreated to the coolness of her chamber, where she could escape both the growing heat of the day and Caroline's vicious tongue. There she remained until the heat penetrated the shuttered windows, making the chamber seem like an oven, driving her to the coolness of the gardens, where a breeze could be found in the late afternoon to break the heavy calm of the summer air.

The castle was astir with speculation about Edward's delay in leaving for the royal estates, and even Brettan seemed on edge from the delay. The mood changed only when a royal feast was given to break the monotony of the endless days of summer. Amidst the many toasts made to the king and queen, Edward announced the impending birth of his second child, dispelling rumors that he had feared to leave London because of rebel threats against the royal family, revealing instead his deference to the young queen and her uneasy health during the first weeks of her confinement. As the announcement was made, Maren's eyes caught Brettan staring at her from across the large hall, where he stood among his knights, and she blushed openly at the secret they shared of their own child. He bowed his head slightly to her. Though he had spoken his approval of the child, she had silently doubted his words, for he had said little more of it in the weeks that had passed. That one look reached into her soul, leaving her breathless and flushed at the realization that he was indeed pleased that she carried his babe. And again, as at so many times in the past weeks, the wild tumult of her emotions left her uncertain, even fearful of what she felt for the bold English knight. She could only be silently grateful that he had chosen not to make a similar announcement, perhaps in an effort to protect her from the rumors and idle gossip certain to accompany such an announcement, particularly should Caroline learn of it and make her own assumptions, knowing the time they had been wed.

In the weeks that followed the royal announcement, Maren occupied her time with the young prince, herself feeling no such infirmities as the young queen, and silently grateful for her own good health. Indeed, she seemed to grow more radiantly beautiful with each passing day, as if the child she carried gave her a glow of vitality. And that glow was not lost to others who watched her with keen eyes, so that she more and more sought the refuge of the privacy of her chamber, to avoid the inquiring glances or bold questions that she wished desperately to avoid, although she knew the day fast approached when she would no longer be able to prevent her condition from being made known to everyone at the English court.

The first week in August, Edward made the announcement that the royal family and his court would travel to their country estates for the remainder of the summer, before his return to Wales and the final campaign he waged against Llywelyn. As Duchess of Norfolk, Maren was to accompany the royal family, together with several members of the court. From there Brettan intended to travel to Norfolk before his return to Wales with the English army and Edward. It was a matter she fearfully chose not to discuss with him. The journey to Wales was one she hoped to make with him, and she had not found words to make him understand her need that her child be born in Wales. Nor could she hope he would consent to it. She occupied herself with the final packing for the trip to the royal estates, silently grateful that they would soon be able to escape the unyielding heat of London, for it had begun to wear on her, making her more vulnerable to Caroline's barbs and criticisms, always easily spoken when Brettan was not about.

One morning the young maid entered her chamber unnoticed, and Maren spun upon the young girl defensively, making her back away in hasty retreat. She had a visitor, she was told. She hastily made her way down the long stone stairway to the hall below, impatiently wondering who might possibly be asking for her, when her only acquaintances were those at the English court, who maintained a polite distance. Coming to the last step, Maren whirled around the column of the stairway, her softly slippered feet brushing faintly against the stone flooring. She stopped in midflight at the sight of the oddly familiar figure just inside the massive doors of the castle. She would have recognized the slightly stooped, round-shouldered form of the old maid anywhere. Casting aside all formalities, Maren swooped down on the old woman, causing both the stern guards at the portal to stare uncertainly at her uncontrolled enthusiasm.

Agnes' arrival lifted Maren's spirits no small measure, for the messages she brought from Maren's father dispelled the anger between them at Monmouth, and she felt the warmth of his love in the words he had sent. No word had been received of Edmund, only rumors and speculation that traced his path from Cambria to the North of Wales, but nothing that might give word of his captors or their purpose. The unbearable silence, more so than any message of the lad's death, seemed to weigh heaviest on her father. Indeed Agnes spoke of her fear for his health those first weeks after his return, for he seemed like a man possessed, ranting to see the murderers punished for the deeds committed against his family. Only when the days slipped into weeks and no word came of Edmund's fate did his manner give way to a deep, brooding silence more frightening than his ravings for revenge. Catherine seemed much improved. The weeks of seclusion at the abbey had worked a healing magic on Maren's sister, so that Agnes felt secure enough to leave the girl in the care of the good sisters. Catherine seemed restored to her gentle, caring self, her thoughts bright and clear, though she refused to speak of the attack on Cambria or the death of their mother. The pain and uncertainty that Maren had carried with her all those long weeks, since she had been captured by the English, eased somewhat. What Agnes knew of the marriage remained unknown, for she kept her thoughts to herself, only making comment that Maren seemed greatly changed, then idly assuming it was the ordeal of the weeks and months past. Yet once the first days after her arrival passed, Maren was certain the woman eyed her slender waistline keenly, and had already guessed the truth. Still Agnes remained silent in the matter, mercifully allowing Maren the opportunity to speak of the matter herself. Of her brother Andrew, Agnes informed Maren that he had escorted her as far as the English border and then proceeded to lead her father's men to the north of Wales. Indeed, her father made his own plans to rejoin the fighting, the final campaign against Llywelyn, remaining at Cambria only to attend to the final details of Catherine's welfare before returning to the north. Knowing her father, Maren pondered his purpose in following alone to the north country, and realized it had to do with Edmund's abduction and her father's private quest to see the lad safely returned.

Within a matter of days the final arrangements for their journey to the country had been made. The young queen appeared more frequently to oversee the final preparations. Even Caroline's vindictiveness seemed to have eased somewhat, for she too was to accompany the royal household to the country estates.

The day of their departure from London dawned warm, but Maren welcomed the morning, for it gave her the opportunity to ride beside Brettan and his guard in the long, heavily guarded column, far from Caroline's prying glances and honeyed comments to her husband. Agnes made little comment of the woman's waspish attitudes or her attentiveness to the Duke of Norfolk, seeming to understand what had not been said. With great skill Agnes had managed to become a protective buffer between Maren and the jealous mistress who still hoped for so much, often waylaying the tenacious lady with

324

some skillfully spoken bit of information of the queen's disapproval of such conduct, which temporarily caused Caroline to abandon her direct pursuit of Brettan. Each stolen moment of privacy helped strengthen the fragile relationship between Maren and Brettan. Though Agnes would not yet admit to liking the English knight, she had somehow silently taken up his cause, having won a small but significant victory against Caroline in suggesting that Maren and Brettan ride near the front of the column, where the young queen might enjoy their company. She had artfully arranged that Caroline ride near the rear where a steady cloud of dust filled the air from the horses' hooves. Though Maren could not have been certain of the woman's schemes, she indeed felt more confident that, although she could evenly meet any attack Caroline might give, her back was well-guarded by the loyal maid, not yet realizing that Brettan had already taken his own measures to protect his duchess.

Beyond the confines of the stone walls of the castle and the cobbled streets, which ran open with the stench of raw sewage, the air seemed to clear, and the heat somehow became more bearable in the early morning hours when the royal party made its way into the open countryside beyond London, for the two-day ride to the royal estates in Essex, north of the city.

Maren marveled at the green of the countryside, while they rode beside the cooling waters of the Roding River. Spirits seemed to lighten, and the queen seemed less afflicted with the early discomforts of the child she carried.

Late in the afternoon the queen seemed to grow weary of the ride, so they made their camp upon the open field, to complete their journey the following day. A long row of tents was assembled, and large fires laid to roast the pheasant and partridge that had skillfully been hunted for the evening meal. The large camp took on the atmosphere of a small town, while the lords and ladies of the court enjoyed the evening's festivities and the freedom from the stifling clime of London. Musicians strolled through the camp, the sweet strains of the lute and the zither filling the night air.

Brettan joined his king before the blazing fire, to partake of a last toast after the meal before retiring for the evening. Agnes had long since retired for the night to her own pallet, made in one of the far tents for the ladies' maids. Though no conversation had passed between Brettan and the old maid, Maren was aware of a tacit truce between the two, and was silently grateful that Agnes did not persist in burdening her with endless criticisms of Brettan when Maren was plagued with enough of her own doubts.

Maren sought the refreshing coolness of the night air. She walked from the fire before Brettan's tent, and her attention was drawn to the royal enclosure, where she watched in dismay Caroline approaching Brettan. Caroline pretended a chill from the evening air, begging him to escort her to her own tent. Maren's cheeks flamed brightly to witness the exchange, though the distance was too great for her to know the exact words spoken. She could well imagine Caroline's honeyed pleas for him to accompany her to the privacy of that enclosure. Brettan finally relented and rose to walk with Caroline along the row of tents to the far end, where Caroline's tent had been set. Maren turned away abruptly, suddenly at a loss to understand the wrenching feeling deep inside her. Though she would heartily have denied it, there was a nagging doubt that her feelings went beyond her first thoughts of the marriage vows she had spoken with Brettan. As if in response to her sudden vexation, Maren felt the first faint stirrings of Brettan's child deep within her womb. The one thing she might be certain of was the

326

child she carried. It was not imagined, but very real indeed. Maren had seen the look on Brettan's face when he had looked upon his mistress. Had she seen desire? Had he indeed sought his pleasure with Caroline those many evenings, when he had failed to return to her chamber? Did he but take his pleasure with Maren as was his wont, only for her to lose him to his fair-haired mistress, as Caroline had once promised, when she herself grew round with his child? Maren's temper flared to think of all the sharp words Caroline had given her. Gathering up the thin woolen shawl and wrapping it firmly about her shoulders, Maren stalked off into the evening, intent upon relieving some of the hostilities and anger that nagged at her. Seeking solitude from the others who gathered about the large campfires, Maren wandered in the direction of the long line of horses tethered between the stands of trees at the edge of the greensward. She heard a low nickering that she knew well, and she looked for the gray head above the others. Brettan's stallion whinnied a soft greeting. She snatched a thick handful of soft grass just beyond his long reach, and offered him the tasty lush mouthful. Though it was easily capable of crushing her with one sideways step, Maren stood calmly beside the gray, her calm, fearless spirit flowing from her fingers to the large beast that chomped lazily on the proffered tidbit. Thoughtfully, Maren stroked the heavily muscled neck. "I should like to be like you, my friend. When you are angry, you toss your head to the wind and race until the anger is gone. I run from my anger and fears but find myself soundly caught for them. You have bonds but are free. I find that, no matter how I struggle, I cannot break the bonds that hold me." Maren rubbed the velvety softness of the gray nose that brushed her shoulder inquisitively, for the stallion sought another treat from her hand.

"You gray rogue, you are no better than your master. With one fine treat you seek another, and then I am certain another. Methinks you have kept his company far too long. His bad habits have become yours." Maren patted the finely arched neck, while the stallion nudged at her playfully. She turned to return to the camp, but stopped when she heard the breaking of twigs underfoot. Someone had approached very close.

"Struggle no more against those bonds, Maren, but let me take you from here."

Maren spun about with such fright that her movement startled the gray, sending him snorting, his head tossing wildly in the air, at the scent of the stranger who approached. In the meager light Maren could see the figure of a man, but his whispered voice held no recognition for her. Maren's first thought was to run from the stranger but, before she could turn and flee, her wrist was firmly seized in an unrelenting grasp. The man's other hand quickly drew back the hood of his tunic, so that she could clearly see his face outlined in the flickering light of the campfires.

"Geoffrey! Merciful father in heaven, what are you doing here? Do you not realize the danger you are in?"

"My dearest Maren, I have followed you across Wales and England these months past. Can you not understand my purpose in risking so much? I am here to take you home," Geoffrey whispered from the seclusion of the trees, pulling her away from the light of the campfires. "Indeed I had despaired of any success, but this journey of Edward's has provided me the opportunity for your escape."

"Geoffrey, this is madness for you to risk so much, with so many of the English guard about. You must leave, it is not safe for you to remain here, and I could not bear it if any harm should come to you. Please, Geoffrey, I cannot allow you to risk your life." Maren glanced uneasily over her shoulder, fearing her absence might have been noticed, for she was well guarded.

"Maren, I have pledged myself to you. I shall not abandon you as your father has. I will not leave England without you."

"Geoffrey, there is much you do not know, so much has happened since we left Cambria. My father has not abandoned me, he willingly gave his consent that I come to England." Maren's gaze pierced the darkness, that she might see his face to know of his reaction to her words. "Geoffrey, I cannot leave England. The Duke of Norfolk is my husband." Maren's voice was hardly more than a whisper. She had spoken the words for the first time, as if in that moment she had finally accepted the reality of the marriage.

"I know well of the marriage. I was at Monmouth the day your father and Andrew rode for Cambria. Word travels well among the common people. The celebrations of the wedding continued well into the next day, and a young lad in the town gave me word of the occasion. I knew not that you were the bride until that day in the marketplace, when I saw you so well guarded by his men. He must value the prize he has won very highly, to keep so many about you all the time."

"Then you can see that your efforts are hopeless. Geoffrey, please, I could not bear to see you harmed for my sake. Go now, while you may," Maren pleaded earnestly.

"The vows spoken with the Duke of Norfolk are meaningless. This marriage does not exist; I do not accept it. Come with me to Wales, Maren. Live with me as my wife, as once you promised. There is nothing to hold you here in England, least of all the promises of a father who has betrayed you." Geoffrey leaned very close to whisper against her ear, his breath hot and discomforting against her neck.

Maren tried to pull her wrist free of his grasp, but found herself well restrained. She stared into the lean hardness of Geoffrey's face, his gray eyes suddenly seeming so cold. She saw nothing of the boy who had shared her childhood. Maren sensed something dangerous in his manner, that he listened not at all to any of her arguments. She felt again the faint stirrings of her unborn child. The child was her future, no matter the wars or anger that pulled at her, the child was a truth she could not turn from. And she knew of a certainty that, if she chose to leave England with Brettan's unborn child, there was no army on earth that could prevent him from following her, for he had made his feelings in the matter quite clear. Somehow she had to make Geoffrey understand that her decision went beyond her simple desire to return to her home.

"Geoffrey, what may I say that will make you understand what I feel? I cannot say that I do not care for you, for it would be a lie. Indeed I care for all that we shared as children at Cambria, and for your friendship with me. If war had not come, perhaps things might have been very different between us, but the attack at Cambria changed everything in my life forever. I cannot change what has happened, though I wish that I might. My mother is dead, and Edmund is still held captive. Catherine has suffered greatly, and though the wounds would seem to be healed, she shall carry her silent torment with her always, as will I. I would that all might be the same as it was before, but it is not. It can never be. What we knew of Cambria is gone. I have accepted it. You must also accept it, for this is the only truth. My father consented to the marriage, by his words, to keep me safe from what I do not know. I must trust in his decision, for it is all that I have."

"Maren, beloved, this marriage to the Englishman is false. You were given to the marriage by an Englishman," Geoffrey argued desperately, that he might make her see.

"I was given to the marriage by my father! Be he English, or no, he is my father, and I must trust in his word."

"Maren, you have been betrayed at every turn by the English. They are our enemies. Edward seeks to destroy our people. Your father fights beside Edward against your mother's people. Can you not see that you have been betrayed? Leave with me now, while we may go." Geoffrey's grip tightened about her wrist in his desperation to convince her.

Maren felt suddenly uncomfortable at the odd light that played across Geoffrey's pale eyes. "Geoffrey, please, I cannot return with you. Unhand me!" Maren whispered vehemently.

"I have vowed that you will return with me to Meyrick. I shall not leave without you."

Maren twisted away, while Geoffrey tried to smother any further objection with his free hand against her mouth. His intent was clear. If he could not persuade her to leave with him, he would take her by force, if necessary.

Maren thought him surely mad to dare so much within the camp of the English, with Brettan so very near, yet for all she knew, Brettan was well occupied with Caroline and knew little of her plight. "Geoffrey, you must not do this. I cannot return with you to Meyrick. Geoffrey, please, you are hurting me." Vainly Maren pleaded with him, but she knew by the determined look on his face that he had not heard any of her words.

Maren had sought to keep from telling him more, but in her rising panic, in her struggle against his determined hold, Maren realized there were no easy words for what she had to tell him. "Geoffrey, I cannot return to Meyrick with you, because I am with child."

She had hardly guessed the impact her words might have. Geoffrey suddenly ceased his struggling with her

331

and held her at arm's length, his grip still unyielding at her wrists, a look of shock on his face, for he realized well that for the short time she had been wed, the child must have come from her first weeks within the English camp. His shock quickly faded to anger, and rage distorted his face, a low menacing growl coming from deep in his throat.

"So you willingly bed the English dog, and now bear the mark of his leavings upon you. You are a fool, Maren. I would gladly have overlooked that the English had taken you prisoner, knowing not what you might have endured in their camp, but you have yielded that prize you once promised me. I see well now the reason for your father's decision. He would not see you bear a bastard by the English. He could not bear to see you pay the price for your shame. But my dear, sweet Maren, you shall pay the price for your betrayal of me."

"Geoffrey, I have never betrayed you. You sought promises that were never spoken, except in your imagination or as play between children."

"It was never my imagination, Maren. Those childhood promises have given me strength these many months past, to continue to believe that I might yet have you with me. Now I find that the English plants his seed to seal the marriage. I shall not honor this marriage; for me it does not exist. The English come, and they take what they will, but they shall not have you. The promises made in our childhood still bind, Maren. I shall honor them, and so shall you." Roughly Geoffrey shoved her from him, so that she stumbled uncertainly. Panic seized her as she gazed into Geoffrey's enraged visage, which sent a wave of coldness over her in spite of the warmth of the summer's eve. Before she could move away from him, Geoffrey had turned and vanished into the thick covering of trees beyond the clearing.

The gray stallion snorted nervously, pawing at the soft

earth beneath his hooves as if sensing her distress, then suddenly raised his large head, his ears pricked forward at some new sound that approached. Maren whirled to find Caroline standing a few feet away, and wondered how much of the exchange she might have seen.

"You must guard against wandering so far from camp, my dear. There are many wild animals that venture forth from the forest. Without a sword to protect you, you might fall prey to some forest creature on his nightly roamings."

Maren eyed Caroline evenly, certain that she must have heard part of her conversation, yet finding nothing in the woman's words that spoke of it.

"I fear no one, Caroline."

"Still, you would do well to guard against unseen dangers."

"What dangers do you speak of? I see none about," Maren retorted, her voice suddenly sharp after her confrontation with Geoffrey.

"Brettan guards you well, but he cannot always guard against every danger. You are Welsh, and you are the enemy of the crown. Many dangers await those who are enemy of the king."

Maren laughed, suddenly amused at Caroline's seeming concern for her well-being, sensing the warning that lay beyond the well-chosen words. Yet nervousness tinged her voice, as she gazed at the older, more experienced woman, who would pay any price to gain back her favor with Brettan. Maren's wide blue eyes narrowed. "Your concern is well taken, Caroline, but in truth, I find that the true enemy of Edward hides not, but reveals himself in the guise of loyal friend of the crown. I am no enemy to Edward. He must look closer to find the true threat." Wishing no further conversation with the hateful woman, Maren turned on her heel and stalked back to the welcoming safety of the blazing fires that circled the encampment, nearly colliding with Brettan as she stormed toward the tent. His arms reached out to steady her uneven footing, and his glowing green eyes gazed into hers questioningly. She knew of a certainty that he had not expected to find her there. He had followed Caroline, for what purpose she could well guess. Her nerves raw, Maren twisted impatiently from his grip and hastened to the solitude of the tent, leaving Brettan to stare uncertainly at her fleeing figure.

"My darling, I knew you would come. Let there be no more harsh words between us. We may find a sheltered haven, free from prying eyes. Let us share these few hours together." Possessively Caroline slipped her fingers through the opening of Brettan's tunic, tracing her cool fingers intimately across his chest, molding her body against his, swaying her hips seductively against him teasingly, seeking his response.

Brettan stared into the icy depths of her eyes, suddenly aware of the calculating coldness to be found there. He longed to know what words had passed between Maren and Caroline. He could not trust that Caroline would honor the truth of his marriage. Though word of the marriage had come as a shock to her, he would not tolerate her continued attacks against Maren. Though he felt certain Maren could easily handle the fiercest of enemies, he feared for her safety and that of his child. "Caroline, we have spoken of this. It is my intention to honor the vows I have given. I will say no more of the matter."

"Would you not expect that also of your wife, my love?"

"What are you about, Caroline?"

Seeing that she had his attention, Caroline pressed her cause, laying the seeds of doubt, desperate for any advantage she might gain in driving Maren from Brettan, from England. "The girl is Welsh. There are rumors that

334

she is part of Llywelyn's rebellion against Edward and seeks some vengeance against the king. She is not English. How could you believe the words of one whose people are sworn to drive us from Wales? She will not honor her vows. Why must you play the fool by holding yourself to them? Even now she seeks the company of others. And can you be certain of the loyalty of your knights where the girl is concerned?"

"You go beyond yourself, Caroline. Welsh or English, there is no difference when the vows are spoken before God."

"It is said that the Welsh are godless. Must you wait until the girl's betrayal of you is complete, before you will cast aside these hollow vows?"

"Caroline, your tongue will see you soundly caught for your lies. I will speak no more of the matter." Brettan brushed past her and followed Maren's retreat to the tent, at the far side of the camp. Behind him Caroline stood alone, her keen eyes staring at his departing figure. She would use what she had learned this night to gain her rightful position as Duchess of Norfolk. It was only a matter of time, until all was hers, as it should rightly be hers.

Brettan knew well Caroline's maliciousness, and could only guess what might have passed between the two women. Steeling himself against Maren's anger, he sighed heavily before lifting the heavy flap of the tent and entering the enclosure. Across the tent Maren stood in silent thought, her slender back to him as he approached her.

"I am oft reminded of Caroline's vengeful ways. I fear you are now the target of much of her anger, which should rightly fall to me." He spoke gently, trying to guess her mood.

"'Tis nothing. Please do not speak of it." Maren waved him back unconvincingly, turning away from his gaze so

335

that he might not see her face.

Sensing her distress, Brettan gently seized her slender shoulders and turned her slowly until she stood before him, her head downcast, the thick veil of her ebony tresses hidding her face from his view. Tenderly, Brettan lifted her chin with his fingers, so that his eyes could see hers, and the tears that coursed down her cheeks tore at his composure.

"I swear I will see the woman flogged for her words against you." Brettan's anger flared at the sight of the pain in her wide, deep, blue eyes.

"No, please. Brettan, you must not. To do so would only invite more anger. Leave the matter be."

Gently Brettan slipped one arm about her slender waist, his other hand reaching up to catch the warm, salty tears on the tips of his fingers. He gently traced the outline of her cheek, and the high, well-defined bones that made her large eyes slant slightly at the edges. His fingers were warm against her skin, chilled from the evening air. Or was it some greater coldness that seemed to invade her entire being? Slowly he lowered his lips to hers, not knowing whether he would meet with resistance or perhaps only resigned acceptance. Gently his mouth moved over hers, tasting of her softness, the honeyed sweetness that was hers alone, and he felt her fevered response speak of her own longing. He lifted her and bore her to the pallet where first they had lain those many months ago, which now seemed a lifetime. Laying her upon the soft thickness of the pallet, Brettan expertly unfastened the closures of her gown, drawing the garment away, until she lay before him with only the thin chemise to conceal her naked loveliness from his hungering gaze. Moving from her but a moment to snuff the last candles, Brettan returned, his own clothes falling to the floor of the tent. He spread his warm length beside her like a great beast lounging beside its mate, then closed his arms about her, gathering her to him in one easy movement. Slowly his great warmth drove away the chill of the evening. But Maren shivered from some inner coldness that refused to yield. Feeling a need to hold her near, Brettan pulled her into the curl of his body, burying his face in the silken mass of her hair, fragrant with the faint scent of roses from her morning bath. Gently he kissed the hollow of her neck, thinking that never before had he known such complete pleasure. He felt, with her close beside him, as if all wars, all anger held no meaning, and might not have existed, with her nearness to give him ease.

Maren turned within his arms until her gaze met his glowing green one. What horrible truths were there yet to be spoken between them? Was Brettan indeed responsible for her mother's death, though he had fervently denied it? The only truth she was certain of were the moments they now shared and the child they had created, who lay safely nestled within her. Brettan's words had been true and haunted her. She had found pleasure in their lovemaking, even in those first weeks as his prisoner. But it was a truth she had not yet been ready to accept. Now that she longed to accept it, there were those who might yet force them apart. Maren blocked out all the doubts that crowded her thoughts, and reached up, her slender arms encircling Brettan's neck, drawing him closer, so that her lips reached hungrily for his. There was only this moment between them, whatever else she would face on the morrow. She felt his faint surprise when she molded her body against his. Inquisitively, she probed the softness of his mouth with her tiny tongue, as he had taught her, her lips setting his aflame, for her desire matched his. Gently Brettan rolled her over onto her back, gazing down in sudden wonderment at this slender girl, his wife, who possessed a passion to match his own.

In one motion Maren reached up and pulled the chemise over her head. She tilted her head back to stare at Brettan for a moment, uncertain of his desire for her. Propped up on his elbow beside her, Brettan reached over and kissed her in tender response, his one free hand reaching to cup the ripe fullness of her breast. Maren's breath caught in her throat at his warm touch against her skin, and she reached a hand behind his neck. Slowly she guided him to her. Brettan leaned forward, his mouth closing over the taut, rose-hued peak. Gently he teased that crest with his teeth, sending tremors of sweet ecstasy shivering through her. Never before had she known such pleasure, and she arched against him, marveling in the agonizing tenderness of his touch. Slowly Brettan's other arm encircled her shoulder, lowering her to the pallet, one hand gently kneading the soft fullness of her flesh. Maren moaned softly beneath his touch, reaching up to trace lightly the broad flat surface of his chest, and then down along his side, her fingers reaching across the lean, hard flatness of his stomach and hips. A dull aching hunger began deep within her, and Brettan moved over her, his lips burning a molten path where they touched. Maren arched up against him, seeking her release with him, in that ageless union of flesh and spirit. Brettan restrained her passion, though he felt his own building within, wanting to prolong the sweet fulfillment of their moments together, now without anger or doubts to tear at them. His name fell from her lips in agonized pleading for him to take her, but still he resisted, again claiming her lips, his fevered kisses falling across the silken smoothness of her skin, his kisses traveling down her neck and across her shoulder. His tongue teased the other peak to tautness beneath the heat of his advances. Gently he nibbled at that full orb, causing her to respond at that barest measure of pain that was only a moment away from sweet pleasure. Slowly he moved over her, his knee riding between her legs. Maren's hand lowered feverishly and, finding the treasure it sought, closed its fingers over him. For a moment Brettan pulled back in surprise at the passion of the young beauty who lay beneath him. He was at a loss to understand her emotions, why she came to him with a desire to match his own, when he had expected only anger. Unable to delay the sweetness of their joining any longer, Brettan closed the distance between them. Maren's arms closed about him, and she arched upwards to take him fully. Brettan entered her slowly, almost fearful to cause her pain, yet unable to deny the hunger that grew within him at each moment he delayed. Moving slowly against her, Brettan felt her impassioned response. She moved with him, their passion mounting to a fevered pitch. And as that final moment of ultimate pleasure burned through them, Brettan molded her slender form against his own so they were one, and he knew himself lost to her forever.

Chapter Fifteen

The royal hunting grounds of King's Forest spread before the gently sloping hillsides surrounding the magnificent lake. The stone manorhouse stood like an imposing fortress on the far side of the lake. The sun rested low in the afternoon sky the second day of their journey from London.

Word of the royal visit had been sent in advance, and a small army of servants wasted no time in making the manorhouse suitable for the royal family and their guests. Brettan and Maren were given a chamber very near the royal chamber, but a greater distance from the others, so that it seemed the arrangements might have been deliberately planned to remove them the greatest distance from Caroline.

Maren sighed her pleasure in the hot bath provided by the servants, while Brettan and his knights took a late evening meal with the king before the huge roaring fire, which was needed in the evening hours, even in the late summer months. Agnes bustled about the chamber, laying out a light linen robe for Maren to wear after the bath, unpacking the wooden coffers, exclaiming over each richly made gown, and silently thinking that she had judged correctly. Not only was the Duke of Norfolk a man of wealth, but a generous one, for it seemed he had spared no amount of coin for her mistress' gowns, which rivaled that of any queen. Glancing back at Maren, submerged in the warm, fragrant water, Agnes thought how the young girl had now become a woman, and she was silently grateful that Geoffrey of Meyrick had no further claim upon her mistress. She eyed Maren speculatively, handing her mistress a small cake of sweet-smelling soap. "Is his lordship pleased with his child to come?"

Maren's head shot up at the unexpected question, the soft cloth she held in her hand splashing loudly in the soapy water. She eyed her maid. If Agnes was capable of knowing the truth, then others were also likely to know of it.

"We have not spoken overly much of it," Maren replied softly.

"Does he not know that you are with child?" Agnes pressed her.

"I did not say he was not aware of it. I said only that we have not spoken of it at great length."

Agnes sniffed disapprovingly, wondering what the response of the English knight had been to finding that he must now accept the responsibility of his pleasures with her mistress. "It is not a matter which he can long ignore. Surely he has no regrets in the matter. The Duke of Norfolk seems a proud man, and I should think he would greatly welcome strong, fine sons."

"Even if those sons are part Welsh?" Maren eyed the old woman pointedly, at last giving voice to part of her silent fears.

Agnes leaned over Maren, handing her the cloth for her to wash. "There is no shame in your blood, mistress Maren. Your family is a proud one with a heritage rich enough to match that of any English royalty," she scolded gently.

"It is not shame I feel, Agnes, for I am proud of the child I carry. It is my doubts of my mother's death that plague me, and haunt my dreams," Maren whispered softly.

"Then you believe the English to have lead the attack against Cambria? You must not believe such lies. Old William knew well that those who attacked Cambria were Welsh." Agnes stared keenly at Maren. "Look to Geoffrey of Meyrick for the answers about the treachery against your family, my child."

"Geoffrey? Agnes, what madness do you speak? Geoffrey has been like one of our family since we were children. He and Andrew took their training as soldiers upon the same field with my father. Why, even now he seeks only to—" Maren halted abruptly before she had spoken any more, realizing how dangerously close she had come to revealing all to Agnes of Geoffrey's presence in England.

"Have you seen Geoffrey since you came to London?" Agnes eyed her suspiciously, but Maren went about her bathing.

"How could I possibly have seen Geoffrey? You see how well guarded I am. Indeed, I am no different than the prisoner I once was when I was taken from Cambria."

"A prisoner so carefully cosseted? I think not. Nay, you will not find a prisoner so richly gowned or jeweled, nor so lovingly attended."

Maren laughed. She rose from her bath and accepted the linen Agnes brought for her, tightly wrapping it about her body when she stepped from the wooden tub. "Lovingly attended? I think not, Anges. But then I have not told you that the Duke of Norfolk first thought to bring me to London as his mistress. Only my father's intervention succeeded in raising my station from that of mistress to that of wife. And upon my arrival in London, I

343

was beset by that pale-haired whore who is his mistress, and who plagues me at every turn, that she might regain his favor. No, Agnes, by his own words, the only reason the Duke of Norfolk consented to the marriage was out of his sense of duty should I spill forth his bastard child. And indeed his seed was firmly planted, for I now bear the proof of that burden."

"Will you then rid yourself of the child now, as you are well capable, or will you see it brought forth, and then leave both child and its sire, to find some ease for your doubts by returning to Cambria? For the Duke of Norfolk would never allow you to take his child. I know little of the man, but this much I do know. He is a proud man, he would never allow anyone to take something from him that he holds dear."

"Leave my child?" The words cut through Maren with painful reality. She knew it would never be possible, nor would it be possible for her to take her child from Brettan. Agnes had spoken the truth, for he would never allow it.

Sensing the girl's unspoken answer, Agnes draped the light robe about Maren's shoulders and lovingly unbound the thick tresses to brush the waving masses slowly until they shone with a life of their own. Seeing her young mistress safely abed, Agnes doused the last candle at the table and departed the chamber, confident in the man who had fathered Maren's child, that he would allow no harm to come to them.

Brettan retired to his chamber just as the cock crowed at the first light of dawn. The long hours of wise and thoughtful conversation, well-toasted with ample drink, had failed to fatigue his body. Within just a matter of a few hours, Edward would have them all astride their horses and at the hunt, for such sport was one of the king's favorite pastimes. Leaning over the basin of cold water, Brettan splashed the refreshing liquid over his bronzed face, shaking the droplets that clung to his waving, dark hair. Looking about the room, he caught sight of Maren's garments neatly laid aside, her combs and scented soaps arranged across the large table, the mark of her place in his chamber, in his life. Quietly he moved to stand beside the large bed that seemed to hide her slender form in its voluminous soft mounds. Leaning his weight against the heavy wooden post of the bed, he gently traced the well-turned outline of her cheek, brushing aside a stray curl of raven-black hair. What fate had brought him such a winsome beauty to sleep before him, gently cradling his unborn child within her, until the day she would bring him forth? Where lay the reason that one might possess such qualities of virtue, and another could not? As if in answer to his silent musings, Maren stirred from her sleep. There was no fear when she gazed through the gray light of dawn and saw the tall, lean figure of the man who leaned over her, for there could be no other like him. "You come late to bed, milord," she murmured sleepily.

"And how is it that you know I have not been abed all this time, and but now rise?" he replied softly.

Maren stared through the dim light into those glowing green eyes, then nuzzled his warm hand against her cheek. "The bed is large, and cold without your warmth, milord. I would know had you shared your warmth with me. Instead, you stand over me like some hunting beast stalking its prey."

"You are only partly right. More often I feel the naked prey before the power of your beauty, milady. Shall you indeed strike me down, by turning from me for some grave deed you think me guilty of?"

Maren reached up through the cool morning air and entwined her fingers with his. Now in these last moments before dawn, she felt the most vulnerable, as if some unseen danger lurked very near, just beyond the circle of

Brettan's protection. "There is time, milord, before the dawn and the hour when your king shall beckon," she murmured huskily, her voice filled with a sudden longing. She pulled him down to her, and Brettan yielded to the heat of passion that built to consume them both before the golden glow of the new day.

The cool breezes of the forest stayed the summer heat, and the days passed with measured swiftness. The young queen, greatly relieved of her first discomforts, joined Maren for her daily rides about the estate, while the king and his men spent their days at the hunt. Even Caroline seemed less inclined to her usual waspish moods and lent her efforts to planning the feast that the king had announced for the end of the summer. The vast estate was vividly decorated with abundant flowers in the gardens, to which were soon added festoons of the royal colors hung to decorate every tree. Each servant was pressed to complete the plans for the feast days in advance, so that only the slightest effort would be required on the day of the festivities. The good fortune of the king and his men at the hunt provided the ample fare for the great number of guests that were expected, and the ovens of the manor were kept busy for days preparing a horde of pies, puddings, and sweet breads whose aroma spread on the air to entice every appetite. Accustomed to helping her mother plan large meals for the great numbers of guests at Cambria, Maren lent her efficient hands to helping in the kitchens, which also allowed her to maintain the greatest distance from Caroline, whose interests seemed to concentrate on ordering the servants about, causing more than one frustrated maid to fume silently at her meddlesome suggestions. Caroline was soon well occupied with setting the colorful decorations about the estate. The task indeed seemed a contrast to her disposition, but she seemed to enjoy responsibilities that kept her busy, so that she had little thought for other matters.

When her presence was not required in the kitchens, Maren slipped away to the royal nursery to play with the young prince, keeping him entertained for hours on end, much to the delight of the queen, who often seemed at a loss to deal with her energetic young son. Unknown to Maren, Brettan kept a watchful eye on her, uneasy after witnessing her last confrontation with Caroline, yet unable to determine the reason for his wary spirit, knowing well that Caroline's easy manner of late would soon pass, and she would continue her malicious attacks against Maren when she tired of the planning for the feast. Tenacity was one of Caroline's unfailing qualities.

The first days at King's Forest were hectic for Maren, since the young queen relied more and more upon her new friend for companionship. A bond of friendship grew between the two, and it was not long before the queen had guessed the secret Maren had kept for so many weeks. But always, at the end of each day, Maren found herself watching across the lake for the first of the riders to return from the day's hunt, feeling her calm return when Brettan's tall frame came into view at last, handsomely seated astride the large gray stallion. As the days passed leisurely, the lines about his eyes seemed to ease, and his manner became more relaxed, as if he at last felt he might set aside his constant vigilance against danger. Always the soldier, it was some time before the wariness eased from his manner and he was able to enjoy his time with his men and his friends. Maren wondered at the reason for the change in her mood toward him and could only attribute it to the child she carried, for she found herself truly happy only when she knew he was about, completely safe only with his arms about her.

The day of the summer feast dawned bright and balmy.

347

The entertainers, jugglers, and musicians arrived from a neighboring village, summoned days in advance and eager to entertain the royal visitors. The entire estate had become a country fair. Food and drink were brought forth in abundance and laid upon the vast number of tables draped with white cloths and colorful ribbons. The feast was to be the final celebration before returning to London and, though Brettan had mentioned he might travel to Norfolk, he had spoken no more of it, so that Maren wondered if his plans no longer included her. In the last days Brettan's manner had become more closed to her, as if he were hardly aware of her presence at all. Only when they were alone in their chamber did the invisible shield seem to drop away, so that she felt again that she held some measure of importance to him. And she silently feared that he held great doubts about the child she carried, even regrets for the marriage vows he had spoken. The thought of returning to London did little to lighten her mood, but her dampened spirits soon disappeared before the antics of the jongleurs and acrobats. She moved among the entertainers in the cool morning air with the queen and the young prince, who was greatly amused by the colorfully dressed performers. Beside her, Sandlin and Sir Bothwell lent their jovial humor to the spirit of the day, escorting Maren and the queen about the estate. Caroline had been conspicuously absent the entire morning, and Maren was silently grateful for her reprieve, for she had little tolerance for the woman's insults and biting remarks. Feeling at ease for the first time in several days, Maren soon joined in the light humor of the knights who accompanied her. Her one disappointment was that Brettan had chosen not to join them, for he was to compete in the games of the day and had joined the others in sharpening his skills near the lists, before the competition was to begin.

Maren was oblivious to the careful scrutiny of amber

eyes that watched her from across the playing field, or she might have felt less confidence while she moved among the royal guests.

Caroline moved quietly and unobtrusively at the edge of the greensward. Cautiously she avoided contact with anyone she might know, but searched among the great numbers of people for the one she sought, and who she was certain would be there that day. These several weeks since she had chanced upon Maren's meeting with the stranger, she had searched for some sign of the man, confident that he would again attempt to contact Maren. Theirs had been no chance meeting, for their manner had spoken of familiarity, although Caroline could not understand the words that she was certain were Welsh. Caroline carefully searched the faces of each person she passed for some sign of the man she was certain she would recognize. She could clearly see how the man's presence might work in her favor to discredit Maren. Caroline smiled her most radiant smile at Lord and Lady Ashton as they passed by, then pushed her way past the many tents that had been set at the edge of the playing field. She glanced longingly at the large, ornately decorated tent with the blue and gold banners flying, but promised herself that there would soon come a time when she would be mistress of all that the blue and gold colors represented.

Brettan carefully eyed the distance across the clearing to the farthest tree, where a bright red satin cloth had been fastened to the tree trunk as a target. Taking the arrow his man handed him, he set the nock and with great ease drew it back even with his cheek, sighting the target along the shaft. In one clean movement he released the arrow, hearing the shaft split the air and the deadly tip quickly find its mark. He knew he could easily be matched by the other marksmen. It was the greater distances that offered the greater challenge for the afternoon. Moving back several paces to the next line marked in the dirt, he waited his turn at the target, carefully eyeing his competition among the men who stood about preparing their bows, or making some adjustment in the plumage of an arrow, convinced that it might make some difference in the accuracy of the shot. He leaned his well-muscled frame against a large oak tree, carefully surveying the men about him. He tried to shake off the growing tension that played through his muscles, causing him to feel uneasy, while all about him remained calm and unchanged. There was nothing unusual in the manner of the men who good-naturedly hurled challenges to one another, or boasted of their prowess with the bow. Across the green his wandering gaze caught sight of the mauve gown, which he remembered Maren had selected that morning for its more ample waist, that did not bind against the growth of the child she carried. His eyes warmly followed that slender beauty with long waving black hair that swirled about her shoulders and waist, while she moved through the milling crowds. He was pleased that the anger between them had eased of late, although her mood had become more withdrawn, and he could only attribute it to the child. Though his responsibilities often kept him from her for long hours, he increasingly found his thoughts filled with the vision of that exquisite fair face, and silken masses of raven-black hair that draped about her slender form alluringly, as when she slept curled innocently beside him. He had undertaken the responsibility of the marriage vows as he would have any other, with a firm sense of duty, always aware that there remained secrets between them, and doubts. Well could he remember his journey to Cambria and the blind, consuming quest for vengeance that had set him on that path so many months before. He still carried the firm belief that she was the key to that quest. He accepted her first explanations of the medallion, but

350

there was more to the matter that had not been said. He knew well her mother had been murdered in the attack against Cambria, but where she might have obtained the medallion he had not been able to learn from Maren. And he knew well, by the nightmares that haunted her sleep, that she possessed great fears, which he had not been able to take from her. There was another who held the answer to that, and he could not rid himself of the feeling that whoever that person might be, great danger awaited Maren. Her father had believed that England might provide her a safe haven, but Brettan had not been able to learn what that danger might be. The last man stepped from the line, and Brettan handed his bow back to his squire, choosing instead the prized Welsh longbow, a finely made weapon nearly twice the size of the English bow, and made of the finest hand-rubbed wood, found only in the forests of Northern Wales. He expertly tested the tautness of the bowstring, aware of the curious glances he received at having chosen such a large, ungainly weapon, whose lightness of weight belied its size. Setting the arrow, he sighted the target. Taking careful aim, he released the arrow and with great satisfaction watched it find the center of the target. A murmur of appreciation was heard from those who watched, and his knights and competitors gathered about to inspect the oversized bow. Brettan's eyes scanned the royal enclosure for some sign of Maren, not fully at ease with her far from his sight.

The royal party moved along the green, and Maren stopped to sample a tart offered by one of the servants. As if in approval of her choice, her child moved strongly within her, and Maren's hand gently felt the slight rounded hardness of her stomach. Aware that Brettan had not yet felt his child move within her, she wondered at his true feelings about the babe. Eleanore smiled at Maren knowingly and reached out a hand reassuringly at the secret they shared.

Brettan had insisted that he had married her out of a sense of duty to protect her innocence, but there were moments when she caught him looking at her in that strange way of his, that seemed to lock her within his private world, where only the two of them could enter. In the few months since their marriage, he had seemed every bit the faithful husband, sharing her bed with a passion that left her breathless for more, yet always retreating beyond the veil of that golden gaze to some inner place, as if he but waited and watched, but for what she did not know. And the times when he chose not to share her bed, her fears and doubts returned tenfold. As of late they had taken a different form, an honest fear that he would soon tire of her and return to Caroline, when Maren grew round-bellied with his child. Maren forced those haunting doubts from her thoughts, bending to scoop the young prince into her arms and hug him tightly, aware that very soon she would hold her own child, if Brettan would allow it, and not send her and the child away. Slowly they made their way back to the royal enclosure, brilliantly festooned with banners and ribbons that fluttered wildly in the summer breeze. Across the field the targets had been set, and the bowmen took their positions for the competition along the marked line. Maren shaded her eyes with her hand, searching among the knights for the brilliant blue and gold de Lorin colors, her breath catching in her throat at the sight of Brettan's standard, which snapped in a breeze that seemed to send the figures of the golden lions leaping into the wind.

Having spent the greater part of the morning walking about the vast estate, Caroline sighed her disappointment. She had failed to find the elusive stranger she had seen speaking with Maren. She turned about to return to the royal enclosure, intent on not missing any of the contests Brettan was to compete in. Whirling about with great impatience, she collided headlong with a tall servant, who reached out to steady her as she tripped.

"You fool, release me or I shall have the guards set upon you. You!" Caroline stared into the lean face shaded by the heavy woolen hood, her slender hands closing over his arm in a talon-like grip, for she refused to risk losing the man in the crowd. "Wait! I must speak with you." Vainly she tried to restrain him, but her strength was no match for the stranger who twisted away, suddenly alarmed that Caroline might draw the attention of the guards that were all about.

"Wait! I must speak to you of the Lady Maren!" Caroline called after the man, who sought refuge in the milling crowd about them.

Geoffrey halted at the mention of Maren's name. Turning back slowly, he gazed at the fair-haired woman, his eyes narrowing. He wondered suspiciously what she might know of Maren or his conversation with her. She was the same woman he had seen approach her weeks before near the forest, after he had tried to persuade Maren to leave England with him.

"I know you have come because of her. I may be able to help you."

"What concern to you is the Lady Maren?" Geoffrey questioned suspiciously, turning back to the woman.

"She has taken something from me that I would see returned. Perhaps if I help, you may be able to aid me in my cause."

Geoffrey eyed the woman keenly. There was something in her manner that told him he must not trust her, but he might well be able to use her to gain Maren.

"What has she taken from you, that you would make an alliance with an enemy of the crown to see it returned?"

Caroline eyed the Welshman carefully, knowing well she must be cautious in the matter, or she might find

353

herself in grave danger. "Come, I know of a place where we may speak of the matter more privately. There are too many guards about who might become suspicious."

Geoffrey followed Caroline past the tents into the thickly wooded copse beyond the green. From many days of watching and listening, he knew of the woman's relationship with the Duke of Norfolk, and he had already guessed that the marriage had interfered greatly with her own plans to become the Duchess of Norfolk. Silently he followed the pale-haired woman, whose beauty was sharp and hardened, and he decided that in not too many years her beauty, unlike Maren's, would fade, leaving only the harsh lines of greed upon her face. Coming to a small secluded glen, Caroline whirled about, a small, lethal dagger clenched tightly in her fist, her face hard, her eyes glinting maliciously. "I do not mean to harm you, but you are my enemy, as is that whore who has stolen the Duke of Norfolk from me. I only guard against any treachery you might attempt."

"You may put away the blade. I have but one reason for risking such danger, and that is the Lady Maren. Once she is returned to me, I will leave England."

"I too wish for that. Once she is gone beyond his reach, he will forget her and will once again turn to me."

Geoffrey eyed Caroline uncertainly, and she wielded the blade threateningly. "True that may be, but she may not willingly leave England."

"She will leave willingly enough. I know well that she longs to return to her home. Indeed, she has tried many times to escape. But always the Duke of Norfolk has prevented her from leaving, for he feels some sense of duty to the girl, though I cannot say why. But I must find a way to be rid of her. And you may be of service to me in that cause."

Geoffrey sighed heavily and regarded the scheming woman. "I have spoken with Maren. By her own word, she will not leave England. The marriage was by her father's decision, and she feels bound by his word. And she will not easily leave the marriage, or the father of her child."

"What is that you say? A child? I should have known it these weeks past. So soon his seed spills fertile within her. I know him well. You are right, for he would never allow her to take his child. Of that I am certain. Yet there may be a way that she might be convinced to leave him. And we must see that she escapes. She is never left unguarded." A deep furrow lined Caroline's forehead while she gave herself to thought. "There must be some way to lure her away from Brettan's guard, perhaps at night, before he retires to their chamber. The guards are not near then. It must be done soon, before the king and queen return to London. It would be impossible to take her from the castle. Here we have the open countryside on one side, and the forest on the other, to offer protection. But rest assured that your escape will not be an easy one. Once Brettan learns she is gone, I fear he will give chase. His guard is many and, if it is combined with that of the king, escape may be impossible. Are you willing, Welshman, to risk your life for the girl?"

Geoffrey sneered at Caroline. "You English know little of our ways. Even now my men await my return and, though our number is few, we are enough to see the matter done."

Caroline lowered the slender dagger, resheathing it in the jeweled scabbard at her waist, then approached the stranger. The color of her pale eyes deepened with the boldness of their plan. She slowly approached Geoffrey, swaying her hips gently as she walked across the clearing.

"I have heard it said that the Welsh are a wild and ruthless people, and yet you do not seem so dangerous. It will take a ruthless man to steal the wife of the Duke of

355

Norfolk. Is she worth the price you seem so willing to pay, or is there some other reason you seek her return? Certainly your determination is not merely that of a lovesick swain? Indeed, the girl would seem too sullen for you to enjoy yourself with her. What then is the reason that brings you to Edward's camp, risking death for such as her?" Stopping before him, Caroline felt an uneasy excitement running through her veins. She stood so near the enemy, unguarded, and now by her own hands unarmed. Slowly she reached back and pulled the combs from her flaxen hair, letting the silvery mass tumble to her shoulder, a bold contrast to the thick mass of Maren's ebony tresses. Her gaze locked with his, and she tossed her head, setting the thin wisps of pale hair floating about her. The very danger she placed herself in seemed to heighten her senses, and she could feel the building of her passions. She knew well the agonies of the long months since Brettan had come willingly to her bed. Though others had readily extended their favors to satisfy her desires, she still felt that hollow longing that only one man had ever satisfied. She wondered if this Welshman might for a while fill the void within her that Brettan had left. Slowly she raised her hand, instinctively knowing any sudden movement would be regarded as treachery. Geoffrey eyed the woman suspiciously, wondering at her game. His breath seemed to still in his chest when she slowly unfastened the closures of her gown, letting it fall away, stepping out of the pale yellow cloth. Wantonly she slowly wrapped her arms about his waist, drawing him near, so that her small breasts were pushed feverishly against his chest. Geoffrey exhaled slowly, his eyes watching over the top of her head, searching the forest that surrounded them for some unseen danger, some trap the woman might have set without his knowing. Deciding to play her game, but on his own terms, Geoffrey grabbed her hand, drawing her down beside him, none too gently. His eyes traveled hungrily over her slender length, and he unwittingly compared her to that lovelier form that had haunted his dreams for months. Caroline hungrily reached up to unfasten the ties of his tunic. Her touch was warm when she greedily stroked her thin fingers through the light brown hair on his chest, her lips lowering to trace a path of fevered kisses across his stomach. She lifted the tunic, enjoying the power she held over her enemy.

Geoffrey pulled away from her for a moment, stepping out of the coarsely woven breeches and the scuffed boots, before throwing himself down on the moss-covered earth to rejoin the English whore who so willingly offered what he had sought for a lifetime from a dark-haired beauty, whose haunting vision clouded his thoughts even as he coupled with the heated bitch who spread herself so willingly beneath him.

Caroline smiled her superiority over the man beside her and, in one well-calculated move, turned him onto his back so that she straddled his hips. Slowly she lowered her head to reclaim his lips, his hands sliding excitedly down her back and across her hips. With deliberate rhythm she ground her hips into him, promising, torturing, still unyielding. Geoffrey's fingers dug into her skin, but she persisted in taunting him. When his strong hands closed about her ribs and threatened to crush her, she viciously bit his ear, causing him to grunt in sudden pain. Geoffrey reached above his head and drew the slender estoc concealed within the belt he had laid aside. With quiet certainty he leveled the tip of the blade at Caroline's throat, and she pulled back in surprise, thinking she had perhaps misjudged this Welsh heathen. But she calmed herself when she saw the passion that raged within his eyes, and she smiled knowingly. Geoffrey's hand twisted painfully in her hair, but still Caroline refused to show any fear, his threats only adding to her mounting excitement.

"You, milady, are a whore. You ask nothing for your favors," Geoffrey growled at her.

"Then I am not so very different from your precious Maren. She willingly crawled into Brettan's bed when he held her prisoner. Do not condemn me so easily. At least I acknowledge that which I want and do not meekly submit to what others would have of me."

"One such as you can never understand Maren. For you cannot understand that she would place others before herself. But you have your purpose, and you shall serve me well before we see this done." Geoffrey glared at her.

Caroline's eyes narrowed as she resumed her rhythmic movement against him, the tip of that lethal blade never wavering from the spot against her neck. Her hands moved over his chest and across his shoulders, while she swayed seductively above him, each movement sending her small breasts shaking, those upturned peaks growing taut with her passion. Her eyes never left those of her captor, even when she raised herself quickly and in one violent motion settled herself upon him, taking him fully within her, writhing to feel his heat penetrating deep within her. Wildly she picked up the pace of her movement over him, until she suddenly felt herself picked up and rudely thrown against the floor of the glen. Never breaking that intimate contact, Geoffrey slammed into her brutally, again and again, without relenting, bruising, thrusting deep with her, as if by hurting her, he might in some small way relieve some of the silent agony he had borne for months. And yet there was no cry of the pain he brought from her, only a deep-throated laugh, her eyes glistening brightly with the pleasure of her pain. Her cool fingers flew at his chest, raking her nails across his bare skin, leaving blooded furrows where they traveled. Wildly Caroline tossed about beneath the arrogant enemy, meeting each thrust equally, her passion now a guttural gasp, for she felt the waves of his release deep within her. But her own passion thirsted, and she moved against him with a need that became desperation and yet was not sated. Roughly Geoffrey pushed her away from him and moved to gather his clothes. Slipping into the breeches, he cautiously eyed the panting woman, who sat up slowly, brushing the twigs and grass from her matted hair. She cast him a murderous glare. "I should have known a Welshman could give me no pleasure. That arrogant slut you prize so highly, is welcome to your quickly spent rutting. Perhaps that is what comes from coupling with animals in barns." She spat at him.

Before she could take caution against him, Caroline was sent sprawling back by the force of Geoffrey's blow against her cheek.

"I take my pleasure according to my partner. Give yourself no great airs, milady. The bull who but serves to breed a calf has more pleasure than I have found between your thighs. Indeed, you could learn much from those lowly cows."

Caroline glared at him warningly. "Set aside your petty insults, Welshman. You need me to gain the girl. Without me all is lost, and for now I could as easily see you split open, if I thought there were any other way to be rid of the conniving whore." Quickly Caroline retrieved her clothes and dressed, so that, except for the red coloration that spread across her smarting cheek, none would be the wiser for their woodland tryst.

"Make your plans to leave England. We shall meet again in three days' time, at this same spot. And make certain your men do not act hastily. We cannot risk our plans on some foolish act."

Geoffrey nodded, looking at the woman with something akin to disgust, feeling that he had gained little satisfaction within her meager frame. "That is more easily said than done. My men grow restless and quite bloodthirsty. It would aid Llywelyn's cause no small measure to see Edward cut down, so that he might lead no more armies against Wales. See your treachery well laid, woman, but do it quickly. I know not how long I may restrain my men, before one is tempted to strike against the English. Though they are loyal to me, their anger runs deep."

Caroline gave him a contemptuous look. "Such lack of order would not be tolerated among the English. But heed my warning to keep your men in hand. If there should be a mishap against the king, the entire English army would be at your throat. There would be no safe haven in all of England or Wales for you. Heed my words, and I shall deliver the girl to you. Now go, we must not be seen." Pulling the thin wisps of her hair back with the heavy combs, Caroline smoothed the fabric of her gown. When she looked up, the Welshman was gone, silently blending into the forest beyond the glade, as if he might never have been there. Only the bruised ache between her legs gave proof of their meeting. Carefully she retrieved her slippers, then hastened to return to the day's events beyond the glen. Caroline felt more confident than she had in the many weeks since Maren's arrival, feeling certain her reunion with Brettan was close at hand.

Maren turned to the young page who approached and beckoned for her attention. Brettan had requested her presence in his tent before the jousting that was to begin shortly. Knowing well his intentions, Maren's temper rankled at the obvious meaning of his summons. Her deep blue eyes glinted boldly, and she sent the lad back with the message that she would not join him. She could well imagine his temper when he received her message, and a faint smile of satisfaction pulled at the corners of her mouth. Deciding on a walk, Maren enticed the young prince away from his maid and, escorted by two of the King's guards, strolled with the young lad among the musicians and acrobats, delighting when the child gurgled gleefully at the antics of the performers. They stopped to purchase some sugar-coated plums before approaching the lists, where the young prince was captivated by the sight of the knights in their shining armor, astride the great war horses. Maren stooped down beside young Alphonse to wipe some of the purplish confection from his cheeks, where he had smeared some of the sweetness, and she marveled how one sugared plum might adorn so much face. A long shadow fell across their path, and Maren turned to look up into the steely visage of Brettan de Lorin astride the gray stallion, in full dress of armor ready for the jousting to begin.

"You wound me, milady, that you would refuse my request to join me in my tent. A knight of the king often chooses to spend those last minutes, before meeting the lance, with someone dear to his heart."

Maren reached back to the young prince to make one last effort to wipe the sticky plum from his cheek, but he dodged her mischievously. "Then, milord, by all means, you should summon someone dear to your heart, and not cast your requests so lightly on one who does not meet that qualification."

"Aye, my sweet Maren, your words wound me far worse than any blade. But since I now must join the battle in the lists, will you not give me some small token of your affection?"

Maren straightened to gaze fully at Brettan, her deep blue eyes unable to look away from those glowing green orbs that held her gaze. She could not deny how

361

handsome he was, sitting before her so calm, so arrogant, so sure of himself. "But as you can see, milord, I have nothing to give." Impatiently young Alphonse tugged at her hand until she turned to give him her full attention, unable to ignore his silent pleas any longer. With great satisfaction, the child held aloft the bright silken cloth she had used to wipe his face. Before she could snatch it from his grasp, Brettan had lowered the tip of his lance with great ease and in one swift motion pulled it from the child's hand. The young prince laughed gleefully, but she whirled back to Brettan, her anger at his little game obvious in the firm set of her jaw. "As with everything else, you merely take what you want. It matters not that I might have considered giving it to you."

"I fear, Maren, I grew far too impatient. I could not wait for you to decide the matter. The competition might have ended before you finished glaring at me." Urging the gray forward, so that Maren thought he intended to walk over her, he halted the stallion with the gentlest touch on the reins and, bending low, with an ease that belied the weight of the heavy armor he wore, he scooped Maren into his grasp and pulled her against him. Anger flooded through her at his bold display of her before the king, indeed the entire field of English knights, yet she dared not kick out lest she frighten the gray and cause them both great harm for her foolishness. With both hands she pushed with all her strength against the cold hardness of the armor that protected his chest, Brettan's warm, vibrant laugh flowing through her. Teeth clenched tightly, Maren seethed, struggling vainly to gain her release.

"Take care, Maren, lest you find yourself beneath the gray's hooves, and me powerless to protect you."

"You are most loathsome, milord. You care not that everyone is watching us, even the king."

"Indeed, I care not, Maren. I have told you, I but seek

362

some small token of your affection, given freely. The cloth shall accompany me into the heat of 'battle'. But I seek more, something to live within my memory."

Without any warning, Brettan crushed her to him in a fierce embrace that forced the breath from her, his mouth lowering to her, his lips burning feverishly against hers. In the heat of her anger, Maren felt herself responding to his touch and, though she tried to deny the pleasure of it, she could not. Slowly her arms reached up until they encircled his neck, and she held him to her with a passion to match his own, wishing that they might be anywhere but in the midst of the field of spectators, some private place where they might enjoy each other in their ultimate passion of one another. The other knights rode past them, casting appreciative glances toward the slender girl within his embrace. Brettan released her gently and set her back upon the ground beside the young prince. "Guard her well, milord, until my return."

Young Alphonse, quite serious with the purpose of his new responsibility, bowed before the knight, then raised twinkling blue eyes that hinted at his merriment in the game Brettan played with him.

"And you, milady, see that you break no more hearts this day. I think I shall have little strength left after the jousting, to take on a long line of bold knights who come forward to defend your honor."

"You are mistaken, milord, for they all know my honor sorely abused. All I receive are looks of pity for the company I am forced to endure."

Brettan threw back his head and laughed uproariously. "Shall I then tell them, one and all, just how you enjoy my 'abuse'?"

Maren's cheeks flamed brightly. "I would expect such as that from an Englishman."

Brettan bowed his head before her in mock salute. "I thank you for your kiss, milady. Now I may do battle,

363

even risk my life upon the field of honor, taking with me the fond memory of your passion." The last was spoken almost in a whisper, and he smiled mischievously at her, his wide smile sending the dimples in his cheeks dancing in a maddening way that she found absolutely irresistible. In a sudden fit of temper, Maren grabbed young Alphonse by the hand and whirled about to find her way back to the royal enclosure, her hips swaying gently, her slender back rigid as she stomped away. Brettan chuckled softly to himself, thinking there were more pleasures and surprises to be found within a marriage, than outside of it; at least more honesty. And he smiled when he turned the gray stallion toward the lists, and rode to join the others for the jousting.

Maren watched the jousting enthusiastically, marveling at Brettan's strength and prowess upon the battlefield, for he bested each of his opponents and rode from the field completely victorious. She had never really doubted the outcome. There was only one who might have given some doubt to the victory, and the king had chosen to save his strength for the other sports that were to fill the afternoon, reluctantly acquiescing to the queen's request that he not participate in the competition when he was so recently returned from the dangers of war. Brettan rode toward the royal enclosure to receive his tribute, and his eyes watched only her slender form, as she sat beside the young queen. He bowed stiffly before his king, and then, giving Maren a wink and a warming smile, whirled the gray about and sought his tent to prepare for the archers' tournament.

Edward also took his leave to prepare for the competition, leaving Maren with the young prince and Queen Eleanore. Across the green, Maren saw the brilliant blue and gold banners waving above Brettan's tent and pondered his surprise should she suddenly choose to join him there. She smiled at that thought, and at the possibility that he might not be found in time to compete against the other knights of the realm. A group of riders galloped past, and the young prince playfully dodged his mother's grasp. Just beyond the queen's reach, young Alphonse stumbled and fell dangerously close to those thundering hooves passing by. The men valiantly sought to guide their mounts away from the child, but Maren darted among the riders and quickly scooped the young child from the ground, hugging him tightly against her. Her heart pounded wildly at the near mishap, but Alphonse squirmed to regain his freedom, unaffected by the danger and completely unafraid. Maren laughed nervously, then set him to the ground, keeping a firm hold on his hand lest he sneak away and fall into some other danger. She glanced up at the young queen and smiled reassuringly at the young woman, whose look of distress faded into a grim smile while she reached for her son. "I fear he outdoes me. Edward says he carries the true signs of a great warrior, but I am given to doubt that he shall survive to that age. Maren, you are a constant wonder to me. Your love and tolerance are a great gift. Your child shall be most fortunate to have your love."

"The prince is a joy to me. He reminds me much of my young brother, Edmund, when he was that age. He too was a great handful. It required all my mother's attention, not to mention that of my sister Catherine and myself, to keep him from doing himself some great injury."

"You miss your family greatly. I can see you carry much sadness, but you must not despair. The Duke of Norfolk shall ease your sadness."

Maren fought back her sadness at the thought of her brother's uncertain fate, and the young Queen reached out to squeeze her hand reassuringly. "You are friend to me, Maren, and I value that very highly. Always

365

remember that love is a most precious gift and, once given, can never be taken back, but will return to you a score more than that which you gave."

Tears welled within Maren's eyes at the queen's great loneliness, for she could never allow anyone close for fear of betrayal. Queen Eleanore had spoken honestly.

"Milady, you belong here in England. Though you may not see it now, I feel that you belong here. Stay with us. Do not flee us. We offer only friendship."

Uncertain how to answer the queen, Maren laid her hand gently over Eleanore's. "There is so much that must be set aright, your majesty."

"And in time, all will be set aright. You must have faith in those who love you. You must have faith in the Duke of Norfolk, for he loves you."

Maren looked at her doubtfully. "I cannot be certain of what you say. There has been so much anger between us, that at times I fear it can never be taken away completely. I pray that in time what you say may be true, for the sake of the child."

"Time, milady, shall prove to you, that you are indeed loved."

Slowly they returned to the royal enclosure to watch the archers take their places along the line that had been marked in the sod. The signal was given, and each archer set his arrow and at the next signal released it. Each then moved back to a second line several paces behind the first. Again the arrows were set, and again released, all but three finding the targets accurately. Edward seemed highly pleased at the prowess of his archers. They moved back to a third line, and then a fourth, each time a few arrows falling short of their mark. The competitors approached the fifth mark from the target, with more than half the field remaining. Down the long line of men, Maren noticed with pride Brettan's tall, well-muscled frame, and watched the ease with which he set his arrows at the given command and effortlessly released the shaft, the arrow easily finding the target, and she noted with great pride the Welsh longbow he wielded. The distance was again increased, and several more archers failed to hit the target. Brettan exchanged some good-natured challenge with the king, who returned the challenge, and the men again set their arrows. Now only three archers remained—the king, Brettan, and Sir Bothwell, who had also chosen a longbow. Again the distances were lengthened. Maren watched Sir Bothwell carefully eye the target and slowly raise the bow. It seemed an eternity until the arrow was released, finding the center of the target. Brettan nodded appreciatively and took his place at the line. Maren watched excitedly, unaware that Queen Eleanore watched her with a knowing smile of approval, and also unaware that Caroline had returned and sat close behind them, her own gaze openly malicious, for she noted well Maren's glowing eyes upon Brettan de Lorin.

Drawing back the arrow, Brettan took careful aim, his hand completely steady, and quickly released the arrow, the tip easily finding the center of the target. Edward silently cursed the longbows his opponents had chosen, well aware of the weapons' long-distance accuracy, but gamely he took his position. He carefully noted the added distance to the target and calculated the gentle breeze that stirred.

All watched in great anticipation. The king walked to the target to more accurately determine the distance, then turned back to the line.

From the corner of her eye, Maren saw a movement very near the royal enclosure, among the spectators. She looked back toward the targets, while Edward continued his careful scrutiny of the distance. She suddenly felt a chill in the summer air and shivered involuntarily. Her attention was caught by that single figure approaching through the silent crowd. Suddenly uneasy, Maren spun about to see the man charge toward them, the light glinting off the cold, deadly blade clutched tightly in his hand. Abrupt realization spread through Maren, for she saw well the direction of his movement. With one thought, Maren lunged in front of the queen, a warning cry escaping her lips as she threw herself between the attacker and the queen.

Maren's slender weight caught the attacker off balance, and he stumbled momentarily. Maren clutched the front of his coarse, woolen tunic, and her breath caught as she stared wide-eyed into the face of the stranger. She felt only a dull ache when the blade entered her side, and thought that if this were her death, then it was nothing to fear. Unconsciousness crept over her, mercifully delivering her into a blessed darkness where there was no pain. And in those wide, blue eyes that stared disbelieving into his own, the Welsh rebel saw his own certain death by the grave miscalculation he had made.

Within the royal enclosure, the realization of the attack brought chaos and panic as the young queen watched the horrible scene before her. She quickly pushed her young son from harm's way to the safety of his maid, then screamed for the guards. Within moments, a score of the English guard swarmed into the enclosure, equal amount giving chase to a lone figure that fled through the crowds upon the field.

The queen quickly shrugged off the loyal guards who desperately sought to remove her to the safety of the manorhouse, while the call went across the field for the call to arms. Fearfully she knelt beside Maren's crumpled form, grasping her hand as she felt for the faint pulsing in her wrist. Anger welled within the young queen, for she realized well that the attack had been meant for herself, and now one so dear to her lay dangerously close to death.

From across the greensward, the cry to arms was heard instantly. Brettan whirled about and sought the gray stallion tethered close by, his warrior's instincts immediately washing away his fatigue from the days' events. He scanned the entire field as he vaulted into the saddle and, without a backwards glance for his guard, spurred the mighty destrier forward across the greensward, large clods of turf churned up under the mighty steed's hooves. A deep sense of foreboding tore at him when he approached the enclosure, where the royal attendants, the lords and ladies of Edward's court stood in massed confusion. Close behind him, Edward ran the full length of the field, his thoughts immediately for his queen and the young prince, his sword drawn.

Seeing the bowed head of the young queen bent over a figure, Brettan suddenly felt a twisting within, for he recognized the mauve color of Maren's gown. Eleanore looked up when Brettan dismounted and knelt beside Maren, her eyes speaking her anguish. Brettan's warm fingers gently brushed against Maren's neck, and he felt the faint pulsing that beat weakly beneath her skin.

"She took the blade meant for me." The young queen's voice trembled with her emotion as she stared into Brettan's fierce gaze.

Gently Brettan reached beneath Maren, fearing he might cause her more pain if he moved too quickly. His large hand closed about her waist, his other arm went beneath her legs, and he stood effortlessly, her fragile weight borne easily in his strong arms, capable of wielding a sword, now gently bearing her with such tenderness toward the manorhouse, where the royal servants had already received word of the attack.

Caroline vainly attempted to gain his attention, meeting only a menacing glare that caused her to shrink from him. Silently she cursed the damned Welshman and his inability to control his men, for she had no doubts that it was indeed one of them who had wielded the knife. A slow smile spread across her face while she watched the solemn procession into the large stone house, aware that the day's events might well work to her advantage. And, feeling as if she indeed made a bargain with the devil, she prayed that the Duchess of Norfolk might not recover from her wounds.

Brettan kicked open the large door to the first chamber he approached, having quickly gained the second floor. With great care he carried Maren to the large bed and gently lay her on its softness, which hardly seemed to yield beneath her slight weight. His hand about her waist was covered with her blood, and the sleeve of his tunic showed crimson and wet. Down the length of his breeches her blood had run freely. Behind him, a multitude of servants and the young queen filled the room, until Agnes pushed her way through the stunned servants. She stopped abruptly at the sight of her mistress, so pale, and covered with blood, lying upon the thick coverlet of the bed. Her horror-struck eyes flew to Brettan's in silent question, but she hardly waited for an answer, but moved to quickly remove Maren's gown. Eleanore gave her orders for hot water, and clean cloths to bind the wound, sending a score of servants scampering with firm commands that tolerated no question of her authority. Agnes vainly attempted to pull Brettan from the bed, that she might attend Maren. Eleanore came forward, casting aside all formality, and gently took Brettan by the shoulders, his tall frame towering over her smaller height.

"Milord, you must let us clean and dress the wound. The bleeding must be stopped if she is to live. I will care for her myself, and with Agnes' help she may well survive to greet the morrow. You can do no more here. Please let us do what we must." Pleadingly she held his hands in her own, looking into that green gaze that reflected all his misery. But behind the misery she saw the growing spark of his desire for revenge, and she drew back almost fearfully. Brettan turned suddenly and cast one long, hungering glance over his shoulder at the pale young girl who lay so near death in the massive bed.

"See that she lives, Agnes. I could not bear her loss." With those last words, he stormed from the chamber, leaving Agnes and the queen no time to ponder the passion of his words. He had spoken what he had only just begun to realize, that his life would be meaningless without the fiery, proud young girl, who had once been his prisoner, but now held him captive, even so near death.

Chapter Sixteen

Brettan kicked at the bundled form with the toe of his boot. The bundle unrolled, the heavy woolen blanket falling away from the body of a man plainly dressed in the coarse woolen garments of a common servant, so that he might move about without drawing attention to himself. His lifeless body came to rest before the king, who stood across from Brettan. Their gazes locked for a brief moment.

"I gave specific orders that the man was to be taken alive!" Edward roared to his men, who had just a moment before delivered the bundled body upon the greensward.

"Milord, we found the man slain within the forest, already dead by some other hand before we reached him," the helmed guard answered quickly.

With a stiff nod of frustration, Edward dismissed his captain and turned to Brettan. "None can remember seeing the man about. He was merely a nameless instrument of Llywelyn's treachery against the crown, for it is obvious his attack was meant against the queen. I have sorely misjudged Llywelyn. I had not believed he would dare to strike so deep within England. He grows bold in his last hours."

Brettan glanced toward the second-floor windows that reflected the afternoon sun sinking low in the sky, the muscle in his cheek tensing. He turned back to his king, suddenly unable to bear the thought of returning to that chamber. "I shall take my own men and search the forest. I want the one who gave the orders for the attack. He is the murderer I seek, the one who has eluded me these many months. I will have his life for what he has caused this day, even if it means following him to Llywelyn's lair."

Edward sought to ease the cold, brutal desire for revenge he saw behind that guarded visage. "My friend, Llywelyn's moment of truth shall come, that I promise you. I fear that, should the Lady Maren not recover, he may yet find in her death a cause for uniting all of Wales against England, and prolong the agony of this conflict. I shall ride with you. I cannot abide the long hours of waiting, sitting idly before the fire. Perhaps when we are returned, we shall have good news of the Lady Maren. I pray it is so, for I have come to value her proud, brave spirit."

Edward swung into the saddle and spurred his horse hard to catch Brettan's fleeing figure, which charged the gray toward the edge of the forest, driving the stallion as if all the demons of hell pursued them. Mercilessly he drove himself, and his guard searched long into the night for any signs of the attackers in the heavily wooded copse, only relenting at last for Sandlin's earnest plea that they could accomplish nothing more in the darkness that had descended over the dense forest.

Haggard and exhausted, Edward and Brettan returned to the manorhouse. The windows of the entire second floor were darkened, with only a few candles left burning in the main hall to guide their footfalls. Greatly fatigued, Edward waved back a dutiful servant who rushed forward with the evening meal, kept warming on the kitchen hearth. Eleanore greeted him at the base of the steps, then slowly approached Brettan, who stood before the blazing hearth trying to drive the ache from his tired muscles. His hands rested on the mantle that loomed over his head. He seemed unaware of the footsteps behind him. His head hung wearily, his eyes closed in complete exhaustion.

"She is dead?" Brettan's voice was hardly more than a ragged whisper, as if those few words required all his effort.

Gently the young queen reached out to touch his arm comfortingly. "Nay, milord, she lives, though how I am not certain."

"And the child she carries?"

"There was such great loss of blood. It is too soon to know of the child. Please, you must rest. I will have food and wine brought."

Brettan turned slowly, his broad shoulders sagging with his great fatigue. Lines of weariness deeply creased at the corners of his eyes. He smiled faintly at the young queen. "Your life was spared. For that I am grateful."

Eleanore shook her head sadly. "Yea, milord, but at what cost? The life of a friend, one who is innocent, who has suffered so much loss already? 'Tis an unfair exchange, I think. Please let me have food brought for you, milord."

"Nay, I must go to her. And my thanks for the words you bring me, kind lady. They are the only strength I need."

Silently the queen watched Brettan mount the darkened stairway to the second floor. She joined her husband at the base of the stairs, wearily laying her head against his comforting shoulder, and he drew her up the stairs to their own chamber. Beyond the estate, the guards of Edward of England and the Duke of Norfolk continued their search for the unseen enemy.

375

A single candle burned at the table beside the large bed when Brettan entered the chamber, moving silently across the wood flooring. He waited a moment for his eyes to adjust to the meager light, straining through the darkness to see Maren's form in the bed, to gain some assurance that the queen had not been mistaken. Slowly he exhaled, releasing some of the tension he held within, seeing the slender outline of her body beneath the coverlet that had been spread across her. Agnes rose from her chair beside the hearth, where she had kept her silent vigil the hours past. Brettan brushed past the maid, and approached the bed to reassure himself that Maren truly lived, unable to understand how she might have survived such a wound as he had seen many a man lose his life to. As if his memory sought to torment him, he thought he could feel again the warm stickiness of her life's blood upon his hands. He brushed his hands against the velvet of his breeches and stood over her, leaning against the massive oaken post of the bed for support. Her head was turned slightly away from him, and in the dimly lit room, watching her intensely, he could see the faint but rapid pulsing in her neck, the shallow rise and fall of her chest.

"The wound is clean and bound, milord. In truth, I do not know how she lives, but her mother's strength flows within her, and with God's mercy she will live. The next days will tell. All that we may do is wait. I will stay with her, milord. You must rest."

Brettan shook his disheveled head adamantly. "Nay, I will not leave her again. I will care for her myself."

"Milord, the hour is late, and you have had no food or rest this day. There is naught that may be done for her now, only to watch against the fever. What good will you be to her should you fall ill for your worry?"

"It is my intention to remain here. If I must throw you from the chamber to see it done, then so be it. I have no patience for argument in the matter. I brought her to this, and I will see that she is well again." Brettan's voice had changed to a low menacing growl, so that Agnes backed away before taking her final stand. "I'll not have you causing her more harm with your desire for vengeance in this. She is my mistress. I have cared for her since the day she was born, and I'll not have you causing her more harm. She had no care for being here. All that she has ever desired was to be allowed to return to her home, and but for you she might have. Now she lies there, near death, because of it. May the devil take you, and I will not have you dirtying up this room with mud on your boots or the smell of horses on your clothes. You will bathe yourself before you step in this room again, or I will take my own blade to you, I swear I will." Agnes glared venomously at the tall knight who towered over her, refusing to back down in the face of such a formidable enemy. The line had been drawn, and at that moment, despite her meager height and advanced years, Agnes indeed seemed the immovable object before him. Brettan could have bodily removed her stout frame in one easy motion and been done with the matter. But in the old maid he saw only love and devotion for her mistress, who had been brought to this by his own hand. He could not find fault in her words. Sadly, he acknowledged their truth.

"Your tongue is sharp, Agnes. You have no need for a blade to defend your mistress. Your words let blood."

For a moment Agnes stood uncertainly before this tall Englishman, who seemed the size of an oak tree in the small room, the darkness casting menacing shadows across his lean, handsome face. She knew well that more than one bold servant had lost his position, not to mention a goodly amount of his backside, for fewer words than she had dared. The Duke of Norfolk was fully capable of striking her down for what she had dared, yet he seemed suddenly drained of all strength, as if his sadness were too much for him to bear.

"A tub of hot water awaits before the hearth," Agnes suggested softly. "You shall have privacy enough. I'll keep watch over her until you have finished." Anges' tone eased at the silent misery in Brettan's face. He hesitated a moment, uncertain about disrobing before her, and Agnes chided him gently. "Milord, I have seen a good number of naked bodies in my time, all ages, both man and woman, and bathed a goodly number, I might say. If you are shy about it, I will see the matter done myself," she threatened, taking a step closer to Brettan.

Realizing he waged a losing battle, Brettan wearily held his hand aloft to halt her approach. "Enough, woman! I will bathe, if that is your want." Brettan quickly undressed and stepped into the hot water. Within minutes the bathing was completed, and Brettan rose from the still hot water and hastily wrapped the linen about his lean waist, stepping before the hearth to dry.

From beside the bed, Anges grumbled her disapproval. "You cannot have cleaned very well in that short space of time."

"Curse you, woman! Say no more of the matter, or I shall see you soundly thrashed with a whip and confined to the stables for your harassment." With that he seized the linen from about his waist, drying the last droplets of water from his well-muscled thighs, and Agnes turned back toward the bed, a sly smile of satisfaction creasing her round face. Seizing clean garments from the wooden coffer, Brettan hastily dressed and then returned to take up his silent vigil beside Maren's bed.

Again he looked for that faint pulsing at her neck, his muscles relaxing when he saw it, gaining some reassurance from it. Brettan and Agnes struck up a silent truce while they continued their vigil through that first night. As the first gray shafts of light pierced the darkness of the room, near dawn, Brettan lifted heavy eyes to watch Maren's perfect profile. She had not moved in all those hours, so that he feared he might have lost her after all. And yet, feebly, that pulse continued, and her shallow breathing had become more labored as morning approached. Gently he took her slender hand between his two larger ones and, raising it to his lips, kissed her fingertips in a silent, desperate plea to hold her with him. Exhaustion crept over him, so that finally his tousled head rested beside her hand on the bed, his fingers closed protectively around hers.

Through the long hours of that first day, Maren remained unconscious, the fever raging to take its toll of what remained of her strength. Hour after hour, Brettan refused to leave the chamber, ordering Agnes back, allowing no one near to touch her. He pressed cooling cloths against her fevered brow, changing the soiled bandages at the deep wound in her side, closed with Agnes' careful stitches, as if he alone by the sheer strength of will might hold her from the brink of death. With a gentleness that Agnes would not have known him capable of, he forced liquids down Maren's throat.

She seemed to regain some semblance of consciousness the second day. He held her as he would a small babe, stroking her, talking to her, when he could not know if she even heard his words, his voice gently soothing. He promised her brighter days beyond the wars, days when she might again return to her home. Still the fever raged within her, seeming to set her skin aflame, wasting her slender body, causing her large eyes to sink deeper within her small face, so that she appeared not a living thing. Only her hair, dark and vibrant against the linens of the bed, gave a hint of her beauty. The delicate lines of her face made her seem no more than a child. Through those long hours that rapidly became days, Brettan refused to leave her side, taking only the most meager of meals when Agnes threatened him, seeming not to sleep, drawing on some inner strength that allowed him to pursue the life of a warrior. Now he guarded against the oldest enemy of all, death, refusing to let it enter the chamber, refusing to let it claim her. Oblivious to the world beyond the chamber or the silent vigil of the royal household, he waged his silent war, willingly bargaining his life for hers, that she might live.

Within her darkened world, Maren fought the demons of her nightmares that returned to haunt her, clinging like a mindless wraith to that outstretched hand she could not see, which seemed to offer calm from the storm, a haven of safety in the warm strength that flowed from those fingers, which gently stroked and soothed her skin. And when the numbing cold replaced the ravaging heat, she felt that warmth protectively wrapped about her, the only reality in the darkness that surrounded her. And then she knew only silence. She drifted at last free of the fever, those unrelenting hands having refused to release her.

From the deep void of sleep, Maren was vaguely aware of a growing pain that started in a faint spasm and then grew, forcing her from sleep, only to subside, letting her drift for a few moments, before returning with greater intensity. Coming fully awake in the darkened chamber, Maren stared about her uncertainly. She remembered nothing of the last days, only a faint memory of the afternoon of the feast, when she had chased after the young prince, gently holding him from harm's way, after he wandered too near the horses. She blinked, her eyes straining through the light that seeped through the opening of the heavy velvet drapes. Why were the drapes drawn in the middle of the day. Or was it only early morn? Her thoughts were confused when she gazed about the room, seeing that she was alone. Had she only dreamed that Brettan had sat beside her on the bed, speaking to her of things she could not now remember?

Though her thoughts commanded, her weakened body would not obey. Maren feebly struggled to rise from the bed but fell back weakly, her breath coming in gasps from her exertions. She tightly closed her eyes against the sudden dizziness that caused the room to whirl about her, causing her stomach to feel uneasy. Weakly her hand fell back against the coverlet. She struggled for some comprehension of her weakness. A vision swam before her eyes, the vision of a man, and the queen. Suddenly Maren remembered that man and the cold intent in his eyes. He had stalked the queen, that deadly blade clutched tightly in his hand while he approached the royal enclosure. She remembered lunging toward him and throwing herself against his arm when he lashed out at the queen. She saw again the shocked, disbelieving look on his face, which suddenly turned to anger, and then fear. And she felt again that dull ache in her side, then nothing more, only a dark void of what had followed. Vainly she tried to call out for Agnes, but her voice was only a whisper through her parched lips. Again the wave of her pain started anew from deep within.

Maren waited until the pain had subsided and she could again draw an even breath. She again tried to sit up, succeeding in propping herself up on one elbow. Again the pain returned across her stomach, and she struggled to swing her legs over the edge of the bed. She stopped for a moment to catch her breath, leaning heavily against the post of the bed, shaking violently from her exertions, her skin suddenly beaded with perspiration from her efforts. She felt the pain return, cutting through her like that flashing blade, the pain so intense that it required all her efforts to remain upright, while it washed over her. She tried to call out, and again her voice was no more than a whisper. She attempted to stand in an effort to reach the door to the chamber. The room seemed to whirl about her, and she closed her eyes tightly, feeling darkness reaching out to claim her. Maren slumped onto the hard wood flooring, at last yielding to the unconsciousness that engulfed her, mercifully delivering her into that darkness where there was no pain.

As Brettan lifted Maren from the floor, his hands caught in her gown, and he felt with sickening realization the warm dampness of the linen, for blood flowed freely from her.

"Agnes!" Brettan's voice seemed to shake the walls. He turned with Maren in his arms, pleading for the woman's help.

Agnes stood stunned in the open doorway for a brief moment at the sight of the crimson-soaked gown, fighting back the truth she had hoped would not come. Her thoughts came back to reality, and she quickly took command of the situation.

"Lay her upon the bed, and fetch the maid from the hallway. I must have fresh linens, and see that hot water is brought from the kitchens."

Brettan laid Maren gently upon the bed and then stood uncertainly.

"Milord, now! Her life depends upon it. She loses the child, and I must see it properly done, or we shall lose them both."

Brettan bolted from the chamber, nearly colliding with a young servant girl outside the chamber door, sending the frightened lass into the chamber as he bellowed his orders. Within moments a handful of servants rushed into the room, their arms laden with fresh cloth, and others heavily weighted down with ponderous buckets. The queen hastened from the hall below, and one look at Agnes' grief-stricken face confirmed what the young queen had feared. Brushing aside her maid's protests for her own well-being, Eleanore adamantly refused to be taken from the chamber. Before Brettan could return to the chamber, the heavy door had been firmly shut. He

382

stood in numbed silence, staring at the oaken portal, thinking that he could not have known any greater sadness than Maren's loss, but he now realized the possibility that he might lose both Maren and his unborn child. Unable to move, unable for the first time in his life to take command of what passed beyond that portal, Brettan stood silently outside the door, completely drained of all strength, all hope. He felt the firm grasp of a strong hand on his shoulder and turned to gaze through sunken eyes at his king.

"Come, my friend. For now there is nothing you may do to help her. Now you will come, and we will speak of things that I perhaps should have said long ago."

For hours they rode beyond the rolling greensward that bounded the manor, along the perimeter of the hunting grounds, trailed by their well-armed knights, and soldiers who kept their vigil against any attack. Brettan pushed the gray beyond all endurance, racing before the wind until the large warhorse lathered and faltered in his stride, responding valiantly to the demanding hand on the reins that urged him on further, until it seemed both man and beast would surely drop from their efforts.

When Brettan finally realized the strain on the animal beneath him, he lessened his pace, easing the mighty steed to a gentler gait, and then finally to a walk. Side by side they rode, in silence. Edward kept pace, his own mount winded from laboring to keep up with the long-legged gait of the gray stallion.

Reaching the crest of a knoll beyond the manor, Brettan drew the gray to a halt and wearily slid to the ground. Reaching for a handful of green grass, he twisted it in his hand and proceeded to rub down the gray, whose sides heaved with the efforts of the run. Silently Edward dismounted, allowing his own steed to graze untethered, threw himself down on the ground a small distance away, and gazed out over the greensward.

"My friend, I envy you, that the path you follow has always been one of your choosing. You, beyond any man I have known, always see your own direction clearly, and heaven help any who would alter your course. I have often thought those are the qualities best found in a king, and pondered England's fate had you been born to be king. I have made decisions that I know well are not the ones you would have made. We have argued long and hard over the campaigns we have waged through the years."

Brettan threw aside the stalks of grass. Pulling the reins loose over the gray's large head, he let them dangle to the ground. Wearily he turned to face the sun, his thoughts clearer after the exhausting ride. "Do you make an apology, milord, for some decision you believe you have wrongly made?"

"I make no apologies for any decisions I have made, or orders I have given. But there are truths which I have known and, perhaps unwisely, chosen not to reveal until this moment, for fear it might cause unforeseen dangers. As it is, those dangers have struck very close. My one failing was in keeping the Lady Maren safe from those dangers."

"By your order, sire, she is my wife, and the responsibility for her safety thereby falls to me. It is my failure that finds her near death."

Edward looked at his loyal knight and friend. "'Tis true, but in faith, I have not made you aware of the full extent of that responsibility, and that, my friend, is perhaps the greatest danger of all, and so, I must assume part of the responsibility. I truly regret that it has taken this grave injury to the Lady Maren to force my hand. She is brave and true, and the queen values her friendship beyond any other. I shall live with my own grief for your loss this day. But it is my belief that the Lady Maren will live, and that is why now it is even more

384

important that you understand all that has come to pass." Edward rose and turned to face his friend, the weight of his authority heavy upon his broad shoulders.

"The Lady Maren's family is one of the oldest in all of Wales. Her grandfather was the first of the land barons to seek a permanent alliance with England many years ago. He sealed that alliance with the marriage of his only child, a daughter, to Gilbert de Burghmond, one of my father's knights. All of the grandfather's holdings of land and wealth were to pass through his daughter to his grandchildren, a symbol of the unification of Wales with England. He was a man of singular vision, and he received great opposition from the old Welsh prince, who wanted to maintain his absolute control of Wales. The old prince had once hoped for a marriage between the baron's daughter and his son, Llywelyn. Such a marriage would have aligned the north and south of Wales, with great power and wealth, and made my efforts to bring the two countries together as one virtually impossible." Edward turned back to gaze at the setting sun, now much lower in the western sky.

"The old baron fell to an untimely death, leaving his wealth and the vast southern estates to the Lady Julyana. Upon his death, Llywelyn moved swiftly to draw revenge and establish his rule in the south of Wales. Lord de Burghmond was here in England, having been summoned by King Henry in an effort to lay a plan for strengthening England's hold on the south of Wales. The Lady Julyana had remained at Cambria with their newborn son. The old prince traveled to Cambria, it is said, to offer his aid to Lady Julyana after the death of the baron. He remained at Cambria for many days, holding the Lady Julyana prisoner and threatening the life of her infant son, if she refused him. He took his revenge against her father through the Lady Julyana and, in several days' time, he and his men left. Some months later, a second child was born to the Lady Julyana, a girl-child, who is said to have favored her mother's dark-haired beauty. That child is the Lady Maren." Edward turned back to Brettan, uncertain at the silence of his knight.

Brettan stared hard at his king, the full meaning of Edward's words tearing through him. "She is half-sister to Llywelyn! By all that is holy, I should have been told!" Brettan advanced angrily upon his king, all the raw emotions of the last days vivid upon his anguished face, his eyes blazing with barely restrained fury. "A pawn, that is all she is to you. You clearly saw the advantage that might be gained, and you have used her and me in this mad game of war you seek. Now she lies very near death because of this."

"Easy, my friend, lest we speak words in anger that may never be forgiven. Yea, a pawn, if that is what you would believe. But tell me then, milord, what your decision might have been were you king. Llywelyn has sworn to drive my armies from Wales, but to do that he must align the south with the north of Wales. His only hope in gaining the support of the south lies in gaining the alliance of one of the oldest families in all of Wales, certainly one of the richest and most powerful. If the Lady Maren had refused his cause, he would have destroyed her; she would have been a pawn for Llywelyn to use, with her certain death once he obtained absolute power, for it is certain he would never willingly share that power with one who is his half-sister. Fate, my friend, decreed that your path should cross with hers, but the marriage was a means of removing the Lady Maren from Llywelyn's grasp, and from certain death. It was Lord de Burghmond's belief that she would be safe in England. And it was only to that end that he agreed to the marriage. I but sought to right a wrong against the lady for her lost honor. I learned who she was only after I gave the order for the marriage. Think what you will of my purpose in the matter, I have spoken the truth. My deepest sadness is that I was greatly wrong, hoping she might find safety in England, and I shall carry the burden of having failed in that to the last of my days." Edward stared hard at his knight, trying to comprehend Brettan's thoughts behind the wall of his anger. Brettan gazed beyond his king into the distance beyond the forest.

"The order for the marriage was a difficult one. I risked your anger, even the loss of your friendship, for the honor of a young girl, who was but enemy to the crown. I could not be certain that you would obey the command. Only your first words of your intention to bring her to England as your mistress seemed to ease the decision I had made."

"You know me well, milord. Had I been against the marriage, there is no power on this earth, not yours, not anyone's, that could have forced me to submit." Brettan retrieved the trailing reins as the gray stallion gently nudged his shoulder. Stroking the large animal, he turned back to his king, his tone at once sarcastic and slightly mocking. "What now is to be her fate, your majesty? Shall we await to be certain that she lives?"

"I know well your anger, milord, for it is my anger also. Until these last days I was given to question her loyalty, for in truth she never desired to be brought to England. Sad it is, my friend, that by risking her life for that of the queen, she has removed all doubts. Now she must be protected, for Llywelyn shall not be satisfied to leave her within our grasp. She was safe enough as long as he was unaware that she was here. Now, I fear, the danger is even greater. Once he knows that she lives, he will be forced to attempt such as the attack again. He can ill afford for her to remain in England, for his cause in the south of Wales is then hopeless. I shall take the queen to London on the morrow, for I trust not the lack of safety here in the forest. Will you return to London when she has recovered?"

Brettan turned back to Edward, some of his anger having eased, for he knew well the pain in his king's words. "If she lives, I think Norfolk to be a safer haven. She will gain her strength there, and I have a need to see the Lady Helene. I shall keep her safe, now that I know the enemy I must guard against." Brettan's tone was cold and without emotion. Without further words, he turned the gray toward the manorhouse, his only acknowledgement of his king in the slight bow of his head when he turned away.

Brettan sent the stallion across the fields at a full run, toward the lights that now appeared in the windows of the manorhouse, against the growing darkness of night.

Fear pulled at Brettan. He reined the gray to a halt before the long row of stables, the animal's hooves clattering loudly on the cobbled walkway. A stableboy rushed to take the horse, and Brettan gave his orders for the animal's care. He stopped to stare at the glowing lights that shone through the heavily paned windows of that second-floor chamber. Brushing impatiently past the servants who appeared at the doorway, Brettan mounted the wooden stairway to the upstairs chamber. Reaching the door, he rested his hand heavily on the iron latch, hesitantly, almost fearful of what might await him on the other side.

At the top of the wide stairway, a form moved among the shadows. Lady Caroline flattened herself against the stone wall while a young servant passed through the hallway. Only a few moments before, she had heard the sounds of horses in the courtyard below, and known that the king and Brettan returned from their ride. She quickly gained the second floor, hiding herself among the shadows, that she might have a chance to speak with

388

Brettan for the first time in days. The entire manorhouse had taken on the air of a well-fortified garrison after the attack, and the royal family had silently waited for some word of the Lady Maren's health. But as each day passed with her condition unchanged, Edward had grown uneasy at remaining at the estate so far from London, and given the order for their departure the following day. Caroline would be forced to leave with the queen, and could not bear the thought of that departure without some word with Brettan.

She heard the heavy footsteps on the stairway and, while Brettan stood before the chamber door, Caroline emerged from her shadowed hiding place. "Brettan, my darling, I must speak with you. Please do not send me away."

Brettan turned to her wearily, and she was startled by the drawn and haggard look about his face. His eyes closed heavily , for he had little patience for Caroline's schemes or treachery.

"For days you have been closed within that chamber. There has been no moment for us to be alone. Indeed, it would seem as if there were some great plan to keep us apart."

Brettan sighed wearily. "Caroline, there is no great plan, only your failure to understand fully that what we once shared no longer exists. I have no time for this." Brettan made to push past her and enter the chamber.

"Brettan, my love, please hear my words. Edward has given the order that we are to return to London. I could not bear leaving without some word from you that you do not hate me."

"Caroline, I have never hated you. It is only that there are much graver matters that must be attended to."

"Has the Lady Maren worsened?" Caroline could not resist questioning him, for all who had entered the chamber had remained strangely silent by order of the queen, and Caroline had learned little of Maren's condition.

"You would be greatly pleased by that, would you not?" There was a warning edge in Brettan's voice that Caroline knew well. She realized that his anger flared dangerously when he stared at her through the dimly lit hall.

"You will be disappointed, I am certain, to know that my wife shall live. I would not have it otherwise."

Caroline's face contorted in rage at his use of that endearment that should have been hers. She fought for control, lest Brettan know the effect of his words on her. She had dared to hope, even to pray that the girl would not live through that first night. But she had survived, and in the days since the attack, Brettan had refused to leave her side, causing Caroline to fear greatly for her cause in luring him back to her. Now he stood before her, impatient to return to the chamber, and Caroline could clearly see that he had changed greatly from the first days when he had returned to London. Her anger with him for taking the girl to wife now faded, before her dawning realization that his loyalty to Maren went beyond his code of honor or a solemn pledge to his king.

Her desperation made Caroline bold. She stepped from the shadows to stand before Brettan, placing her hands intimately upon his chest, gazing pleadingly into his eyes. "My love, I can easily understand that you feel some measure of responsibility for the girl. Edward, I am certain, reminds you of that daily, as it was by his order that you were wed to her. Though I must return to London with the queen on the morrow, it is important that you understand I but await your word, so that we may put this foolishness aside and be together once again."

None too gently, Brettan grasped Caroline's wrists in

strong hands, drawing her against him so that her face was very near his. Caroline seized the opportunity of the moment and molded the length of her body against Brettan's, hoping to arouse in him the passion she knew him capable of. Brettan's voice was almost menacing as he glared at her, his green eyes glowing unnaturally, so that she felt a sudden fear of him that she had never known, as if she had suddenly confronted some wild, crazed animal.

"I have little patience for the words of a heated bitch who would seek her fortune in my bed. I have spoken these words before, Caroline, but you have chosen not to believe the truth in them. I honor the Lady Maren as my wife. It goes beyond your simple understanding or any order Edward might give. As you know me, you know well that, had I chosen not to marry, there is no power in all of Edward's kingdom that could have forced me to do so. It was by my choice, and I shall honor the vows I have spoken with her before God. And though we have this day lost the child she carried, I promise you there shall be another to ease the sadness we feel now. Now get yourself from my sight, and plague me no more with what you had hoped for. Mark my words well, Caroline, though you were willing to give all for what you desired, you have lost all to one who sought nothing for herself. It is a lesson few learn, but they pay the price with their loneliness."

Wounded by his stinging words, Caroline struggled against his hold, tears of anger welling within her amber eyes. Brettan's grip about her wrists loosened, and he had cause to regret the pain he saw in her eyes. Seeing her advantage, Caroline pressed her cause. "May we perhaps speak again, when you have returned to London?" It was the most she might hope for, in the presence of his great anger toward her.

"I shall not be returning to London. When Maren is stronger, I shall take her to Lionshead. I do not trust her

391

safety in London." Caroline winced at the blow of those words. She had hoped that he would be returning soon, and now to learn that he intended taking his wife to Norfolk, to Lionshead, where she had once hoped to be mistress, was more than she could bear.

Brettan gently released Caroline. Taking advantage of the moment, Caroline reached her arms up about his neck. "I know you well, my love, and you shall yet tire of this girl. I shall await your return." Caroline stretched up on her toes, pulled Brettan's face down to hers, and gently kissed his mouth, before he managed to pull away.

At the far end of the long hall, the queen halted, startled by the sight of the Duke of Norfolk and Caroline outside the chamber, embracing like impassioned lovers, but she was not easily fooled. Eleanore quickly recovered and coolly approached her lady-in-waiting.

"Lady Caroline, I am certain your presence is required elsewhere, for there is much that needs be attended to before our departure on the morrow. You will leave now." Calmly she dismissed Caroline, leaving her no choice but to leave, or fall into disfavor, a fate that even Caroline was not foolish enough to risk.

"You will find the Lady Maren is resting easier now. I deeply grieve, milord, at the loss of the child. You must now look to your lady's recovery. Your decision to take her to Lionshead is a wise one. I fear there would be far too many dangers for her in London." Without further word Eleanore descended the stairway to the hall below, a smile of quiet satisfaction lighting her face, for the first time in many days, when she greeted her husband, for she knew well the healing magic of time shared when two hearts reached tentatively out to each other.

The chamber glowed softly with the light of several candles set near the hearth, where Agnes sat in one of the high-backed chairs, her silver-streaked head bent forward wearily. She had at last yielded to the strain of the past days. Glancing to the large bed, Brettan sighed his relief at the sight of Maren's slender body folded within the mounds of velvet softness. She slept protected, like a rare jewel. He moved quietly across the chamber and knelt beside the large bed. His hand gently felt her forehead, her skin still quite warm, her breathing still rapid and shallow, but her sleep now undisturbed by the pain of losing the child. Gently he wrapped her hand within his strong grasp and raised it to his cheek, feeling the silken softness of her skin. Though the fever still raged within her, she would live, of that he was certain. And silently he vowed that no one would ever harm her again.

"Milord?" Agnes quietly approached the side of the bed.

"The child is lost." His voice seemed not his own.

"There was never any hope for the babe, milord, from the moment she was injured. There was too much loss of blood."

"Was the child a son?"

Agnes suddenly felt a great sadness for this Englishman who had once seemed so fearful to her, but now seemed like any other man who grieved for the loss of something loved. And the sudden realization of his love for her mistress filled her heart with a sudden warmth, after so many days of sadness.

"It was too soon to tell, milord," Ages lied gently.

"Agnes, she had felt the child move within her. She spoke of it. I must know if the child was a son!"

Unafraid of the sudden passion in his voice, Agnes shook her head sadly. "Yea, milord, a son."

Her answer cut through Brettan, as if that blade had been thrust through him instead of Maren. Agnes sought to give him some comfort in his moment of agony.

"The Lady Maren will live, milord. There may be other sons, for she is strong."

"A son." Brettan's words seemed not his own, his voice filled with grief at their loss. "A son I shall never hold and see grow to manhood. Llywelyn has taken that from me. He shall not take her too. I will not allow it."

Agnes stared at the Duke of Norfolk, as if she feared he might have lost all remaining sanity, yet behind the feral gleam in those glowing green eyes she saw complete presence of mind. She stepped back, at once fearful of this man, who she was certain would challenge all the demons of hell had they chosen to enter the room. She made the sign of the cross and whispered her prayers, knowing somehow that they were weak next to the determination of the man who knelt beside her mistress' bed. Any doubts of Maren's recovery faded before his complete determination to keep her with him.

Brettan remained by her side, refusing to leave the chamber for even a moment and, as her fever climbed and sent spasms of shivers through her pitifully thin body, he pushed Agnes aside and built the fire at the hearth until the room glowed red with the heat. He disrobed before the startled maid, sending her fleeing from the chamber, shielding her gaze from his nakedness, thinking him surely mad. He joined Maren beneath the heavy coverlet, adding his great warmth to hers. Gently he drew her against him, careful not to cause pain to the wound in her side. His heart ached as he curled protectively about her. It was perhaps his imagination that her silent shivering seemed to lessen, but he held her near for what remained of the night, speaking softly to her, drawing her back from the grasp of death, until he felt the heat in her body ease, to be replaced by a coolness that he had not felt in days. The gray streaks of first light filled the chamber when at last she slept peacefully and deeply, curled against Brettan's body, her small head cradled against his shoulder, her breathing deep and peaceful, the fever eased. And Brettan also slept, a deep, cleansing sleep. To the old maid who anxiously poked her head into the dimly lit chamber, fearful of what she might find, while dawn broke over the forest beyond the manor, they seemed like two lovers who but slept safe in each other's arms. Carefully she pulled the heavy oaken door closed and whispered her prayers of thankfulness for her mistress' life, knowing that the fierce knight who slept beside her had challenged death and refused to yield. And she smiled wearily as she also found her bed, thinking that perhaps Brettan de Lorin was a man worthy of her mistress. Though he was English, he might be forgiven that one shortcoming.

Chapter Seventeen

Geoffrey of Meyrick carefully watched the activity that had surrounded the manorhouse since early dawn. The procession of carts and saddled horses that stood waiting, while an unending flow of servants carried various items to be packed into those carts, could only mean that the royal family and their guests were preparing to return to London. Geoffrey retreated into the thick foliage of the heavily wooded copse beyond the rolling greens that surrounded the manorhouse.

For days since the attack against the queen, he and his men had barely eluded the persistent English guard, which searched the forest and surrounding countryside for some sign of them. Foolhardy though it may have been to remain so close beneath their very noses, Geoffrey had given the order that they would remain in the forest until he might learn of Maren's fate.

Though his men might have disagreed with Geoffrey's single-minded purpose of taking her back to Wales, none dared speak of those doubts for fear of unleashing his uneven temper of the last weeks. None could deny his right to the lady, but all felt that there was too much risk in riding so deep into England, surrounded by their enemies for a mere girl. Among themselves they had heartily cursed such foolishness, retreating behind their sullen glares when Geoffrey sensed their disfavor. To occupy their time and make good use of their presence, they had spoken among themselves of striking a blow against the English king, to give advantage in the war their countrymen waged against Edward in their own country. Overhearing their grumblings and conspiratorial plans, Geoffrey had overruled their schemes, reasoning their numbers were far too few, and such a plan would only guarantee them all certain death. The man Baskin was the only one of his men who remained unconvinced of the danger. Four days earlier, he had left their forest hideaway well before dawn. Upon realizing the man was gone, Geoffrey's wrath had known no bounds, for he was convinced of Baskin's intent. For the better part of the day, Geoffrey and his men remained well hidden within the forest, many times only a few feet away from the Englishmen, but always safely hidden. Geoffrey had left their camp for a brief time that he might find Baskin among the English, donning his meager costume, only to return alone much later. Shortly after his return, the cry of alarm was heard across the greensward, with the heavily armed English guard drawn to the royal enclosure near the lists.

In the chaos and turmoil that followed, disguised as one of the serfs, Geoffrey had been able to learn that the attack against the queen had failed, leaving the Lady Maren gravely injured. Barely able to control his rage, Geoffrey had returned to his men and given the order that Baskin was to be found and brought to him. Each man had left the camp with an uneasy feeling of dread for the fellow, knowing well Geoffrey's anger. Within the hour Baskin had been found fleeing through the forest, fearing the English, but more fearful of Geoffrey of Meyrick. The trial was a simple one, and the man's fate was certain. He gazed into the cold hardness of Geoffrey's eyes, which held nothing but the man's death in their icy depths. Geoffrey carried out the sentence himself, delivering the deadly blow, withdrawing his blade just short of death, for he thought it better to leave the man to suffer for his disobedience, as he had left Maren.

Gagged so that his moaning would not alert the English, Baskin was carried far from their secluded encampment, his blood flowing freely from the gaping wound. He was left in a pool of his own blood, his life slowly ebbing from his body. He would be found, but far too late to tell the English anything that might be of use to them. Carefully Geoffrey and his men moved deeper into the forest, splitting up into smaller groups, seeking caves or hollow tree trunks for safety from the English. They could not outrun so many English and, now that they had been alerted to the rebel presence, they would search the forest with a vengeance. The only hope for Geoffrey and his men was to remain hidden. And Geoffrey was determined not to leave without some word of the Lady Maren.

That had been four days ago, and now the English prepared to return to London. The rebels dared not venture near the manorhouse to learn of Maren's fate.

Geoffrey turned around to see one of his men returned through the forest from his watch, dragging a struggling figure across the floor of the forest, his fingers tightly clamped across the woman's mouth, the large paw of his hand completely obscuring her face. The man roughly shoved the woman toward Geoffrey, so that she stumbled badly, going down on her knees when her feet tangled in her mantle. In an instant Lady Caroline was on her feet, the hood of the mantle thrown back for her to glare ferociously at Geoffrey and his men, as they approached her.

"Tell them to keep their hands off me. Tell them, or I

swear I shall bring down the entire English guard on your head." Caroline's bosom heaved with her efforts, and she whirled first on one man and then on another who dared approach too close.

Silently Geoffrey gave the signal for them to hold.

Caroline turned on him. "You fool! What could you have possibly thought, sending your man against the queen? Though I heartily approve his final choice of victim, my regrets are that he blundered so badly. And now Edward has strengthened his guard of everyone, and prepares to return to London. You fool!"

Geoffrey grabbed Caroline by the arms and shook her roughly, staring earnestly into her face. "Then the Lady Maren lives?"

"So eager are you for your Lady Maren, that I believe you would take the wasted wench as she is. Yea, she lives, much to my disappointment. You cannot know what pleasure her death would have brought me. Truly a worthy solution for that one."

"But hardly one of my choosing." Geoffrey's grip tightened on Caroline's arm, so that she flinched at the pain he caused. "Her death would hardly serve my purpose. I want the Lady Maren alive."

"Then you have what you want, for she lives. I overheard one of the maids say she is greatly weakened from the fever and the loss of blood. And Brettan remains by her side every moment of the day and night, refusing to leave even when the maid would change the bandages."

"Then she is too weakened to travel?"

"That is what I have come to tell you. Edward returns this day to London, but your Lady Maren and the Duke of Norfolk are to remain until she is strong enough to travel. Though I warrant that will be some time. You will be pleased, as I am, to know that she has lost the child

400

she carried."

"Can you be certain of this?" Geoffrey stared at Caroline anxiously.

"I have not been allowed near her chamber since the attack. Only the Queen, the Duke of Norfolk, and the maid are allowed in the chamber, no one else. But I have the information in good faith. You may rely upon it."

"If this is true, then there no longer remains any reason for her to remain with the Duke of Norfolk. Have you any word when he plans to return to London?"

"They are not to return to London. The Duke of Norfolk has given word to his men that, as soon as the Lady Maren is strong enough, they are bound for Norfolk. You see well my concern, for he remains most protective of her even with the loss of the child. I had hoped that, when the child no longer existed, he would grow tiresome of the burden of this false marriage. I fear he carries a deep sense of responsibility for the girl. That is why you must follow them to Norfolk. I am bound for London with the queen, but I shall follow shortly, and then we may lay our final plans to remove the Lady Maren from his care. If you want your precious Maren, you must follow them to Lionshead."

Geoffrey turned away from the Englishwoman, who pressed closer, leaning into his arm. He felt no response to her wanton gestures, though she pressed her breast into his arm. A frown creased his face when he compared her open lust, like that of a bitch in heat, to Maren's soft delicate beauty that masked a hidden passion he had only dared dream of. And yet his doubts nagged him. He had promised his men success and a quick return to the North of Wales before summer's end. That success eluded him, for Brettan de Lorin seemed determined to keep him from Maren. Angrily he slapped the leather gauntlets against his leg, contemplating his decision. "Time grows short.

Soon the seasons will change, and winter will be hard upon us. I do not choose to remain in England until then. The winter snows will make travel difficult. I must return to Wales before the first snows."

"Then you must act with all possible haste. Before month's end, I shall travel to Norfolk. I have a cousin with a small estate near Lionshead. I shall meet you at a place called Southwold, on the coast, on the morn of the Christmas celebration. There is a small inn where we may meet and not be noticed. Lionshead is very near there."

"The delay will be costly."

"Only if you should fail this time. You must be there, for it is the only way you shall have her. The Lady Maren could not survive the journey to Wales now. She would be dead before the first day's end, though I care little what happens to her. But in that time, she will be stronger, and perhaps now, with the loss of the child, she shall willingly return to Wales."

"It would seem I have little choice in the matter, though I do not care for her to remain with the Duke of Norfolk."

"Nor do I, but I cannot see that we have any other choice. Will you follow to Norfolk?"

"Yea, I will follow," Geoffrey answered resignedly. "And this time there shall be no mistakes."

"I must return before I am missed. Remember the inn in Southwold, on the day of the Christmas celebration." At the man's nod, Caroline wrapped her mantle more closely about her shoulder, suddenly chilled by the morning air. She pushed her way through the thick growth of the heavily wooded copse, carefully retracing her path to the manorhouse. Geoffrey quickly waved back one of his men who would have followed her. He watched Caroline's fleeing figure steal along the half-wall that enclosed the gardens, then cut through the gardens to take up her place among the other ladies in waiting, astride their horses, waiting to begin the journey to London.

Brettan made his farewells to his king. And in the second floor chamber, Queen Eleanore sat beside Maren's bed, gently holding her young friend's hand, bidding her silent goodbye. The young queen rose abruptly at the sound of the door opening. Brettan had entered to bring word that the king awaited her.

"Keep her safe, milord, and let there be gentleness between you. I think you know not the treasure you hold."

"In that you are greatly mistaken, Your Majesty. I have pledged to keep her safe," Brettan smiled gently.

"If anyone is capable of it, milord, it is you. I shall pray for your quick return to London. I am selfish, milord. I long to have my friend with me once again."

"I am also selfish, milady. Her first responsibility, I pray, shall be to me."

Brettan bowed low before his queen, holding the door open for her. Eleanore gazed again at the sleeping girl in the large bed. "Then you must guard your lioness carefully until she is strong once again. And bind her to you with truth and kindness. I have heard it said that the lioness can be a most formidable foe."

"Most certainly, a worthy adversary. But then, none should know that better than I. But it is not my intent to take up the sword against the Lady Maren. I think perhaps to tame the lioness."

For the first time in the past days Eleanore smiled at the handsome knight who stood before her, a faint glimmer of the old smile gracing his well-curved lips. She could easily see how half the ladies at her court had given favor to Brettan de Lorin, while the rest were either too old for pursuit or too young to care. A young maid bobbed into a low curtsy before the young queen, reminding her of those who awaited. Eleanore turned once more to Brettan, gazing earnestly into those vivid green eyes, which seemed to glow like those of a cat. "Guard her well, milord. Though there are those who are certain the attack was against me, I fear there is danger that awaits your lady."

Without waiting for his response, Eleanore turned and descended the wooden stairway to the guard who waited below. The call was given for the guard to mount their horses, and the long procession moved slowly down the pathway to the main road that would take them to London.

Peaceful quiet descended on the manor. Brettan's guard was posted to their watch, while several of his loyal knights took up their guard within the manor. The sounds and smells of the evening meal filled the air, and the men, eager for a diversion, set up a match of arm-wrestling at the large table in the dining hall.

Restlessly Brettan found his steps seeking that chamber at the top of the landing, finding calm only when he once again reassured himself that Maren slept peacefully. There remained a faint coloration at her cheeks after the ravaging of the fever, somehow making her look as if she might never have been ill.

Brettan moved to place a log on the meager fire that had been freshly kindled, the flames leaping eagerly to consume the heavy wood, casting a golden glow about the room, the fire driving back the coolness of the evening. At the sound of her faint stirring in the bed, he approached from across the room. Staring through the dark shadows that lay across the bed, he felt the wide blue depths of her eyes on him while he moved. The flames leaped higher at the log on the hearth, and the shadows were driven back, so that he saw the soft delicate oval of

404

her face. Faint circles remained beneath her large eyes but could not detract from the exquisite beauty of her skin, or of the dark lashes that thickly fringed those brilliant blue eyes, only faintly tinged with the last of the fever. She carefully watched him approach the side of the bed and bend to sit beside her, his greater weight sinking into the heavy covers. With great effort, Maren reached out a slender hand that shook with her effort, and gently traced the line of Brettan's face until her fingers crossed his lips.

"Forgive me, milord." Her voice was the barest whisper, but her words clear. She closed her eyes at her effort, then opened them again to stare at him. She moistened her parched lips before going on. "I never sought the death of our child." A ragged sob escaped her trembling lips, and the tears that threatened would not come, she was so weakened from the fever. Gently Brettan gathered her into his arms, and the tears that fell were his. He buried his face in the silken mass of her hair. He had feared losing her, too, but now he knew of a certainty that she would live. She had reached out to him as she had not done before, and he would not risk losing that one small gesture.

Gently Brettan kissed her shoulder through the thin gown she wore. "We shall begin anew. This day shall mark a beginning between us. From here we shall learn of one another, and I vow to you there shall be no more nightmares to haunt your dreams." Brettan kissed her temple as she lay with her head against his shoulder. She did not move but remained perfectly still, her breathing deep and even, and Brettan realized that she slept and had not heard his words. "Sleep peacefully, my little one. I shall keep you safe always." It was a solemn promise. He laid her gently back upon the softness of the bed, then joined her a few moments later, frowning Agnes to silence when she returned and would have protested at finding him in her mistress' bed.

Silently cursing all Englishmen but particularly those who seemed forever capable of finding a warm bed with a beautiful young maid, she closed the door behind her, leaving her mistress' safety to the fierce knight who lay beside her, confident that no danger dared approach such a man, who might defy the fearful Llywelyn himself to keep her near.

Within a matter of days Maren insisted on leaving her sickbed, arguing with Agnes that she would only become more weakened if she continued to spend each waking hour in bed. Knowing the temper of her mistress, Agnes remained silent but fretful, watching Maren take her first tentative steps in many days. Her goal was the large wooden tub that steamed with warm water before the glowing hearth. The wound in her side had closed sufficiently, leaving only a long angry scar that marked the perfect satin texture of her skin. Maren gave little thought to the ugly red line, but stripped away her gown with hands that trembled visibly, and then gratefully accepted Agnes' help to cross the short distance to the tub. Startled by the sudden opening of the door, both women turned surprised gazes toward the tall knight who stood in the doorway, his heavy broadsword strapped to his side. "What is the meaning of this?" His voice set the walls shaking, and he charged into the room and, setting Agnes aside, quickly gathered Maren's meagerly clad frame into his strong arms. In one quick movement, he whirled about to return her to the bed.

"Nay, I shall not return to that bed until I have bathed." Firmly, Maren laid a slender hand against his chest, her fingers pressing against his bare skin at the

406

neck of his shirt. Brettan felt the heat of that touch, her hand pressing against him. "Milord, these many days I have been bathed one leg or arm at a time, but never allowed the comforts of yonder tub. And I swear there are creatures stirring in my hair for lack of washing. I will have a bath and wash my hair. Surely you cannot deny the need?" A playful smile pulled at the corners of Brettan's mouth and sent the dimples in his cheeks even deeper, while he gazed into the wide pools of her deep blue eyes, thinking how much he valued just the sound of her voice, or her deep even breathing when they lay together at night. Gently he nuzzled against her neck, breathing in the fresh clean smell of her that seemed unchanged. But he could hardly resist teasing her when her mood seemed so much improved.

"In truth, milady, I had noticed a certain fragrance about you, that could fair rival the smell of my men after a good match at wrestling."

Maren smiled up into his glowing green eyes, thinking how good it felt to be held so near, feeling his warmth radiating through his garments to warm her bare skin, so that she felt no need for clothes against the coolness of the evening.

Agnes grumbled her disapproval of such behavior, even between a man and his wife, especially when the wife had so recently suffered such a great injury and the loss of a child. "It shall be on your head if we lose her yet for all your whirling her about, so that she may catch her death of the ague after being so ill."

"She shall not catch the ague, Agnes. She is stronger today than yesterday, and she shall be stronger yet on the morrow. Now get yourself from the chamber while I attend milady's bath."

At the wide-eyed expression on Agnes' face both Maren and Brettan laughed heartily. The woman fled the chamber, mumbling something under her breath about the foolishness of youth.

Brettan gazed down into the face of the lovely young girl he held firmly in his arms and wondered about her true feelings. It startled him to realize how very little he really knew of this girl, this woman, who was now his wife. So much they had shared, yet so little did they know of each other.

"Are you determined to see this through, milady?" Brettan questioned her playfully.

"Yea, milord."

"Then so be it." Gently he swung her about, until he held her over the tub of water. Carefully he pulled away the thin linen she had wrapped about her and, casting it aside, gently lowered her into the steaming water. For a moment Maren's arms clung about his neck, holding him near, then very slowly she released him.

Pulling off his doeskin tunic, Brettan rolled back the sleeves of his linen shirt and, sitting down on a small stool beside the tub, seized the fragrantly scented soap from her hand.

"Milord, is my fragrance such that you feel compelled to see the washing done yourself, to make certain that it is done properly?"

Lathering the rose-scented cake, his favorite, Brettan playfully dropped a mound of lather on the tip of her small nose. "I have learned, milady, that one of the finest pleasures to be shared between a man and a woman is the leisurely time spent bathing. Though there are those who frown on such frequent practices, I find them to be quite enjoyable, especially when shared in such desirable company. Until such time as you are fully recovered and capable of enjoying the pleasures to be found in my bath, milady, I shall have to be content in doing these favors for you, and receiving what pleasure I might from it."

Maren pretended to be shocked at such information, and silently wondered where he might have enjoyed such pleasures. No doubt in the company of the ever-willing Lady Caroline. Her good mood seemed to dampen, and she became silent, while Brettan reached a finger beneath her chin, lifting her face so that he might look into her eyes. "There are many pleasures that I wait to share with you, Maren. I have promised you that we would share a new beginning. And so we shall." At the perplexed look on her face, Brettan laughed gently. "If I remember correctly, milady, you were asleep at the time. Indeed, you seem to be sleeping much of the time lately. But that shall pass when you are stronger." Slowly Brettan lowered his head very near hers, so that she could feel a warmth that had nothing to do with the water in her bath. Maren could feel the rapid beating of her heart and thought certainly it must be from her exertions, but when she stared back into the depths of those glowing green eyes, which held hers as if by some unseen bond, she knew it to be not from the strain of bathing, but the strain of being so near him, and wanting to feel him closer about her. Her breathing seemed to stop when Brettan's lips moved softly over hers, his warmth igniting her with a flame that glowed brightly within her, driving away the sadness and darkness of the last days. His kiss lingered, and he seemed to give her breath back, and she felt a rush of sensation, as if she need never breathe again, except it be his warmth that gave her life.

Brettan's own composure was sorely tested from the many days he had been forced to endure without even kissing her, allowed only the briefest of contact, when he lifted her or held her close at night. Still, that had been the most comforting feeling he could have imagined, until a moment ago. Now he found himself struggling for control, to keep from pulling her bodily from her bath and taking her to the bed, with no thoughts of her injury or the babe she had lost, but only the basest need of her. Still he restrained his desires, knowing he could not press her yet, but solemnly vowing to himself that there would come a day, hopefully in the not-too-distant future, when they would again share all the passion of those weeks and months before the attack.

Carefully Brettan resumed his bathing of her, washing across her slender back and down the gentle curve of a hip. He then washed the roundess of her shoulders. She lay back against the edge of the tub, luxuriating in the pampering she received. As his lathered hands wandered near her breasts, he hesitated for a moment, so that Maren glanced up expectantly. Locked in silent challenge, they stared at each other, each wondering what the other's thoughts might be. Gently Maren reached to seize the linen cloth to finish the bathing, but found it firmly held in Brettan's grasp. Her eyes never leaving his, she gazed back at him unafraid, and his hands lowered over the full mounds of her breasts, his touch sending a shiver of delight through her, those rose-hued peaks growing taut. Quickly Brettan finished bathing her, at last surrendering the cloth so that she might finish washing her legs, while he lathered the thick mass of her hair. When every part of her was clean, she leaned back in the tub while Brettan poured a bucket of clean water over the length of her hair. Then she stood, wringing the sodden mass, while Brettan wrapped a long linen about her, then carried her to the chair before the fire. There Maren sat while the thick, dark waves of her hair dried before the heat of the flames, and watched him strip away his garments and take his own bath.

"I think it highly unfair, milord, that you should take such advantage of me while I bathe, yet I am not allowed that same privilege with you."

410

Brettan eyed her lazily as she sat before the hearth, her ripe, full breasts outlined against the linen by the glow of the fire behind her.

"I had considered that, milady, but given that this is your first day out of the bed, and that you might not escape further injury were you to test me as you did a few moments ago, I reconsidered the matter and decided it should best wait until we can share a bath together."

Maren relaxed back into the high-backed chair, a cushion easing her back. It had been placed against the hardness of the wood to ease Agnes' discomfort during so many hours spent watching while Maren lay ill. She felt oddly calm and serene closed within the chamber, watching this most intimate yet natural act of bathing, of a man who was her husband, yet quite simply a stranger to her. As he continued relaxing in the warm water, Maren's thoughts strayed to days passed, and the fate that had brought them together so many months ago. She struggled to fight back the melancholy that threatened to consume her. Brettan at last emerged from his bath, shaking droplets of water from his tousled mane of dark, waving hair, so that she was dampened from his playfulness.

Brettan dressed quickly in a tunic and breeches of dark brown edged with gold braid, which seemed to make his eyes glow even more brightly, and the dark, rich color made him seem more handsome than she had thought possible, for it was the same color as his hair, set warmly aglow by the light of the fire. And she thought she could well understand Lady Caroline's hurt and anger to find he had wed another, when she had thought to wed him.

"Come, you are tired. I shall see you are comfortable, and then I shall have a tray brought up, so that we may take the evening meal together."

Gently, Brettan lifted Maren, the light linen cloth

411

falling away so that he lifted her naked from the chair, carrying her slender weight easily to the bed. "I shall have Agnes bring you a gown. Though I much prefer to see you as you are, I fear the meal would grow cold from lack of attention if you remain unclothed."

Oddly, Maren felt no embarrassment at his casual perusal of her nakedness, only a glowing warmth that he should be pleased with her. Gently setting her upon the bed, he reached across her to draw up the coverlet, his hand brushing against the soft flatness of her stomach. His hand lingered for a long moment, and Maren placed her smaller hand over his, holding him to her.

"I never felt the babe move." Brettan's voice was suddenly filled with great sadness.

"It was very faint at first, then later, much stronger. He was a strong child, and I think he would have been a fine son for a father such as you." Maren's voice trembled with overwhelming emotion, so new that it was painful for her to speak, and yet she forced herself to reach through the pain she saw for the first time in those glowing eyes. She had not known how much Brettan had wanted the child. Now it was too late.

"I will give you another child, Maren, if you will have it. A child made of love, not of violence. We shall remember the child we have lost, but we shall find our joy in the children yet to be, for what we have lost."

Tears trickled softly from Maren's eyes, the first she had cried since losing the babe, the first she had allowed herself to mourn her loss, which she now realized was his loss also. Gently she reached up to caress his handsome face, filled with so much pain and, closing her eyes, kissed him tenderly, a kiss that spoke of all her sadness, all her fears, and all her hopes. She felt his warmth as he responded to her kiss, his own lips burning across hers with a passion that matched her own, the taste of him mingling with the saltiness of her tears. Gently he

412

gathered her into his arms and sat upon the large bed, cradling her in his protective embrace, comforted just to hold her safely near. And it was some time later when Brettan ordered up a tray for the evening meal and roared for Agnes to attend to her mistress, lest she be taken with a chill for her lack of adequate care.

Chapter Eighteen

The days had grown milder, with a certain chill in the early morning and late evening that foretold of the new season that was upon them. A heavy dew was upon the greensward each morn, and the wind carried a certain sharp fragrance of leaves and grass dying beneath the early frost.

Brettan's mood became restless, whether from the enforced inactivity of their confinement at King's Forest, or perhaps some greater desire to rejoin his king, Maren could not be certain. Several messengers had arrived from London and, with each one that came, Brettan's mood seemed to darken, as if before a gathering storm. As the days passed, Brettan spent more hours of the day away from Maren with his men, leaving her heavily guarded and in Agnes' capable care. When he returned at the end of each day, Maren had begun to detect small lines of worry about his eyes, as if he carried some great burden but, when he thought she watched, the worry seemed to fade as if a mask were suddenly dropped into place, so that the face that greeted her carried a smile. It seemed as if he sought to keep something from her, something she had not been able to learn in all the hours spent quietly in their chamber. By night Maren lay gently curled within his arms, the heavy thudding of his heart beneath her cheek a constant reassurance of the safety he had promised her. And by day she gained her strength, when Agnes was not about to nag her that she pushed herself too soon, venturing further each day about the large manorhouse, until she could slowly walk the wide sweeping stairway, if she held very carefully onto the posts to steady herself against the occasional lightheadedness that warned her she strained too much. Always strong, always sure of herself, Maren found her recovery slow and frustrating, when her body did not respond as she willed it. Only occasionally did her mind wander to thoughts of the babe she had carried for that brief time, whose gentle life she had felt stirring within her, and was then gone. It brought her too much sadness. She could not yet fully understand, and she found it better if she pushed the memory from her thoughts. Yet there were times when the memory, so fresh within her mind, could not be willed away, as if the loss of her child were part of her greater loss of her mother and the uncertainty of her brother's fate. But she found with each passing day that her sad moments were fewer before the assault of Brettan's gentle caring, and she found herself quite surprised to admit that her feelings for the English knight who had once held her his prisoner had changed much over the weeks past. Or had the change come before that? She only knew that, though there might be no physical bonds to keep her with him, now that the child was gone, she was silently grateful that he had not offered to release her from the marriage, for the bonds that now held her fast were deeper and stronger than any chains or length of rope that he could have placed about her.

On this morning, Maren sat obediently before the blazing warmth of the log at the hearth, while Agnes busied herself with setting some order to the chamber. Maren's appetite had returned over the last days, and she quickly downed the ample fare of hard-boiled eggs, fresh-baked bread with honey, and the freshly sliced apples Agnes had placed before her. Silently Agnes beamed at the glowing health that bloomed in Maren's cheeks, frequently offering up a prayer of thanks that her mistress had survived the wound. She enjoyed her authority over her mistress, which she had not been able to enforce for a good many years, since Maren was a child. Now, with the combined efforts of her determination and Brettan's silent but effective authority, they had managed to enforce her slow convalescence. And yet Agnes could have sworn that Maren was not at all fooled by their efforts, for she knew her mistress well.

Agnes brushed through the waving mass of Maren's hair, which cascaded down the length of her back. "Aye, milady, in a few more weeks you shall be as strong as before, though I would swear none could tell by looking upon you that you were ever taken ill."

"Agnes, most certainly it must be the good care I have received these last weeks, yet I feel the Duke of Norfolk would be greatly relieved if we could leave for Lionshead soon."

"His lordship shall bide his time. His one concern is for you. He shall not risk your health for the sake of reaching his home a week or two earlier."

"Agnes, what do you know of the man who attacked the queen? I have heard it said that he was found dead in the forest. I have also heard that he was Welsh." Maren studied the maid's reflection in the silvered mirror, but Agnes continued brushing her hair in silence.

"Why would one man risk so much, with the English all about, and so far within England? Most certainly he paid a dear price for that which was doomed to fail. Why would his own men see him slain?"

Agnes cast a wary glance at her young mistress, then smoothed a last curl into place. "I can well see that you have too much idle time, to listen to rumors and gossip about the manor. As for the man's failure, 'tis true that he failed in his attack against the queen, but only by your intervention. As for the answers to your other questions, who may say what the purpose of such men might be? It is well known that Llywelyn grows desperate in this war against the English king. It is not unreasonable that he would attempt such an attack. Even now, the king prepares his armies to return to Wales for the final campaign. I pray for peace. There has been enough killing. It is time this war was ended." Realizing that she had said more than she intended, Agnes quickly gathered up the last of the garments. She saw a sudden flickering of uncertainty in Maren's eyes, at the realization that the Duke of Norfolk would be part of that campaign against their people.

"I would see you safely to the hall below, if that is where you are bound this morn. I'll not have you risk breaking your neck when your legs are still so weak."

Maren whirled about in the chair, her mouth flying open in quick denial of the maid's words, then closing just as quickly, for she realized Agnes knew everything of her wanderings of the last few days.

"You will say nothing to his lordship?"

"I will say nothing as long as you promise not to walk about unescorted. It is for your safety, mistress, or I shall be forced to tell all."

Maren fumed helplessly, for she well realized Brettan's certain anger if he learned of her daily walks.

"Very well, but I will not remain a prisoner in my own chamber. I will come and go as I please. Nor do I have need of a guard to follow me about. The manor is well protected. Surely Brettan cannot think that there would be another attack?" As if that knowledge suddenly flared

418

brightly within her brain, Maren turned on the maid. "What is it that the Duke of Norfolk guards so well against?"

"I have no time for idle chatter. There is much that needs be done."

"Agnes! I will have an answer from you. What is it that Brettan fears? Surely he cannot fear my betrayal? Is that what he guards against? Agnes! Answer me."

"It is not you he fears, milady. Methinks he guards against an attack such as the first. It is natural for him to think of your safety."

"Then tell me, Agnes, why does Sandlin or Sir Bothwell always remain within easy sight? It is the same as when I was first his prisoner. Nothing has changed. Can he think so little of me that he thinks I would flee at the first opportunity?" Maren's voice had risen sharply, and she turned on the maid with growing doubts. Could she possibly have been mistaken in their last days together, when she had thought all the old doubts and conflicts at last laid aside? Brettan had spoken of a new beginning between them. Had he only sought to keep her close with kind words that were subtle lies?

"Mistress, there is much that needs be attended. You must not worry needlessly of matters that do not exist."

"Very well, Agnes, you may go." Maren sighed after she dismissed the maid, realizing she would learn nothing more from Agnes. Her thoughts raced over her conversations with Brettan of the last days. She sought some answer to her nagging doubts, yet could find nothing in any of the words passed between them to give her alarm. Indeed, his manner had been most loving and gentle. But in all truth, what did she know of men or the concealed thoughts behind spoken words?

Calmly, Maren waited until she knew Agnes would have reached the hall below. The maid would not yet have had time to summon Sandlin or Sir Bothwell to guard outside the chamber. Quickly she seized the lightweight woolen shawl from the wooden coffer and, wrapping it about her shoulders against the early morning chill, carefully slipped from the chamber to the end of the hallway that descended to the servants' chambers, and beyond that to the gardens that surrounded the manor. She listened carefully at the landing for voices of any servants who might have remained below, then slowly made her way down the stairway, stopping at the bottom to catch her breath, her heart racing wildly from her unaccustomed exertion. Passing down the narrow passageway to the heavy wooden door, Maren carefully lifted the heavy latch and let herself out into the gardens, where the last of the fresh vegetables grew, carefully tended for the royal household. No one was visible, and Maren quickly made her way along the stone half-wall. Rounding a corner that would lead her to the front of the manor, she heard the voices of two young servant girls approaching and quickly adjusted the shawl over her head to conceal her features while she bowed her head and passed the maids. Gaining the front of the manor, Maren glanced quickly about her, like a mischievous child on some wild adventure. She had managed to elude both Agnes and her ever-present guards, and the excitement sent her blood racing. She inhaled deeply of the fresh, crisp air that marked the early days of autumn. Hardly weakened by her efforts, she felt strength flowing through her at her success in gaining her freedom, if for just a few moments, before she would be forced to return to the manor. Maren slowly made her way toward the stables, knowing she would find Brettan attending the gray stallion, as he did every morning, choosing to care for the large warhorse himself. More than one stable boy had suffered bruises or worse from the spirited animal's wild nature.

Her light footsteps made faint crunching sounds in the

thin mantle of frost that covered the greensward. She found him as she had thought she might, and the spirited steed snorted a greeting at her approach, causing Brettan to look up. His face paled beneath the glow of his bronzed skin at the sight of her, his concern obvious in the worried frown that creased his face. Quickly he threw down the brushes he held in his hands and, crossing the distance that separated them, gathered her to him, his lean, well-muscled arm going around her slender waist, while his other arm went beneath her legs, swinging her up into his arms and quickly carrying her to a bench just inside the stables, where he sat down, drawing her into his lap like a disobedient child. Maren hardly protested his concern.

"God's mercy, what are you doing here?"

Maren glanced impishly into his green eyes, which sparked his anger at her foolishness. "I grow weary of my prison, milord. I but sought some fresh air and a bit of freedom. It would seem there are those who would seek to keep me securely held within the walls of my chamber."

"Where are Sandlin and Bothwell? They were told to stay with you."

"And I assume, milord, that they are at their posts, as you have ordered. I merely slipped past them by taking another direction. You may remember well that I have great skill at such." Maren smiled innocently up into his glowering gaze.

Brettan's grip about her tightened, and she saw his anger in the outline of the thin scar that shone white along his cheek. "You, milady, are a fool."

"You have said that before, milord."

"You could have been injured attempting this. Must I forever have you bound in chains to see that you do as you are told?"

"Am I then your prisoner, milord, as I was when first

you captured me and took me from my home?" Her manner was suddenly quite serious. She stared boldly at him, demanding a truth that he was not prepared to give.

"You are not my prisoner. Indeed, I believe that our roles are now reversed. I forever find myself a prisoner to you, milady. A prisoner who at times finds himself powerless to keep you safe. I merely seek to keep you from further harm, as I have promised."

Maren's anger eased at his words, but she remained uncertain. He pulled her gently into the warmth of his embrace and brushed a kiss tenderly against her forehead. His words were softly muffled in the mass of her hair. "There was one attack; there could easily be another. I could not bear your loss after the days and weeks we have shared. Can you not understand, little one?" Gently he held her from him, so that she might look into his eyes and understand more fully his anguish. "Those first days, when you lay so near death, I would gladly have bargained my life for yours, and then, when you lost the child, your pain was my pain. You have become as much a part of me as living and breathing. I did not plan for it to be so, indeed it might have been better for you had I not come to care for you as I have. How can I make you undersatnd? There are matters beyond you and me, beyond what we have come to feel for one another, that may yet take you from me. I could not bear that loss. I know that now, as I know myself. That is why I have you guarded. Not to keep you in, but to keep others out."

"Others? What others? Brettan, I do not understand. The attack was against the queen. My injury was an accident, nothing more. What is my importance, that anyone would choose to harm me? Brettan?"

He gathered her into his arms, the muscles in his jaw tightening, and fought against what he must soon tell her. "You are Welsh, my love, and I English. With the

422

war that rages about us, is that not enough cause for my concern, that someone might wish to see you harmed?"

"Brettan, I am half English by my father. I have lived my entire life caught in this war. And as for someone who might wish to harm me, I can well imagine Lady Caroline's great joy were it to come to pass."

"Caroline? Nay, she is not that foolish. She realizes her cause is lost. It was lost that first day I saw you at Cambria, among all the smoke and the ruins."

"I remember well your intentions, milord. I believe you thought to return to England with me as your mistress. Pray tell, how thought you to keep two mistresses?"

"Aye, those were my thoughts, but I think this arrangement far better. My family would highly disapprove of my bastard children running about England, while their Welsh mother lured every heart at the English court."

"Your family?" Maren was startled by his casual reference to that of which he had never spoken before.

"Yea, milady, my family. Even the lowliest whoreson is born of a family of sorts. I believe that is what you once called me?"

Maren blushed uneasily, vividly recalling the long list of English and Welsh names she had called him.

"Your family is in London?"

"Nay. My mother and sister care little for court life in London. My mother is at our family estate in Norfolk. Since my father's death, she has chosen to remain there. She finds the attentions of the old fools at court quite unbearable. My sister has most recently returned to Normandy, after spending the last year with our mother."

"Are there other sisters or brothers?"

"My brother Philip served Edward as a young knight and was lost at the battle of Lewes."

"Oh, I am sorry."

"There is nothing to be sorry for. It is a matter I feel nothing of. Philip was several years older than I. We never knew each other well."

"Yet he was your brother, milord, and that is a bond that cannot easily be cast aside. Was he also a friend of the king?"

"When a man is king, Maren, there is no one he can truly call his friend, no one he can truly trust. For there are always those who would challenge him. But if Edward was to have a friend, it would indeed have been Philip, for he gave his life to spare a young prince new upon the field of battle."

"But the king calls you his friend. Is it not a true friendship?" Maren questioned, at a loss to understand Brettan's meaning.

"As much as he may allow a friendship, that he shares with me. I know well that, were I in need of his help, he would give it, but always with the understanding that it is because of the strength of the house of Norfolk."

"Milord, do you say that the king fears you?"

"Nay, it is not fear, milady, but respect born of the knowledge that, though he may be my king, Edward is still a man, the same as I or any of my knights."

"And if he were in need of your help, would you give it?"

"I am pledged to do so by the honor of my knighthood."

Maren glanced at him uncertainly. "But beyond your vows of knighthood, would you obey Edward in all matters?"

"Beyond my vows, Maren, I would do whatever might be necessary to keep what is mine."

"And what if Edward had not ordered the marriage, but spoken against it? What then would you have done, milord, Duke of Norfolk? Would you have risked all that is yours, and the favor of your king, to keep me as your mistress?"

"Edward's orders had little to do with the matter, milady. I pledged myself to you beyond even my loyalty to my king."

"How can you say that?" Maren was horrified at his honesty.

"'Tis truth I speak, Maren." She stared aghast at him, unable to comprehend what he was saying. Brettan smiled gently into her wide, blue eyes. "'Tis a thing born of passion, milady. I was quite soundly lost when first you came to my bed."

"Came to your bed? You forget, milord, it was force that brought me to your bed," she reminded him.

"'Tis true, Maren, the force of my passion for you." Playfully he nibbled at the tips of her fingers, sending shivers of delight up the length of her arms. Abruptly Brettan stood, pulling her up along with him, molding her body against his, so that he was pressed intimately to her. "Then so be it, milady. If you are strong enough to venture to the stables, and idly pass time fondling a poor knight of the realm, then I would venture you are strong enough for the ride to Norfolk."

Maren's mouth flew open in quick denial of his lewd reference to the moments they had spent in the stable, but was quickly silenced when his mouth moved over hers hungrily, tasting the softness of her lips. His tongue intimately pressed between her lips, seeking that honeyed velvet softness beyond, and he tasted too her sweet response, which drove his passion to new heights, so that he was tempted to throw her down in the straw in the nearby stall, and take his ease within her, with little care for whoever might find them there. A cautious warning restrained him. He struggled against the heat of her desire and was sorely pressed to set her from him, before he took her, like the heated animal she had once accused him of being. Her eyes widened at the sight of his aroused passion, which pressed feverishly against the inside of her thigh. But in her eyes he saw only an invitation to finish what he had started.

"Enough of this, milady. Or we shall both be forced to explain to Agnes not only your absence from the hall, but your disheveled appearance, if we linger in the stables."

Maren's hand flew to her mouth. She giggled, and then her manner grew more serious as she stared into his emerald eyes. "Only if you vow that we shall finish what we have begun, milord, when more time allows for a slower pace. I fear my strength is not yet adequate for trysts taken quickly in the hay."

Brettan gathered her against him in one quick motion, gently breathing in the sweetness of her hair. "Again, you have my solemn promise, Maren, that we shall continue what we have begun."

Within two days' time, all was in readiness for the journey to Norfolk. Brettan had grown increasingly uneasy as autumn set its mark of change upon the countryside, the first leaves taking on their brilliant red and gold colors. He could not risk traveling to Norfolk and having the weather turn uncertain, and therefore gave the orders that all must be made ready for the journey.

Agnes fumed and fussed over his decision, openly doubtful of his wisdom in matters that concerned Maren's health, until Maren was forced to intervene, quickly silencing the woman's heated protests with an authoritative command, which caused all present to turn and stare at her in stunned disbelief, that one so beautiful could possibly be possessed of such will. Brettan had turned away to hide the amused smile that had spread across his face, for with each passing day Maren became

426

less the invalid, and more the lady of the manor. More than any words, it gave him certainty of her return to good health.

Determined though she was to ride her own horse on the morning of their departure, Maren found herself completely exhausted after only an hour's ride from her efforts to remain in the saddle, a feat that would have required no great effort before her injury. One glance at her strained face, and Brettan's orders were quickly given that she was to ride with him, atop the large gray warhorse. Fatigued beyond any objections, Maren silently yielded the reins of the small black mare to Sandlin and gratefully welcomed the strong, safe haven of Brettan's arms, gently lifted from the saddle and deposited into his lap. Maren's faint smile of gratitude was reward enough for Sandlin, who led the mare to the end of the procession. He had long considered Maren his special "prisoner" and took much delight in the great changes he had seen in his master since that day at Cambria so many months before.

The brilliant chill of the early morning air, which marked the changes of the seasons, drove Maren back into the secluded warmth of the heavy mantle Brettan drew across his shoulders, enclosing her against the solid strength of his chest.

Maren's muscles tensed and trembled violently but, as the moments passed, she relaxed into the gentle motion of the gray's easy stride and slumped wearily against Brettan, drifting into peaceful slumber with his strong arms wrapped protectively about her, his lips gently brushing the top of her head.

They traveled north through Essex, and Maren seemed to gain strength each day, the fresh air and sunshine and crisp cool mornings revitalizing her. She slept most of the first day they traveled and, when Brettan ordered the camp made early that first afternoon, she hardly remembered his lifting her from the saddle and carrying her to the tent. Nor did she remember the meal he forced her to eat before gently laying her upon the thick, soft pallet, where she had first lain with him. The following morning she awakened early and quietly left the tent to take a short walk beside the river where they made their camp. Brettan found her there after near tearing the camp apart upon waking to find her gone. So great was his anger and fear for her safety, that he had been sorely tempted to thrash her, when at last he found her sitting silently beside the stream. But when she had turned to him, so great was his joy to have her safe that he had instead gathered her into his arms, suddenly at a loss to deal with the new emotions he felt.

The three-day journey to Norfolk lengthened to twice that number, for Brettan ordered camp made early each day, while several hours of light still remained. Though his men were eager to reach the northern estates, they well understood the slower pace he kept, and none challenged his decision. Brettan took particular pleasure in keeping Maren close under his hand, satisfied with just the nearness of her, while they rode through the vast countryside that made up the de Lorin estates. Maren understood how Edward might highly value her husband, whose wealth she had only just begun to comprehend. By night they shared their warmth and, in the cold of early morn, Maren was drawn to the vibrant heat of Brettan's body beside hers, separated from her only by the thinness of the chemise she wore. With each touch, each gentle caress, she felt a deep, aching need grow within her, and their journey came to an end all too quickly.

"We shall reach Lionshead near midday tomorrow. All will be in readiness. I have sent word that we will be arriving. I would not have you first see Lionshead all closed and dusty from the months past since I was last here." Brettan carefully polished the broad flat blade of his sword in the soft glow of the candlelight that flickered when an occasional breeze drifted through the closure of the tent, their last night before arriving.

"Is your mother not at Lionshead?" Maren looked up from the fine stitching she had set to one of Brettan's linen shirts.

"Lady Helene finds Lionshead empty without her family about her. She prefers instead to occupy a smaller manor nearby."

"But she is the Duchess of Norfolk. Certainly it is not fitting that she should be cast out of her home."

"Lady Helene has hardly been cast out of her home. It is her choice that she remain at Harrow House. My father gave it to her as a wedding present on the day of their marriage. Indeed, they spent more time there than at Lionshead. Harrow House is hardly some meager hovel. It is a grand house, and quite suited to my mother. Since my father's death, she has chosen to remain at Harrow. It gives her comfort to be near something that was a part of him. And by my marriage to you, milady, you are now the Duchess of Norfolk."

Maren eyed him skeptically, noting the odd gleam that sparkled in those glowing green eyes, which seemed to take on the glow of the candles burning brightly about them.

"And what might be the Lady Helene's thoughts of that? I can hardly believe that she will be greatly pleased." Uneasily Maren remembered Lady Caroline's reaction at finding she had been replaced as Brettan's betrothed, and she could only think that Brettan's mother might feel that same bitterness at the loss of her title.

Laying the blade aside, Brettan rose from his cross-legged position before the fire and quietly sat down beside her on the soft pallet, where she sat fresh from her bath, her skin aglow with good health and youth, her eyes like sparkling sapphires that glowed with unmistakable warmth. Gently he lifted her chin, so that she was forced to look into his eyes. "You do the Lady Helene an injustice. You must not judge her by the acts of others."

Maren set down her sewing, gazing into his handsome face, bronzed by long hours spent practicing his warrior's skills astride the gray warhorse. His dark hair, long and shaggy like a mane, lay in thick waves about his face and neck, a stray curl falling loosely over one eye, so that she felt the greatest desire to reach up and smooth it back. What manner of man was he that, though once her enemy he could draw all hatred and fear from her? Only once had she asked him of his part in the attack on Cambria, and only once he had given his answer, and yet she had no doubts that he had spoken the truth. But what secrets did he still hold from her behind that guarded gaze, that she found staring back at her now as if he could look into her very soul? And what now of their marriage, now that the child was lost? Was it as he had said, that he was bound to her and she to him, from that first moment at Cambria? Or did he now feel some small regret for the vows that had been spoken between them? Was it his intent to take her to Lionshead because of a greater duty to his king, only to return to London and his mistress when that duty was fulfilled? Maren stared into those emerald depths with intensity, so that she might find answers to all her questions in that glowing gaze. Finding none, she stubbornly forced her doubts from her mind, reaching up to smooth back that stray lock of hair, her warm fingertips gently brushing against his skin. Brettan inhaled suddenly at the heat of her touch, losing himself in the depths of her wide-eyed gaze, feeling his resolve weaken before the passion he saw stirring in her gaze. His warrior's strength to hold himself from her crumbled when Maren slowly slipped her fingers through his hair, gently pulling his face to hers. Her eyes closed, and her lips sought his, conveying her desire for him in the heat of her lips moving against him. They clung to his, while her tongue sought the warmth between his lips. Brettan's thoughts reeled under the assault of her wanton attack on his senses. Never before had he known such honest response, and he felt his weakened control melting before her ravaging ardor.

Pulling away from him suddenly, Maren rose to her feet and crossed the width of the tent to snuff the candles that cast their warm glow about the enclosure. Wrapped in darkness, Brettan leaned back on one elbow, wondering at her game, his eyes straining for some sight of her in the meager light that glowed through the walls of the tent, from the campfires beyond. In an instant his searching ended, for he felt her nearness, the warmth radiating from her body in the coolness of the night air, which entered through the fabric walls. Her rose-scented fragrance was all about him, and he felt her hand lightly upon the linen of his shirt, and then the heat of her fingers slowly untying the closure of the shirt, slipping her hand through the opening to caress the soft furring of dark hair that spread across his chest, lightly tracing his collarbone, then traveling down the length of his side. And then her hand disappeared, and he felt a gentle tugging while she pulled the shirt from his breeches and drew it over his head. Never before had he known such boldness from a highborn woman, much less a young girl who was his wife, and a virgin when first he had taken her. His composure shaken, Brettan leaned back to await her next move.

Maren pushed him back against the softness of the pallet, pressing lingering kisses across his chest, her small tongue trailing a sweet path down his side and then across the flat hard surface of his belly, following the path of dark hair, which narrowed at his waist and disappeared below the belt of his breeches. Gently Maren

431

pulled the leather belt from his waist, her hand lingering ever so briefly against the inside of his thigh. He fought for restraint, and her laugh was low and warm in her throat when her hand closed over him. She fully enjoyed her mastery over the bold English knight who had so often held her within his power. Gently she lay across him, the naked fullness of her breasts searing him where they brushed against him, driving Brettan beyond all endurance. In one urgent movement, Brettan pulled her beneath him, gently pinning her onto her back, his weight holding her against any possible escape. "What foolishness is this, Maren?"

"No foolishness, milord. Only an end to your saintly attentions toward me."

"You know well, Maren, that I do not deliberately seek the life of a monk. I came close to losing you, and I shall not risk causing you some harm now that might injure you further."

"That, milord, is your foolishness. You have never caused me pain when you have come to me."

"Not even that first time?"

Maren stared through the meager light in the tent into those glowing eyes. "At first there was pain, born of my fear of that which I had never known, but later the pain became an ache of my own need for you, an ache that can be eased only by you."

"Then do you not desire an end to the marriage?" Brettan's voice was hardly more than a whisper against her ear. He gathered her slowly to him, her breasts pressed against the soft furring that covered his chest.

"My greatest fear, milord, is that you would seek that end, now that there is no child to bind you to the vows spoken before your king."

"I have told you, Maren, my vows were spoken to you before God. It is my intent to honor those vows. You must also remember that I once promised to give you

432

another child but, before this passes between us, this night, before another child is made of my seed taken deep within you, I must know what you feel in your heart."

Maren looked deep into his eyes and saw that the shield that had before concealed his innermost thoughts and emotions had been cast aside. She now saw only the agony of his pain should she now choose to cast him aside, and that truth more than any other bound her to him for all eternity. Gently she took his hand in her own and laid it across her breast. "Feel my heart beneath your hand. Feel how it beats at your slightest touch. Against my will you have become my life's blood, so that I am certain, if your life should cease, so would mine. It was not so at first. Were I to say so, you would know it to be a lie, but the vows I have spoken cannot measure against the vows I now speak. Brettan, you are my love, you are my life. Give me the seed of your love, and I will lovingly hold it within me until it comes forth, a child created of that love. Or send me away if that is your wish, but once it is done, never call me back with tenderly spoken words, for once this love I feel dies, it can never be given life again."

Fiercely Brettan held her small face between his two hands that could easily have crushed the life from her. "I could never send you from me, for you are the very air I breathe. To send you from me would be to seek my own death." Brettan's voice broke with a passion he had never before acknowledged, so that tears filled Maren's eyes as she stared back at him.

"Then hold me, milord, and let there be no more words between us this night."

Slowly his hold loosened, and Maren felt the fierceness easing from his body, lying across her. Tenderly she sought his lips, her arms reaching up to close about his neck, pulling him to her. She felt his sweet response when the warmth of his body flowed through her. She stretched full length against him, moving her legs between his, arching upwards against him. Brettan's hands caressed the skin across her back, then lowered across the gentle curving of her hip, pressing her to him. She felt the heat of his passion. His lips left hers and traced a molten path aross her cheek, her eyelids, then gently nibbled at her ear, sending shivers down her back, so that she wriggled in delight against him. He lightly kissed the ridge of her collarbone and the rounded smoothness at her shoulder. He raised her hand and pressed a lingering kiss into the palm. Then his lips returned to claim hers, more intensely, for she felt the passion building within him, no longer straining to deny what they both sought. Maren moaned softly when his mouth closed over the peak of her breast, feeling sweet agony as he gently teased that rose-hued tip, gently kneading the fullness of her breasts while his tongue tasted her softness. Brettan rose to remove his breeches, letting them fall where they might, and rejoined her, the warmth of his long body seeming to wrap about her when he gathered her to him once again. And again his mouth sought the fullness of her breast, driving her breath from her at the intensity of that pleasure. She felt that ache deep within her and abandoned herself to his touch, his caress, aware only of him all about her, taking her to new heights of pleasure. With a passion born of desperation, Maren tasted of him, caressed him, drew him closer to her, so that no part of them did not touch, and then, faintly at first, she whispered her plea for him to take her. But Brettan resisted, building within her the flame of his own desires. Still he teased her, tormented her, until she seemed like a wild creature beneath him, her gleaming white body as smooth as satin where he touched, the wild cascade of her hair tumbling about them in complete disarray, while his kisses traced a fiery path over every part of her skin, so that she seemed

434

aflame from his touching her. And still he resisted that final, ultimate pleasure to be found within her, but sent her to new heights. Maren felt the wild pulsing in her veins, moaning softly, pleadingly for sweet release. And then, with deliberate slowness, Brettan's knee moved between her legs, and she opened to him, and even more slowly he lowered himself to her, so that she felt only a first faint pressure. She stared up into the strong, handsome face of her English knight, but he seemed to hesitate for one last moment, as if suddenly uncertain.

His name on her lips was her final plea, and Maren arched up against him, forcing him deep within her. Her breath caught in her throat at the surprise of that entry, and yet she did not cry out. Slowly Brettan moved against her, gently. But it was her need of him that forced her passion to new heights, and Brettan moved with her, feeling a need of her so deep and consuming that he was lost to her. They soared higher, until the waves of passion that broke within them were as one, and Brettan pressed her to him in that final moment of sweet agony.

Slowly the waves of their passion ebbed, leaving them resting gently in each other's arms, Maren's raven tresses swirling about them in wild abandon, and that one bond between them remained unbroken. And some time later, when they awakened, still held firmly in each other's grasp, they took their pleasure of one another more slowly, with a joy that surpassed any known before.

Chapter Nineteen

Lionshead rose majestically, like an imposing guardian that protected a portal to the sea. It had been built at the order of William the Conqueror, a northern fortress for the Norman hordes invading England. The fortress and the entire region that surrounded it, bounded by the sea on one side, had been presented to Brettan's family years before, as a reward for securing a foothold for the bastard king. Now, nearly two hundred years later, the vast holdings that were Norfolk spread beyond the hillsides and valleys bounding the imposing stronghold.

Lionshead indeed seemed to Maren like some large beast guarding the hillside, from which it commanded a breathtaking view of the sea beyond. Brilliant blue and gold banners flew from each turret and tower, snapping wildly in the autumn breeze, and their arrival was heralded with all the pomp and ceremony that might have been accorded the king. From where she sat in front of Brettan, astride the tall warhorse, Maren was able to see all about her. The entire guard at Lionshead was presented for Brettan's approval, and a flood of servants and serfs lined the vast courtyard, straining for a glimpse of the newly returned lord of the manor and the lady he

437

had brought as his wife.

At the top of the stone steps to the great hall, a tall woman stood in splendid array, her head held proudly, watching the procession slowly approach. Lady Helene, Duchess of Norfolk, cast aside all formality when she rushed forward to greet her son upon his arrival.

"Brettan, my son." Her smile radiated her love and warmth. She extended her hand to her son, then gathered him into her embrace. Gently Brettan pressed a kiss against her cheek. "You are well, and beautiful as always."

"I am well and lonely, with my children so far from me. I fear too soon you will be gone again on some crusade our king pursues, when he has finally succeeded in making Wales and England one. You have set us to complete turmoil with your message that you would arrive in five days' time. And where is your bride?" Her strikingly beautiful face, which bore a strong resemblance to her son's, searched beyond him to the young girl still mounted astride the gray. "My son, at times I think you have no more sense than that great horse of yours. What can you be thinking of, leaving your wife to ride after her illness?" Lady Helene quickly descended the wide steps, calmly but effectively chastening Sandlin for allowing his mistress to be so handled by his lord and master.

"Milady, I think you shall find the Lady Maren sufficiently recovered from her illness." Brettan chuckled at his mother's pretense of great anger.

Sandlin easily assisted Maren to the ground, and then stood aside while the two women stared at each other with open interest.

"We had word that Brettan had taken a wife of great beauty. I thought the man might have exaggerated his story. I can see he has not. My dear Maren, welcome to your new home. Welcome to Lionshead." With that

438

Lady Helene swept Maren before her, up the stone steps into the great hall beyond, leaving an amused Brettan to wonder what he could have doubted in their meeting.

Their days at Lionshead were the happiest since the days before her mother's death, though Maren could not imagine that she could have been happier than those last days of traveling to Norfolk.

With each passing day she learned more of Brettan than she had thought possible, coming to know his home, his people, and his family. Brettan remained occupied with reviewing the past year away from the estates. Long hours each day were spent with dispensing his soldiers to their own families in the area, if only for a short time, or meeting with the vast numbers of servants and serfs that tended the immediate holdings of Lionshead. Crops that had been planted and harvested were studied with great care, as were the increased flocks of sheep and herds of cattle, not to mention a highly prized herd of fine-blooded horses that were Brettan's passion. The priests from a nearby village came to offer their welcome to the lord and master, and petitioned for the necessary coin to begin a school of higher learning for the young boys and girls of the village. In many instances Brettan gave some instruction to his steward for the handling of a certain matter. In others, he was forced to ride out into the countryside, sometimes forcing an absence of two or three days to see to the endless responsibilities that had fallen to his steward over the last year. But each evening, when he greeted her across the vast table in the dining hall, Brettan drew her into his world with the telling of his day, and he gently questioned Maren of her hours spent with the Lady Helene. By night all their thoughts were cast aside save for one, for they lay safely within each other's arms, freeing themselves to the wild passion

439

of their love, while he sought to fulfill his promise to her.

Autumn passed with fleeting swiftness, the days cool and brisk, frosty nights giving way to the shorter, gray days of winter, and Maren found all her hours occupied with the Lady Helene and the planning of the Christmas feast at Lionshead. During Brettan's absence of the years past, Lady Helene had celebrated the holiday at her smaller home at Harrow House. Indeed it had been many years since the holiday had been taken within the vast stone walls of Lionshead. But when the word of the master's return spread about the countryside, the plans were made, and all eagerly waited for their parchment invitation, neatly lettered with great care by the scribe who had been called to set his letters for the guests.

Great stores of food were brought forth from the storerooms beneath the castle, which could easily have housed and fed an army of thousands for months, even years, during the siege of William the Conqueror. The townspeople whose homes were secured within the mighty walls of Lionshead lent their vast efforts to the holiday spirit, rejoicing at their master newly returned from Wales with a fine, beautiful young wife, whose kindness was already known to many. Indeed there were those with illness or injury who had quickly learned that the Lady Maren possessed great knowledge of herbs and medicines which brought healing magic to the afflicted. Soon Maren found herself traveling out among the people of Lionshead, as her mother once had for the people of Cambria. With Sandlin or Sir Bothwell at her side, she often stayed long hours into the afternoon, only returning when her guardians kindly but forcefully reminded her that the Duke of Norfolk would not take it kindly if she were to fall ill herself from fatigue. Yet the joy Maren received in helping the people of Lionshead seemed to give her a purpose among Brettan's people, so that when she returned to him in the evening and they spoke of their days, he was not unaware of the light that glowed in her vibrant eyes, which told him more of her happiness in her new home than any kindly spoken words.

Only occasionally, at night, when she lay beside him in the quiet darkness of their chamber, and all other thoughts were laid aside, did her memory fill with the sights and sounds of the last days at Cambria and the uncertain fate of her family. Never, in all the months since her marriage to Brettan, had her father or brother sent her any word of Cambria. Only because of Agnes had she been able to learn of Catherine, and that no word had been received as to Edmund's fate. And that had been several weeks before, with no word since, so that she could only fear the worst for the lad. Her eyes would fill with silent tears of sadness when she thought of her mother's death, and the strange fate that had brought her to Lionshead.

As if sensing her great sadness, though he slept beside her, Brettan would gather her into his arms, pulling her close, keeping her safe, as he had vowed, kissing away her tears until her sadness vanished before the heat of their consuming passion.

The brisk autumn wind whipped the heavy mantle about the lone rider, who sat astride his mount and stared into the distance, beyond the trees lining the road to the fortress atop the hill. Each day for the past two weeks, the stranger had watched carefully for some point where he might find entrance to the fortress, always discouraged to find that even here, so deep within England, the fortress was constantly guarded by an army that would have rivaled that of the English king. And at the end of each day, the stranger retreated to some unknown point to take his shelter against the coming winter, which closed in with each passing day.

Not until today had the stranger stayed on the hillside to linger more than a few moments before riding on. Now, as he watched the small village at the base of the fortress, his eyes watched with keen intent the figure of a slender young woman, riding to one of the thatched houses that bordered the village, followed by two of the guards from the keep. Dismounting from her horse, the young woman threw back the hood of her mantle to greet the woman who stepped out of the house. His breath froze in his throat, while Geoffrey of Meyrick watched the young woman from his secluded vantage point, the bright sun of the crisp, clear day glistening off raven-black hair, pulled back from the delicate oval of her face. Though her features could not be seen from that great distance, the stranger had no doubts of her title, judging by the richness of her mantle and the close guard kept over her by the two knights. A smile spread slowly across his face, while Geoffrey gazed down on that fair figure. The prize he sought was indeed at Lionshead, and good fortune had now presented him the opportunity to seek her out.

Geoffrey watched the house long after Maren had disappeared inside with the woman, contemplating his plan. He would not leave matters entirely to Lady Caroline. After all, she was English and for that alone could not be trusted, even though she sought Maren's return to Wales as much as he. He shivered in the early morning breeze and drew his heavy mantle more closely about him, before urging his horse down the hillside through a thick outcropping of trees that offered shelter. He would seek out the inn at Southwold on the appointed date as he had agreed, but in the days left before that meeting, he would lay his own plan, to make certain there was no failure this time. He could not afford to return to Wales empty-handed, nor had he any intention of remaining in England longer than was absolutely necessary. If the Duke of Norfolk interfered in the matter, then that would be his own misfortune. Geoffrey smiled at the thought that he would find great pleasure in making Maren a widow. And when she no more wore her widow's weeds they would marry, for he could well imagine Maren's loyalty to the vows spoken before God, which would never allow her to live as wife to another man, when her husband still lived. That smile of satisfaction curled into a tight-lipped glare at the thought of the Englishman whose blood he would enjoy seeing flow freely.

The next days, Geoffrey rode the entire perimeter of Lionshead, always discreetly out of view of the well-armed English guard who patrolled the countryside. By watching carefully, he soon learned their pattern and avoided traveling where he knew he could be certain to find the guard. Three days later he found the opportunity he sought, sitting warming in the early morning light, safely sheltered in a large stand of trees that formed a small hunting park beyond the castle. On this same day, the two weeks past, Maren had ridden out early before venturing forth into the village, riding well ahead of her guard, as if she sought some momentary freedom before they caught up with her. To his satisfaction, Geoffrey saw that this morn was no different. He instantly recognized that slim figure when Maren emerged through the smaller gate of the keep, astride the fine-boned black mare he had seen her riding before. As if suddenly seized by some mischievous spirit, she leaned low over the mare's neck and gave her free rein, starting the black on a wild pace that sent the heavy velvet of Maren's mantle billowing out behind her, like large wings about to give her flight. Her ebony tresses broke from their fastenings and streamed behind her in the wind, while she sent the mare at a devilish pace over the greensward. Behind her the guards had not yet discovered her absence. Geoffrey realized with sudden clarity that, if he were to have any opportunity to speak with her, it must be now, before the guards followed and saw him approaching her.

In sudden decision, Geoffrey spurred his own mount forward, toward the edge of the river that ran its course beside the fortress to the sea. He saw well the line of Maren's flight and rode hard to catch that fleeing figure.

Maren reveled in her sudden burst of freedom, letting the mare take the bit firmly in her teeth and stretch her slender, long legs over the rolling turf. She gave little heed to the growing distance between herself and her faithful guards, as Sandlin emerged from the same gate she had left a few moments before. She gained more time while they sat astride their horses searching the horizon for her fleeing figure before giving chase, each thinking of their master's anger should any harm befall the Lady Maren. Only Sandlin seemed confident of her abilities in handling the high-spirited mare, for he highly suspected one temperament richly deserved the other. His greatest fear was another danger that might lurk beyond their protective guard. Catching a glimpse of a single rider racing across the green, Sandlin instantly recognized the ebony black mane of Maren's hair and urged his mount ahead, calling to the rest of his guard.

Feeling the mare begin to strain beneath her, Maren applied a firm steady hand to the reins. At first the mare fought the restraint and refused to yield, racing over the field of dried grass, now browned from the heavy frosts of the last weeks. Maren felt the mare's firm hold of the bit ease a small measure, and she pulled back firmly, until the mare slowed to a rolling gait and finally to a walk, arching her lovely, long neck defiantly, while Maren spoke to her gently. The black mare snorted her excitement, and Maren knew well she would have bolted at the slightest ease on the reins. Maren laughed gaily, reaching down to stroke the mare. She turned to gaze back to the castle that loomed into the brilliant blue sky and saw the tiny distant figures of Sandlin and the other guards giving chase. "Ah, my pretty one, I fear our moment for freedom is at an end. Even now our guard descends upon us, to see that we are returned to our walled prison. But we shall not return without giving them a good run, eh, my pet?" She could well imagine the disapproving looks she would receive from Sandlin when at last they caught up with her; if they caught up with her. She urged the mare on at a slower pace, turning back in the saddle to look beyond the river that stretched before her. In the distance she saw a single rider approaching. She shielded her eyes from the sun's glare, with her hand.

There was something familiar about the rider who approached. A memory stirred within her mind but remained beyond her grasp. She slowed the mare's pace, but the rider came toward her at a hard gallop. There was something in the cut of his clothes and the odd position he maintained on the back of his mount, almost as if he were very old or perhaps crippled. Or perhaps sought only to give that impression. Maren's eyes flew open in stunned surprise.

"Geoffrey!" She stared at him, at last seeing his face beneath the heavy woolen mantle and recognizing him. Far behind her a warning cry was sounded by Sandlin, for he too saw the rider, and drove his men hard against the clear danger he saw, with her still beyond their protection.

Maren glanced quickly over her shoulder to see Sandlin and the guard quickly closing the distance to her. She turned back uncertainly when Geoffrey approached and reined his horse to a stop. She saw in his eyes that he too had seen the guard, and knew instantly that he would not risk a confrontation with the English.

He controlled his nervous horse, continuing to stare beyond her at the approaching guard, and then for a moment his eyes locked with hers. "I must speak with you Maren, but not here. There is too much risk. Some place where we may speak in private, away from your 'loyal' guard." The last was spoken with a note of derision in his voice, and Maren was taken back by the fierce expression that played across his face, which seemed to have aged so much since she had last seen him.

"Geoffrey, do you bring some word from my father?"

"There is no time now. Where may we meet, where you will not be followed? The Duke of Norfolk must value you highly, to keep you always so close under his hand." Geoffrey sneered at her.

"Geoffrey, you need have no fear of the Duke of Norfolk. The news you bring me may be spoken before him."

"You are a fool, Maren. I would hardly have expected such loyalty, for the man who ordered the attack on Cambria, and your mother's death."

"You are wrong, Geoffrey. The English are not responsible for the attack."

"Your faithful hounds approach, Maren. There is no time for this now. We must meet, and soon, for time grows short. I shall come to you again. Do not attempt to find me. I will seek you out. Your English would glady cut me down were I found near you. I shall not give them that opportunity." Casting another uneasy glance over his shoulder at the riders who approached, Geoffrey whirled his horse about.

"Until we meet again, my love." With a vengeance he drove the horse hard for the river's edge, then plunged across, quickly gaining the coverage of the trees beyond. Maren had no time for further thought, for Sandlin and the guard descended upon her, two of the guard riding hard to give chase.

"Please, no, Sandlin! The man merely sought directions from me. There is no harm done."

Sandlin eyed her steadily, as if he did not quite believe her words. "Did the man have a name, milady?"

"He gave me no name, he only asked of a farm."

"Which farm did he ask of, milady?" Sandlin deliberately sought answers he knew well she did not have.

"I cannot recall, it was not a name known to me."

"'Twould seem strange, would it not, milady, that a man merely seeking directions would depart so hastily."

Maren turned the mare about, seeking to draw Sandlin's attention away from the direction of Geoffrey's escape. "He seemed in a great hurry, I know nothing more of the matter."

Sandlin eyed her keenly. He knew well more had passed between her and the stranger. "There are many dangers about, milady, even here in Norfolk. I must make this known to the Duke of Norfolk."

Maren suddenly felt her defenses flaring, and yet she could well imagine Brettan's anger when he learned of the matter. She sighed heavily. The afternoon quickly took on a certain foreboding chill, and she resignedly turned the mare back toward Lionshead.

Brettan's wrath knew no bounds when later, at the evening meal, he questioned her heatedly about the encounter. He paid little heed to Lady Helene's earnest pleas, but lectured Maren for several moments of the dangers surrounding Norfolk, of treacherous thieves that abounded the forests, and desperate sorts of every size, shape and description, when Maren suddenly rose from her seat at the long dining table. She slammed the ornate goblet down on the hard surface of the wooden table, in a deliberate show of defiance, the loud noise suddenly silencing his tirade and drawing three pairs of eyes in her direction. Sandlin quickly lowered his gaze and absently toyed with a piece of roast fowl on his plate, seeing the warning light that glinted in those enormous blue eyes, which sparkled like the richest sapphires, and he silently prayed for deliverance from the storm that quickly gathered. True to his word, he had had no choice but to tell Brettan of the stranger seen near the river, who had eluded his guard, and yet even as he had done so, knowing it for the Lady Maren's safety, he had regretted the confrontation he knew it would bring. For if there was anything he had learned in the months past, in the company of the lady of the manor, it was that her temper was one to be regarded with utmost care. Quickly he glanced up and caught a momentary glimpse of the Duke of Norfolk, who stood before his own chair, his weight propped forward menacingly on his two hands, braced against the surface of the table. And Brettan's voice echoed through the stone hall, bellowing the full force of his anger.

"Mistress, if you cannot obey the rules of this house, then I will see you soundly prevented from riding about the countryside. I make no concessions in this matter."

Maren's voice was low and she leaned forward to accept his challenge. "I will not be prisoner in this house, nor any other. Once that was so, but never again. I will say this only once, there was no harm done by my speaking with the man. Is it your intention, milord, to have me bound in chains and held as your prisoner, as once you did?"

"That may still be arranged, Maren. Whatever it takes to keep you safe, I will see it done. Be it that you must be chained and bound, then I will give the order."

Glancing first at her son, and then at the seething anger and defiance she saw within the depths of those flashing blue eyes, Lady Helene rose abruptly from the table and, seizing a large carving knife from one of the platters of roast boar, slammed the tip of the blade down into the smooth surface of the table, suddenly more fearsome than all those about her.

"I will not take my meals among such bickering and anger. Brettan, your father never allowed anger to come to this table, and I shall not allow it now. From what I hear, 'tis a petty thing you squabble over. So take yourselves away and see the matter set aright. There is too much anger here. I will not see it enter this house."

Maren stared across the width of the large table at Brettan's stony countenance, knowing she had dared much. But she could not ease the tight constricting knot in her stomach, her proud defiant gaze locked with his. The worst part of it was that he was right, and she knew it to be so. What drove her anger beyond reason was his treatment of her, as if she were some possession that he must safely lock away, and guard against someone else's taking from him. She stared into that smoldering gaze, and all she could see was his anger. Not waiting for his reaction, she whirled on her heel, suddenly unable to face his anger any longer, and fled the hall for the courtyard beyond, ignoring the cold of the gusting wind that had come up. Mindless of the path she followed, Maren flew into the dark of night, seeing only the distant glow of lights in the stable beyond, which offered a sanctuary. She turned her steps toward that quiet haven, where she might escape Brettan's uncertain and biting anger.

Brettan looked to the two who remained at the table, and knew the full weight of the criticism in their solemn glances. Sandlin cleared his throat uneasily and reached to drain his goblet, hastily standing to take his departure. "You do the lady an injustice, milord. She should know the truth of what you guard against."

"And perhaps place her in more danger by doing so?

449

Can you say what you think her reaction might be to this?" Brettan looked from his man to the Lady Helene, knowing he had gained their complete disgust by his treatment of Maren the last days. "There is no need for you both to look at me so. Continue your meal. I cannot see that it should be ruined for everyone."

"My son."

Impatiently Brettan turned back to Lady Helene, having started for the door.

"Remember, my son, that words spoken in anger may not easily be taken back. Do not be harsh with your lady, lest you cast aside something of such immeasurable value, that may never be found again."

The dark fury left Brettan's face while he listened to her words. Slowly he rounded the end of the table to stand before the tall woman. Even now she possessed a timeless beauty that would always be hers. "I am oft reminded, of late, that too often I choose the armor of battle. There are times when I would see a matter resolved as I would with one of my soldiers, had he disobeyed an order and endangered not only himself but others as well."

"My son, your Maren is not a soldier. She is not a man. She is gentle and vulnerable. And your silence makes her more so. Do you doubt her so greatly that you cannot trust her with the truth? You must find a way to set aside the trappings of war. Trust in her, and I believe you will find in her a weapon more fierce than any blade you could hold at your side, if you will but let her be. Go to her, my son, and let this matter be settled gently between you."

"And what if she should choose to return to her people, when she knows the truth? Must I then keep my own wife prisoner to prevent it?" Brettan stared at Lady Helene, all his uncertainty reflected in those emerald depths.

"You must trust in the love that binds her to you. She might well have left you weeks ago, but chose not to. The bond that keeps her here is strong and grows stronger with each day, but you must trust her."

Brettan bent low and pressed a kiss on Lady Helene's cheek before standing back to gaze down at her. "Ever the peacekeeper. I have wondered how you survived all of us when we were children. I swear, we were forever at odds with one another."

"I applied the same measures that I may yet find a necessity for. A green sapling switch is oft the only remedy to restore order to a household."

"Do you threaten me, milady?" Brettan teased lightheartedly.

"Only if you persist in this manner, where the Lady Maren is concerned."

Brettan's face sobered when he caught Sandlin's eye and then looked back at his mother. "The matters of which I speak are of grave concern."

"Then, my son, your wife should know of them." Lady Helene held out a restraining hand, for he seemed about to tell her something. "I have no need to know of it. I accept the Lady Maren as she is. I have learned more of her in just the last weeks than you may know in all your time together. But set this aside, and do not let it come between you. I have a need to see my grandchildren running about these halls, and I will not allow you to set those plans aside."

"Who has said that woman is weaker than man? I would heartily wager for a handful of women in any battle." A playful smile pulled at the corners of his mouth, and his humor seemed restored. "Have Agnes keep the meal warm. I go to find a wayward bit of a girl with more stubbornness than good sense." A loud slamming of the oaken portal marked his passage. Brettan fled the hall in search of a black-haired beauty who was

451

both his greatest treasure and his worst torment.

The storm grew apace with Maren's anger as she fled across the wide cobbled courtyard, mindless of the gathering storm that blocked the stars and the moon from view, casting the courtyard into darkness. Winter unleashed its first assault on the countryside, sending a sudden heavy rain that quickly turned to blinding torrents, which drenched her before she could reach the stables. The air had grown colder through the evening and threatened to bring the first snow, and the rain turned to blinding sleet that stung at Maren's eyes. She struggled to reach the heavy door that had been drawn closed against the mounting wind. Lifting the latch, she threw her meager weight against the stable door, hardly budging the solid portal. Her gown was soaked and clung to her like a second skin, and her hair hung in long, dark streamers down the length of her back. The cold and wet of the storm, together with her inability to open the door only added to her frustration, and in sudden fury, Maren stepped back and launched a well-placed kick at the unyielding portal. The intense pain that shot through that injured member only fueled her frustration and anger, and she thought miserably that she had probably succeeded in breaking every bone in her foot. Before she could launch a second attack at the stable door, she felt herself swung off her feet, in arms that bore her weight with little effort and opened the massive doors at the same time.

Having spotted her slender figure huddled against the stable doors, Brettan quickly lifted her and, throwing open the large doors, easily carried her within, closing the heavy portal behind them, blocking out the fury of the storm, which assaulted the stables with growing strength. Unceremoniously he deposited her on a pile of hay in the first stall.

"You, milady, are a fool of the grandest sort."

Maren jerked her face away from him, so that she would not have to look at those piercing eyes which seemed to know her every thought before she could speak it. "You are most faithful in reminding me of that, milord. I wonder that you do not tire of my foolish company and send me away, so that you might not be bothered further."

Brettan lunged for her, roughly seizing Maren by the arm so that she cried out, whether in pain or surprise he did not know.

"Enough!" he roared. "I will have no more of this. I sometimes think that your father might have been quite pleased to be rid of you. You have the capacity to drive a man beyond all reason!" Roughly Brettan shook her, so that Maren feared her head might snap at her neck. Whether from the cold of her soaked gown or her raw emotions she could not be certain, but her teeth chattered loudly while she stared back at him.

Brettan glared down into the sapphire blue depths of eyes that seemed to draw from him his will to do else but hold her, crush her against him until she cried out, that he might force upon her some understanding of his fears, some understanding of what she had come to mean to him. Instead he folded her within the growing warmth of his embrace, fiercely drawing her against him, feeling the soft, alluring sweetness of her body against his.

"No!" Maren's heated protests were smothered beneath his kisses, his mouth covering hers in a contact that ignited within them both a flame that threatened to consume them. And slowly, against her will, Maren felt her own betraying response, for she leaned into his embrace, feeling as if she could melt into him until they became one, and never have a desire to be separate again.

Slowly Brettan lowered her to the fresh, sweet hay that

453

lined the floor of the stall, his lips never leaving hers, exploring the honeyed, softness of her mouth. He left her for but a moment, returning with a soft woolen blanket laid aside by one of the stableboys. In that one moment Maren stubbornly sprang to her feet to face him warily when he returned, refusing to yield to him so easily.

The dim light cast by the tallow lanterns cast a soft glow across her face, and Brettan was aware of the grim determined set of her slender jaw. She backed away from him defiantly.

"Maren, I grow weary of your childish pranks. Come, you must get out of that wet gown or you will catch your death of the fever."

Maren held out a restraining hand, her eyes flashing her refusal to bend to his will. "Nay, milord, I know well your intentions. You shall not find me such easy prey. This issue shall be settled between us once and for all. I will not live as your prisoner. If that is all you think of me, then allow me to return to my family, for there is then nothing to bind me to you."

"Maren!" Brettan's tone was quietly menacing. He slowly approached her, giving little heed to her words.

"Come no further, or I vow I shall see every guard, every stableboy, every servant at Lionshead knows what passes here."

"Your threats have little meaning for me, Maren. You should know that well by now. I care little who may hear what passes here. I am lord and master of this hall, and none shall interfere in my personal affairs."

Knowing he spoke the truth, Maren bolted for the heavy stable doors drawn against the mounting storm, but her flight was a moment too slow, for she found her way blocked by Brettan's tall frame. He quickly reached out, seizing her about the waist.

Maren fought against his greater strength with all the cunning and skill she had often used against her brother

454

Andrew, when they had played as children. She would not easily submit. Before Brettan could close his other arm about her, Maren had twisted within his grasp and ducked under one arm, gaining her freedom except for the sleeve of her gown. Brettan sought to restrain her at the last moment she fled his hold. With a rending tear the fabric separated when she pulled away, leaving the gown gaping, the bodice fallen away from her heaving breasts. So great was her surprise at the sudden coolness of night air against her bare skin, that she halted for the briefest moment. A moment was all Brettan needed. He lunged for her, his shoulder catching hers, his heavier weight sending them both sprawling headlong into the hay.

Maren wriggled beneath the length of his tall frame, her air cut off by his greater weight. When at last he rolled from her, Maren breathed in deeply and, once she had breathed, the air was filled with her vivid references to his character and questionable breeding, all flowing forth in the Welsh language that was lost on him. Wildly she thrashed about in the hay, her slender arms striking out at him, her left arm striking him square on the side of the head, so that he was forced to grasp both her arms, pinning them over her head so that she might not cause them both more harm.

"Maren, I say hold, now! Or, I swear by all that is holy, I shall turn you over my knee and thrash you until you cry for mercy. At this moment it is my sound belief that a spanking would serve you well."

Again Maren struggled upwards against him, her eyes flashing, her anger barely checked by some spark of caution that he might indeed do as he threatened.

"Maren!" he roared at her. "Do not force my hand."

"Will you see the guard removed?" Maren flung at him, lying panting beneath him.

Brettan glared down into the wide expanse of vivid blue eyes that glared venomously at him from the soft

455

oval of her delicate face. She really had her temper up this time. He could think of a score of delightful things he would rather do with her than pin her to the floor of the stable, but he could easily see that this matter must be resolved if there was to be any peace between them.

"Maren, since you have brought this between us, then listen to my words, as if your life depended upon them, for indeed it does. I do not keep my guards about you to make you my prisoner. Indeed, you are given complete freedom in my home, in all that is mine. Tell me, what prisoner may say the same? The guards are for your protection. Already you have nearly died because of an attack. It is far too dangerous for you to roam about unescorted."

Maren seethed with uncontrolled anger, staring back into those glowing eyes that seemed to bore into her very soul. "What price have you been given to keep me in England? What game does Edward play, that I have become his pawn?"

Brettan stared at her in momentary surprise that she could unwittingly have struck so close to the truth. And yet had it been mere chance, or did she perhaps know something of what her father had told the king? Was she merely leading him on, hoping to gain some information she thought he kept secret from her?

"Maren, why is it so difficult for you to understand that I love you? I could not bear your loss, nor could I say words that might send you from me forever. So you see, my lovely Maren, I am caught at cross purposes, desiring that which by right is mine, and yet constantly I must guard against those who would take you from me. I have paid the highest price to the bastard Llywelyn, in the death of my unborn child. I shall not give more. He shall not have you." Brettan's voice broke with his sudden emotion and became hardly more than a whisper. He suddenly released her arms, gathering her into a warm

456

embrace that shielded her bare shoulders from the cold. He rolled with her so that she was suddenly sprawled over him, pinned against his chest, staring uncertainly into his face, golden in the light from the lanterns.

"What secrets do you hold from me, milord, that I must forever rant and rave like a mindless shrew until at last I force some small word from you? You know all there is to know of me, yet I am left to guess what dark secrets haunt your dreams." Gently she reached up to hold his face between her cool palms, staring into his gaze. "You see into me and know all there is to know, my very thoughts, the words I would speak before they are spoken, and yet you keep all that you feel hidden from me, so that I must forever challenge you to learn one small thing. What is your agony, Brettan de Lorin? What is it that sends you and your men so deep into my country, far from your king, far from the battle that sets our two countries against one another? Milord, if not to strike against my family for some nameless revenge, then what brought you to Cambria? Was it perhaps someone you thought to find there, as you found me?"

Brettan's lean, handsome face was like a mask of stone. He turned his eyes away from her, not yet prepared to tell her the truth, yet knowing the time fast approached when he would no longer be able to deny her and still keep her beside him.

As if sensing the silent battle that raged within him, Maren gently touched his cheek with her fingers, which burned where they touched, forcing him to look at her. All anger of the moments before fled when she saw the torment in those green eyes and, in a gesture that conveyed more than all her words, she slowly lowered her mouth to his, at first tentatively, then more forcefully. She felt the need to ease in him the pain she had seen a moment before. Her eyes closed as she lost herself completely to his warmth, her tongue probed

457

gently between his lips, and the coldness she had felt moments before from the sodden gown faded before the flames of their mounting passion, which flared brightly to consume them.

Brettan surrendered completely to the fever of her kisses, responding with a heat of his own, pressing molten kisses along the gentle curve of her neck and across one gleaming white shoulder, left bare by the torn fabric. Slowly his hands sought the warmth of her skin beneath the torn garment, and in one quick movement the last of the gown easily separated and fell away from her, leaving Maren clad only in the thin chemise, and it too disappeared, until she lay beneath him, her long slender body bathed in the soft glow of light from the lanterns, the full, ripe mounds of her breasts glowing warmly, pressing against him, stealing from him some of his warmth to drive away the chill of the night air against her naked skin. Beyond the walls of the stable the sounds of the storm grew to a fevered pitch, the wind driving the first pelting rain hard against the weathered stone and wood of the impenetrable fortress. Within those walls, Maren lay in the protective warmth of her knight and surrendered to the passion that neither could deny. Slowly Brettan built within her a consuming desire that none but he could satisfy. His kisses fell across the gleaming surface of her body, teasing, tantalizing, taking her to new heights. And her hands reached out to caress beneath the velvet of his clothes, quickly pulling the garments away until he lay beside her, like a lean, dark beast capable of great harm, yet within his arms she found only sweet pleasure, and an unspoken promise to keep her safe. Slowly the distance between them closed. Brettan pressed her against the soft wool of the blanket, bringing a startled gasp to her lips at that first contact that burned through her, like a fiery shaft that threatened to brand her soul with his passion. He pressed deeply within her, finding in that joining that which made him whole, and Maren responded, arching upward to accept him fully, molding him to her with a fury that matched the mounting storm raging about them. Higher and higher they climbed, driven by the heat of the flames about to consume them, higher, until Maren felt as if she stood on the brink of some great abyss. Slowly Brettan pushed her beyond that point, so that she drifted on the waves of her passion and felt his passion become one with hers, washing over her, gently sending her drifting back to the soft glow of the stables and the sweet smell of the fresh hay, and the rain that now fell softly against the roof of the stables, for the storm outside, like the storm within, subsided. Brettan pulled her tightly against him and draped the woolen blanket about them, carefully tucking the edges in about her. Her first deep sigh marked her sleep beside him.

"Sleep, my love. Sleep, and speak no more of these words that have passed between us tonight. Were you to know the truth, I fear a great danger I might not be able to protect you from. Sleep, milady, and let us hold what time we may." Maren stirred gently beside him, as if in sleep she silently accepted his words, and then Brettan rested beside her, breathing in the fresh fragrance of her hair that lay beneath them, like a luxuriant pillow upon the hay. And in time he too slept, for a while holding back all danger, all fear, until the light of morning. Danger must be met in the light of day, when one can see the enemy clearly and know his purpose.

Chapter Twenty

Maren stood outside the large oaken doors that were the main entrance to the great hall at Lionshead, in the crisp, cold morning air, greeting first one guest and then another, of the many who had come to share the holiday feast with the lord and lady of the manor.

Easily capable of housing several hundred, Lionshead seemed to come alive with all the joyous good spirit of the holidays and the gaily exchanged greetings of old friends and distant relatives, who came forth for the first time in several years to greet Brettan de Lorin, Duke of Norfolk, and his lady.

Maren's jaws ached with the efforts of a constant smiled greeting since the earliest hours, and her hand had been soundly crushed for the hundredth time in the pudgy fist of someone she could not remember. She smiled her most radiant smile at the wizened Earl of Montrose and his extremely young and virginal-looking wife, and Maren knew a moment's gratitude that Brettan was not like the feeble gentleman. Although she heartily suspected he might give his young bride a surprise or two, for he had given Maren a most enthusiastic and ardorous welcome. Her gaze traveled the length of the procession

461

of lords and ladies who continued to arrive, and her attention was drawn to six lavishly clothed knights and the lady who rode before them, their banners flying the colors of the Earl of Blanding. Beside Maren, Lady Helene stiffened visibly, for she also watched the flaxen-haired woman and her escort approach the steps of Lionshead Hall. The woman boldly refused the assistance of one of her knights to dismount, but awaited assistance from the Duke of Norfolk. Lady Caroline was resplendently dressed in velvet of a soft gold color, fitted tightly to her slender waist, and elaborately trimmed in a gold braid intricately woven with lover's knots, stitched about the edges of the sweeping sleeves. Her mantle was of a heavier velvet, trimmed in a rich, luxurious fur of a deep brown color, which seemed to glow with a life of its own. Maren felt a certain uneasiness, smoothing her hands over the soft velvet and satin of her own gown, heartily wishing she had chosen one of more elaborate decoration. In the next thought, she chided herself for her vain airs before the openly wanton advances of Brettan's mistress. Yet Maren could not ignore a sudden pang of jealousy for what they had once shared, so that she grew increasingly uncomfortable before the artful coyness of the Lady Caroline. Maren had not known the woman would be a guest for the feasting. She was aware of Lady Helene's calm demeanor while they awaited the arrival of the next guests at the top of the steps.

"Always remember, my dear, that on the field of battle it is best to face one's enemy straight on. If you show your back for one instant or let down your guard, your enemy shall have the advantage, and strike you down in an instant."

Maren eyed Brettan's mother speculatively. "I was not aware that you were so accomplished in such matters, milady."

"'Tis a lesson I learned long ago from Brettan's father

and, though he offered it from his experience on the battle field, it has served me well in other applications."

"I have no fear of the enemy well met, milady. It is the enemy who cannot be seen that proves the greater danger."

Lady Helene turned her appreciative gaze upon the young girl who stood beside her, and wondered that such innocent beauty masked so keen and perceptive a wisdom.

Below them Caroline leaned intimately against Brettan, who lifted her from the back of her horse, depositing her gently beside him. She pressed against him, whispering some message, and Maren felt a sudden stabbing pain that tore through her composure and twisted cruelly, to watch her husband in such close contact with his mistress. His face was unreadable when he bent low to catch Caroline's words, making it impossible for Maren to know his mood at this reunion, which he had no doubt known of well in advance. Maren struggled for composure, refusing to let Caroline or Brettan know how their touching of one another affected her. She greeted more guests who had arrived. Her hands clenched into tight fists at her side, for Maren found Brettan's actions unbearable. She longed to turn her back on them and seek the safety of her chamber, but indeed, what safety might be found there, when Brettan brought his mistress into his home? Beside her Lady Helene remained calm, but the warmth of her smile a moment before had cooled noticeably at Caroline's approach. Or was it only Maren's imagination that Caroline desperately hoped to find consolation with Brettan's mother? Lady Helene made her greetings to Caroline with an unmistakable air of stiffness, acknowledging the woman with only the briefest nod of recognition, and then waiting for Maren to offer her greeting. But it was Caroline who sought to gain favor with Maren, with a greeting of open warmth that seemed to all a genuine gesture. Caroline's smile was radiant, until she swept past Maren, her golden, amber eyes seeming to devour Brettan while she entered the hall on his arm. Maren glanced away in sudden confusion, and only Lady Helene was aware of the cold viciousness concealed behind the intruder's guarded gaze. It made her gasp to witness the silent challenge Caroline hurled at Maren.

Over the next days of feasting and sporting that marked the holiday season, Maren sought more and more the solitude of her chamber or the warmth of the kitchens, where she could escape Caroline's relentless assault of quietly spoken criticisms of whatever task Maren might be at, or some sly comment regarding Brettan's likes and dislikes, of which his mistress seemed to be the only one possessing such knowledge. Before Brettan or Lady Helene, Caroline maintained the common courtesies due the Duchess of Norfolk, relying on her unspoken gestures of intimacy with Brettan to accomplish slowly her attack on Maren's confidence. What should have been a joyous and merry holiday quickly turned into a nightmare for Maren, who realized well the extent Caroline might go to maintain her status as Brettan's mistress, or better yet, his wife. Indeed he seemed not to notice Caroline's deliberate attacks against Maren, or chose to ignore them. His responsibilities to his guests took him away from Maren for long hours each day, leaving her vulnerable. Even Lady Helene had chosen to return to Harrow House for a few days' respite before the celebrations on Christmas Day. Only as now, when Caroline had accompanied several of the lords and ladies to hunt in the forests that bounded Lionshead, did Maren find succour from the woman's waspish moods, which seemed so effectively to fade into honeyed warmth when Brettan entered the room.

Having seen to the many foods that were to be prepared for the Christmas meal the following day, Maren sought the crisp, refreshing air beyond the stone walls of the hall, that they might help clear her thoughts and ease her troubled spirit. She seized an apple from the basket in the kitchen and, wrapping her heavy mantle about her shoulders, stepped out into the brilliant sunshine, whose promise of warmth was heartily challenged by the piercing cold that left frost crunching underfoot, even under the midday sun. She had sorely missed Lady Helene's quiet, calming spirit of the last days, and heartily wished she could have retreated to Harrow House to escape for even a few hours Caroline's embarrassing attentions to her husband. Seizing upon the idea, Maren quickly made her way across the courtyard to the stables, stopping just inside. At the far end she saw the finely chiseled head of the black mare. The spirited animal greeted her with a gentle nibble at her outstretched hand, searching for the usual apple Maren brought.

"Ah, you are clever, my black beauty. You are always certain I will bring you some sweet surprise. Well, you are quite right. It seems small reward for the pleasure you bring me. You above all seek nothing more than this small apple, when others are sworn to my destruction. And now they have left you behind, have they not, to enjoy this fine day, when you must remain behind. Two of a kind are we. Well, not for long. I feel a need to stretch my muscles, and I think a visit to Harrow House would provide that."

Maren quickly bade the stable boy saddle the black mare and, flashing him her most radiant smile of gratitude for his part in her reprieve, she easily sprang into the saddle, sending the spirited mare across the length of the courtyard, departing the confining walls of the stone fortress.

Maren, exhilarated at the feel of the lean, well-muscled beast beneath her, sent the mare flying over the frosty greensward, the cold wind biting at her skin until it was numbed, and she could no longer feel the tingling sensations in her nose or her chin. She briefly reined in the black at the crest of the hill beyond Lionshead, which gave her an unequaled view of the castle, and a sweeping vista of the greensward and the line of the trees around the fortress, and beyond that the rocky cliffs dropping to the sea below. Seeing it as she did now reminded her much of Cambria. Had she allowed her thoughts to linger on other holidays, passed with her family, she might have yielded to the overwhelming melancholy that had stolen over her the last days. Instead she whirled the mare about and sent her flying down the far side of the hill in the direction the stable boy had told her, oblivious to gray eyes that watched her with open desire and longing from the seclusion of the forest.

Harrow House was much smaller than Lionshead, meant to house one family and the servants, rather than protect an entire village. Built as a retreat from hectic demands on the Duke of Norfolk, it was hardly more than a large cottage, nestled discreetly amidst a large stand of spruce trees, which protectively sheltered it from view. No massive stone wall rose imposingly around Harrow House, for safety from enemies had been left to Lionshead. Instead the grounds about the cottage rolled gently away to the stables on one side, with vast gardens and orchards on the other. The trees' limbs had been stripped of their foliage before the onslaught of the winter's cold but held the promise of abundant beauty when spring came once more upon the land.

A young servant rushed quickly forward to take the black from her and, before she could reach the steps, the large portal to Harrow House was thrown open in greeting. A young maid peeked out curiously, then stepped aside hastily when Lady Helene came forward to see who her guest might be. A warm smile of genuine pleasure spread across her lovely face upon seeing Maren at the foot of the steps. "My dear, I had wondered how you fared with such a great houseful of guests. You must forgive me for abandoning you, but I fear I much prefer the quiet solitude here to the boisterous and often loathsome company that descends upon my son. And indeed, you manage so well, I felt that I was no longer needed. Although it was truly my intent to return on the morrow for the Christmas day celebrations. But tell me, has Caroline managed to drive you from your own home?"

"I accept your kind apologies, milady, but I fear it shall be some time before I can forgive you for leaving me to that loathsome witch, whose one cause seems to be Brettan. I grow weary of facing the enemy at every turn. Indeed, I fear I shall be forced to draw the blade in defense."

"So at last Lionshead has a worthy mistress. I am pleased. As for Caroline, she seeks only to bring you pain for what she has lost. She little realizes that it was never hers. But come, you are chilled. We will sit before the hearth and see what solution might be had for this pestilence in the form of a flaxen-haired woman."

Maren sat in one of the high-backed chairs before the blazing hearth, still wrapped snugly in the heavy folds of her mantle. The chilling ache of the ride began to leave her fingers and then her hands, until she was forced to push back the mantle, feeling the warmth about her. She sipped a steaming brew of cider laced with spices, brought forth by a young maid and gazed about the large room that was the main hall and dining hall of Harrow House. Brilliantly colored tapestries covered the stone walls of the room, casting a warm glow that made the chamber seem comforting and somehow smaller. The opposite wall had been richly set with a warm, mellow wood paneling, the beauty of the grains shining in the dancing firelight from the hearth. Large windows set with heavy panes let in bright sunlight during the day to help warm the rooms, and at night were covered by heavy velvet drapes, now drawn back to each side by a length of heavy gold cording. Everywhere about her, the rooms of Harrow House were bright and warm, reflecting the touches of the mistress who resided there. At their feet a sleepy hound lazed before the warmth of the fire, the light graying of his dark muzzle marking his preference for comforts, while the younger hounds had taken up the duties of the hunt. Here at Harrow House, Maren felt the peacefulness and warmth springing from a love shared over many years between the master and mistress of the house. This had been their hideaway, and was now the haven of memories for Lady Helene.

"I understand why you prefer Harrow House to Lionshead. There is a warmth here that cannot be found in stone walls."

Lady Helene smiled warmly at Maren. "There is perhaps only one thing more I might ask to grace this house. I have a need to see my grandchildren here. This house needs the sounds of their laughter and playfulness, and even a good confrontation now and again. Each of my children was a treasure for me, but alas, they are grown so quickly, and children no longer. But when this house is full of laughter and voices, I shall again be most contented, for I shall steal them away and spoil them endlessly."

Maren glanced away uncomfortably from Lady Helene's searching gaze, the memory of the child she had once carried and then lost still painful for her. Lady Helene reached out a gentle hand, seeing the dark

468

sadness that clouded that blue visage. "Time, Maren, heals even the greatest of wounds. I have every faith there will be grandchildren enough for even me. I have faith in my son, and in you. It would not surprise me greatly if the next Christmas feast should find me cuddling my first in my arms, and that shall be the finest gift of all."

Maren felt a warmth spreading across her cheeks at the memory of the weeks since they had arrived at Lionshead, and indeed she could find no fault in the moments she and Brettan shared alone, in the seclusion of their chamber. His loving of her seemed to know no limits, for he sought her out at any hour and would steal her away to some secluded tryst, always finding some clever excuse when they returned some hours later, to find the servants and his guard highly alarmed at their absence. Only his knight, Sandlin, seemed to find some source of amusement in all of it, casting a glance of satisfaction at Brettan, as if making some silent point that his master had succumbed to the charms of his Welsh captive, and was now soundly caught. Only in the last few days, since Caroline had arrived, had they been allowed fewer moments together, for the woman seemed intent on occupying Brettan's every moment, and Maren had grown increasingly uncertain of him. She gained some small comfort in the way he always sought her out once the day ended, retiring with her to the privacy of their chamber, and she found that her thoughts were continually filled with the hope that she was again with child. She had been easily caught with the babe from her first time with him, those many months before, and she could only hope that it might happen again just as easily. She raised questioning eyes to Lady Helene.

"Have you no other grandchildren? What of your daughter?"

"My daughter has been wed for some time, and still

there are no children, though I know she would dearly treasure a child. I pray she may yet have a babe of her own, for her husband is a man of title and great wealth, and must have an heir if his family is to retain their estates. But they are far away in Normandy, and I fear I could not be easily satisfied with seeing her children every few years. As the Duke of Norfolk, it is of great importance that Brettan have a son who may one day succeed him. Though I love my daughter dearly, she is not capable of holding all of Norfolk as my husband did, and the king would not favor the idea that her husband might control the de Lorin estates. Brettan is the rightful Duke of Norfolk, and it must pass to his sons."

"Brettan has spoken little to me of his family. He only mentioned his brother, who was much older. More than that I do not know of him."

Lady Helene cast Maren an odd glance. "I see that he has not told you of Damon. Philip was my husband's firstborn, by his marriage to the first Duchess of Norfolk. She was a frail girl and did not survive the birth of her son." At Maren's look of surprise, Lady Helene nodded understandingly. "I see there is much my son has not told you of our family. I was but fifteen when I was first presented to the Duke of Norfolk by King Henry. Brettan's father was twice that age, but my father thought it a brilliant match. You see, my dear Maren, the land here, all about Harrow House, and much more to the river and beyond, belonged to my family. By our marriage, the vast holdings of both families were aligned. My own brother died as a child from a fever, and there were no other sons to succeed my father. He had long admired the holdings of the old Duke of Norfolk, and saw the alliance of our families as a means of preserving his own wealth. You see, dear Maren, you are not the only one given to a marriage of suitable arrangement."

"Yet Brettan has said that your marriage was a bond of

470

love." Maren gazed questioningly at his mother.

"I could easily have been given to a loveless marriage, as so many of my friends were. 'Tis my good fortune, Maren, to have fallen in love with the Duke of Norfolk. I knew it the moment I first saw him, and he is the only man I have ever loved, and I love him to this day." Lady Helene stared into the glowing flames at the hearth, as if unaware that any other occupied the room with her. "He was my soul, my passion, the very essence of my existence, as if nothing had existed for me before he came into my life." Her voice was barely more than a whisper, and Maren felt suddenly uncomfortable, as if she had intruded on something very private. Yet she understood completely what Lady Helene had said, because for the first time words had been given to her own feelings for Brettan. And that realization was very frightening to her. She sought to draw Lady Helene back to the present moment.

"You spoke of another brother?"

Lady Helene smiled apologetically. But her mood seemed sad as she rose from her chair and refilled Maren's cup from the pot simmering over the hearth. "Yea, my youngest child, my son, Damon. Had he lived, he would have been not much older than you. There were two babes born after my daughter, but neither survived. I had long given up all hope of another child when I learned that I carried Damon. He was a fine young man, and he so loved Brettan. After my husband's death, he looked to Brettan more as a father, for the guidance a son might need. He was but seventeen when he earned his knighthood. That was only two summers past. He was most eager to follow Brettan and Edward to Wales, but Brettan refused him. After Brettan left Norfolk that last time, Damon took his own guard and followed. He and his men were attacked one night while they slept near the Welsh border. I was told that, had it not been for the captain of the guard, all would have been lost. They were murdered in their sleep, with no chance to draw their own weapons."

"They were attacked by Welsh rebels?"

"The captain of Damon's guard spoke only of one man he saw that night. Brettan has sworn to see that man die for the attack. He seeks his death, more than any loyalty to this war or to Edward."

Maren's hands shook with a sudden weakness, so that she was forced to set the cup aside in order not to spill the steaming cider. A haunting memory stirred within her thoughts, of old William's words that last day at Cambria, of the cowards who attacked from within the castle, so that no man was given the chance to draw his sword in defense, a coward's attack. She turned her glance toward Lady Helene. "Brettan once spoke of a murderer he followed. It was that which brought him to Cambria. He thought that I had something to do with his brother's death."

Lady Helene saw the horror-stricken look that crossed Maren's lovely face, and she leaned forward and gathered both Maren's trembling hands in her own. "You must never think that. I know my son, and I know he never thought you responsible for Damon's death. Nor do I."

"He said he followed the murderer to Cambria." Maren mused thoughtfully. "That must mean that the ones who were responsible for Damon's death are also responsible for my mother's death and Edmund's abduction. But why? To what purpose? I do not understand any of this."

"Maren, I have told you of this because, unlike my son, I believe knowledge can be a very useful weapon. He only seeks your protection, you must believe that."

"My protection! Always Brettan speaks of keeping me safe, but safe from what? What have I to fear from anyone? I am half English, but also half Welsh, and yet

472

my father delivers me to the English king and gives me in marriage to an Englishman. So many questions remain unanswered, and still I find I am no closer to the truth of my mother's death." Maren stood, suddenly unable to remain seated any longer, a wild energy surging through her. "What is it that everyone knows, but I may not?"

Lady Helene also rose to her feet, quickly wrapping her arms about Maren's slender shoulders and gathering her into a comforting embrace, like a mother attempting to soothe her hurting child. "You must have faith in Brettan, my dear. Have faith in his love for you, for I know it to be a true love. In time all will be known, but for now he has chosen to keep some part of it from you. Have faith in his wisdom. I have never found it lacking."

"But he is the sworn enemy of my people. Even now, Edward plans his final march against Wales. Messengers have arrived daily from London. I know they ride against Llywelyn soon. How may I have faith, when the man I have married now must ride against my people? What faith is there, when I have willingly given myself to the very man who has sworn to cut me down?"

"Maren, my son is not sworn against you. He could more easily take his own life than harm you. It goes beyond the vows of his knighthood or his loyalties to Edward."

Maren stared at Lady Helene, her eyes wide in wonderment at this strong woman before her. "Brettan once spoke those same words."

"Then you must not doubt the truth of them."

Maren looked past Lady Helene out the heavily paned window, suddenly aware that much time has passed since she had arrived. Already the December sky had lost its wintry glow, and the sun sank low in the western sky. "The hour grows late. I must return to Lionshead."

"My child, please remain for the night. I shall send word to Brettan, and then we may return together on the

473

morrow. The hour grows late, and I should fear for you to journey alone so close to nightfall."

"The black is swift and shall carry me quickly the short distance to Lionshead. You need have no worry for my safety."

Lady Helene smiled warmly at Maren, knowing well that the girl sought the comfort of her husband's presence. "If I have no cause to worry in your traveling about in the night, then perhaps I shall have cause to worry for my own safety, should I allow you to return alone and have my son learn of the matter. If you insist on returning this day, then I shall see my guard accompanies you. I would not have it upon my head, if some harm were to come to you. And for my own purposes, I must protect the future of my grand-children."

Lady Helene summoned three of her guard to accompany Maren. Within a few moments they stood awaiting her, and the black stood nervously pawing the hard frosty turf, eager for a last run. Maren bid Lady Helene farewell. Lady Helene stood on the front steps of the manor, watching the riders disappear into the growing darkness.

Darkness had fallen about the countryside when Maren and the guard arrived at the castle, and she was silently grateful that Lady Helene had insisted on sending the men with her. Two of the guards at the main gate heralded their arrival, and she felt the warmth of the glowing lights in the small windows of the main hall. Maren could hear the loud spirited songs of merrymaking from inside the great hall. Hoping to slip unnoticed through the large doors, Maren drew back in sudden surprise when they abruptly swung open wide, Brettan's towering height outlined in the golden glow of light that flooded the doorway. His stance was stiff and unyielding, and Maren was immediately aware of his ill humor, for she felt the heat of those emerald eyes piercing through her. "Where the devil have you been?" Roughly he leaned forward, seizing her arm in a viselike grip that threatened to snap her slender bones. "I was forced to send half my guard about the countryside in search of you. I demand an explanation for this, milady!" Roughly he drew her inside the great hall, so that they stood just beyond the entire company of their guests, secluded in the shadows at the entry to the hall. Though she should have been frightened by the anger she saw in his face and the menacing glow in those golden eyes, she felt oddly relieved that he should have cared for her safety. Her hand rested warmly against his chest, her fingers lightly touching his bare skin at the neck of his linen shirt. That one touch seemed to set them both aflame. Liquid heat coursed through them, giving undeniable truth to their fears for one another, their desires for one another. The long moment passed and was broken when Caroline stepped into the shadows, her hand slipping possessively through Brettan's arm, seeking to draw him back to the festivities of the evening meal. Her frustration mounted with each passing moment, for she found herself unable to break through that long, intimate moment that passed between Brettan and Maren, as the glowing eyes of the lion burned into that deep, blue gaze. "My love, your guests are anxious for your return, as am I. You must not ignore your responsibilities to them or me," Caroline suggested alluringly.

"Then may I suggest, Caroline, that you do not disappoint them. You should return immediately," Brettan answered, his gaze never leaving Maren's. They seemed locked within some private world Caroline could not enter.

Caroline clearly saw her advantage disappearing and pressed more boldly. "But my love, it is you they wish to see, and not this Welsh prisoner you have brought back

475

for Edward."

"I shall return presently." It was an order more than a statement, and Caroline knew instinctively that she dared press no further. A slight frown creased her forehead, and she quickly returned to the table, ordering more wine from a young servant girl. Caroline quickly drained the ornate goblet and ordered it refilled, glaring into the shadows near the doors of the hall, knowing Brettan and Maren lingered there, yet unable to know what passed between them. That, more than anything, goaded her beyond all reason.

"Your hands are cold. We shall speak of this anon. I shall have Agnes draw you a warm bath and bring you a tray. I will join you later." Brettan's voice had suddenly lost all traces of its anger of moments before, and he gazed warmly into her eyes.

"Later?" Maren's disappointment was obvious in the tone of her voice.

Brettan pulled her roughly against him, nearly crushing her in his strong embrace, before releasing her to depart up the stairs to their second floor chamber. Maren turned back to gaze down at him, her blue eyes glowing brilliantly down at him. "You promised, milord, not long ago, to give me another child. I find your efforts of late sorely lacking."

Unable to free himself of that haunting gaze, Brettan smiled up at her, a sly grin pulling at the corners of his mouth, softening the harshness of his anger, so that she ached with longing for him, so handsome was he in the light that flickered from the candles in the hall.

"I would suggest, milady, that you hasten to your bathing, or you shall find your bath sorely lacking and be forced to find adequate warmth in our bed."

"I have never found our bed lacking for warmth, milord." When she hesitated a moment longer, Brettan

476

advanced up the first steps, heartily determined to carry out his threats. Maren retreated up the steps and closed the door to their chamber with a loud thud. Brettan chuckled to himself as he returned to the dining hall, sorely at a loss to understand the moods of his wife, but heartily convinced he could withstand anything for the promise of the moments between them he would enjoy later. He skillfully avoided Caroline's persistent ploys, finding himself weary of her attentions, which bordered upon an embarrassment. She finally occupied herself in flirting with one of the other guests near the hearth, casting him only an occasional glance. Certain that his guests would hardly notice his absence and were quite capable of continuing their celebrations, Brettan made his excuses and quietly stole up the stairway to that second floor chamber that held the promise of such pleasure.

Closing the door softly behind him, he searched the dimly lit chamber for sight of Maren, first at the bath. Finding it had been removed, he looked then for her in the large bed. The bed was empty. What the devil was she up to now? Had she possibly taken ill after the cold ride, now seeking some healing balm from her maid? Before he could turn about in search of her, Brettan found himself soundly held about the waist by long, slender arms. Taking her hands in his and turning about to face her, he caught his breath in his throat at the sight of her slender naked body, gleaming like fine satin through the open folds of the heavy velvet robe she wore. But it was her eyes that caught his gaze, staring wantonly at him, those wide blue orbs softly fringed in dark, long lashes, seeming to draw him outside of himself, so that he knew himself lost to her will. The thick ebony masses of her waving,

477

tumbling hair swung about her shoulders loosely, cascading down the length of her back. She slowly walked away from him to stand before the fire at the hearth, then lowered the robe until it fell about her feet to the thick tapestry on the floor. The warmth of the fire glowed on the finely curved lengths of her legs, and she turned back to him, a rose-hued tip of one breast thrust impudently through the mass of her dark hair, enticing, teasing him beyond all reason.

In one movement Brettan was beside her, gently pushing back the thick veil of her hair, exposing that glorious peak that seemed to beckon his touch. With the tip of his finger he lightly traced the tip, and then the fullness of that tender orb, and Maren closed her eyes in rapture, her breath faint between her parted lips. When she again opened her eyes, his hand had closed possessively over her breast. He softly kneaded her flesh, and she reached up to untie the fastenings of his shirt, slipping it over his head, exposing the expanse of his chest beneath her fevered hands, which explored the muscles covered with dark, curling hair. Tenderly she raked her fingers through the soft furring, until she held him about the waist. His face lowered very near hers, and Maren's lips sought his, her senses reeling at the exquisite warmth of his mouth against hers. Slowly her fingers worked the fastening at his breeches, at last freeing him to stand against her, his naked warmth pressed full length against her own body, which ached with an urgent longing to be consumed by him. Boldly she pressed against him, his mouth moving over hers, his tongue probing the honeyed softness of her mouth, his hands roaming over the entire length of her, until no part of her remained untouched. Urgently she pleaded with him to take her and, unable to deny his own impassioned desires, Brettan lowered her to the tapestry, his

478

arm beneath her gently cushioning her back against the flooring, while his thigh pressed between hers. The mane of her black hair swirled about them, and Maren rose to meet him with an urgency that only heightened his desire for her. Bruisingly he pressed deep within her, unable to resist any longer the feel of her closing about him. The momentary pain seemed to increase her desire for him, for she felt his molten heat boring into her. She arched up against him, the pain subsiding to be replaced by that aching desire. Maren felt the sudden searing flame of her own passion, which thrust her to new heights, and she took him with her, so that the final moment of ultimate pleasure was theirs together.

In the early light of dawn, Christmas Day, Caroline stole silently from the hall. Within moments she had gained the stable and coerced the sleepy stable boy into saddling a horse. Threatening him to silence, she made her way through the heavily guarded gates of Lionshead. The guards, ever wary of those entering the fortress, gave little thought to those leaving.

Southwold was little less than an hour's ride from the fortress, safely tucked into a small harbor. Unescorted, Caroline had to remain on the main road for fear of meeting with some miscreant, but she caused little attention when she moved through the small village, only just beginning to stir to celebrate the Christmas Day. Many already celebrating the feast lay about the inn, heavily into their cups of ale or wine, or sleeping off the holiday spirit of the night before. Giving her eyes a moment to adjust to the darkness inside, Caroline stepped cautiously over the body of a sodden customer and made her way to the only figure remaining upright, in a darkened corner on the far side of the inn, near the back door.

"You are late!" the man whispered vehemently.

"It was difficult to leave unnoticed."

"What word do you bring?"

"We must make our plans immediately. I want the Lady Maren removed from Lionshead by tonight. The longer she remains with him, the less our chances for success in this matter. In the time I have been to London the bond between them has grown stronger, and I want that bond severed."

"I have watched the fortress and seen her about. Of late, his attentions are required elsewhere, for he often rides afar early before first light, returning well after the lanterns are lit."

"Of late perhaps, but just last eve, he took his leave of his guests early and sought their chamber. It must be this night. I cannot abide his touching her. Do you understand, it must be tonight, or I shall make my own plans to have her removed. As I have said, it matters little to me her fate once she is gone from here, but I will have my rightful place beside him, and then I will be the Duchess of Norfolk!" Caroline's eyes glistened unnaturally in the dim light, her desperation having pushed her to the brink of madness.

Geoffrey watched the woman through the darkness that separated them. "It shall be tonight. Already the frost is heavy upon the ground. I must return to Wales before the first snows are hard upon the land. We shall make our plans. My men await my orders nearby, and we shall both have what is ours."

While the first shafts of light streamed into the chamber, Maren curled against Brettan's warmth, her legs entwined with his, his arm flung across her breasts, his large hand in the soft tangled mass of her hair. In her

480

half-sleep, Maren grew suddenly chilled and snuggled deep within his embrace. Yet the elusive fears that haunted her dreams and her thoughts would not be willed away. She forced back the day for a few moments longer, snuggling into the safety of Brettan's chest for a little while longer, steeling herself against the dangers he guarded against, but could not stay forever.

Chapter Twenty-One

Christmas Day dawned bright and clear, and Maren and Brettan joined their guests in the large chapel at Lionshead for the mass. All the countless marriages, births, and deaths of generations of his family had been blessed within that holy place, and she felt an odd serenity, as if by partaking in the elaborate ceremony there by his side, more than any marriage vows, she was joined with him for all eternity, as his father had been joined with his mother, and his father and mother before him. Through the long hours of the ancient Christmas ceremonies, Maren was aware of Caroline's scrutiny some distance away. But even Caroline seemed to hold some respect for the occasion that was marked by this day, restraining her critical comments of Maren and seeming to enjoy the high spirit of the holiday. At the evening feast Brettan rose to toast his guests, then offered a special toast to his duchess. Maren was unaware of the momentary scowl that crossed Caroline's face and in the next instant changed to a strained smile upon her thin lips.

Later that night, in the privacy of their chamber, before the blazing fire Brettan built upon the hearth, he drew Maren to the high-backed chair and, seating her before the warmth at the hearth, bade her keep her eyes closed until he returned. Within moments he returned, approaching from behind her. She could hear the movement of his leather boots against the wood flooring. She felt the gentle pressure of his hands upon her shoulders, the warmth of his fingers resting lightly against her neck. Her thoughts were suddenly of another time, when his hands had closed about her throat in a crushing grip that she had feared meant her death. How strangely so much had changed between them in the past months, so that she felt no fear of him now, only a calm feeling that she belonged with him, there, for always, and yet the words she might have spoken to him of that feeling would not come, but left a tight feeling in her throat, so new were they for her. His fingers left her for a moment, and then she felt a heavier weight placed about her neck, and the cool, smooth feeling of metal against her skin.

Brettan came round the chair and knelt beside her. "You may open your eyes."

Slowly she looked down at the ornately carved medallion he had placed about her neck. Brilliant blue sapphires had been set in the intricately molded figure of the lion's head that was the de Lorin crest, matching the ring Brettan had given her on their wedding day.

"The medallion was given to my mother by my father, and is to be passed on to each son who becomes Duke of Norfolk. I give it to you now with the hope that you will accept it, as my wife, as my duchess, and that you will accept Lionshead as your home, and the home for our children." His words were solemn and, though his glowing green eyes twinkled at her, she held no doubts of his sincerity. Maren gazed down at the medallion and, when she lifted her eyes to his, the large blue depths had filled with tears. "It is a most lovely gift. Far more than I deserve. Milord, I have done nothing to warrant such as this. It should rightfully belong to the Lady Helene."

"The Lady Helene has no desire for the medallion or the title it carries. Her greatest pleasure is taken at Harrow House, and occasionally in venturing here to Lionshead, as now. I warrant that in the future, her presence will be more noticeable here. She has most definite plans to enjoy the babes she is certain we shall bring forth, and she would not see you alone here at Lionshead."

"Alone?" Maren's head lifted in surprise at his words.

Brettan gathered her slender hands into his larger ones and bent his head to place a soft kiss upon her fingers. "Would that I might spend all my days with you here at Lionshead, and my nights discovering the pleasures to be found with such a fair maid. But the time draws near when I must return to London, and from there, I must return to Wales." The full meaning of his words tore through Maren like a well-honed blade.

"Then I shall return to London with you." Maren gazed into his glowing green eyes, which held only warmth for her, seeming to bathe her in intense heat, and drove back the cold of all her fears. Tenderly Brettan reached to brush back a stray tendril of raven-black hair that seemed to beckon his touch, the back of his fingers lightly touching her cheek. "Would that I might always keep you near me, my sweet, for I vow, your company is far superior to that of my men or that lumbering warhorse, and I find of late I grow weary of pursuing causes. More and more I find my head and heart seeking gentler moments." Her somber gaze locked with his.

"You return to war against my people?"

"Llywelyn prepares even now for his last campaign, and indeed it shall be the last. His men are scattered, his supplies all but cut off. Even now he is rumored to have taken refuge in his fortress at Snowdonia. Yet he hopes to

485

rally the south of Wales against Edward."

"And if he should succeed in raising strong support in the south?" Maren held onto his strong fingers. He rose from her side and turned to stare into the flames that licked at the large yule log he had placed at the hearth.

"Then he may yet succeed in pushing Edward out of Wales."

"Would that be such a dreadful outcome? The war would be at an end."

"Maren, you do not understand. Llywelyn shall not be satisfied with victory now, but shall continue his struggle to establish himself as supreme ruler of Wales, and at a dreadful price for your people. Long ago, both Llywelyn and his father fell from favor with the old prince, who refused to name either man as his successor. Now, Llywelyn seeks revenge out of greed. Your people matter little to Llywelyn. If there were coin and land enough to satisfy his greed, he would gladly yield his cause."

"And is Edward so very different?" Maren questioned with stinging honesty, her words sharp, turning to him.

"I have known him long, fought beside him in many battles. For all that he is King of England, riches and title hold little meaning for him. He is determined to make Wales one with England, because he believes that Wales can be made strong again. His only cause is to bring this war to an end. Indeed, many times he has attempted such and offered Llywelyn an honorable end, with enough land and wealth of his own to maintain his titles, but always Llywelyn has cast aside all overtures for peace, so that now Edward no longer offers an honorable end. He will not yield until it is done." His voice was grim, and he stared down at her.

"Then I fear, milord, that the cause may already be lost. Though Edward may strike down Llywelyn, he will never crush the spirit of my people. Too long we have lived independent from England. Edward cannot hope to hold Wales by force alone. My whole life I have known of the wars between England and my country. Always I have lived soundly caught between the two, both part of me. I fear it shall always be so. My people would never accept Edward as their ruler. They must have their own Prince of Wales."

Brettan poked absently at the log glowing brightly with the new flames. Slowly he turned back to Maren, considering her words, the heat of his gaze drawing her eyes to his. She had unwittingly struck upon the heart of the problem that confronted Edward at that very moment. How to establish English authority over Wales, yet allow her country autonomy. An odd smile pulled at the corners of his mouth while he contemplated the fragile beauty of the young girl before him, ever at a loss to understand fully such wisdom in one so beautiful. Ever had he believed that beauty and wisdom were not well matched, finding it only once before, in the woman who had given him life. How oddly fate had brought to him another such, who with all her fire and defiance had unknowingly bound him to her, as none had before. Slowly he extended his hand to her for the first time, a silent request rather than a demand of her love.

Maren stared into the depths of that warm, green gaze, mesmerized by the soft glow that held her beyond her own will. She answered his silent plea, accepting his hand and melting into his embrace, his strong arms closing about her. His voice was oddly muffled in the thickness of her unbound hair, flowing loose about her shoulders, as he murmured her name.

"Milord, let me return to London with you," she pleaded, knowing his answer before it was spoken.

"Nay, I cannot allow it. Here you are safe, with my guard to protect against any danger. In London, I fear I might not always be able to keep you safe. I could not bear another attack against you such as the first."

"Brettan, what danger do you fear for me? Surely there can be no danger when I am with the king and queen at the palace."

"The greatest threat may be found close at hand."

"You speak in riddles. Brettan, what danger is it you fear? If it is so great, then do not return to Wales, for it may find you also, and I—" Maren stammered uncertainly, catching herself at the last moment before speaking what was in her heart.

"My love, can you not trust me now with your true feelings? Must you forever hold me at arm's distance, for fear of some harm you think I might bring you? Maren, for all that has passed between us, can you not now speak from your heart, as I have a need to hear it?" He implored tenderly.

"What is in my heart is all that is truly mine alone, milord. Would that I might exchange it for that secret you hold from me," Maren answered, challenging him in a most subtle way.

Brettan sighed heavily, realizing that there was still much that remained unspoken between them, and a deep, cold fear rose within him, that he might not be able to keep her safe from the dangerous web closing about her. He crushed her against him in a fierce embrace that drove the breath from her lungs, but she clung to him, somehow sensing the desperation within the strength of his arms about her. "Always remember, my love, the vows I have made before God are sacred. I do not make them lightly. My life would glady be forfeit before I would break them."

"Then you will not say what it is you fear?" Maren pressed one last time.

Brettan's hands gently cupped her face to stare down at her, then gently lowered his mouth to hers, feeling his soul come alive at that molten touch. "I fear only that you shall turn from me."

"Milord, you have nothing to fear in that regard."

Brettan raised his handsome head to gaze down at her questioningly. It was the most she had offered him of her feelings. "I pray what you say is true, Maren. I shall live for it." Slowly he drew her into his embrace, his senses filled with the sight, the scent, the feel of her, and he knew that no greater pleasure was to be found beyond those four walls that for a time held back all wars, all strife, all fear.

Agnes had not returned to aid Maren in her morning bath, so she finished bathing herself and dressed, and now stood before the silvered mirror, gathering back the thick waving masses of her hair with a length of blue satin ribbon, which matched the elaborately woven trim about the sleeves of her gown.

Brettan had risen before first light and pressed her back into the warmth of their bed, gently ordering her back to sleep, with the excuse that he only attended to some of their guests who chose to rise early and catch the first light for an early morning hunt. With the cold crisp air in the chamber nipping about her bare shoulders, she had sleepily complied, burying herself beneath the heavy down coverlet.

Now, having given her appearance a final inspection, she departed the chamber to seek out Lady Helene, whose company Maren had come to treasure greatly over the last days, with so many strangers about.

Her mood was light when she descended the stairway, noting the lateness of the hour, and that many of their guests had already departed the hall for the brilliant warmth of the sunshine outside. She warmly greeted Lord and Lady Broadhurst, who departed the large dining hall for a leisurely stroll through the gardens, which still held the last rose blooms on protected bushes, refusing to yield to winter's icy touch.

In the kitchens, the cooks and a host of servants were already hard at work preparing the evening meal, which had been planned days in advance. A vast assortment of freshly dressed fowl lay upon the long tables, waiting to be skewered and set at the roasting pit, while various kettles and pots simmered with puddings, stews, and fruits in heavy sauces, all to entice the hearty appetite. The efficiency of the servants never ceased to amaze her, and Maren departed the kitchens confident that all was in very capable hands. Making a hasty retreat from the kitchens, Maren headed for the heavy double doors of the main hall, halting just at the portal, her hand resting lightly at the large latch, when an unmistakable voice drifted to her from across the hall.

"So, the lady of the manor rises. I have waited most of the early morn hoping to speak with you. I had hoped that you would perhaps join me in a late morning ride about Lionshead," Caroline ventured sweetly, tilting her golden head enticingly, her manner all innocence.

"The Duke of Norfolk has asked that I join him at the hunt," Maren replied uneasily, uncertain of Caroline's sudden polite manner.

"My dear, all the knights and lords of the realm have long taken to the field and the forest beyond. We shall hardly be missed until their return. Come, let us ride, and I shall show you Lionshead. There is much you will need to know if you are truly to be the lady of Lionshead."

"I am certain, Caroline, that whatever I should need to know, my husband shall give me aid," Maren replied wearily, having grown increasingly impatient with Caroline's badgering and bantering of the last days.

"Very well, if not about Lionshead, then there are perhaps things you must know of this marriage you have so easily accepted, and Brettan's purpose in the marriage." The slightest trace of maliciousness edged

490

into her words.

"I know well your purpose. You seek to regain what you have lost. I have no use for your lies," Maren retorted icily. "Nor will I accept your presence here any longer. You will take your leave immediately." Maren's hands clenched into tight fists while she struggled for control over her rising temper.

"You are a fool. You cannot see the truth when it is before your very eyes. I shall not be leaving Lionshead. I am here now at Brettan's invitation, but I see you were not aware of that. He has made it clear to me that he wishes me to remain here at Lionshead," Caroline offered bravely, for there were no others to give denial to her lies. "You thought foolishly to bind him to you by carrying his child. How little you know of him. He cares little for such responsibilities. Once I too carried his child, that I might gain his promise of marriage." Caroline eyed Maren coldly, feeling no small amount of satisfaction at the startled look that filled those blue eyes. "I can see that he has chosen not to speak of the matter to you. Shall I then tell you of your husband? He was with Edward on the crusades in Palestine when the child was born. My child only lived for a few days, but even that was not enough to gain his vows." Caroline glared at Maren, seeing the effect her words had on the young girl.

Maren whirled away from Caroline, refusing to listen to any more of the woman's lies. But before she could leave the hall, Caroline seized her by the arm, halting her flight. "Do you think the child, or any momentary passion he might feel for you, would be enough to gain his vows? There is only one who could have forced Brettan de Lorin into this marriage. His loyalty to Edward is unfailing. That, and his desire for revenge against your people for his brother's death."

Maren wrenched her arm free from Caroline's clawlike grasp, which left bruises on Maren's tender flesh where

491

she held her. "No! I will not accept what you say. You are poisoned with your own hatred. I cannot believe these lies."

"Would you then believe the bargain Brettan has made with Edward? It is a bargain for great wealth and holdings of land in Wales, once this war with Llywelyn is at an end, in exchange for his marriage to you. It is a little thing, really."

Maren turned her gaze upon Caroline, her large, blue eyes glinting with feverish desperation. "But to what purpose? What is there to be gained by keeping me in England?"

Caroline's eyes gleamed with her satisfaction to see Maren's confidence wavering. "Edward is no fool. He knows well the power and importance of your family in the south of Wales. And the south is Llywelyn's last hope for victory. If he fails to unite the south, then his defeat is at hand. By your mother's death, the power within the south falls to you. You are the one hope he might have to gain the support of the southern families."

A slow dawning pierced through Maren's resistance. Though she struggled to deny it, she could see no other explanation for the long months she had been forced to remain in England. Had not Brettan spoken of the importance to Llywelyn of rallying the south of Wales against Edward? Was this then the secret Brettan had kept from her? Was her father also part of the plan to keep her from returning to Cambria? She closed her eyes tightly in an effort to gain some measure of control, her thoughts tumbling in confusion. Yet it was an easy explanation of the raid against Cambria, if the English had sought to gain control over her mother in her father's absence. It could be the only explanation, for she could never accept that her father had willingly sacrificed her mother's life, and Edmund's. Nor could she accept that he would willingly agree to the marriage.

Was there something more that they held over his head? Did they perhaps bargain Edmund's life in exchange for the marriage? Somehow she had to get away from Caroline. She must think of what she had learned, and try to comprehend the meaning of it.

"Leave me. I will not speak of it further."

"You must listen, for there is only danger in your remaining here in England. At this moment, there is one who awaits to take you back to your home, back to your people."

"What are you saying? Who awaits?" Maren turned back to Caroline, and suddenly she knew. Geoffrey. Geoffrey awaited to take her back to Wales. Geoffrey, who had always loved her and now sought only to protect her.

Caroline saw Maren weaken and sought to press her advantage. "Even now Brettan makes his plans to return to London, there to join Edward's army for the last march against your country. How confident they are of their victory, with you securely held here at Lionshead. And victory shall surely be theirs, as long as you remain in England. Can you deny that you are guarded at all times? Can you deny that you are still a prisoner, as ever you were in the beginning, when first you came to England?"

"I must have time to think on this," Maren cried out in sudden desperation.

"There is no time. In five days, after the new year, Brettan will take his guard to London, from there to march against Wales. And once England is victorious, what shall then be your fate, once you have served your purpose? You will be considered an enemy of the crown, and you shall be removed, and all shall be as it was once before between Brettan and me. Your only hope is to leave Lionshead with this man who comes now for you. Stay, and your fate is certain." Caroline hissed her final warning.

Maren leaned heavily against the stone wall of the hall, the heat from the hearth suddenly unbearable, threatening to smother her, making breathing difficult. She tried to clear her muddled thoughts. And yet what argument could she possibly have against the glaring truth Caroline had spoken? The woman's purpose was clear, as it had always been, and yet that alone did not explain all the questions that had remained unanswered for so long. Now it all seemed so simple that she could not understand how she had failed to know it from the beginning. Even more painful was that she had so willingly believed Brettan's words, so easily yielded to his touch. Her cheeks flamed warmly, for she remembered all the times she had lain within his arms, yielding to him with a passion that he had built within her. Her heart constricted that she could have been so easily fooled, nothing more than a pawn in Edward's war against her country, against her people.

"You must leave while you still may. Even now Geoffrey of Meyrick awaits. There is no safety for you here in England, only death. I will take you to him. We must ride before Brettan and the guard return." Caroline brushed past Maren, hurried out the large doorway, and then turned back one last moment. "You must at least agree to speak with him, so that you will know I speak the truth."

Wearily Maren nodded, the rough stones cool and soothing against the heat of her flushed skin. Her thoughts refused to accept anything other than the glaring truth of Brettan's lies to her. Her hand trembled when she reached out to steady herself before mounting the stairs to her chamber. She could not deny the simple truth of Caroline's words. She inhaled deeply, realizing with sudden finality that she could not remain in England.

Maren mounted the wide stairway to the second floor.

She stood silently in the open doorway of the room she had shared with Brettan, gazing at the rich, opulent tapestries that decorated the walls, the heavy chairs carved from rich woods. On the table lay the fine combs and brushes and the assortment of rich-smelling soaps Brettan had given her as a gift. Everything seemed unreal to her. Her feelings, her senses seemed numb. She felt as if she had received a blow, yet could feel no pain. She felt nothing while she gazed about the room. And then a cold, lonely aching washed over her. Maren inhaled deeply, for she heard Caroline returning. She pulled on the heavy mantle and drew it tightly about her shoulders against the cold of the winter day. There was no time to search out Agnes to give the woman an explanation, and she could well imagine the woman's temper at learning that she was leaving to meet with Geoffrey of Meyrick. The woman's dislike of Geoffrey was intense, though Maren little understood the cause for such ill feelings. Quietly she left the chamber, her slippered feet brushing noiselessly against the flooring as she descended the wide stairway.

The stableboy cast an anxious glance at the two women, but quickly saddled the black mare and a fine gelding Caroline had chosen. His unspoken doubts were reflected in his young face, watching the two women mount and depart the fortress, quickly gaining the crest of the distant hill, then disappearing in the coolness of the wintry day.

Maren eased the mare to a stop beside the stream, not yet swollen with the runoff from the heavy winter storms. The black lowered her fine head and drank of the brisk water, then tossed her head in alarm, as if aware of Maren's uneasy mood. Beside her, Caroline slipped nimbly to the ground, roughly jerking the gelding's head back from the water, though he sought to drink liberally. The animal snorted his displeasure at her treatment,

495

rolling his eyes, sensing her menacing attitude. Maren stroked the mare to calm her, while the animal nuzzled a soft velvet nose into her shoulder. "Let us be done with this. Where is Geoffrey? You said he would ride to meet us." From behind her Maren heard a faint snapping sound, that of a twig yielding underfoot. Maren whirled about, her nerves raw, to see the shadowy figure that moved cautiously through the lowhanging branches of the dense trees, using the shelter of the forest for protection from cautious eyes.

Lean, and clothed in the meager doeskin garments of a lowly servant, Geoffrey of Meyrick emerged at the edge of the copse and looked warily about before satisfying himself that no others followed the two women. In quick, even strides he crossed the stream, using the flat even stones for steps across the water.

"Maren, so many times have I ventured from this forest in hopes of speaking with you, only to have your guards constantly preventing it." His gaze swept over her slender frame longingly. He reached out gently to push back the edge of her hood that he might gain a better look at her, as if to satisfy himself that she was indeed standing before him after so many months. "I see you have recovered from your wounds. You must believe me when I say that there was no greater pain than mine when I saw you injured. The fool who caused you harm has paid for his grave mistake."

"What do you know of the attack?" Maren missed the glances exchanged between Geoffrey and Caroline. He gently seized her hand in his and drew her to a more private place, where they might speak without Caroline hearing their words.

"These things are in the past, and best left forgotten. Suffice it to say that the man has paid for his deeds with his life."

"But, Geoffrey—"

Impatiently Geoffrey raised his hand to silence her. "There are other matters of grave import that we must decide, and so little time. Maren, I have come to England to see that you are safely returned to Wales. I know well you were forced to speak the marriage vows with the Duke of Norfolk. I shall not hold you to honor those vows. The time for escape is now at hand, and you may leave all this behind you."

"Geoffrey, these arguments between us are old. You must understand that this marriage was made by my father's blessing. I cannot go against his wishes, though I may little understand his purpose."

Geoffrey hung his head in grim determination. "Maren, in truth, you are a victim of your father's betrayal."

"Stop this. I will never accept your words against my father. I was taken prisoner by the English. My father sought the marriage only out of honor."

"Honor? Bah! Your father sought the marriage because it was the only means by which he could guarantee Edward control of the southern families. Have not his loyalties always been completely to the crown? Maren, think! Can you not see that you alone are the one guarantee Edward has of victory against our country? As long as your mother lived, Edward could never be certain of her loyalties."

"No, I cannot believe what you say. Brettan has told me that it was not his men who struck against Cambria. William told me that the men who attacked were not English. I cannot accept what you say."

Seeing his cause waver dangerously before Maren's desperate will to believe in her father, Geoffrey grabbed her roughly by the wrists, drawing her against him. "Maren, you were not meant to survive the attack of Cambria. Do you not see? With the strength of your mother's family broken, Llywelyn would have been powerless to raise an army against Edward. Now, with this mockery of a marriage, Edward has the final weapon against our people. With you held prisoner in England, Llywelyn is doomed without the strength of the southern families."

Maren twisted free of Geoffrey's grasp, stumbled backwards, struggling for some understanding of what he was telling her.

Geoffrey advanced a few steps toward her, but halted when he saw the wary, uncertain look that crossed her face. "How may I know that what you say is true? Is not one deception as good as another? You are asking me to believe in my father's betrayal. You are asking me to believe that he would willingly permit my mother's death and Edmund's abduction. And what of Edmund? Where is he now, if he lives? There has been no word of him in all these months."

Geoffrey could see his arguments had not swayed her, and his anger grew tenfold at the realization of Brettan de Lorin's hold over her, a hold he had never possessed. "Your brother suffered the same fate as the Lady Julyana. My men have learned that he was taken to an English monastery, there was taken ill with a fever, and died some months ago."

"No! You lie!" Maren whirled on him, her pain at his words clear upon her beautiful face. "It cannot be true." She turned away in stunned disbelief at what he had told her. So great was her pain, she was not aware of the look that passed between Geoffrey and Caroline, or she might have realized the truth in that one look. She shook her head in stubborn denial, her small chin set firmly, refusing to accept his words.

Realizing he had failed to convince her, and that she would not easily accept further argument, Geoffrey moved with amazing swiftness born of his desperation. He lunged for her, pinning her arms to her sides, and his

498

stronger arms closed about her, lifting her clear of the ground.

Maren was too stunned to realize quickly what was happening to her. She attempted to free herself but found she was firmly held in his unyielding grasp. Then Caroline sprang forward. Seizing a length of leather from her horse, she came forward and none too gently bound Maren's wrists in front of her.

"Geoffrey, you must not do this," Maren cried out in anger, realizing the trap she had fallen into. "You must release me at once, before I am missed."

"I cannot, my love. I must leave for Wales this very night, and you shall leave with me."

"Geoffrey, that is impossible. You must release me while I can still bargain for your life."

Behind her, Caroline laughed menacingly. "You have no authority here. You are bound for Wales. Take this and bind her mouth, lest she cry out. I'll not have the entire guard at Lionshead descending down upon us at the sound of her alarm."

Geoffrey seized the folded length of linen Caroline provided him and spun Maren about. Before he could tie the cloth in place, though, she seized her final chance for escape. With all her strength she brought her foot down on his instep, causing Geoffrey to grunt in surprise at her attack, the pain shooting up his leg as he drew back. Her feet unbound, Maren whirled about and fought the heavy folds of the thick mantle tangled about her. With strength born of desperation, Maren ran and stumbled to gain the crest of the hill, frantically lunging to gain her freedom, but she hardly considered Caroline's grim determination to be rid of her. Maren saw only the crest of the hill looming before her in the fading light of day, and then a sudden burst of white light that blinded her vision, and intense pain at the back of her head, and then nothing, darkness closing about her in that last instant.

She saw neither the stunned look upon Geoffrey's face when she suddenly crumpled and fell to the ground, her strugglings silenced, nor the gleam of satisfaction that sparkled malevolently in Caroline's pale eyes, the heavy stone dropping from her hand with a dull thud.

"You have what you came for, now take her and be gone."

"What of the Duke of Norfolk, once he realizes she is gone? He will certainly follow."

"I will see that he does not follow. Once he learns she has chosen to return with you, he will quickly lose his keen interest in her. And I shall be there to console him in his hour of need. Now go! Though I may detain him, I cannot be certain of his guard. They are quite taken with her, though I fail to understand their reasons, and might not be so easily convinced that she has left of her own choosing. I will give you as much time as possible. For now, your cause is mine."

Geoffrey checked the growing bruise at the back of Maren's head. There was little loss of blood, though she would not soon regain consciousness. Perhaps all the better that she would not immediately know of his treachery against her. Carefully he secured the linen cloth across her mouth, then gently lifted her. Like a cloth doll Geoffrey laid her across the front of his saddle and then, mounting his horse, pulled her across his lap so that her slender weight rested against him. Quickly he motioned for Caroline to bring Maren's mare. They would have need of the mare's strength in the days to come. He watched the fair-haired woman from behind his guarded gaze, as she approached with the mare and handed him the reins. Geoffrey reached down, grasping the folds of her mantle in his one hand, and tightened his grip threateningly on the cloth. "See that the Duke of Norfolk does not follow. I hardly think you would care for him to learn of your part in this matter."

Boldly Caroline snatched the mantle from his grasp, her amber eyes glaring her defiance of the man she regarded as her enemy, and used only for her own purposes in regaining what was rightfully hers. "I shall not easily yield what is mine again. Take the whore, and see that you fulfill your part. I will see that you have the time you need. Should you be unfortunate enough to fall into the hands of the English, your fate will be assured."

Enemies, with their hatreds set aside for their common purpose. Geoffrey turned his horse about and, leading the black mare, disappeared through the thick, low-hanging branches of the juniper trees, riding hard until he had gone a great distance. Only a faint rustling sound marked his passage through the forest. There, rejoined with his small band of men, he rode north for the few hours of daylight that remained, taking shelter in an abandoned cottage for a few hours' rest before continuing their journey.

Maren was aware only of a penetrating cold that seemed to surround her. For a few moments she lay still, listening for any sounds. Vaguely she remembered riding with Caroline out to meet Geoffrey. When she struggled against her bonds, she remembered too his treachery. The stone flooring beneath her was unyielding, and a sharp corner of a stone poked painfully into her side. She was immediately aware of the bonds about her wrists that restricted her movement, and the constricting cloth that prevented her calling out. Wearily she lay back, attempting to gain her strength. Her mouth was parched, and the cloth so tight against her tongue caused her to gag against the dryness. Where was Geoffrey, or Caroline? And who had struck her from behind. Caroline, no doubt, for the woman was a constant source of treachery. All at once she was reminded of that blow by the pulsing ache at the back of her head, which only increased her misery. Her arms and legs had grown numb

501

from lying in one position for so long. Frantically she flexed her fingers and toes in an effort to drive off the cold and gain some movement. She was vaguely aware that she lay against a stone wall. Total darkness surrounded her, but through an open space she could see into the night beyond. Stars twinkled brilliantly in the cold night, with clouds spread across the moonlit sky. She knew not where she might be, only that someone had brought her to this small cottage within the forest, for she could see the faint outline of the treetops in the night sky, once the moon rose high. Much later, or was it only a few moments, she heard a slight shuffling sound and the gentle nickering of horses. The door of the cottage creaked slightly as it was opened and shut, then Maren was aware of someone kneeling very near her, and a voice came from a second person near the doorway. Their voices were thick with the Welsh language.

"Has she awakened yet?"

"Nay, she has not moved since we came here. He keeps her well guarded."

"Aye, and ye had best keep your hands off her. Lord Geoffrey has his plans for her."

"Aye, he has his plans, but then maybe we have our own plans. The reward would be handsome for one such as her."

"But only if you live long enough to collect it, and there is nothing to say that the Duke of Norfolk would not slit your throat first. We have taken a great deal of risk in coming here. All I care about is returning north. I would not care to see the English hunting us in these woods."

The first man who entered poked lightly at her shoulder. Maren instinctively remained still, so that the men thought she remained unconscious.

"Leave well enough alone, I say. His lordship shall

502

return soon. He'll not take kindly to your handling of her."

"Ah, he be welcome to her. I have no use for one who would whore herself to the English."

"No whore this one, Davey. 'Tis said she be the wife of the Duke of Norfolk."

"Aye 'tis true enough. But still a whore. But you be right. I've no notion to end like poor Robby, for all his bravery. I've no desire to feel that cold blade across my throat. She must be some rare prize, that his lordship would risk so much in coming to England and staying so close all these months." Again the man poked at Maren and then, apparently satisfied that she still slept, he rose to rejoin the other. The door creaked at their leaving.

Maren sighed her relief. Somehow she had to find a way to escape. What could Geoffrey's purpose possibly be in seeking her out like this? Was this then the measure of his undying love for her? This was no act of love, but the act of a madman, and his cruelties were obvious. He had said that Edmund was dead all these months past of some fever. No, she could not believe that. Would not Agnes have known of it then? Maren attempted to shift her position and then tried to loosen her bonds. It seemed the more she tried to loosen the leather strips, the tighter they became about her wrists. At last she laid her head back in exhaustion, her breath coming in gasps from behind the cloth that pressed tightly against her mouth. When she had regained her strength, Maren again worked at loosening the bonds. This was madness. Geoffrey could never hope to take her from England. And yet, what if he was successful in eluding Brettan? For weeks, months, he had managed to remain beyond the grasp of Brettan's guard. What if he did reach Wales? What then was his purpose? And what was her part in all of it?

Maren struggled against her bonds, until her arms trembled with her weakness and the ache of the growing coldness of the night. It seemed that she had worked the bonds for hours, when the door again opened. Maren lay silent. A lone figure crossed the small room and knelt beside her, drawing a heavy woolen blanket across her for warmth. Not daring to look through the darkness, Maren remained motionless. It required all her control not to react against the hand she felt against her cheek, gently stroking, smoothing back the tumbled mass of her hair. And faintly through the darkness she heard Geoffrey's voice whisper to her through the darkness.

"Long you have been promised to me, Maren. Now we shall see the promise kept. Now you shall be mine forever. I will take you to Wales, and then we shall see these wars at an end. Rest, my lovely Maren, for the morrow we shall ride." Gently he leaned over her and pressed a kiss against her cheek, his lips oddly cool, almost clammy against her skin, so that she felt herself cringe at his touch of her, so intimate, as only one other had ever touched her. When at last Geoffrey settled himself across from her and his even breathing marked his sleep, Maren's jumbled thoughts betrayed her bravery. She remembered the safe, secure warmth of Brettan's arms and wondered miserably if he had learned of her disappearance. She could well imagine the cunning lies Caroline might tell him. Warm tears filled her eyes, for she realized the hopelessness of her predicament. Surely Brettan would find her, surely he would come for her. She could not believe the lies Geoffrey had spoken against Brettan and the king. At last she fell back exhausted and miserable, the only light in her thoughts the memory of the weeks, the months and seasons she had shared with Brettan. For all that they were enemies, he had never harmed her. Indeed, he had risked his life to protect her, pledged his honor to her, and loved her, if not with love then with a passion that had claimed her soul as no other ever had. What now was to be her fate?

The warmth was gone from the day, and a biting chill was carried on the air. The hunters urged their weary mounts across the greensward that lay beyond Lionshead. Good fortune at the hunt, with several stag brought to ground and a good number of boar taken, had called for hearty celebrations before a blazing open fire, while the animals were gutted and hung for the return trip to the castle. Weary but jubilant, the knights praised their own prowess and that of each other, raising their cups in celebration of the fine day.

Now they returned, riding before the last light, day yielding to darkness.

A multitude of brilliant lights could be seen in the towers that formed the outer wall of the ancient fortress. The large gates had been left open, although well-guarded in anticipation of the master's return, and a pack of excited hounds yelped loudly at the scent and sound of the returning men and the fresh game carried over the extra horses. Boisterous voices echoed loudly against the stone walls, which loomed high into the rapidly darkening sky as the English reached the stables within the keep. A full score of servants and stableboys quickly rushed forward, taking charge of the weary mounts and dispensing the game to the kitchens. Brettan tossed his reins to a stableboy and gave his orders for an extra ration of grain for the gray. He gently stroked the soft gray muzzle that was thrust into the folds of his tunic, seeking some hidden reward. Finding nothing of interest, the gray snorted and rolled his eyes discontentedly.

"You spoil the animal, milord. Already he has grown so temperamental that no other may come near, save perhaps your lady. See what your indulgences yield."

Bothwell teased goodhumoredly, having more than once received a painful nip from the animal when passing too near.

"You are envious, my friend. There is no finer beast in all the realm. Countless times have I owed my life to this one's fierce spirit. Edward has offered me much gold to possess him. But I have other plans. When this warring is ended, I shall turn him loose upon the greensward with the finest mares to be found, and we shall then see the proof of his strength. The black mare shall be the first, for she is of the finest Arabian blood, of the desert tribes. They shall produce offspring, of strength and endurance never before equaled."

"I hardly think the black will cower before his fierce moods. She is a fine, spirited animal. Any offspring they yield will truly be a mount worthy of a king. But first we shall see if the gray is capable of taming the mare," Bothwell offered lightly. "Much the same as your lady, would you not say, milord?"

"My friend, you must always remember that high spirit may oft as not be tamed with a gentle but firm touch, rather than force. The gray knows well the true spirit of the black."

"Ah, at last we have the truth of how you have tamed the maid and gained her favor," Guy de Brant offered, with much rolling of eye and good-natured teasing.

"I must confess, that more than once I feared the cause lost. The lady is possessed of great spirit and cleverness. Indeed, my good friends, had Llywelyn half her cunning and spirit, he would indeed be a formidable enemy," Brettan responded truthfully. He turned when the captain of his guard entered the stables. By the somber expression on his captain's face, Brettan knew the matter of grave importance. It was not like the captain of the guard to bother with some trivial affair that he himself could easily attend.

"What is it, man?" Brettan questioned, unfastening the bridle from the gray's soft muzzle. An uneasiness grew within him when his man remained silent, then finally broke the silence, his voice somber. "The lady Maren is gone, milord." His captain's voice carried the weight of his message as he stood before his master. A sudden quiet settled over the entire company of men in the stables.

"Tell me now, what has happened?" Brettan's voice carried a note of deathly purpose. He quickly motioned for Bothwell and the others of his knights to follow him to the great hall, his long, muscular legs carrying him quickly across the cobbled stones of the wide courtyard. Dressed in heavy chain mail and hauberk, prepared for battle, the captain of the guard struggled to keep pace with Brettan.

"The maid Agnes can tell you more, or mayhaps the Lady Caroline," the captain responded, entering the hall behind Brettan's towering frame, which seemed to fill the portal.

"Lady Caroline? What has she to do with this?" Brettan demanded sharply.

"Milord, she was the last to see the Lady Maren. When they were set upon by three horsemen."

"You have sent the guard to patrol the countryside?"

"Yea, milord. Sandlin remains afield with a goodly number of the guard. I have searched the entire countryside to the west as far as the river. I returned to await your orders. Darkness shall make our search difficult."

"Give the orders that we ride immediately. My horse is spent, so have another saddled. I must learn more if we are to search further this night, and the weather bodes ill, for a storm gathers on the horizon. Await my further orders."

The captain knew well the fierce purpose that lay

quietly controlled beneath the stony exterior of that bronzed visage. He had seen it countless times before, and knew the grave price that would be paid by those who had dared so much. The captain strode from the hall to prepare his men for the long night ahead. He held no doubts that no man would be spared until the Lady Maren had been found. He only prayed she was unharmed, for no power in Edward's kingdom could prevent the deadly vengeance that would be unleashed if she had come to harm.

The Lady Helene rose quickly when Brettan crossed the hall. "My son, she has been gone since late this morn. Caroline says that they rode beyond Lionshead together. Brettan, you must not jeopardize her safety for your own vengeance. Remember that there is more to be gained with a well-laid plan than a hasty attack."

"Yea, milady. Always the calm strength in the midst of the storm. But there is treachery here that I shall not abide, and there is more lost this day than the maid. I fear my heart goes with her, and I shall perhaps be too late to save her," Brettan answered truthfully, gazing into that gentle visage that somehow soothed his angry spirit.

"Once the treachery is known, my son, then you may know the proper weapon, but for now do not speak hastily and yield your cause for a show of temper. Meet the enemy with cunning, and the day shall be yours. It is a lesson your father taught you well. It is the strength that flows within the house of Norfolk." Lady Helene offered, laying a comforting hand on his sleeve.

"I will remember, milady." Brettan's voice was solemn. He turned to Agnes.

Agnes rose quickly when Brettan approached the hearth, her ancient feet moving her well-rounded frame with a quickness surprising in one of her advanced years. "Milord, she gave no word that she was leaving. I but returned to find the chamber empty after I had drawn her morning bath."

"You must tell me what you can remember, Agnes, anything that may have been amiss. Was she unhappy over anything, or perhaps fearful of something?" Brettan pressed, seeking some reason for Maren to have left Lionshead without his guard. The woman shook her head sadly, for there was nothing more she could offer him. "Cook spoke with her, but there was naught that was amiss. She has said that the Lady Maren was quite cheerful. Lady Caroline ordered two horses saddled. They rode from the castle together." Agnes' lips were pressed together in a grim line, and she wrung her hands. Beyond the old maid, huddled before the blazing fire that had been set at the hearth, Caroline sat with her head bowed, the hem of her gown torn and stained, her golden hair matted and disheveled, as if she had met with some great mishap. She lifted soulful eyes to Brettan when he approached and stood over her. Her lower lip trembled visibly as she stared up at him, at the same time allowing the thin woolen shawl that covered her shoulders to fall away, exposing the bare curve of her bosom beneath the torn gown. With great effort, Brettan fought for control, realizing that Caroline might very well be his one link to Maren. He stared down at his mistress, seeing nothing but the pathetic creature who had hoped for so much, and caused him nothing but endless aggravation. He looked deeply into her eyes and saw the lustful longing there, feeling repulsed by her unbridled wantonness.

"And how is it, milady, that you have escaped the attack? You must tell me everything that has happened. I must know who did this. Who has taken Maren?"

A ragged sob escaped her thin lips. Caroline feebly attempted to stand, and would have collapsed. Brettan was forced to catch her in his arms. Silently, he cursed under his breath and helped her back to her chair, her hands clinging to the front of his tunic as she drew him back to her. "Please do not leave me. Brettan, you must not leave. These men are dangerous, I fear for you if you give chase."

Brettan leaned forward so that his hands were braced upon the arms of the chair. He leaned over her, his face not a hair's breadth from hers, fighting to remain calm, realizing that with each passing moment Maren was taken further from him. "Caroline, you must try to remember anything that might tell me of the men who have done this."

Caroline reached a trembling hand to her brow, as if trying to clear away an invisible fog that clouded her memory. "They came upon us so fast, there was no warning. The Lady Maren had suggested that we ride upon the greensward. We rode just to the river when they were upon us. There were three of them, though I cannot say who they might have been. By their language, I am certain they were Welsh, and the Lady Maren knew their leader. She spoke most familiarly with him. Indeed, she seemed most pleased to see him."

"What of the other men?" Brettan pressed, the muscle in his cheek working beneath his bronzed skin.

"They held me fast so that I could not escape. They did this to me." Caroline spread her hands over the torn and rent garment.

"You are certain milady knew this man?"

"Brettan, how may I tell you, that you will not be hurt by what I say? The Lady Maren said the man was her betrothed, and that she had long waited for him to take her back to Wales."

"She lies. The woman lies. Milord, you must not believe these words." Boldly Agnes sprang from her own chair across the room beside Lady Helene, daring much before the heated glance of the one who had done so much to gain Brettan.

"Milord, her words are false. Long have I known my

510

mistress, since she was a small babe. I know her as I would know my own. She had found happiness here these last weeks at Lionshead. Though much had given her cause for great sadness, she had come to feel safe here, milord. You must believe what I say is true. The Lady Maren would never have left without some word. She would never have left the gentle caring you have given her."

"Brettan, surely you will not believe the rantings of this old hag. She thinks only of her own station now that her mistress has flown, leaving her behind. My darling, you must believe what I say. All these months she sought only to return to her people. Indeed, when you first found her, you held her as your prisoner, to prevent her escape. Can you not now see that she has merely done what any prisoner would attempt?" Desperately Caroline clung to Brettan's arm, for she felt her cause failing before the truth of the maid's words.

Brettan straightened, his back stiff and unyielding, forcing Caroline to loosen her grasp on his arm. He stared down at her thoughtfully while a single, pathetic tear trickled down her cheek and spilled into her lap. Never had he known her capable of tears through all the years he had spent with her, not even at the death of the child she had claimed was his, those few years before. Was this now a ploy to gain his sympathy, and then perhaps his favor, if he failed to find Maren? Brettan stared into the golden flames of the fire, contemplating Caroline's part in all of this. She most certainly had much to gain from Maren's leaving England. And of course, there was Llywelyn, for he held no doubts that Llywelyn was responsible for this. In his heart, he knew Maren would never have left willingly. There was no lie in the happiness they had found in each other these last weeks, since coming to Lionshead. Though clever and cunning to equal any man, Maren was not capable of deceit, that much he had learned of her in the months since Cambria. His decision suddenly made, Brettan whirled about, dispensing orders to servants and his guard, crossing the great hall to begin his search.

Seeing her cause fail, Caroline rose from the chair with unexpected agility for one who had suffered so much that afternoon. "Brettan, you must not do this. The lady Maren has made her choice to return to her home. Can you not see, my love? She goes willingly, she spurns you for another."

Reaching the large doors to the hall, Brettan halted momentarily and turned back to Caroline, who drew back, startled at the fierce expression that was like a mask of death on his handsome face. "Do you believe that I would so easily accept your lies, Caroline? I know not fully your part in this, but I am convinced it is there. I go now to bring back my wife, and pray, Caroline, pray to all the saints in heaven that she is unharmed, for I promise you that vengeance shall be mine if she is harmed. Take yourself from my house, you lying whore, and never darken my door again. Be thankful that I do not now take time to seek some satisfaction in applying the lash for your lies. As you know me, believe I shall have what is mine. Your cause is lost, Caroline. It has been lost since first I saw the Lady Maren, and it has little to do with honor or vows. I would seek her out unto the depths of hell itself, for she is my soul. Do not let me find you here upon my return." Angrily Brettan whirled about, halting only when Agnes reached a hand out to him pleadingly.

"Milord, may the saints watch over you and hasten your return."

"Be of good faith, Anges, I shall not return without her, for I fear my life would be meaningless if she were not to share it."

"Milord." Agnes beckoned him back, fear lining her

care-worn face.

Brettan stared down at the stout woman, whose great love and devotion to her mistress were borne in every fiber of her being, and his fierce countenance softened, for he realized the helplessness of the woman to aid her mistress in her hour of need. Now Maren had been taken from him, of that he was certain. He would never believe that she had left willingly, and he saw that same belief in Agnes' eyes. He squeezed the woman's shoulders reassuringly.

"I shall bring her back to Lionshead, Agnes, of that you may be certain. Do you believe that I would so easily relinquish her?"

Agnes stared up at Brettan, surprised at the emotion that broke in his voice.

Brettan's eyes softened at the thought of the slender girl and the brighter days they would share. And then he was gone, disappearing into the darkness beyond the hall, until Agnes again saw his tall frame outlined in the golden light glowing from the stables. The courtyard was filled with the sounds of the armored soldiers who mounted their horses. The order was given for the gates to be opened, and the long column of riders faded beyond the light of the stables into the bitter cold of the winter's night, in search of the Lady of Lionshead.

Maren was roused from her uneven slumber by a rough shaking at her shoulder. The first gray light of day poured into the humble cottage. Outside, the weather had become ominous with the threat of a storm. Her throat was agonizingly dry, for it was impossible for her to swallow with the linen cloth so tightly bound across her mouth.

Geoffrey appeared in the doorway of the cottage and gently pulled her to her feet. "I do not wish to hurt you,

513

Maren, but the cloth must remain in place until we have gained more distance. If I could be assured you would not cry out, I would loosen it."

Maren nodded pleadingly, leaning heavily against him. Somehow she must escape, but for now her greatest need was for something to drink. Geoffrey hesitated momentarily and then lowered the cloth.

"Water. Please, I must have some water," Maren croaked, her throat parched from the heavy linen stuffed in her mouth through the long night.

Geoffrey held a small cup for her while she drank, then drew her outside the cottage, after pulling the cloth back into place. She was allowed some measure of privacy in the dense foliage beyond the cottage, but her movements were greatly hampered by the leather ties that bound her wrists together in front of her. When he guided her back to the cottage, Geoffrey again loosened the cloth, then pushed her down onto the floor.

"Here, you must eat. It is not my intent to have you die before we reach Wales. Maren, you must understand what I do is necessary. It is our destiny."

"Geoffrey, please, you must allow me to return to Lionshead. Brettan will not stop until he has found us, and then your fate shall be certain. I do not wish your death, but you invite it willingly," Maren pleaded, trying to reason with him.

"I will not speak of this further. If you do not choose to eat, then I shall replace the cloth, and we shall be on our way. My men grow impatient. And as to your thoughts that he shall follow, perhaps he shall not. The Lady Caroline shall convince him that you have left of your own choice. How eagerly would he give chase to one who spurns him?"

"Geoffrey, you can never understand what has passed between Brettan and me. You hope for something you

514

believe was promised when we were children. It can never be."

"You are mine. You shall always be mine," Geoffrey growled fiercely, so that Maren knew clearly his dark determination. "Eat now. We ride long this day. There will be no rest until well after dark."

"Geoffrey—" Maren attempted to plead with him further, but was halted by the stinging pain of his hand striking her across the face, the blow sending her to the floor.

"You are mine, and that is an end to it. Do not speak of it again." He stood over her, an unusual light glowing dangerously in his eyes, so that she feared he might cause her more harm if she pressed the issue. Silently she nodded her submission for the moment, realizing that if she were to escape, it would have to be well thought out, for he would never yield to her pleadings. A short while later she was lifted atop the black mare, her hands tied securely to the pommel, the reins firmly tied about Geoffrey's saddle, preventing any possible escape. True to his word, the cloth had been roughly jerked back into place over her mouth. Maren forced herself to concentrate on the path ahead, so that she might remember it if she were able to escape. But beyond the cottage, the path disappeared into the thick foliage of the heavily wooded forest, so that it was impossible to know which direction they traveled, and perhaps equally impossible for anyone to follow.

The long hours spent atop the black mare seemed endless to Maren as the day stretched before them. She was watched constantly, allowed no moments of privacy. Her only accomplishment was in slowly working the leather ties that bound her wrists, so that they were quite

515

loose when they stopped at midday to rest the horses. With a dark scowl, Geoffrey checked the bonds and glaring at her suspiciously, jerked them even tighter, so that they cut cruelly into Maren's soft skin, leaving angry red welts where they bound too tightly. Through the long afternoon she struggled to remain upright in the saddle, so great was her fatigue. An occasional sound in the woods brought her upright, for she imagined that Brettan and his guard followed closely behind. But each time, she slumped wearily back over the saddle, hope fading with each passing hour. They continued long after darkness had fallen in the forest, following the winding course of an unknown river that took them farther and farther from Norfolk. They slept a few brief hours on the floor of a cave, then continued before first light. Eventually morning faded into afternoon, and afternoon into night. Three days became four, and then five. They rode hard through bone-chilling drizzle, and then the first flurries of snow that drifted lazily one afternoon to blanket the earth in a mantle of white splendor. The storm continued throughout the fifth day, so that they were forced to stop and seek shelter from the blinding snow. Geoffrey heartily cursed the delay, sending first one man and then the other to keep constant vigil for any who might follow, yet realizing that, if the English followed, they too must yield to nature's greater force. By early morn the storm had ceased, and Geoffrey pressed them onward, sparing neither man nor beast in his desperate struggle to leave England. Constantly, Maren watched for some unguarded moment, some change in their routine, that she might gain an advantage and slip away through the forest, but always she was bound, and only now had the linen cloth been removed. Constantly she worked the leather ties that bound her wrists, becoming loose in the damp coldness only to tighten when they dried, binding her more firmly than before. Geoffrey's mood darkened at any delay in their progress, but Maren constantly begged for time to rest, desperately hoping that her efforts would gain Brettan some advantage, if he followed. And deep within her heart lay the hidden fear that perhaps Caroline had been successful in convincing him that she had chosen to leave him. But each time she forced back her doubts, refusing to accept that he would so easily succumb to Caroline's lies. All her hopes lay in her firm belief in the love they had shared. Without that faith, she would surely have been lost.

They came to a river crossing, and Maren knew of a certainty that they would soon rejoin Geoffrey's men at the Welsh border. Geoffrey crossed ahead of them, the black mare securely led by one of the other rebels. The third guard had crossed to ride ahead and search the countryside for any English patrols. The cold water swirled about the horses' legs, the biting cold quickly slowing the animals' movement, making their footing uncertain while they felt their way over the uneven terrain. The horse in front of Maren suddenly lurched into the depths of the river, stumbling on the rocky bottom of the river. The guard was momentarily unseated, his hold on the mare's reins loosened, while he grasped to remain atop his horse. Maren seized her opportunity and lunged over the mare's neck, grappling to retrieve the reins. The black mare whirled through the churning water in the direction they had just come, and Maren urged her forward, desperate to gain the shore. Immediately the cry was sent up, and Maren had a brief glimpse of the one guard attempting to turn his mount around. Across the river, Geoffrey's face darkened when he realized the man's failure. In one motion, he sent his own horse crashing into the icy depths of the river, giving hasty pursuit to that struggling figure who so desperately sought to guide the black mare to shore.

Freedom was at hand. Maren drove the mare hard. She

517

felt the black stumble uncertainly when her hooves found footing at the water's edge, but the mare struggled gallantly. Behind her, Maren was aware of the thrashing sounds in the river, and that Geoffrey bore down on her with amazing swiftness. Without a moment's hesitation she sent the mare headlong into the forest, mindless of the branches that swiped at her and threatened to unseat her while she frantically drove the mare onward. Her grasp on the reins was uncertain, her movements greatly restricted by the leather ties that bound her wrists, but she urged the mare forward, at the same time maintaining her precarious balance in the saddle. She was oblivious to all else save her flight to freedom. The loud crashing sounds in the forest behind her were cruel reminders of the man who pursued with such demonic persistence.

Maren glanced back briefly, her attention drawn only momentarily from her uncertain course, but in that one instant the mare lunged through lowhanging branches and went down, fighting to keep her footing. The undergrowth tangled about her legs, sending the mare down badly. Maren loosened her hold of the reins. The mare rolled, sending Maren slipping from her back, gently depositing her on the floor of the forest.

Before she could look up, Maren heard the mare's thrashing. The black struggled to stand. Realizing that she had suffered little more than a few bruises, Maren bolted upright, but moved too late to restrain the startled mare, who lunged away from her, eyes rolling wildly, crashing off through the forest, mindless of Maren's soothing words.

She stared after the fleeing horse. Behind her in the distance, she could hear the approach of a rider. Geoffrey drove his horse through the dense forest in pursuit. Now she was afoot, with little hope for escape, unless she was able to remain hidden in the forest. Maren quickly scampered to her feet. Further flight was senseless. Geoffrey would only overtake her. Desperately she glanced about her for some place in which to hide, realizing her time grew short, for the crashing sounds grew closer. Her gaze fell on a downed timber nearby. Quickly Maren dropped to her knees and peered into the dark depths of the hollowed out tree, rotted away with decay. Her thoughts were suddenly filled with the idea of some fierce animal that lurked within those darkened depths. With grim resolve she decided that whatever creature might await her could be no worse than the mindless creature now bearing down on her with such a vengeance. With great effort Maren crawled into the timber, reaching forward with her bound hands, sorely cursing her restraints. Once safely hidden inside the tree, she closed her eyes and listened for Geoffrey's approach. The heavy bark of the timber muffled outside noises, so that she was forced to strain for some sound of him. Her breathing quieted. She lay within her wooded hideaway, the steady thudding of her heart the only sound, listening intently. And then she heard it, voices and the sounds of horses moving through the lowhanging branches and undergrowth that lined the floor of the forest. Maren's breathing stilled. She lay perfectly silent, listening to the voices come very near and then move away. It seemed an eternity that she lay there. How much time had passed, she could not be certain. For a while longer, she lay safely secluded within the heavy walls of the timber. With certainty she realized she could not remain there forever. Eventually she would have to leave that haven and begin her journey back to Norfolk.

Long moments passed, or had several hours come and gone? Maren shifted her position, for a rough piece of bark pressed painfully into her back. Slowly she regained her crawling position and edged her way out of the timber. Just beyond, she could see the light of day looming before her. She stopped to listen again. No sounds came to her from the forest beyond. Carefully she continued until she emerged from the timber, the fresh, sweet air of the forest filling her lungs. Maren glanced about warily. There were no signs of Geoffrey or his men. But which way lay Norfolk? The leaden sky that could be seen through the crowning treetops offered no clue by the position of the sun. She chose her direction and moved through the forest with silent resolve. Carefully she picked her way over a fallen timber. As she crawled across the timber and stood on the opposite side, she was suddenly grasped and swung clear of the ground. Maren's vision was blurred by the thick veil of her hair which fell across her eyes, but she struggled against the firm grasp that held her like a band of steel. Like a wild creature suddenly run to ground she lashed out viciously, realizing her efforts were in vain against Geoffrey's greater strength.

Frantically Geoffrey tried to subdue her flailing arms, which beat at him furiously. He reached to grasp her wrists, and Maren blindly lashed out at him, seeking any advantage she might gain as long as her strength remained. Her long fingers found soft skin and, seeking to cause some distraction, Maren viciously dug her fingernails into his flesh, leaving long talon marks that drew blood across his cheek. Geoffrey shrieked like a wounded animal, flinging Maren from him so that she fell to the ground. He whirled on her, that unnatural light in his eyes making her suddenly fearful that he might yet cause her harm in spite of his avowals of love for her. She cringed, trying to gain her footing. In an instant he was upon her, roughly pulling her to him, his face a dark mask of blind rage. Viciously Geoffrey struck her with the back of his hand, sending Maren sprawling to the ground. Her head reeled with sudden dizziness. "You will never escape me. You are mine, Maren, as you have always been mine. Do not test me further, or I swear I shall seek out the Duke of Norfolk and have him brought before you to receive his punishment for taking you from me."

Maren reached up a slender hand to wipe the small trickle of blood that ran from her lip. "You are mad. There is no place on earth where you may hide from him."

"I fear no Englishman, least of all one who must hold a woman prisoner to bed her. Rest assured, Maren, I hold no grand illusions of such men. You are mine, and I shall take my pleasure of you. This marriage with the Duke of Norfolk shall cease to exist, and you shall be my wife."

"Nay, Geoffrey, I shall never yield to you. I see that what you once promised as love is nothing more than a blind sickness that threatens to destroy you. Do you believe for a moment that, having once tasted of the sweetest of love, I would accept this bitter gift you offer? No, Geoffrey, though you may take me afar, you cannot remove from my memory the beauty of the love I have known. I can never be yours, though you might bind me with all the chains upon God's earth. Death is your mate, Geoffrey, and she shall consume you," Maren hissed, boldly defying him.

Geoffrey lunged at her, seizing her wrists in his stronger grasp. "Come, milady," he commanded jeeringly. "Your escort awaits you." He whispered at her ear, pushing her roughly ahead of him through the thick undergrowth.

Through the long, cold hours of that first night, Brettan pursued an unseen enemy, stopping only when

521

the trail they followed disappeared into the dense foliage and would not be found without the most careful searching. He chafed at the slower pace they were forced to keep. At first light, he ordered half his men to return to Lionshead for fresh horses and provisions for the journey. Though he followed an elusive trail that led them ever northward, he knew eventually the path would cross the border into Wales. Doggedly he followed the faint tracks left in the soft dirt that quickly became mud, and then lay blanketed with the first mantle of the winter's snow. His guard would rejoin him at Montgomery on the Welsh border. At dawn he dispatched his messengers to Edward.

For days, Maren was led like an animal through the drifting snows of winter, the English countryside fading into the stark beauty that was Wales. Though her heart felt a momentary joy at seeing her homeland, she feared her fate. Geoffrey pressed them hard through the long hours of daylight and well into each night, rising before first light to continue their desperate journey. Only when they had reached Wales did his fierce temper seem to lessen, once they were joined by more of his rebel army. But instead of turning southward toward Cambria, Maren was aware that their course led steadily north. Her worst fears had come to pass. Geoffrey had no intention of returning her to Cambria, where she might have hoped for the aid of her family. Instead he was taking her deeper into the coldest climes, always avoiding the small towns and villages.

A single-minded purpose grew deep with her, that she would never submit to his wishes. He might hold her prisoner, but he would never rule her heart. As long as there was breath in her, he would never have her. And she blocked out the bitter cold that penetrated her mantle

522

and set her teeth to chattering. She closed her mind to all else but the memory of golden days, those brief seasons of splendor she had known with Brettan. And eventually she no longer felt the cold or heard the leering remarks of the Welsh who guarded her, or Geoffrey's menacing threats. She knew only that she would survive, and one day she would again return to the love she had known, if Brettan would have her.

Chapter Twenty-Two

The northern fortress of Snowdonia loomed like a large bird of prey, sitting high atop a tall mountain that seemed impregnable.

Maren stood shivering in the damp coldness of the hall, refusing to meet the gaze of the man who sat before her like some gloating, self-satisfied fox who has just driven the hare to ground. A penetrating chill held the vast room, the numerous candles flickering wildly, for uneven drafts of air gusted about the hall like menacing ghosts stealing through the shadows. Maren drew the sodden mantle more closely about her shoulders, as if to protect herself from those unseen spirits.

Slowly the man rose from his chair and walked toward her, his face concealed by the shadows until that last moment when he stood no more than an arm's distance away from her. Maren felt his careful scrutiny but boldly refused to cower before his powerful dominance. She unfalteringly returned his even gaze, her blue eyes flashing like brilliant sapphires and meeting that paler azure gaze, breathtakingly cold and unmerciful. Still Maren refused to yield.

"Well done, my friend." The man spoke in the heavy

Welsh tongue. Geoffrey stood a few feet away, refusing to meet Maren's gaze. The man turned to speak to her directly in flawless English. "I trust your journey has not been too difficult."

"I demand my immediate release. You cannot hold me here." She spoke in a clear voice that belied her trembling spirit.

"My dearest Maren, I regret that I cannot release you," the man answered, obviously already aware of who she was, when she was still unaware of his identity. "At this moment, Edward drives his armies deep into our country from a score of locations along our border, in the belief that he shall be successful in dividing our country, and conquer us by severing each region from the other."

"Then it would seem the cause is lost. I should think the wise decision would be to surrender before many more lives are lost in this senseless warring."

"You little understand my purpose, my lovely Maren," he responded sarcastically.

A slow dawning crept over her while she stared at the man she had only heard stories about. "I understand that Edward has managed to raise an army more powerful than you might ever imagine. By their number alone, the English shall overpower you."

"We shall see, although I am not given to discussing point of strategy with women. However, I might be willing to make an exception with you. Would you not find great satisfaction in seeking your revenge against the English who are responsible for the destruction of your family?"

Maren boldly turned to face the man who now stood mockingly before her, his face lined with the excesses of too many years spent warring, too many ill-gotten pleasures, and now the cold brutal loneliness of this isolated fortress, whither he had retreated. Llywelyn the self-proclaimed prince of Wales presented a pathetic sight. He waited for her answer. "You would have me believe that the English are responsible for the attack on Cambria and the death of my mother. I cannot accept it. My father's steward has attested that the men who attacked were Welsh."

Llywelyn cast an uneasy glance at Geoffrey, realizing that he confronted no docile young maid. He studied the girl before him carefully, suddenly aware of boldness he had not expected in one so young and beautiful. "Your father!" he roared angrily. "All would have you believe that the English lord is your father." He glared at her.

Geoffrey intervened, his cold demeanor suddenly yielding before his concern that Llywelyn might divulge far too much, things for now best left unsaid. "Milord, there are other matters of more import. Now is not the time to discuss this."

"She must realize where her loyalties must lie!" Llywelyn spat at the younger man.

"Not here, milord. Not in this manner, lest you cast aside something of importance in the heat of the moment," Geoffrey insisted, stepping forward to halt the Welsh prince's hasty words. "Milord, the journey has been long, and all are weary. Surely the morrow would be soon enough for this?" Geoffrey pleaded, his voice carrying a hint of urgency.

"Yea, perhaps 'tis true. Have the Lady Maren taken to her chamber, and mind you, well guarded." He spoke under his breath, and then in a louder tone, suddenly calmer, he turned to Maren. "Forgive me, milady. I fear I have forgotten myself. You are guest here, and so shall be treated accordingly. Go now with the servants, for you will find a chamber has been prepared for your arrival."

"If I am to be treated as a guest, milord prince, then it is my choice to take my leave immediately," Maren dared, refusing to be taken in by his sudden change of mood. She saw the warning glint in Geoffrey's eyes but

527

gave no heed. She plunged ahead, determined to have the matter out. "It is my wish to leave now."

Llywelyn approached her slowly. Did she note a menacing danger in his movements? There was nothing to lose in challenging this rebel prince. Somehow she clearly understood that he loathed cowardice but held some respect for spirit even in the face of overwhelming odds. The Welsh prince halted just a few paces away from her, his hands folded behind his back, his feet planted in a wide stance, carefully studying her flawless features.

His voice was deathly quiet when he spoke to her. "You will come to understand, milady, that what you would have is of little import. I choose to call you my guest, but make no mistake that you will obey my commands. If it is prisoner you prefer to be, then that may be arranged. But be forewarned." He held up a finger menacingly to give emphasis to his words. "Any treachery on your part shall be dealt with accordingly."

Maren returned his challenge, refusing to cower before his bold threats. "There is no punishment that you might inflict upon me that will force me to yield to your schemes." She returned his glare unwaveringly.

"We shall see." Silently he gave a signal to one of his guards, who immediately left the room.

Suddenly aware of Llywelyn's intent, Geoffrey turned to him. "Milord, you gave your word that you would not press this matter now."

"Do not question me in this. The Lady Maren has chosen this confrontation. We shall now see how boldly she defies my word." From behind them, Maren heard the distinct sounds of the guard returning, and turned about to see the man enter from the passage beyond, dragging a struggling form beside him. When he pulled the youth into the light from the hearth, Maren gasped in stunned disbelief.

"Edmund!" The lad's struggling halted for the briefest

moment at the sound of his name. His head spun toward her, and he hung momentarily suspended within the guard's grasp, staring at Maren. And then, like a whirlwind, he lashed out at his guard, swinging one foot with deliberate aim to catch the unwitting guard in the groin. Immediately the man's grip on Edmund was released, and the guard crumpled to the stone flooring. Wasting no time, Edmund was on the man in a moment, pulling the heavy sword from his sheath with an ease that belied the boy's youth.

"Maren, you must not give them what they want. It is he who was responsible for the attack on Cambria." Edmund's face was flushed with excitement. He skirted the perimeter of the chamber, just beyond the reach of the guard who attempted to recapture him, fearful of that menacing blade that Edmund waved with surprising ease.

Maren whirled upon Llywelyn, her fatigue of their journey falling away before the cold realization of the truth that had eluded her for so long. But when she turned on the prince of Wales, she was hardly aware of the guard who advanced on her and in one quick moment held her firm within his grasp, one arm tightly about her while the other held a slender blade against the column of her throat.

"Now we shall see who has authority here." Llywelyn turned on Edmund. "Lay down the blade or she dies. It is a simple matter, but one that only you may decide. And I think you may know that I shall do as I say."

Edmund's conflict was clear upon his boyish face. He glanced first at Llywelyn, then at the guard who held Maren fast. He hesitated a moment, and the guard tightened his grip about Maren, forcing her to cry out, and pressed the blade more firmly against her throat. The sword clattered loudly as Edmund threw it from him. Immediately Maren was released, so that she fell to the flooring, the guard stepping from her. Edmund ran to her side, throwing his arms about his sister's neck, suddenly the child again, with such joy at seeing her. For a full, long moment, Maren clung to her younger brother, feeling such joy at seeing his tousled black curls and his mischievous blue eyes that she might have forgotten those who stood about them, so long had she believed him surely dead.

Geoffrey laid a restraining hand gently on Maren's shoulder. Maren jerked away from his touch, as if she had been burned with a hot iron. "You are part of this. You have betrayed me!"

"Maren, there is much you are not aware of. Once you have learned the truth, perhaps you shall feel differently."

"Murderer, liar!" Maren hissed at him. "You have blood on your hands. William said that betrayal came from within. How true his words. You betrayed my family. You above all had access to Cambria without question, and might pass before the guards without suspicion, and none were left to tell of it." Maren felt herself wavering dangerously toward losing control as she rose to accuse Geoffrey, oblivious to the others who watched the confrontation. She reached up and in one cruel motion tore the small gold medallion from her neck, the one she had worn since that last day at Cambria. Oddly she felt no pain when the chain cut into her flesh, and she thrust the medallion at Geoffrey, the light of the candles glowing brightly off the bold gold lion emblazoned on a field of blue. "This was in my mother's hand when she died. Taken from her murderer at that last moment. How easy it was for me to believe that the English were responsible for the attack. I saw only the medallion. I ignored William's words that the men who attacked the castle were Welsh." Maren's eyes gleamed feverishly, and she refused caution. "Brettan told me that he followed his brother's murderer to Cambria.

530

Geoffrey, how came you by this medallion?" Her voice was hoarse with her emotion while she stared into Geoffrey's startled gaze. This was not as he had planned it. He could not find the words to admit his guilt, unable to face the reality of his actions.

"The attack of Cambria was by my orders." Llywelyn's voice was cold and without remorse, echoing through the stone hall.

As if she had not heard his words, Maren's gaze remained locked with Geoffrey's. Within those deep pools of blue, Geoffrey saw his cause lost.

"Geoffrey, why? We played together as children. It was you who first taught me to ride. You and Andrew were the same to me as brothers, my mother accepted you as if you were her own child. How could you have done this?"

"Maren, what words might I say that you would believe? That it was all a tragic accident? You were all that I wanted. All I have ever wanted. But your father denied me that. He refused to allow our betrothal. How different it might all have been if he had but allowed the marriage. Before he left for the north country that last time, I pleaded with him to announce the marriage, but he remained firm. I knew that this war between England and Wales would take you from me. But I was given another chance to gain your love. Llywelyn promised that once Wales was his, we could be wed. Your father and the English tried to prevent it by taking you from me, but now you are here, and we can be together for always, as it should be. You must believe, Maren, I never meant to harm the Lady Julyana. I did not know of her death until later, when I returned for you."

Maren stared at Geoffrey incredulously. "How could you believe that I would ever accept marriage to you when you are responsible for my mother's death, and Edmund's abduction? I cannot accept what you offer."

531

Maren spun around to face Llywelyn. "My mother's family is one of the oldest in the south of Wales. Surely there is none more loyal in all of Wales. What then was your purpose in this act of cowardice against Cambria? Does the Welsh prince seek to endear himself to his people by murdering innocent women and children?"

The prince of Wales raised his head slowly, studying the young girl before him with quiet deliberation. "Edward seeks to make Wales one with England. It is his one true cause. I can never allow it to be. For hundreds of years, our people have defied English domination. We must be victorious. We must not allow English rule within Wales. Our heritage will be destroyed should that come to pass. But my armies grow weary with Edward's unending assaults. Sympathies are divided. It was so with your grandfather. He welcomed the English and gave his daughter in marriage to an English nobleman. Did you know that my father petitioned the baron for your mother's hand in marriage? But the Baron of Cambria refused, insisting on an English alliance. And the Lady Julyana was wed to Lord Gilbert de Burghmond. But always within my father burned the hatred of his humiliation. Even long after he wed my mother, he could not set aside his wish for revenge against your grandfather. And he took his revenge. He took his revenge against your mother for spurning him." Llywelyn's chest heaved with great emotion, his eyes glistening with an unusual light. "After the death of the old baron, my father traveled to Cambria when he knew Lord de Burghmond to be away. He took his revenge, for he took his pleasure of the Lady Julyana, which had been cruelly denied him."

"No! I will not listen to this. You are poisoned by your own delusions and greed, so that you must lash out at those around you. Do you think I would easily accept the lies you speak?" Frantically Maren pressed her hands over her ears to block out his hate-filled words. In one quick movement, Llywelyn reached her, roughly seizing her wrists in his strong hands, forcing her to listen to his words. "You are the child of that union. You are my sister, by virtue of our same father."

The vast room fell silent. Maren stared at him disbelievingly, then lunged at him like a creature gone wild. "You lie! My father is Gilbert de Burghmond. I will never accept your lies!"

Llywelyn flung her from him so that she fell to the stone flooring, Edmund immediately kneeling beside her.

Maren's breasts heaved with her silent agony. She glared all her hatred at the man who stood over her.

"Gilbert de Burghmond knows well who is the sire. Can you deny his purpose in seeing you wed to the Englishman?" Llywelyn roared at her, feeling himself losing control before her proud obstinacy.

Maren fought back the hysteria that tore at her, threatening to crumble her composure before this man who was her enemy. She struggled to keep her voice calm, pursuing the answers she must have. "If what you say is true, then what is your purpose in bringing me here now? Would not a bastard child be best forgotten?" she hissed from between clenched teeth.

"Nay, you will bring me the support I need to win my final campaign against Edward." Llywelyn grinned maliciously, staring down at her fair beauty.

"What are you saying? How can I possibly have any importance in this war of yours?"

"You are the daughter of the Lady Julyana, granddaughter of the old Baron of Cambria. By your words, one of the oldest families in all of Wales. And by virtue of our common father, you hold great importance as the sister of the prince of Wales, whether I like it or no. You shall give me your support in rallying the south of Wales against Edward. Once the land barons of the south understand that you support my cause, they shall follow. With the strength of the armies of the south, nothing shall stop me. Wales shall be mine." Llywelyn stared past her into the darkness at the edge of the room.

"You are mad!" Maren stared at him, only just beginning to comprehend the extent he would go to proclaim himself ultimate ruler of Wales. "And what of the people of Wales, in this bloody conflict you hasten to? What shall be their fate, when you have defeated Edward? Will you then become the benevolent ruler concerned with the ills of the people of Wales, or will you continue to tax our people unmercifully, so that they cannot survive under the burden of your authority?"

"Wales is mine. It is my birthright, cruelly denied me by this war Edward wages against our people," Llywelyn argued, his eyes gleaming with a brilliance that was frightening, his entire body possessed with his crazed passion. He paced about the hall, unable to remain still, as if a multitude of demons warred within him.

Maren refused to yield to her rising panic, though she swallowed hard. "Hardly your birthright, I think," she flung at him. "Your grandfather refused to name his successor. Could it be that he clearly saw you unfit to be prince of Wales?"

Llywelyn whirled upon her, his surcoat hanging in loose folds about his fleshy body. "I shall be prince of Wales. You shall be my weapon against Edward. You shall see my power is far superior to the English, including the Duke of Norfolk. You shall aid my cause. It is your duty, your destiny." His voice was little more than a harsh whisper. He bent over her, his sour, hot breath burning through her, so that she was forced to turn away.

Llywelyn turned from her and crossed the room to stand before the meager fire at the hearth. "Take her to her chamber, and the lad as well. See that they are well guarded. I want no mistakes." Maren and Edmund were being roughly hauled toward the doorway when Llywelyn delivered his final blow. "If she should attempt to escape, see that the boy is put to death."

Maren's horrified eyes locked with his, and she knew the truth of his words in that gaze that held only the look of death.

"You see, milady, you shall give me what I seek, and quite willingly, I should think." While being dragged from the hall and down the long passageway to a narrow flight of stone steps, she heard his wild, mindless laughter echoing against the walls. It was a sound she knew would haunt her for the rest of her days.

"If you harm my sister, I swear I shall see your throat opened from ear to ear." Edmund lunged at one of the guards, who retaliated by lifting a heavily armored gauntlet to deliver a blow that could have meant Edmund's death.

"No! Please, do not harm the boy," Maren intervened. "Edmund, leave the matter be. There is naught to be gained by your death too." Quickly she pulled her young brother into her arms and gently sent him on up the stairway. Just beyond the landing, the heavy portal to a chamber was swung open, and Maren was roughly shoved toward the doorway. Half the guard moved further down the hallway with Edmund firmly in their grasp.

"No. Please, allow the boy to remain with me. It has been near a full year since I have last seen my brother. He is but a child. Could we not be allowed to remain in the same chamber? Surely there would be no harm in the matter. I have word of our family. Mayhaps even it would ease his rebellious nature if we were left together." Maren saw that the lead guard wavered, seeming to consider her words.

"What harm might there be in keeping two prisoners

535

in one chamber? 'Twould allow for only half your guard. Surely the guard of prince Llywelyn is capable of watching a woman and a mere child?" she continued beguilingly, gazing innocently up at the man.

The man grunted thoughtfully. "Very well. Allow the boy to remain here. But I warn you, I have my orders. If there is any trouble, the boy's life is forfeit," he warned threateningly, in the heavy Welsh tongue that he knew well she understood. None too gently, Maren and Edmund were pushed into the large chamber that had been prepared for her arrival. A small fire glowed feebly at the hearth, offering little warmth against the damp, penetrating cold that threatened to overwhelm the new flames, which flickered and sputtered with great effort.

The heavy portal closed behind them with a deafening thud, and Maren heard the heavy cross bar slipped into place sealing any hopes of escape through that doorway. Maren was confident that at least one of the well-armed guards would remain outside the portal to guarantee the prisoners did not attempt escape.

Edmund crossed the chamber and knelt before the hearth, attempting to give life to the meager fire by breaking up small twigs and branches that had been laid nearby. Immediately the flames leaped to consume the fuel, and Edmund fed the hungry flames with larger pieces of peat and branches until the fire glowed brightly, casting a golden glow about the room, driving back the fearful shadows that crept forth from the corners. When the fire seemed sufficiently restored, Edmund added a heavy log that would guarantee several hours of warmth.

Maren watched her brother for a long moment, realizing that he had changed much over the months since she had last seen him. Still a lad, he had grown taller, but she noted sadly that much of the boy had now disappeared, replaced by a more serious youth. How she longed to see his impish smile once again, for it would

536

have greatly restored her confidence, which was so sorely lacking. Wearily she searched about the chamber for candles to give them more light, finally finding several long tapers set upon a large table against the far wall.

The golden light of the fire joined the glow of the candles, and the room seemed to take on a more cheerful air. Maren noticed with some surprise that the chamber had been carefully furnished in anticipation of her arrival. The ornately carved wooden chest and table belied the austere coldness of the stone fortress, and she silently wondered if some lady of Llywelyn's family had once occupied this chamber in another more peaceful time. An intricately designed tapestry of the finest wool hung at the head of the large bed, which was covered with a lavishly woven coverlet, and hung about with heavy velvet hangings. Two high-backed chairs carved of rich golden wood sat before the hearth, and the stone flooring was covered with another heavy tapestry of a simpler design, its softness underfoot helping to drive back the chill. Maren was greatly surprised that a prisoner could warrant such furnishings. Inwardly she shuddered at the thought that she might share a blood bond with Llywelyn, and her trembling seemed to consume her with the cold of fears that no flame could drive away.

"What of Catherine? And Father, and Andrew?" Edmund asked, poking at the large log he had placed on the hearth.

"Catherine is safe and well. She was taken to the abbey of St. David's after the attack. Father and Andrew shall soon return to the north country, if they are not returned already," Maren replied evenly, with a voice that seemed not her own.

"They march against Llywelyn," Edmund noted flatly. "Maren, do you believe Llywelyn's words about Mother?"

Maren was drawn from her own uncertain thoughts by

537

the mournful sadness in Edmund's voice. She crossed the room and quickly gathered him into her arms, hugging him to her fiercely, his young, strong arms encircling her in an embrace that spoke of all his loneliness and fears of the months past. Gently she kissed the top of his head and smiled, lovingly rumpling his tousled black curls, like her own waving tendrils a gift from their mother.

"I believe that desperate men oft say desperate words. My whole life I have known but one father, and the generosity of his love. He is your father, and he is mine also. I have no other." She could offer him no more. In her heart, she somehow knew that fatherhood was more than sharing the same blood. It was caring and protecting and loving. And in spite of what he believed to be true, Gilbert de Burghmond had given her those gifts as he had given them to all his children. No! She stubbornly refused to accept Llywelyn's words. Her one true father was Edmund's father. It was the only truth she would accept.

Gently she set Edmund from her, gazing into his boyish face, wondering at his courage in one so young. "Now, little brother, we must plan our escape."

"Escape? But how? You have seen how well-guarded the fortress is. You have heard Llywelyn's threats. He will leave nothing to risk. Indeed, I have tried countless times to escape. There is no way out of this chamber, save through the door. There are guards posted at every entrance."

"Except perhaps one, little brother." Maren turned thoughtfully to gaze about the room. "If we fail to escape, then all is lost. In time, Llywelyn shall force me to yield my support and thereby align the southern land barons. He will then have the army he needs to march against Edward. Edmund, there will be many deaths, perhaps even Andrew and Father shall fall. Llywelyn is mad, and he must be stopped. The warring must end, and the only way it may end is for Llywelyn to be halted before he can raise that army."

"Maren, even if we are able to escape, we are only two. How may we possibly stop Llywelyn and his guard?"

"Think, Edmund! If we escape, then Llywelyn no longer holds the power to align the land barons. And there is one who can stop Llywelyn, so that never again will he divide our country with this endless warring. I pray he is near." Maren's voice was hardly more than a whisper, her thoughts filled with the vision of a tall English knight, with dark waving hair, and golden green eyes that filled her with such warmth that for a moment, so vivid was his memory, the room seemed to lose some of its coldness. And a deep longing grew within her, so that she wrapped her arms about herself, hoping she might for a moment hold that memory close enough to give her courage.

"We must plan the escape for tonight," Maren determined, turning back to Edmund. A faint smile played across her delicate features when he seemed to catch some of her excitement, his boyish sense of adventure overwhelming his doubts. "They will hardly expect it of us this night. They shall believe us too tired and frightened. That is the reason we must act immediately. What rooms are along the passageway?"

"Several other chambers, much the same as this. Mine was at the end of the hall. There is no other way out except the stairway we came."

"What of the floor below?" Maren questioned, striding to the one window, which was heavily shuttered against the wind that seeped through and rattled the heavily paned windows.

"I remember a smaller dining hall beyond the main hall, and kitchens beyond that, and I think a small chapel, but I am not certain."

"There might be a way out through the chapel," Maren mused thoughtfully.

"Nay, there is too much risk in it. We must first pass the guards at the door. Downstairs, there are more guards. Nay, we cannot go through the chapel, with no certainty that there is an outside door."

"When do the servants bring the meals?"

"One meal is brought at first light, and then not again until the evening meal. I always saved a portion of the morning meal for midday. I was always hungry then."

Maren smiled at her little brother indulgently, suddenly reminded that he was hardly more than a child, for all his bravery.

"Which direction lie the stables?"

Edmund's eyes lit up, for he at last had a question that he could answer. "The stables are across the bailey, to the far side." Edmund took great pride that he had been clever enough to gain that bit of information in the time he had been there.

"Escape will be impossible without a horse," Maren thought out loud, carefully working the latch that held the glass windows secure.

"We will have need of two horses. One could hardly carry us both through the mountains with all the snow," Edmund corrected her.

With great concentration, Maren pried open the heavily paned windows, stopping momentarily when one squeaked loudly, metal grating against metal. "One horse shall suffice, for one rider." Just as carefully, Maren unlatched the heavy wooden shutters, which swung to the inside of the chamber. Just as she had feared, the wind gusted into the room, carrying with it a swirling mass of new snow, which quickly melted once it drifted to the stone flooring. Maren stared at the heavy iron bars crossing the opening from top to bottom. It would have been too much to hope that the window was unbarred.

She quickly pushed the shutters closed, gently dropping the latch back into place against the freezing cold of the wind that rattled them on their hinges. She closed the paned windows and drew the heavy velvet hangings across the portal, to give them added protection from the storm building with mounting fury outside the fortress. The storm might undo all their plans. Or perhaps not. What better cover might there be than foul weather? Though Edmund's progress might be greatly impaired, so too might that of any who would follow.

"Maren, what are you saying? One rider? We both go." Edmund spoke with authority, suddenly assuming command over their plans.

"No, Edmund. You shall go alone. It would seem our only hope for escape is through that window, and your smaller size makes you the one who shall go."

"I shall not leave without you. Father would never approve of this." Edmund halted, his eyes wide and fearful. "I cannot leave you."

"Edmund, there is no time to argue. It is our only choice."

"Maren, I cannot leave you here. Once they learn I have escaped . . . I fear for you."

"You need have no fear for me, little brother. I am the one Llywelyn must have to gain his army. He intended only to force me by threatening you. He knew well that I would never allow any harm to come to you. Once you are gone, he will not easily use me in his mad scheme. Come, there is not a moment to lose."

Edmund stared at her incredulously. Maren drew back the heavy coverlet on the bed and began stripping off the heavy linens. When that was done, she pulled one of the heavy chairs from before the hearth and stood atop carefully to unfasten the heavy velvet hangings that hung about the bed. When all the bedding and hangings lay in a large mound on the floor, Maren searched

541

through the wooden chest tossing any piece of cloth or garment that might be of use onto the growing pile in the middle of the chamber. "Edmund, listen at the door. Tell me if anyone comes," she whispered furtively, emptying the chest. She quickly set about tying each length of cloth to the other, careful to double the knots so that there was no danger of their coming untied. Some time later, Edmund motioned to her frantically that someone approached, and Maren quickly gathered the odd-looking rope and the extra linens and dumped them in the chest, lowering the lid just as the wooden latch was lifted from the door and it swung open. The servants quietly entered the chamber, quickly setting the evening meal on the table. Without casting a single glance about the room, the two women then shuffled out the door, the door closing with a heavy thud behind them. From beside the hearth Edmund glanced at Maren, his eyes wide with his excitement, leaping to his feet and resuming his position near the door. She felt as if her heart were in her throat. Slowly she let out the breath she had held since the door was first opened, and quickly ran to the chest, resuming her frantic tying and knotting.

"They shall not return this night. I was always left alone after they delivered the evening meal."

"We can leave nothing to chance. If the guards were to discover what we are about, we would both be chained and bound. We must take great caution."

When the last piece of cloth had been tied to the growing length of rope, Maren tested each piece with her own weight. She smiled triumphantly when each tie held fast. Carefully she coiled the crude-looking rope, fastening a sling at the very end. The hour had grown late. Edmund moved to place another log on the fire, while she seized her mantle and inspected it thoughtfully. She would have little use for it now. Summoning Edmund to her, she measured the mantle against his shorter frame. The dark blue color of the velvet would be a sharp contrast against the white of the snow, but the fur that lined the inside might shield him from searching eyes and provide extra warmth for his journey. Maren quickly loosened the seams of the mantle, separating the lining from the velvet. In a matter of moments she had fashioned a long tunic of fur lining which, when tied with a strip of cloth about Edmund's waist, would afford him great warmth from the cold of the winter storm raging beyond the stone walls.

When Edmund at last stood before her, heavily wrapped in the odd-looking garment, Maren had a moment to doubt her hasty planning, yet she knew there was no other way. The longer they remained captive, the more certain would be Llywelyn's success.

"I am going to lower you through that window to the ledge below. The line is not long enough to reach beyond to the ground. I will release the line, and you must secure it to the bars of the window below this one. From there you may drop to the ground."

Edmund seemed to grow excited at the adventure on which he was about to embark. "And from there I shall make my way to the stables."

"The stable may be well guarded. You must take great care, perhaps cause a diversion to draw their attention away long enough to reach the horses."

"Maren, what of the gates?"

Maren glanced at him uncertainly, realizing this was the one part of which she was least certain. "The gates were left open when Geoffrey and I passed through. All may be lost if they have been closed."

"I shall find a way out." Edmund spoke with determination, his excitement lighting his face with a look she had not seen since Cambria. "It cannot be much different than scaling the walls at the old fortress near Cambria."

Maren turned a surprised look upon her younger brother, realizing that he too had found great adventure in those crumbling walls. Quickly Maren wrapped the meats and cheese and bread brought for their evening meal, and thrust them inside the heavy fur of his tunic.

"I shall not take that. You will have nothing to eat," Edmund protested.

"Your need shall be far greater than mine, little brother. Morning shall come quickly. I can wait till then for food." She smiled at him confidently, knowing that she hardly fooled him. Once it was discovered that Edmund had escaped, her own fate would be highly uncertain. But she could not let him see the fear that grew deep within her. "There is a black mare, if you can find her. She is strong and sure, a fine, loyal beast, and will carry you till she drops. She will know the way."

"The way? What are you saying?" Edmund wriggled beneath her hands, which checked the fur tunic for snugness against the cold.

"She carried me here, and she will find her way through the mountains. From there you must find the English, for I am certain their camp will not be far. There you must find the Duke of Norfolk. I am sure he is near." Maren's voice broke, but she fought back the tears that threatened to shatter her composure, and continued.

"But how will I find him? How will I know him?"

"The black will find him for you, and you will know him by this." Carefully she placed the gold medallion in Edmund's hand, the gold of the lions catching the light of the fire and glowing brilliantly. Edmund's eyes grew wide in wonderment at the heavy medallion.

"You must find him, Edmund, the one who carries the standard of golden lions on a field of blue. You must find the Duke of Norfolk and bring him here. It is our only hope."

Edmund stared down at the gold medallion, his

544

youthful spirit suddenly serious, realizing that the moment for escape was at hand. There was no fear in him when he looked up at Maren.

"Would you have me deliver a message to the Duke of Norfolk?" he questioned, never doubting that he would find the man he sought.

Maren looked at him thoughtfully, her heart filled with a sudden warmth. "Nay, little brother, I will save what I would say until I may tell him myself. Give him the medallion, and he will understand."

Edmund looked at her uncertainly, not understanding the hidden thoughts behind her words.

"The hour grows late, and the storm has lessened. You must go now, little brother."

Maren listened carefully at the door. All was quiet. She crossed the chamber and carefully opened the paned windows. She unfastened the latch at the shutters and opened them wide, though a heavy snow still fell through the opened window. With great care she secured the line, again testing it with her weight to see that it held fast, then turned back to Edmund and motioned him to her. She quickly lowered the loop about him and then, dragging a chair to the window, helped him toss the slack part of the crude rope from the window and squeeze himself through the bars. Tightly she pressed his hand. He looked back at her one last time, his youthful face filled with confidence. And then he was gone, carefully letting himself down the length of rope until he reached the ledge below.

Maren felt a tugging on the line and quickly unknotted the rope, releasing the line to her brother, into the darkness below. Now all she could do was wait, and pray for his safety. Carefully Maren closed the shutters, and then the windows. She had used the velvet drapes as part of the line for Edmund's escape, but she cared little that a draft seeped through the portal. She placed another log

545

on the hearth and huddled in one of the high-backed chairs whose unyielding frame added little to her comfort. There were no blankets to warm her, for they had also been used. She stared into the flames, her nerves taut and on edge. If Edmund were caught, she would know soon enough. But if he were successful, there would be no word of his escape until morning, when she was the only prisoner found in the chamber. Uneasily she waited and listened for some sounds beyond the walls of her prison, but the wind was the only sound she heard, and as each moment passed, she grew confident that their plan worked. Eventually exhaustion overcame all else, and Maren drifted into uneven slumber, disturbed only by her dreams, no longer filled with the horror of her mother's death, but with the warm golden glow of emerald eyes, and the strong knight who rode to find her.

Edmund eased himself down the length of rope that Maren had tied, bouncing sharply against the outer wall of the main hall, which housed the chamber where he had been held prisoner only moments before. He swung precariously, tossed by the gusting wind, searching with his feet for the stone edge of the window. Hand over hand he lowered himself, the loop secure beneath his arms. At last he felt his foot brush against something that jutted out from the wall. Swinging to his left, he caught his foot on the ledge and, grasping the edge of the portal, pulled himself onto the ledge. The swirling snow hampered his vision, but below he could barely make out a large structure that adjoined the main hall, possibly the garrison that housed the soldiers. He turned his gaze to the opposite end of the large courtyard but could see nothing, for the snow and the darkness closed about him.

Edmund jerked the line one, two, three times. Immediately it fell past him, disappearing into the

546

darkness below, the weight of the heavy fabrics nearly pulling him from the ledge, had he not grabbed at the iron bars that crossed the window. With great effort he hauled the rope back up, securing one end through the iron bars. Stopping for a moment to catch his breath, Edmund then lowered himself from the ledge the final distance to the ground below. The line grew taut when he lowered himself the last length of line, and he realized with a sudden fear that the line was not long enough to reach the ground. His feet still hung in mid-air. His decision quickly made, Edmund wriggled out of the loop that encircled him, and released his hold. The bone-jarring drop that he expected never came, for his slight weight fell into a soft snowdrift, depositing him gently at his destination. Jumping quickly to his feet, he glanced anxiously about. Hearing that someone approached, he made his way along the wall in the direction of the stables.

The stables lay beyond the main entrance to the inner bailey, to the south. Across the courtyard a horse whinnied in the night, and Edmund followed that sound, approaching so close in the darkness that he was thrown back when one of the stable doors was suddenly thrust open. A lone guard emerged and disappeared into the darkness, weaving unevenly as if he might have consumed too much wine, to ward off the cold of the night, and his boredom.

Edmund quickly regained his footing and shot through the open door, before it was again blown shut by a gust of wind that set the portal clattering loudly behind him.

A single lantern glowed at the opposite end of the stables, leaving much of the long building in darkness. Most of the stalls were occupied, for few chose to ride out in the foul weather.

Carefully Edmund crept along the long row of stalls, moving slowly so as not to startle any of the horses. In the last stall, softly illuminated in the glow of the lantern, he saw the finely chiseled head and satin sheen of the black mare. The mare tossed her head uncertainly when Edmund unlatched the gate and entered the stall. Slowly he stretched out his hand, giving the black an opportunity to gain his scent. Immediately her fine ears flicked forward expectantly, for she seemed to pick up Maren's scent. Edmund spoke to her softly, gently stroking her fine head, reaching beneath to secure the bridle. The mare stood quietly while Edmund set the saddle on her back, pulling the cinch firm about her, then leading her from the stall. A tall roan in the adjacent stall nickered softly as they passed, and Edmund halted just inside the door to mount the mare. Opening the door just wide enough to pass through, he guided the black from the stables into the gusting wind that set the snow whipping about his face. The mare sidled uncertainly but calmed when he spoke to her. Edmund turned the black in the direction of the main gates, knowing that all would be lost if they had been closed.

The darkness of night and the fierceness of the storm offered him protection, but his hopes fell when he reached the massive portal and found the gates soundly closed and barricaded. A light appeared above on the battlements, and a voice called out in the night. "Who goes there?"

Edmund slipped from the saddle and quickly held the mare's fine head against his chest to prevent her from making any noise. Again the light was cast against the blowing snow, only now much closer, and Edmund realized the guard was coming down the stone steps that led to the watchtowers above.

"What are you about?" A second voice called out from the darkness to his left, and Edmund realized that another guard had emerged from the gatehouse nearby to give aid to the first man. That could only mean that for the present the front gatehouse stood open. Seizing his opportunity, Edmund leaped onto the back of the mare and dug his heels in, sending her headlong toward that small gate. Knowing well that his discovery was at hand, Edmund let loose a bloodcurdling yell, as if all the demon spirits pursued him. Startled by the unexpected sound, the guard was thrown back into a drift of snow, the black's chest having caught him full force against the shoulder.

In one brief moment Edmund was through the gate, sending the mare flying across the width of the outer bailey. The mare slipped on the cobbled stones and fought to regain her footing, while Edmund urged her to his right, where he knew the second gate lay.

Behind him he heard the cry go out, and knew that very soon the guard would give chase. Again the mare stumbled on the slippery stones, but lunged forward as if sensing Edmund's urgency.

Having heard the cry of alarm, the unsuspecting guard emerged from his post at the gate.

With all his strength Edmund kicked out at the guard, sending him sprawling headlong onto the cold stones, his face immediately buried in the snow. With a jubilant cry, Edmund charged through the second gate, into the cover of darkness beyond Snowdonia.

Chapter Twenty-Three

Brettan stood at the edge of the crude shelter, heartily cursing the foul weather that impeded his journey.

For days he had driven his men across the whole of England and Wales, in pursuit of the man he had sought for more than a year. Now he faced their ultimate confrontation with deadly calm. The moment he learned that Maren had been taken prisoner, Brettan had spared neither man nor beast in his quest to overtake his brother's murderer. The remainder of his guard had joined them while they crossed into Wales, their numbers making progress slow, so that Brettan had chosen a handful of his loyal knights and, stripping away their cumbersome armor, had proceeded ahead at a greater pace. That had been several days before. Now they camped at the foot of these towering peaks in the dead of winter, with this new storm making passage impossible.

Within him, Brettan fought back the silent torment of Maren's fate at the hands of Llywelyn. He had known the great danger to her, but even the combined strength of his guard and that of the king had not been enough to keep her beyond Llywelyn's evil grasp. His thoughts, his dreams were filled with the memory of her, of silken black hair that fell about them like a heavy velvet mantle when they lay together, shielding them from the outside world, or of eyes the color of priceless sapphires that sparkled with a fire and a life of their own, and bored into his soul until he was not his own man, but lost to her forever, to wander mindless if ever she should cast him away. He remembered the delicate outline of her face in the first light of morning when she lay so trustingly beside him, the gentle curve of her neck, and the soft pulsing that could be found there. And he remembered too her silent strength in moments of sadness over the last months, knowing that he had been responsible for some of that sadness. He grew angry when he thought of their last weeks together at Lionshead, so cruelly taken from them, and the fragile trust that had grown between them, and out of that trust a bond stronger than any steel. A cold anger grew within at the loss of his unborn son, Maren's son, and he silently vowed he would have his revenge.

Edmund drove the mare as hard as he dared in the darkness, finding himself nearly unseated when she stumbled in the drifting snow and then regained her footing, only to lunge headlong into another drift. It seemed they had wandered for hours, and when at last the first light of day lifted the darkness about him, Edmund found that indeed the mare had carried him along a road that was hardly visible in the uneven mounding of snow.

Edmund pressed the mare until her sides heaved with her efforts. Quickly he dismounted and struggled with her for footing in the drifting snow. Now, with full light only a short while away, he knew of a certainty that the guard would be hard upon them. His only consolation was that the guard's progress would be as difficult as his own.

Maren startled from her dozing and bolted upright in the hard chair. She listened carefully, straining for some sound that might tell her what had awakened her. Then it came again. A cry of alarm. Edmund? How long had he been gone? She cursed herself out loud that she had not remained alert, for she had no way of knowing how long he had been gone, or if there had been enough time for his escape. What if he had been caught? She glanced back at the hearth. The fire had died low. He must have been gone at least an hour. Now she was torn with silent agony, that she might have sent him to his death. She heard the heavy footsteps beyond the portal and then a clanking sound when the bar was lifted away from the door. The heavy door swung wide, and Geoffrey strode into the room, followed by two of Llywelyn's guards.

Geoffrey descended upon her, his hand striking with brutal force against the softness of her cheek. Maren was thrown to the floor by the force of his cruel blow. "You fool! Do you realize what you have done by aiding the boy's escape? Now the English will be hard upon this fortress, and I am powerless to defend it." He turned to the guards. "Have this prisoner taken to the dungeons and chained. We shall show the Lady Maren how we reward treachery," Geoffrey ordered, that unnatural light gleaming in his eyes. Maren was roughly seized and hauled to her feet.

She whirled upon him, brushing back the veil of unbound hair that had fallen across her shoulder, her deep blue eyes meeting Geoffrey's with a look that was as cold as death. "Llywelyn is the fool, and you eagerly believe his lies. His fate is yours." She spat at him venomously.

Geoffrey lunged at her, his fingers closing with bruising strength around her arms, and Maren returned his gaze with stubborn defiance. A second stinging slap crossed her other cheek, a small trickle of blood showing at the corner of her bruised lip.

The forest about him lightened, and Edmund stopped to rest. Digging deep inside the fur tunic, he retrieved the small bundle Maren had insisted he take with him. He downed the few slices of dried meat and cheese, saving the bread for later. A movement caught his attention at the edge of the clearing, and the mare snorted uneasily. Edmund saw the shaggy coat of an animal quietly stalking them, only to disappear behind a snow drift. Wolves! Wide-eyed, Edmund tried to calm the black mare, but she seemed to know his alarm and lunged away from him, her eyes rolling wildly with her fear, having picked up the scent of the beasts that lurked beyond the clearing. Whirling about and stumbling in the deep snow, she lunged away from his grasp into the thick coverage of the forest. Edmund dove for the trailing reins and tried to hold on. With sickening finality he felt the leather slipping through his hands, but then it held firm, and the mare dragged him for several paces. Unable to keep his hold on the reins, he felt his grip weakening. The reins slipped from his grasp, and then the mare was gone, her uncertain passage marked only by the thrashing sound in the undergrowth as she lunged through the snow.

Edmund lay motionless for several moments, reality overcoming him. The loss of the mare meant certain death in this wilderness. Slowly he turned over, feeling the heavy burden of his failure. When at last he opened his eyes, a large shadow loomed over him.

Edmund screamed in complete terror, his thoughts filled with the visions of the wolves descending upon

im, tearing him apart, their pink tongues lolling out the
ides of their mouths while they closed in for their kill.

A gruff voice penetrated through Edmund's blinding
error. He was pulled from the snow by the scruff of his
eck, his head snapping backwards while he was roughly
haken by powerful hands. He had no strength left to
ight off the large man who pushed him ahead through a
arting in the trees, along an uncertain path that
radually descended the steep mountain.

Before midday they reached the small encampment.
heir numbers were few, but Edmund could easily see
hat they were well-armed and traveled lightly for speed,
ot greatness of numbers. He was prodded across the
amp until he came to a secluded shelter crudely formed
rom long heavy branches, laid across a downed limb to
rotect from the falling snow. It was a meager shelter, but
ffective. The man behind him roughly halted him before
he shelter, and another emerged. By his size alone,
dmund would have known this man to be their leader.
Ie swallowed uneasily, realizing that whoever he was,
his man could quite easily end his life with little effort.
Iis lean, bronzed features spoke of endless hours in the
un, perhaps atop a horse on the field of battle, for he
eemed at ease with the heavy broadsword that hung
rom his waist.

"What game have you snared today, Sandlin?"

"I found the lad in a snow bank. He had recently
arted company with his horse, a fine black mare who
vill be easily found. She has not wandered far. But this
ne, I think his greatest fears must have been the wolves
saw lurking nearby. They frightened the black."

Brettan nodded to his man and approached the lad, a
rim expression fixed on his handsome features.
Dangers abound in the forest, lad. You are best advised
o seek your home and take shelter from this miserable
veather, for I fear next time one of my knights shall not

555

be near to render aid. And I would know how you came by a black mare."

Edmund stared up at the man in wide-eyed wonder "You are knights of the realm? Edward's knights?" he questioned in flawless English.

An odd look flashed between the tall knight and the one called Sandlin, who had brought him to the camp

"Aye, knights of the realm. And whom do we have the honor of addressing?"

Suddenly cautious, Edmund looked at the tall knight warily. "I seek the camp of the Duke of Norfolk Mayhaps you can take me to him."

"And what might your purpose be with the Duke of Norfolk?" A startled look crossed Brettan's face.

Edmund swallowed hard, fearful that he should not trust so completely in these men, yet at the same moment aware that without his horse, lost within the forest, he might well roam for days and still not find the Duke of Norfolk. These English knights were his only hope.

"I carry something of value for the Duke of Norfolk My instructions are that I am to deliver it only to him." Edmund answered firmly, with an unmistakable air of authority.

Brettan let out his breath slowly, his gaze locked with Sandlin's over the boy's head. "You may give me what you carry."

"Nay, I am to deliver it only to the Duke of Norfolk. I shall not give it to another."

"I am the Duke of Norfolk," Brettan replied patiently "Now what is it that you bring?"

"How may I know that you are the Duke of Norfolk?" Edmund questioned warily.

Brettan sighed heavily, reached within his tunic, and brought forth a shining gold medallion, worn upon a heavy gold chain about his neck. Three gold lions were elaborately carved into the gold, a medallion identical to

556

the one Edmund carried from Maren. "This is the crest of the house of Norfolk. It is known well throughout the kingdom."

A broad grin split the boy's face as he reached within the crudely made fur garment, but before he could retrieve the medallion, he found himself roughly seized about the shoulders and lifted from the ground.

"This fur you wear. How came you by the garment?"

Edmund choked out his reply. "It was made for me, against the cold." Sandlin intervened, his strong firm hand restraining Brettan, so that he finally set the boy upon the ground. Edmund glanced uneasily at the tall knight from under the shaggy mane of his raven-black curls, which had grown long and unkempt over the past months. And though they were lighter in color his eyes were that same wide shape, darkly fringed with thick sooty lashes, that made him seem almost too handsome for a lad.

Brettan looked again at the boy, his attention held fast by that fleeting expression he had seen before on the lad's face. Was it possible, or was the anguish of the last days finally beginning to tell on him? Dear God, but he saw her face in the lad's, an expression that was gone in the next moment. The boy's words drew him back. He reached within the garment and, holding his hand before Brettan, slowly opened it to reveal the medallion identical to the one Brettan wore about his neck.

"How came you by this medallion?" Brettan's voice was a harsh whisper.

Edmund smiled faintly, staring at the tall knight. "It was given me by my sister, before I escaped from the fortress. She bade me carry it to the Duke of Norfolk."

Brettan stared hard at the boy, unable to grasp his words, yet knowing the truth of them in the resemblance the lad bore to Maren.

"What is your name, lad?" Brettan asked gently,

having recovered from his first shock.

"I am Edmund de Burghmond. I have been held captive in Llywelyn's fortress, beyond the pass in the mountains. He now holds my sister prisoner. I fear for her safety."

Brettan fought back his emotions, realizing the bravery of such a young lad to ride into the night in the midst of a storm, on an uncertain journey in search of someone he could not know he would find. But more than that, he knew now that Maren had not left by her own decision, and that she awaited him now.

"Come, Edmund, you must tell me what you know of Snowdonia. And you must leave nothing out." Gently Brettan laid his strong arm about the boy's shoulders, drawing him inside the small enclosure before the fire.

Geoffrey grabbed Maren cruelly by the wrists and yanked her into the dark, damp dungeon below the main level of the fortress. At his signal a guard bound her wrists in heavy irons secured by a length of chain, looped through a large ring moored in the stone ceiling. Slowly the guard drew the length of chain taut until Maren hung suspended by her wrists, her toes barely brushing against the stone flooring. Her head was thrown back, the long mane of waving black hair cascading wildly down her back.

Geoffrey was sorely reminded of his months of waiting and longing while Maren was held by the Duke of Norfolk. He stood beside her now, gazing down into the depths of those brilliant blue eyes that had haunted his dreams, and now flashed her silent anger. Slowly he brushed the backs of his fingers across the velvet softness of her cheek, feeling the vibrant warmth of her skin beneath his hand. Maren jerked her head away from his touch, feeling as if she had been tainted by something dark and evil. Helplessly bound, she met his longing gaze with open defiance. It left a cold, hollow feeling deep within him, and he suddenly knew of a certainty he could never possess her. And that thought, more than any love he might have professed, goaded him beyond all reason.

"My dear Maren, fool that you are, you cannot see that your hatred against me is futile. At this moment Llywelyn and his guard leave Snowdonia for the south, across the mountains. He shall have his army and be triumphant. And all of your proud defiance will have been for naught. As for the Duke of Norfolk, I pray Edmund finds him. I would take great pleasure in ending his life here, where you may watch."

Maren swung about, the heavy iron cutting deeply into her wrists. "You will never take him. Never!"

Behind her Geoffrey's crazed laughter echoed against the hard cold walls. He left the chamber, the heavy door closing behind him with a deathly finality, leaving Maren alone in the damp chamber dimly lit by one candle that flickered at the gusting of wind through the open portal, and was suddenly snuffed once the door closed. Maren was left to her silent agony deep with the dungeons below the main fortress, securely bound by the cold chains, which no amount of struggling could loosen. But her worst agony was that she had unwittingly become Geoffrey's pawn in leading Brettan to certain death. Tears of misery flowed down her cheeks and spilled onto the velvet of her gown, stained and torn from the journey of the last days. She knew her greatest loss would be Brettan, and she was powerless to warn him of the danger that awaited.

Within the hour of Edmund's arrival, Brettan and four of his men were ready to ride to Snowdonia, one man remained with Edmund, and another was sent to take word to Brettan's army of their location.

Daylight faded, with darkness closing about them like a protective mantle, while the five riders carefully wound their way through the pass in the mountains, the black mare Sandlin had recaptured leading them to even footing along the uncertain path.

They reached the base of the fortress as the first light of day lightened the morning sky, the horses' hooves making soft squeaking sounds in the fresh snow.

Leaving one man with the horses, Brettan and his men continued on foot to the south entrance, and the small postern gate Edmund had used two nights before in his escape. The lone guard stood at his post and stretched with fatigue, gazing along the perimeter of the forest that bound the fortress. He turned back to the gatehouse, beating his arms about his body to drive off the cold of the long night. Brettan motioned two of his men to the far side of the clearing, and then he and Sandlin waited while the men deliberately caused noise in the trees, as a diversion. The one guard appeared to investigate the noise, and Sandlin quickly stole up behind him, his quick blade ending any possibility of discovery. Brettan motioned to his men, and they quickly gained entrance to the outer bailey, flattening themselves along the inner wall, against the possibility of being seen by one of the guards in the watchtowers. A quick glance confirmed what Brettan had first thought. There were no guards in the watchtowers, only the one guard they had encountered and possibly one more at the gate to the inner bailey. The fortress was oddly silent, for a garrison full of Welsh soldiers.

Like ghostly shadows creeping in the gray of first light, Brettan and his men quickly crossed the outer bailey and sought the gate to the inside of the fortress. It was exactly as Edmund had told them it would be, and only one guard stirred at his post. The man was quickly bound and gagged and left in a snow drift, where he might be found later. Brettan felt a certain uneasiness at the deserted watchtowers. He quickly dispensed Sandlin to the stables and Guy de Brant to the garrison hall. Within moments both men had returned. The garrison hall was empty, and no more than a score of horses remained in the large stables. Llywelyn had fled. Two more guards left the main hall, and Brettan and Sandlin quickly rounded the corner of the stone fortress in the direction of the kitchens. His two men followed, and in a moment they had gained entrance through the small door at the end of the passageway near the kitchens. A servant stirred some mixture in a large kettle over the open hearth, while they passed by on silent feet. Emerging at the end of the hallway, Brettan sent one man toward the servants' quarters, while he and Sandlin cautiously crossed the main hall, wary of any guards who might suddenly appear. It was their good fortune that most of the men had departed with Llywelyn, leaving the fortress barely secured by a handful of men. Some moments later, Guy de Brant returned from his search, dragging a bedraggled servant girl, who fought against his hold with meager spirit. Wide frightened eyes like that of an animal rolled wildly when the girl saw the other three men before her. She cringed back into Sir Guy's grasp, the taller man approaching with an almost menacing air about him.

"What is this?" Brettan questioned with quiet calm.

"I found her cringing in one of the chambers at the top of the stairs. I also found this." He held aloft the remnants of Maren's mantle, reduced to nothing more than several strips of blue velvet after making the tunic for Edmund.

Brettan seized the torn fabric. "Where is the maid this belongs to?" he questioned menacingly, holding the velvet beneath the girl's nose. She only stared back at him with uncomprehending terror in her eyes. Fighting

561

for control, Brettan tried again. He gestured to the girl and then to the fabric, realizing that she hardly understood his language. Again he pointed to the girl and then to the velvet. Slowly an understanding look spread across her face, and she nodded. Sir Guy kept a firm grasp about the girl, who guided them to a wooden door at the end of the passage.

The heavy door groaned. Brettan forced it open to see a narrow stone stairway descending into complete darkness.

Taking one of the torches from the passageway, Brettan gave his men his orders, then carefully made his way down the length of the stairway. The landing at the bottom led to another set of steps that descended further beneath the castle, while on either side were heavy wooden doors.

Taking the war-ax from his belt, Brettan swung wide at one door, missing the heavy chain in the flickering light of the torch. He swung again, the steel blade of the ax easily separating the chain links. Brettan slid the bolt back and swung the door wide. Moving carefully through the portal, Brettan moved the torch in a wide arc, the glow of the flame dancing off the rich satiny texture of raven-black hair hanging over white shoulders.

Maren's face held a look very near sheer terror. The glow of the torch reflected off the damp walls of the dungeon, illuminating Brettan's lean features and causing his emerald eyes to glow like those of some beast, coming at her from the darkness.

In an instant he was beside her, crushing her within his embrace, lifting her gently to release the pressure about her wrists, which were raw and bleeding, her name a soft whisper on his lips.

"How I prayed you would come," Maren's voice broke into a ragged sob, muffled beneath the roughness of Brettan's kiss.

"You must take great care. Geoffrey has set a trap for you." Maren struggled to speak through his grasp.

Quickly Brettan set to the task of releasing the irons about her wrists.

"What of Edmund?" Maren questioned uncertainly.

"Edmund is safe with my men. And now I must take you from here."

"But how were you able to get inside the fortress?"

"Llywelyn and his men have all fled for the south, in his last hope of rallying the southern land barons against Edward." Carefully he worked at the chain that held her, finally twisting it free of its crumbling mooring. Tenderly Brettan gathered Maren into his arms, and she knew no haven could have given her greater comfort. She clung to him, at last giving in to sobs of fear that racked her slender shoulders. She gazed into his handsome face, and in the flickering of the light from the torch, her face became a mask of terror, for she saw the sudden flash of steel above Brettan's head, while he bent over her.

Warned by that look upon her face, Brettan pushed Maren from him, mindless of any safety but hers. The flat edge of the broadsword fell a glancing blow at the back of his head as he rolled across the flooring.

Brettan's world reeled from the blow, the chamber suddenly bursting forth in a brilliant glow of reds and oranges like a score of suns whose light had been fused as one. Then slowly he rolled into a deep abyss of darkness. He felt Maren slipping from his grasp, and the ax clattering loudly to the stone flooring.

Maren scrambled across the cold stones in the meager light, lunging for the heavy war-ax, realizing that Geoffrey would never allow them to leave alive. In an instant she reached the heavy weapon, but Geoffrey was upon her, striking her wrist with a heavy blow that sent the ax beyond her reach. In a blind rage that bordered on hysteria, Maren turned on him, lashing out at him viciously with her fists, her hands, raking long nails across his face, while he sought to ward her off and she took flesh where her frenzied attack fell. But her weakened strength was no match for his, and Geoffrey pinned her arms behind her, cruelly twisting one, forcing her into submission. Roughly he shoved Maren to the floor. "Now, milady, Duchess of Norfolk, you shall watch as your husband dies. I vowed that no one would take you from me, and now I will end his miserable life."

"No Geoffrey, wait! Let him live, and I shall give my word that I will do whatever you ask."

From far away, Brettan heard Maren's voice, and then it seemed to come closer. His head cleared, and he struggled to gain some awareness of his surroundings.

"Maren, no! You must not. Nothing you say will change what he has planned." Brettan came up on his hands and knees. His head reeled from the blow, a warm trickling of blood at the back of his neck.

"How right you are, milord. There is nothing you can offer, Maren. Llywelyn has already promised you to me. That was the price for bringing you here, that and great wealth, once Wales is free of England once and for all."

"Geoffrey, it is too late. There is no hope for Llywelyn. He is doomed and, unless you stop now, you are doomed with him," Maren pleaded, trying desperately to gain Brettan time for his senses to clear.

"No, my lovely Maren. Can you not see?" Geoffrey pulled her back with him, his voice at once gentle, almost pleading, but somehow it could not mask his evil intent. Again he cruelly twisted her arm behind her, until she thought it would surely break. With his free hand he reached up and caressed the full outline of her bosom. With utter revulsion she attempted to pull away from him, but could not break his hold of her. He then reached up to untie the corded satin ties of her gown, pulling each loose slowly, glancing beyond her to make certain that

564

Brettan was afforded a full view of his touching of her. With sickening realization Maren knew his game. Wildly she twisted away from him, crying out in pain, for he again twisted her arm.

Boldly Geoffrey pulled back the edge of her gown at the neck, revealing the pale skin across her collarbone, as soft as satin beneath his touch, daring what no other man had ever dared.

Brettan also knew well Geoffrey's game, but refused to allow his further handling of Maren. He lunged at Geoffrey, his voice no more than a feral growl that seemed to come from the soul of some untamed beast, which lurked within and awaited only to seek out its prey. In the face of that awesome fury, Geoffrey backed away, pulling Maren along with him.

From the door there was a shuffling noise, and the portal was thrown open, Sandlin and Guy de Brant charging into the chamber. In one swift movement, Geoffrey seized the sword from his belt and held it dangerously near Maren's throat, continuing to pull her backwards with him toward the far door, across the chamber. "Come no further, or she dies," he threatened when Brettan's men advanced on him. But they halted when Brettan held aloft a restraining hand.

"He is mine!" His voice was barely more than a whisper. He stared after Geoffrey's retreating form backing through that far portal, dragging Maren with him.

Up the winding, narrow steps, Maren stumbled and fell, Geoffrey dragging her with the purpose of a man possessed. Behind them she thought she could hear Brettan's even footsteps on the stones, but she could not be certain.

Vainly she tried to slow Geoffrey's progress up that long flight of steps, fearful that his men lay in wait at the top of the stairway. When they emerged, Maren stared about her, struggling to regain her footing. They had emerged inside the empty garrison, used to house the soldiers.

Close behind them, Maren now heard those footfalls, and in another instant Brettan burst through the portal. Roughly Geoffrey shoved Maren against the far wall of the hall, then turned to meet his adversary, his sword clutched fiercely in both hands, taking his stance.

Brettan moved with catlike grace to meet Geoffrey's attack, the deadly war-ax held with an agility that belied its wieldy weight. Without warning Geoffrey lunged at Brettan, his sword meeting empty air, for Brettan quickly stepped aside. But when he wielded the heavier war ax, Geoffrey quickly recovered and stayed Brettan's blow across the hilt of the sword.

Again and again Geoffrey drove the blade against Brettan, each time halted in his thrust, for Brettan met each blow, each thrust with growing strength. Geoffrey held no honor for the battle he fought, but struck coward's blows. And as the moments passed Maren could see that Geoffrey's arm weakened, while Brettan continued to meet each blow evenly, swinging the heavier ax high to deflect another blow, then driving hard against Geoffrey, hooking the blade of the ax behind the hilt of the sword, and in one quick movement jerking the blade from Geoffrey's grasp. The heavy steel sword clattered loudly to the floor, but Geoffrey refused to yield. He seized the slender blade secured within his belt and advanced against Brettan.

Brettan cast the heavier ax aside, his intentions to meet his enemy evenly. He glanced away for but a moment to set the ax aside, but Geoffrey seized his last opportunity and lunged at Brettan, a loud bloodcurdling scream coming from his throat, slashing at Brettan with demonic strength born of his desperation. Brettan met the blow, grasping Geoffrey's wrist in his own hand, and they struggled across the width of the garrison. Geoffrey drove Brettan back hard against the far wall, that deadly blade dangerously close to Brettan's face, while Geoffrey sought to drive it home and end his own torment. The blow to his head and the desperation of their struggle began to tell on Brettan, and his hand shook visibly. He tried to draw on some greater strength to hold off that blade. All his muscles were tensed, attempting to stay Geoffrey's blade.

In that last instant, when Brettan was certain no strength remained, Geoffrey's desperate grasp loosened unexpectedly. Brettan looked into his eyes but saw only a disbelieving look of complete surprise upon the man's face, which stared back at him. The blade fell suddenly from Geoffrey's grasp, clattering to the floor of the garrison, and he sagged and then slumped to the floor, his body suddenly lifeless, the long shaft of an arrow protruding from his back.

Brettan quickly knelt beside the fallen man, then slowly raised his eyes to meet that deep, blue gaze across the hall. In an instant he was beside Maren, gathering her in his arms, the deadly crossbow falling from her hands. And slowly the tears she had denied for so long fell upon her cheeks.

Outside the garrison they could hear the sounds of steel against steel, as Brettan's guard stormed the gates. And then all fell silent.

A moment later Sandlin burst through the door at the far end of the garrison, followed by a score of Brettan's guard.

Chapter Twenty-Four

Maren snuggled deeper into the warmth of Brettan's heavy mantle, while they rode through the melting snows that gave some sign of yielding to the new season that was upon them. Yet only the night before, when they had slept in a small farmhouse, the sky had darkened with clouds, sending swirling masses of new snow to slow their journey to Caernarvon. More than one hundred men, nearly half of Brettan's personal guard, had roused the poor farmer from his sleep, declaring that their abode was being taken in the name of the king. The man had been little impressed, although his manner had softened at the sight of the slender, beautiful young girl who rode with them. The guard had taken shelter in a series of small outbuildings that were intended for the farmer's goats and sheep. Brettan and Maren were given their own chamber within the farmer's home, there to await the storm's end, and they built a warmth within that small farmhouse that had little to do with the fire upon the hearth.

Now, continuing to Edward's northern stronghold, Maren grew uneasy, for she and Brettan had spoken little of the days she had been held captive by Geoffrey, or of the truths she had learned at Snowdonia. Maren pushed the thought further away, wishing to hold forever the sweet, blissful days they had shared since Brettan had found her at Snowdonia. But she grew fearful of what awaited them at Caernarvon, feeling safe only within the circle of Brettan's arms, as if for the moments he held her no danger, no frightening truths could enter into their world.

Maren stirred against him, preferring the firmness of his chest to riding atop the black mare, and Edmund had taken great delight in being allowed to ride the black, finally prying a promise out of Brettan for the first foal the mare would have, sired by the gray stallion. Maren had been greatly pleased at Brettan's generosity, for he had often spoken of his plans for the offspring the gray and Maren's mare would produce.

"What are your thoughts, my sweet?" Brettan murmured softly against the top of her head, his strong hands gently guiding the gray over uneven footing.

"'Tis nothing, milord, only bothersome thoughts that will not leave."

"Tell me of them, so that I may take them from you forever, for I swear I prefer the brilliant blue of your eyes, and not these, dark, stormy ones that look upon me now," he teased gently. Maren tilted her head back and gently kissed his chin, thinking that never before had she known such happiness, as she did now.

"Will you not tell me what it is that troubles you? Surely with Geoffrey dead you have nothing to fear."

"'Tis not Geoffrey that haunts my dreams. Those nightmares ended with his death. 'Tis another I have grown to fear for what may come to pass in the days to come."

"You have trusted me with your life and your heart. Can you not trust me now with your thoughts, and let me take this fear from you?"

Maren bit at her lower lip uncertainly. "What is it to be, milord, when we reach Caernarvon? Am I to be taken prisoner by the king of England, or perhaps quickly sentenced to death as an enemy of the crown?" Maren stared up at Brettan, aware now as never before that she might endure any fate but that of being parted from him forever.

Abruptly Brettan reined the gray stallion to a sudden halt, causing the animal to dance sideways. When the gray had calmed, he swung down from the saddle and roughly reached up to drag Maren into his arms, leaving the whole of his guard to remain patiently in the middle of the road until his return. Reaching a secluded clearing in the trees that surrounded them, Brettan deposited her, none too gently, on a fallen timber.

"I swear by all the saints in heaven, I cannot understand a woman's thoughts. I give chase across the whole of England and Wales, in search of a maid who may be nothing more than a memory, who may reject me at the final moment in favor of another. I choose to ignore Caroline's words that you chose Geoffrey over me. I defy my king and come very near to breaking my vows of knighthood. I order my men into unknown danger that is not their cause. Yet they follow willingly, though why I may not say, save that they too have been bewitched by the beauty of a mere girl, whose treachery and cunning is matched perhaps only by her stubbornness. I risk my life to keep you near me, against all who would set us apart. Can you now doubt me? What more would you have of me, to prove that beyond all else I am pledged to you body and soul? Say it now, so that I may know whether my cause is lost, before I go forward another step on this fool's errand."

Maren could see his silent agony in the emerald depths of his eyes, and her own gaze became blurred. He had reaffirmed his love for her, tearing away at the wall of fear she had placed between them. "I would but remain at your side forever, milord. It is a small request, yet one I fear you cannot grant." Maren's voice trembled once she gave voice to her silent fears.

In an instant, Brettan was kneeling before her, folding her within the warmth of his strong embrace, the heat of his body penetrating through to drive away the sudden chill that had seized her and set her teeth to chattering, even in the glow of the midday sun.

"As you believe in my love for you, never doubt that I will keep you with me forever. I have grown to need the very sight of you to brighten my day, the feel of you, as I need food or drink. I could not long survive if you were taken from me. I would surely become as mad as Llywelyn if that were to be."

"But what if Edward commands that I be sent away? Could you defy your king merely to keep me with you?" Maren stared up at him, wanting only to lose herself in those glowing green depths that warmed her as no flame could.

Brettan's face relaxed, and he chuckled softly. "My love, I have already defied Edward to have you," he whispered matter of factly, raising her hands to his lips and pressing a warm, lingering kiss against her fingers, which sent a river of molten heat coursing through her veins.

"What are you saying?"

Brettan smiled at her indulgently. "You are wondering, are you not, if I choose to deliver the sister of Llywelyn to the King of England? The answer is, I do not. This war between our countries shall end soon. Edward shall proclaim himself ruler of all England and Wales. I go to Caernarvon but to pay honor to my king, and give what aid I might to his cause."

"But what if Edward should seek to hold me prisoner to gain some advantage with my people?" Maren pressed.

"You must trust in me, my love. It shall not happen," Brettan replied softly against her cheek, with an air of complete confidence that she found maddening.

Maren turned back to him uncertainly, still unconvinced of his determination. "How can you be certain?" Maren stared at him, all her uncertain emotions reflected in those shimmering pools of blue.

"Because, my sweet, my guard outnumbers Edward's." He replied so simply that Maren was certain he made some jest. She laughed and pulled away from his grasp, but he remained perfectly silent, and Maren realized that he made no jest but spoke with complete honesty.

"You would send your men against their king to keep me with you?" She gaped at him incredulously.

"In truth, Maren, it is not a decision I would wish to make. But it is there if needs be. I once told you that Edward valued highly the strength and wealth of the house of Norfolk. Edward is no fool. He will not risk splitting England apart for a mere girl."

It took a moment for Maren to absorb completely the import of what he was telling her, and when she finally turned back to him, a look of devilment lit the depths of her blue eyes. "Then, milord, mayhaps you can explain to me the purpose a knight of the realm might have for such a 'mere' girl, if her importance is so insignificant." Maren bowed low before him in mock deference to his title, seeking to lighten his mood. Before she could look up again, Brettan had risen and quickly scooped her into his arms, with a strength she could not have broken if she had chosen to.

"You cause us much delay with your woman's foolishness, milady." He grumbled playfully in her ear, bearing her back to the long column of his guard, who awaited patiently. Maren turned her head away, a crimson flush spreading across her cheeks at the attention they had drawn. But each knight only looked straight ahead, as if they saw nothing amiss with their master's making off with a young maid into the forest in the dead of winter; all, that is, except Sandlin, who met Maren's embarrassed blue gaze with a slight bow of his head, his eyes twinkling with good humor at seeing his master so attentive to the Lady Maren, when he had once greatly doubted that few words could ever pass between them without causing a confrontation. He saw no sign of that anger now, only a knight and his lady fair.

Brettan lifted her atop the gray, then mounted behind her, pulling her firmly back against him, tucking the folds of his mantle in about her legs, casting Sandlin a withering glare that smothered any amused comment. He gave the signal to ride.

"In answer to your question, milady, my interests in such a maid are for many reasons, not the least of which is the pleasure you bring to our bed. But I find in the most difficult of moments a wisdom within you that is uncommon, and a courage beyond all fear. I find that I cannot pass a day without looking upon you, touching you, having you near me. It is something not easily explained. It came upon me that first time I saw you lying in the dust and ash at Cambria, so proud, so beautiful, and so defiant. I knew then I would be lost if I could not have you, although it was not so clear as it is now."

Tears welled within Maren's eyes at the raw emotion of his love for her, silently ashamed that she could have doubted him.

"And now, milord?"

"Now I fear I could not long survive without your presence, for even in the moments of your worst temper, I see a beauty within you that I cannot deny." His mood lightened. He smiled down at her, the dimples in his cheeks undeniably desirable. "There is something I would have of you, something you have long denied me."

Maren turned about in the saddle and gazed into his handsome face questioningly, while he urged the gray stallion forward.

"What nonsense do you speak? What have I left that could possibly be of value to you? My mantle lies in shreds in yonder fortress. Edmund has refused to return the black mare, except for a promise from you of her first foal. Indeed, the only thing I possess is the gown I wear." Maren spread her hands wide before her in complete bewilderment. "If you would have the gown, then I would beg of you to wait a time, that I may replace it, for I would not long survive the winter's cold." She stared into the depths of those glowing green eyes, which teased her serious mood, a smile pulling at the corners of Brettan's mouth. Playfully, he leaned forward to kiss the end of her nose.

"Milady, I speak of your avowals of love. Do you not realize, Maren, that you have never spoken what is in your heart? I know well the passion you find in our bed, but I have a need for you to say it." Brettan kissed the side of her neck tenderly, the touch of his lips against her skin sending shivers of delight down the length of her arms.

Maren stared ahead at the vast, snow-covered peaks that surrounded them, her mood suddenly quiet and somber.

"I once feared saying the words that are in my heart, for fear you would use them against me." Maren turned and gazed into his golden eyes. She reached up and tenderly caressed his face until her fingers disappeared into the thick waves of his dark hair, drawing his face down, her lips seeking his, conveying all her love for him in the passion he tasted upon her lips.

"You are my love, my strength, my reason for life itself, so that I cannot imagine a moment without you. It has always been so, even when I was forced to hate you for what I believed you had done to my family, and my greatest fear was that you would soon tire of me and perhaps return to your mistress."

Brettan gazed down into the delicate oval of her face. He saw more there than she had spoken.

"Are there other doubts that darken your thoughts, milady?"

Maren bit at her lip uncertainly. "Caroline once spoke of a child she had carried, which died shortly after it was born. She said you had cared little for the child and seemed relieved that it had not lived. You have never spoken of it to me." Was she mistaken, or had she felt a stiffening in his arms that gently held her against him?

"You must remember well the source of such information, my sweet. My firstborn child lies in a small grave at King's Forest. One day I shall return and carry him to Norfolk, to rest with his ancestors. I have never spoken of the child she bore, because it was not mine. The child she bore was born nearly a full year after I had left for the crusades. The sire shall never be known and, from what I have heard of those years I was gone, even Caroline cannot be certain of the father," Brettan answered quietly, with no emotion in his voice.

Maren snuggled further back against him, somehow calmed that Caroline had never been capable of giving him a child, and she knew the woman's lies would never again cause her to doubt the man who rode with her.

Before the last light of day, they reached the town of Caernarvon. Brettan turned in the saddle when a shout went up through his guard, and a messenger approached. Gently he shifted Maren's sleeping form where she had dozed for the last hour, the night chill having driven her deeper into the warmth of his heavy mantle. She stirred while the rider approached, and sat up when Brettan gave some reply. She peered out from the fold of the mantle and, seeing that they had stopped just at the edge of the wn, glanced curiously up at Brettan.

"What is it? Is something amiss?"

Brettan pulled her back against the firmness of his
chest. "One of my guard has arrived from the south, near
the Wye Valley."

Maren was keenly aware that something of grave
importance had happened, and she waited for Brettan to
tell her of the news.

"Llywelyn is dead, Maren. The war is ended." Gently
Brettan urged the gray on, riding through the town
toward the large castle that rested with quiet grace
upon the crest of a far hillside.

Silently the words tumbled over and over in Maren's
thoughts, while she tried to make some sense of her
emotions. "I feel nothing. If it is true that he was my
brother, should I not feel something? Perhaps it was all
nothing more than a lie after all."

"I have learned, my sweet, that there is more that
makes the bond than mere blood. Your love for your
family is the proof of it." Brettan held her tightly against
him, riding through the fading light, his voice muffled
against the silken mass of her hair. "It is done now. The
truth of it died with your mother, Maren. We must let go
of it now."

Gently she laid her hand over his larger one, feeling
the silent strength that flowed through his fingers, which
held the reins firmly, strength that had forever protected
her, even from the first, when she had thought him her
enemy and feared him. "Yea, milord. It is done."

The days that followed their arrival at Caernarvon
were filled with great anticipation, for Edward awaited
word from the southern land barons after the death of
Llywelyn. With each passing day more messengers
arrived and, the final one arriving from Cardiff, Edward

was assured of his rule over all of Wales. All would striv
to bring a permanent and lasting peace between their tw
countries. Long hours were spent drafting the length
proclamations to be signed by each land baron, pledgir
his allegiance to the English king. From early light unt
far into the night, Brettan attended his king, giving h
advice as both a friend and knight of the realm to th
important matters that lay before them.

Maren's time was to herself, which she chose to sper
in the company of the young queen, who had presente
the king with a second fine son only days before the
arrival at Caernarvon.

One fine, clear winter morning, Maren sat before th
warmth of the bright sun that filtered through th
heavily paned windows of the royal chambers, working
a fine piece of linen that she carefully stitched into
small gown for the new prince. The lady-in-waitir
entered hurriedly to inform Maren she had bee
summoned by the king. Maren glanced uneasily at th
queen, whose attention was suddenly drawn to the so
sounds of her son, as she put him to her breast. Eleano
smiled up encouragingly and grasped Maren's han
silently comforting her friend's unsteady nerves. Car
fully Maren folded the delicate piece of linen ar
followed the queen's lady from the chamber.

Maren walked down the long hallway to the stairwa
and then descended to the great hall below. She foug
back a rising panic without Brettan's calming streng
beside her. What if Brettan had misjudged the kin
What if he now called her forth to inform her that sh
was his prisoner, and would spend the remainder of h
days locked away in some remote prison?

Maren's thoughts were firm, while she followed th
lady-in-waiting to the large hall, but her trembling kne
belied her calm demeanor, so that she feared all mig
hear them shaking. Maren glanced about the large ha

nd then, taking a deep breath, walked slowly forward to earn what her fate was to be.

Edward was lavishly dressed in an elaborate velvet unic and breeches, of a deep, rich brown. A long flowing nantle of the same color, richly trimmed in a soft fur bout the edges, flowed out about his wrists. He wore no rown, only a large medallion heavily set with priceless tones and intricately fashioned into the shape of a crown eavily draped about his neck, the massive links of the old chain worn impressively about his broad shoulders. Ie sat in a high-backed chair placed before a massive 'ood-carved table, on which several pieces of parchment nd maps had been lain. He looked up at her with keen iterest when she approached. To his left and behind the able, Brettan sat with an expression on his face that gave er no clues to Edward's mood, yet she saw nothing in his anner that might have warned her that something was miss.

Maren curtsied deeply, her hands shaking while she eld the skirt of her gown. Before she could rise, Edward ad come forth and gently seized her hand, drawing her o her full height. Silently Maren drew a deep breath, eeking to calm her nerves before the assault of his areful scrutiny, aware that little escaped that piercing lue gaze.

"Milady, we meet again. It is good to see that you are ecovered from your accident this summer past, and I ust your good health has returned. I have asked you ere because I must make an important decision, and I elieve you may help me with that choice." Edward poke deliberately and with great care, as if he handed own some grave sentence. Indeed, Maren wondered if is decision were of her own sentence. She looked ncertainly at Brettan and saw only the warmth of that lowing green gaze, which warmed the blood within her eins and gave her courage. He smiled at her, offering her

579

more confidence in that one gesture than any words h
might have spoken.

"I believe, milady, that you hold the answer to m
dilemma."

"I will help in whatever way I might, milord," Mare
responded evenly, without the slightest indication of th
fear she felt.

"With the deaths of Llywelyn and his brother Dafy
pass the last of those of Welsh blood with claim to th
Welsh throne. In a matter of days, I shall issue
proclamation to the people of Wales, naming myse
sovereign over the whole of England and Wales, but I ar
well aware, Lady Maren, that a king must rule the peopl
as well as the land. Pray tell, milady, what may you offe
me that might ease my cause of making Wales an
England one?"

Maren stared at the king in complete dismay, that h
would think her capable of such answers, and yet withi
his words she had found a silent promise that Llywelyn'
fate was not to be her own. She pondered Edward's word
and found no easy solution to his problem.

"Your majesty, I hardly understand these matters o
grave importance, which demand much care an
attention. But I do understand that defeat is difficult fo
anyone to accept, but for a proud and stubborn peopl
even more so." Maren glanced at Brettan, knowing h
would find great humor in her words, for he had ofte
accused her of those same faults. "It would perhap
lessen the pain of defeat if my people could look upon
sovereign of their own."

Edward gazed at her thoughtfully. "It is my full inter
to be their sovereign. You have said nothing I do no
already recognize."

Maren inhaled deeply to steady her nerves an
continued slowly, a vague idea taking hold as she spok
"Most certainly you will be their sovereign, but if yo
were to give my people a gift rather than the chains o

efeat, it might lessen the hardship of the days and weeks o come."

Edward stared at her thoughtfully, waiting for her to ontinue.

"Your majesty, you must give my people a sovereign orn in Wales, educated in the Welsh language and ustom, one who by birthright may hold that title."

Edward rose to his feet, his manner suddenly guarded, nd moved toward Maren.

Maren looked to Brettan, who quickly rose from his hair, his entire body like that of a poised cat, motionless, ll muscles tensed a final moment before striking down ts prey, and she immediately realized that Edward had nisunderstood her meaning. Maren quickly rounded the ong table and placed a restraining hand on Brettan's rm, her touch gentle but commanding, for she realized vell that he had fully intended to stand between her and iis king if necessary, for her protection.

"Your majesty, within this castle lies a babe born in his land. By his birth he is Welsh. Give my people their ²rince of Wales. Make your son their sovereign. It shall e a new beginning between England and Wales, a chance or peace." Maren glanced uncertainly at the warrior ing who stood before her, an expression of pleasant urprise gracing his lean features.

"You remind me, milady, that too often I think as a oldier and not as a king, though in me they are one and he same. Very often an answer cannot be found with the word, but must be met with wisdom. You do me honor, nilady. Pray forgive me for having doubted your incerity."

Maren's eyes misted, looking first to Brettan and then o Edward, and she realized the tension that had grown etween the two men while she stood before them. The onflict was now ended.

* * *

581

Brettan retired late to their chamber, and Maren ros[e] from the warmth of their bed while he stirred the dyin[g] embers at the hearth.

"You come late to bed, milord," Maren observe[d] sleepily, her hair fanned out about her like a rich, dar[k] mantle that spread across the bed. Brettan's gaze warme[d] at the sight of her, which he had held so often within hi[s] memory.

"You, milady, have this day given a valuable lesson i[n] the delicate matter of politics."

Maren tossed her lovely head absently, then sat up. "[I] have little knowledge of such matters, but I know wel[l] what is in the heart of my people, for it is within my ow[n] heart."

Brettan turned from where he crouched before th[e] hearth, where a few flames stirred lazily and then burne[d] brighter. "Pray tell Maren, what is in your heart?" h[e] asked softly, his voice sending warm, vibrant wave[s] washing over her.

"A desire for peace. Too long these endless wars hav[e] torn our people apart and left scars upon the land. No[w] that Llywelyn is dead, perhaps peace may begin," sh[e] sighed wistfully.

Brettan saluted her with the poker he held in his han[d] before prodding at the glowing fire. "Ever the eloquen[t] statesman. Tell me, milady, is that the only desire tha[t] lies within the heart of the Duchess of Norfolk?" Whe[n] he rose and approached the bed, there was a devilis[h] smile curling the corners of his mouth, and Maren['s] heart ached at the sight of his lean, handsome face. Sh[e] reached out a long, slender arm, the dark veil of her hai[r] falling away to reveal that she wore nothing beneath th[e] linen covers, and her voice was like warm, rich wine tha[t] soothes the senses while lighting a fire of its own withi[n] the blood.

"There is but one more desire within me. I have a nee[d]

582

to feel your child stirring within me. It is a wish only you may grant, my husband."

Brettan's pulse pounded in his veins at the sight of her silken skin, so fair and lustrous, like fine satin giving stark contrast to the ebony tendrils of waving hair that swirled about her. She came to him like some wanton creature of the night, one no mortal man could ever hope to possess.

With nimble fingers, Maren untied the closures of Brettan's tunic and carefully undressed him until he stood before her like some magnificent bronzed god of ancient lore, come to join her for but a night. In breathless wonder she reached softly to caress the broad expanse of his chest, her fingers momentarily lost in the darkness of the thick mat of hair. They moved slowly up until they entwined gently about his neck, drawing him near, so that the soft rose-tipped peaks of her breasts were pressed into him, burning him with a molten heat that seemed to reach into his soul.

Brettan gathered her to him in a fierce embrace, as if he might draw her within him. "Then, milady, you shall have your desire, for I vow this night I shall give you a son, to hold within you until the day you shall bring him forth, a fierce warrior, proud and strong, born of our passion." He pressed her into the downy softness of the bed, pinning her arms above her head and pressing a feverish kiss against the hollow of her throat. His lips traced a molten path across her cheek and then lingered for a moment, before claiming her lips in a kiss that drew the breath from her.

Maren's hands were freed while Brettan explored the softness of her eager, young body. His rough, callused hand wandered across the silken planes of her stomach, then gently caressed the slim curve of her hip. Maren felt as if her soul were aflame with desire for him, and she returned the passion of his kiss, her lips traveling along a

583

well-muscled shoulder, the palms of her hands feverish against his bronzed skin, drawing him to her. All the lies and deceptions of the last months, which had torn them apart, had fallen away. Brettan murmured softly against her ear, and Maren felt her power over him. Her hands wandered freely down the length of his hard body, and a deep shudder passed through him. Her name was a ragged whisper through the golden firelight that bathed the chamber, but Brettan stayed the desire that raged within him. His greatest pleasure was to be found in hers. Eyes the color of glowing emeralds pierced through the darkness, seeking the truth of her own passion.

Poised at the threshold of complete abandon, Maren gazed back at him in silent wonder at the sight of their bodies entwined, his lean, well-muscled, and golden brown from the sun, hers pale and small beneath the crush of his weight across her. Maren felt the urgency of her own need, a need he had built within her, and she abandoned herself to but one purpose, fulfilling that need. She reached up her slender hand to meet his larger one, slowly entwining her fingers with his, her gaze never leaving Brettan's, conveying a silent message of her love in that brilliant blue gaze that never wavered. She kisssed the bronzed shoulder beside her head, and then his chest, savoring the taste of him, the feel of his skin against her lips. Tenderly she bit at him, but where there might have been pain, Brettan felt only pangs of passion that demanded release.

"Maren!" His voice was a whisper, a command, an urgent plea for her love. Hungrily his lips sought hers, and he felt her sweet response, for her lips parted and she welcomed the touch of his tongue. The passion that flamed within them fused them as one, except for that final fulfillment. Maren felt her own aching desperation and arched against him, seeking her own release.

"Brettan, let me feel you within me. Please," she

whispered, her small hands urgently pressing him to her. And then her breathing seemed to stop, for she felt his heat surging through her, like fire that burned without pain, heat that consumes the soul, so that it may never again live without the flame. And the fire that grew within them exploded, casting them upon the waves of their passion, swirling and drifting as one.

Three days later, in a magnificent and solemn ceremony at Caernarvon Castle, Edward I of England proclaimed himself sovereign over all of England and Wales.

Maren stood quietly beside Brettan for the ceremony, surrounded by his knights and soldiers of his personal guard, all resplendently dressed in their finest garments, blue and gold standards held aloft.

With great care the king took his newborn son from the young queen and held the sleeping babe within his large hands, giving the solemn order that his son would be Edward II, Prince of Wales, and that the title was to pass through the royal line of each King of England. His loud voice booming in the hall, Edward vowed his son would learn the Welsh language and the Welsh customs, promising the child would spend a certain number of his years within the country of his birth and title. Edward then crossed the large hall to stand before Maren.

"Milady, will you now accept my son as Prince of Wales, in the name of your people?" Gently Edward, King of England, held out his sleeping son.

Maren stood uncertainly for a moment until she realized the full import of Edward's gesture. It was a gesture for peace and hope that only the three of them fully understood. Maren's eyes filled with tears, and she reached out to take the babe from his father.

"Yea, I will accept your son as Prince of Wales."

Brettan's hand was calm upon her shoulder. She felt the warmth of pride in his gaze when she looked up at him. Immediately a loud cheer was sounded throughout the hall, and Englishman and Welsh alike gave their approval of Edward I, their king, to the new peace between their two countries, but most of all to Edward's wisdom in proclaiming his newborn son Prince of Wales.

Within her arms, Edward II was startled from his sleep at the sudden burst of noise about him. Maren gazed down at the tiny infant, who yawned sleepily, unaware of the import of the months past. Coming more fully awake, he turned his small face in toward the warmth of the full breast beneath the velvet at his cheek.

Maren smiled down at him softly. "I fear, little one, that I cannot help you there. For that we must find your mother."

Brettan walked ahead of her, clearing a path through the crowd of titled noblemen and knights of the realm. Maren crossed the hall behind him to where Queen Eleanore stood with her ladies-in-waiting. Reluctantly Maren surrendered the young prince to his mother.

"It is only for a short while, my love. I have promised that, before the passage of another winter, we shall hold our own son, and none may take him from us." Brettan's voice was warm as he gently guided her from the hall to a small chamber. He left her but for a moment. Hearing a sound behind her, Maren turned. The man in the doorway extended his arms to her. In the next moment she was in his arms, a flood of tears suddenly drenching them both while she clung to her father.

Brettan found Maren alone in the gardens beyond the hall, still covered with the last traces of snow. They clung to the brown twigs which were all that remained of flowers that had bloomed in the warmer months. Here and there a patch of ground poked through, the warmth of the last days having forced back the cold white mantle that had covered the ground for so long.

"I have saddled the gray. The day is warm, and I thought perhaps you would care to ride."

Maren smiled at him gratefully, always at a loss to understand how he knew her moods better than she.

Together they rode beyond the stone walls of Caernarvon. They followed a stream that flowed very near the castle, until it meandered across a small meadow. Brettan reined the gray stallion to a halt and dismounted, reaching up to lift Maren from the saddle, and they walked a small distance to an outcropping of rocks warming in the late afternoon sun.

"You have spoken with your father?" Brettan looked at her keenly, leaning back against the larger rock.

"We spoke of all the things that had been left unsaid," Maren replied softly.

"Then all is well between you?"

Maren smiled up at Brettan, reaching out tenderly to caress his cheek, where the small lines formed whenever he pondered some matter of great import.

"Yea, milord, all is well between my father and me."

Brettan smiled his relief that the old wounds and sorrows could at last be laid aside.

"It is good that this affair has been laid to rest once and for all. Shall he remain in Wales?"

"For a time he will remain at Cambria, giving support to Edward in aligning the southern land barons. They have already spoken of it. But even now, my brother Andrew takes on many of the responsibilities of Cambria, and my father has a need to see England again."

"What of Edmund and your sister?"

"Catherine shall remain at the abbey. She is stronger now, but for the time perhaps it is best that she remain with the sisters. They have given her strength and love. I know well, it is the best balm for her. As for Edmund, I fear he is determined to become a knight of the realm." Maren laughed, looking up at Brettan. "You are to blame for that, milord."

"But how may I be responsible for what the boy has decided?" Brettan asked incredulously.

"Oh, milord, I fear he was quite impressed when he first laid eyes upon you. Much the same as his sister, so I cannot find fault with him. And now he spends much time with Sandlin, and I vow you will have him well underfoot. He has asked to be allowed to come to England when he is of the age for training for knighthood."

"Then so be it. Edmund is a brave lad. He shall make a true knight. He reminds me greatly of my brother Damon, when he was a boy. No doubt he shall find his way into the Lady Helene's affections. By all means, we shall have him to Lionshead."

Maren leaned forward, laying her hand against Brettan's chest, and pressed a kiss upon his cheek. "You bring me such happiness that I wonder whether I deserve it, and fear that it shall all pass away and be naught but a memory."

Brettan pulled her into his gentle embrace, cradling her head against his shoulder, feeling the faint beating of her heart against his own. "You deserve such happiness because you have brought it to me." Softly he kissed the top of her head, breathing in the faint rose scent of her hair.

"Now that you have spoken with your father, would you also wish to journey to Cambria? I would understand if you chose to go there now."

Maren smiled up at him, all her love flooding her eyes with a soft glow, and reached up gently to caress his cheek. "Nay. I have thought upon it. Perhaps when I have the child you have promised me. I should like for our son to see Cambria and to know his Welsh heritage

But for now I have a deep longing to see my home, and to feel the safe comfort of Lionshead about me."

Brettan lowered his head and softly kissed her lips, a kiss filled with passion, and love, and promise. He tenderly raised her hand to his lips and kissed the tips of her fingers.

"Then, my love, we shall go home. We shall go to Norfolk." Brettan turned her in the warmth of his strong embrace and drew her back against him. They watched the setting sun together, which had become a bright crimson ball in the fading gray light of the winter's day. A warm, gentle breeze stirred their thoughts of the season that was upon them, and all the seasons that were promised, the seasons of splendor.

THE BEST IN ROMANCE FROM ZEBRA

EXCITING BESTSELLERS FROM ZEBRA

JEWELLED PATH   (1504, $3.95)
by Rosalind Laker
In the glittering turn-of-the-century settings of Paris, London, and Monte Carlo, Irene was as unique as the jewelry she created. Two very different men, drawn to her emerald eyes and lustrous pearly skin, forced her to choose one as her destiny. One stirred her body, and the other her heart!

A WOMAN OF THE CENTURY   (1409, $3.95)
by Eleanora Brownleigh
At a time when women were being forced into marriage, Alicia Turner had achieved a difficult and successful career as a doctor. Wealthy, sensuous, beautiful, ambitious and determined—Alicia was every man's challenge and dream. Yet, try as they might, no man was able to capture her heart—until she met Henry Thorpe, who was as unattainable as she!

HEIRLOOM   (1200, $3.95)
by Eleanora Brownleigh
The surge of desire Thea felt for Charles was powerful enough to convince her that, even though they were strangers and their marriage was a fake, fate was playing a most subtle trick on them both: Were they on a mission for President Teddy Roosevelt—or on a crusade to realize their own passionate desire?

STORM TIDE   (1230, $3.75)
by Patricia Rae
In a time when it was unladylike to desire one man, defiant, flame-haired Elizabeth desired two! And while she longed to be held in the strong arms of a handsome sea captain, she yearned for the status and wealth that only the genteel doctor could provide—leaving her hopelessly torn amidst passion's raging STORM TIDE. . . .

PLEASURE DOME   (1134, $3.75)
by Judith Liederman
Though she posed as the perfect society wife, Laina Eastman was harboring a clandestine love. And within an empire of boundless opulence, throughout the decades following World War II, Laina's love would meet the challenges of fate . . .

Available wherever paperbacks are sold, or order direct from the Publisher. Send cover price plus 50¢ per copy for mailing and handling to Zebra Books, Dept. 1587, 475 Park Avenue South, New York, N.Y. 10016. DO NOT SEND CASH.

THE BEST IN HISTORICAL ROMANCE
by Penelope Neri

PASSION'S BETRAYAL   (1568, $3.95)
Luke Steele, his glance meeting the green eyes of the masked bank bandit, knew this was no gun-slinging robber. Looking at sensuous Promise O'Rourke he gave her a choice: spend her life behind bars — or endure just one night in the prison of his embrace!

HEARTS ENCHANTED   (1432, $3.75)
When Lord Brian Fitzwarren saw the saucy, slender wench bathing in the river, her fresh, sun-warmed skin beckoned for his touch. That she was his enemy's daughter no longer mattered. The masterful lord vowed that somehow he would claim the irresistible beauty as his own . . .

BELOVED SCOUNDREL   (1259, $3.75)
When the handsome sea captain James Mallory was robbed by the scruffy street urchin, his fury flared into hot-blooded desire upon discovering the thief was really curvaceous Christianne. The golden-haired beauty fought off her captor with all of her strength — until her blows became caresses and her struggles an embrace . . .

PASSION'S RAPTURE   (1433, $3.75)
Through a series of misfortunes, an English beauty becomes the captive of the very man who ruined her life. By day she rages against her imprisonment — but by night, she's in passion's thrall!

Available wherever paperbacks are sold, or order direct from the Publisher. Send cover price plus 50¢ per copy for mailing and handling to Zebra Books, Dept. 1587, 475 Park Avenue South, New York, N.Y. 10016. DO NOT SEND CASH.